CODE FIVE

BOOKS BY FRANK G. SLAUGHTER

Code Five
Countdown
Surgeon's Choice
The Sins of Herod
Doctors' Wives
God's Warrior
Surgeon, U.S.A.
Constantine
The Purple Quest
A Savage Place
Upon This Rock
Devil's Harvest
Tomorrow's Miracle
David: Warrior and King
The Curse of Jezebel
Epidemic!
Pilgrims in Paradise
The Land and the Promise
Lorena
The Crown and the Cross
The Thorn of Arimathea
Daybreak
The Mapmaker
Sword and Scalpel

The Scarlet Cord
Flight from Natchez
The Healer
Apalachee Gold
The Song of Ruth
Storm Haven
The Galileans
East Side General
Fort Everglades
The Road to Bithynia
The Stubborn Heart
Immortal Magyar
Divine Mistress
Sangaree
Medicine for Moderns
The Golden Isle
The New Science of Surgery
In a Dark Garden
A Touch of Glory
Battle Surgeon
Air Surgeon
Spencer Brade, M.D.
That None Should Die
The Warrior

UNDER THE NAME C. V. TERRY

Buccaneer Surgeon
The Deadly Lady of Madagascar

Darien Venture
The Golden Ones

CODE FIVE

Frank G. Slaughter

DOUBLEDAY & COMPANY, INC., GARDEN CITY, NEW YORK
1971

*All of the characters in this book
are fictitious, and any resemblance
to actual persons, living or dead,
is purely coincidental.*

CODE FIVE

CHAPTER I

As the cab drew to a stop before the main entrance to St. Luke's Hospital, Jud Tyler leaned forward to study the remembered jumble of dark brick buildings, with its metal roof showing an even thicker layer of green canker than it had when he'd left Framingham. The conviction that coming back was a mistake had been growing on him since the plane from Washington had started its descent through the thick layer of smoky cloud that lay over the city, a pall fed night and day by the tall stacks of the steel mills and textile plants that were the lifeblood of this southern industrial center. Now the sight of the old hospital building and the decay which had so obviously attacked it, only deepened that conviction.

Past happiness, he admitted to himself, could not be recaptured; it was foolish even to try because memory always gave that happiness a glow in retrospect it had never really possessed. Seized again by the same sense of futility he had felt, when he'd awakened in Letterman General Hospital nearly a year ago, the right side of his body paralyzed from the explosion of a rocket shell in the midst of the hospital he'd commanded at An Tha, he was on the point of telling the cabdriver to take him back to the airport and the refuge represented by his room at Walter Reed Hospital in Washington, when the man spoke.

"You sure you want the *front* entrance, mister?" the cabdriver asked. "The Outpatient Department is around the corner, a half block away."

"I'm *not* a patient." Jud's voice was sharp as he took a bill from his pocket with his left hand—the right often failed to obey the commands of his will, particularly when he was troubled or tired—handed it to the driver, and received his change. Conscious that the man was watching him as he opened the cab door and set the tip of his cane against the curb to support himself, in case his right leg gave way, he knew he was more than usually awkward, but could do nothing about that either.

1

"Need any help?" the driver asked solicitously.

Jud shook his head but resisted the impulse to hurry; bitter experience again had told him that aphasia—the lack of free communication between brain and muscle—was a relentless enemy, waiting to trip him when he least expected it by robbing him of co-ordination. Stepping back from the curb, as the cab moved on, he examined the surroundings at somewhat more length than had been possible through the window of the cab.

Ventura Boulevard, once a wide, shady street with a park in the middle where beds of tulips formed a riot of color in the springtime, was now a six-laned superhighway, the flowerbeds long since sacrificed to the gods of community progress. A fluid barrier of roaring trucks and darting cars, the boulevard divided the area Jud had known as Irontown into two sections which, judged now by externals only, might as well be worlds apart.

Beginning at the corner half a block to the north, St. Luke's Hospital occupied the east side of the boulevard where Jud stood, a sprawl of dark red brick walls and sooty mullioned windows little changed, it seemed, since he'd left ten years ago after completing his internship. Perhaps the buildings were a little shabbier and the windows even more grimy, if that were possible, from the polluting smoke of the mills across town. And, the flashing sign at the corner indicating the entrance to the Outpatient Department—another half block down Mountain Avenue—no longer quite spelled "EMERGENCY"—with the "E" and "C" missing.

West of Ventura Boulevard a sprawling urban renewal project encompassing at least a dozen blocks had leveled the shabby weatherboarded houses he remembered. In their stead, two towering office buildings rose from the slope on the side toward Downtown, plus what appeared to be a high-rise motel. In the nearer foreground was a busy mall-type shopping center with a ferris wheel and other rides of a typical portable carnival used to advertise such centers easily visible in the bright March sunlight. He wasn't able to identify the impressive structure of steel and tinted glass located on the slight rise directly across the boulevard from St. Luke's, until he glanced up at the roof and saw, in letters that could be read easily a block away, the words PROVIDENT HOSPITAL.

Ten years ago when, medical bag in hand on externe duty, Jud walked the shady streets, the somewhat dingy, middle-class blue collar district on both sides of Ventura had appropriately been called Irontown, since it was inhabited largely by workers in the steel mills. The black invasion had just begun then; now, judging from the number of black children playing on the sidewalk farther along the boulevard, the sprawl of almost identical row houses that still extended eastward from Ventura Boulevard and St. Luke's Hospital had become the same kind of human rabbit warren that was slowly destroying the heart of many another American city.

With a brand-new Harvard M.D. attached to his name, Jud had been busy and happy during the two years he'd spent in the old hospital, helping care for the stream of patients who daily poured into both the hospital and the busy Outpatient Department, traditionally the family physician to the people of Irontown. Even the past ten months spent as a patient in two of the Army's finest hospitals had not totally erased the memory of St. Luke's or his longing to return, so Chuck Rogers' letter had been like a ray of sunlight through a cloud, injecting hope into a future that had seemed dark indeed for a surgeon, whose right hand as often as not refused to obey the commands of his will and whose right leg tended to move at times in a dragging shuffle.

Chuck—the Reverend Charles Rogers, with degrees from Sewanee and Union Theological Seminary—had been chaplain for the hospital at An Tha. While combating the terrible ravages a war without civilized rules could inflict upon friend and foe alike, Jud and Chuck had found a common purpose and a deep bond of brother-hood—until a bad case of malignant malaria had sent Chuck back to the States for treatment two years ago and returned him eventually to civilian life.

Jud had lost track of Chuck until the letter had come to him at Walter Reed a few weeks before. As long as Jud had known Chuck, he'd been in a hurry, and the letter was typical in its brevity:

Dear Jud,
    I am assistant canon at the cathedral in Framingham, with the chaplaincy at St. Luke's Hospital as an unpaid bonus.
    We badly need an experienced surgeon as Director of Emergency Services here to train and supervise the work of the Foreign Medical Graduates on our resident staff. When I read that you had been awarded the Medal of Honor for your work among the Montagnards, I dared to hope you might be interested in coming back to St. Luke's. Even if you aren't able to operate full time yourself yet, your knowl-

3

edge will be invaluable to us, and it would be like old times for us to work together again.

I do hope that you will agree to come.

Best,
Chuck

With his aphasia a nagging reminder that he might never be whole again, Jud had seized the opportunity Chuck's letter offered. He'd even dared to hope that in the hospital where he'd first begun to polish his own skills, a miracle of healing might somehow occur and the barrier between will and action inside his brain be removed. But now, as he compared the new glass and steel structure across the street with the cankerous copper roof and dingy old walls of St. Luke's, that hope seemed as foolish as his coming back had been.

Halfway up the slope between the street and the hospital, the flagstone walk divided to form a circle, in the center of which stood a pedestal. Upon it was a statue of the man whose name the hospital bore, the physician who had accompanied St. Paul on many of his journeys, ministering to the ailing apostle much as St. Luke's itself had ministered to many thousands of sick and afflicted in the nearly seventy years of its existence.

An old Negro was nodding in the warm sunlight on a bench near the statue, his lips moving in a mumble of words that had no meaning. Yet, though his cheeks were sunken from lack of teeth and the hands clutching a bottle of medicine in a white paper bag from the hospital pharmacy were gnarled by rheumatism, there was a look of peace upon his countenance. And circling the statue, touching the flagstones lightly with his cane so as not to awaken the sleeper, Jud felt his spirits lift a little when the shadow of the statue fell upon him like the healing touch of the "Beloved Physician."

II

A middle-aged woman at the Information Desk in the hospital lobby looked up reluctantly from the movie magazine she had been reading. "Can I help you?" she asked.

"I'm Dr. Judson Tyler—used to be an intern here ten years ago."

"St. Luke's was a busy place then." Her tone was wistful. "But not any more—except in the Outpatient Department."

"Did the new hospital across the street do this?" Jud indicated the largely empty lobby with his cane.

"People that can afford to go to Provident wouldn't be caught

4

dead at St. Luke's," the receptionist said scornfully. "Who did you wish to see, sir?"

"Mr. Rogers."

"The chaplain's office is in the Outpatient Department." The receptionist's voice had lost what small amount of warmth it possessed, and Jud wondered what Chuck had done to rub her the wrong way, a facility his old friend possessed to a remarkable degree, when he was intent upon accomplishing some purpose connected with his calling.

"I know the way," Jud told the receptionist and was turning away when she spoke again.

"What did you say your name was, Doctor?" she asked.

"Tyler. Dr. Judson Tyler."

"You must be the one Mr. Ford is expecting. He said you were to come to his office as soon as you got here."

Jud couldn't remember the name from any correspondence he'd had since Chuck's note had arrived at Walter Reed—but then his memory wasn't everything it had been before the disaster at An Tha either.

"Mr. Ford is the hospital administrator," the receptionist explained. "His office is across the lobby to your right."

In sharp contrast with what Jud had seen so far in the hospital, the suite of the administrator was luxuriously furnished.

"I'm Asa Ford, Dr. Tyler!" The florid looking man behind the desk rose when Jud was ushered in and pumped his hand as enthusiastically as a Rotarian running for the district governorship. "I can't tell you how pleased we are that you're going to work with us. Doctors of your caliber aren't easy to find these days."

Jud started to voice his own indecision about remaining, but Ford continued on exuberantly:

"When Mr. Rogers told me he'd persuaded you to become our new Director of Emergency Services, I was more than pleased."

"I didn't realize the appointment was final yet." Jud reserved an option to still say "no."

"This hospital needs someone like you very much, Dr. Tyler," said Ford. "You can be sure your application will go to the city personnel office with my full approval."

"Isn't St. Luke's still private?"

"The people of Irontown have always been a charity burden. It finally got too heavy for St. Luke's to carry, so the city and county

5

had to step in. I came here three years ago from the city finance office to keep an eye on things."

"I guess I'd better talk to Chuck Rogers before I come to a final decision," said Jud. "After all, my correspondence has been with him."

"Of course," said Ford. "Rogers is chairman of the selection committee of the Board of Trustees that hires physician personnel."

The word "hires" grated on Jud's somewhat sensitive nerves, but he kept his irritation under control.

"The chaplain likes to be where the action is—in the Outpatient Department," Ford continued. "After you've seen him, you can fill in the application blank and my secretary will type it for you to sign. I'll see that it gets immediate approval downtown and then we can have the reporters in and make the newspaper announcement."

"Is that necessary?" Jud asked, a little sharply.

"Necessary?" Ford's laugh boomed. "A hospital like St. Luke's doesn't get the most decorated medical officer in the Vietnam War as Director of Emergency Services every day. We've got every reason to crow a little, Dr. Tyler, and we're certainly going to do it."

III

Like most large hospitals built near the turn of the century, St. Luke's was a sprawling structure occupying most of a city block. In its heyday, it had housed almost four hundred patients and, when Jud was an intern, the passages had been jammed with people at this hour of the morning, hurrying to and from the hundreds of activities that made up the daily routine. But now, he saw, when he left the foyer and turned into the main corridor toward the Outpatient Department, the normal pace seemed to have slowed almost to a halt, further proof—if he'd really needed it—that the old hospital was dying.

Nevertheless, he still felt some of the remembered stirring of excitement in a young intern hurrying through this same corridor to duty in the Emergency Room, where unsure hands had gained skill suturing wounds, setting broken bones, and applying plaster casts. Even with the past still a vivid memory, however, he wasn't prepared for what met his eyes and ears when, at the end of a long side corridor, he came through a set of double doors above which was stenciled in long since fading paint OUTPATIENT DEPARTMENT.

Beyond the barrier of the doors to the Outpatient Wing, the

6

corridor to the Emergency Room itself was jammed with people. Roughly half, he estimated were black; the others about equally divided between Mexican-Americans—drawn northward by the rapid expansion of Framingham in recent years with the proliferation of textile mills—and migrants from the mountains of Appalachia, attracted much earlier by the same magnet.

The slurred tones of the southern Negro fused smoothly with the liquid Spanish accents of the Chicanos to create a pleasant undercurrent of sound, jarred occasionally by nasal tones bespeaking the Appalachian Mountain origins of most among the whites in the crowd awaiting attention. Above the buzz of conversation arose still other layers of sound: the wailing of the sick and injured; the hysterial screams of a black girl in pain; the cursing of the drunk weaving in a chair against the wall, clotted blood matting his woolly hair where his scalp had been split by a policeman's billy club; the stink of sweating bodies, congealing blood, and the excreta of the incontinent old man snoring in coma on a stretcher against the wall mixed with the strong odor of disinfectant from a mop wielded by an orderly in a vain attempt to scrub away some of the filth that littered the floor of the corridor—all of it fused into a stench that almost made Jud retch.

In his day the corridors had been jammed much of the time too—especially on Saturday nights when razors, switchblades, and even lowly rocks had taken their toll of human flesh. But order had always been enforced by a policeman who stood beside the door, while now only chaos seemed to reign.

"What are you doing out of line?" a voice demanded sharply in Jud's ear.

Startled, he turned to face a nurse in a green hospital gown with a line of tiny bloodstains across the breast. Her eyes burned angrily as she took his elbow and shoved him toward the end of the line of waiting patients with a dexterity that spoke of long practice in handling the sick and crippled. Even as he moved to obey her, Jud noted that the rather shapeless operating gown failed to hide the fact that the woman beneath it was far from shapeless, just as the cap she wore failed to cover the dark red ringlets, damp from perspiration, escaping from it.

"If you've finished the physical, get back in line," she snapped but, even mussed and perspiring, she was a Juno-in-white. Or, he thought, more appropriately Hygeia the goddess of healing herself, on leave from Olympus.

7

"I'm sorry," he mumbled. "I—"

"You'll have your turn just like everybody else," she said, and turned to pick up a black baby in the type of spread-legged body cast used to treat congenital dislocations of the hip. Moving toward the Emergency Room, she carried the baby with the skilled tenderness of a highly trained and dedicated nurse.

The confusion of the scene fascinated Jud but he was careful to stay in the line of patients while he observed it. Only once could he remember seeing anything like it before; when he'd answered a Medevac call to a field dressing station, where a single medical officer was trying to cope with an avalanche of wounded following an ambush, while gunships cleared the area so helicopters could land and take out the wounded. He knew now that Chuck Rogers hadn't been exaggerating about the need at St. Luke's; if ever a medical situation cried out for someone experienced in bringing order out of this sort of chaos, it was here.

"Dr. Tyler!" A tall white-haired Negro in white ducks greeted him warmly.

"John! John Redmond!" Jud shifted the handle of the cane to his forearm and held out both hands to grip those of the tall orderly. "Don't tell me you're still working?"

"I've got another ten years at least." John Redmond's laugh boomed out. "After all I'm only eighty, Doctor."

"Your sons must be out of college by now, John."

"A Ph.D., an M.D., and a Master's degree from Hunter College." John Redmond's eyes shone proudly. "And my grandson finishes at Harvard next year."

"I'll bet you still ride that bicycle to and from work."

"How would I get my exercise if I didn't?" A gentle black hand touched Jud's where it rested on the handle of the cane. "I heard about your injury, Dr Tyler. Is it still bad with you?"

"At times; you know how brain injuries are, John."

Redmond's eyes moved to the Emergency Room where a struggling youth with blood streaming down his face was being carried in by two policemen.

"We really need you here, Dr. Tyler," he said. "I was very happy when the chaplain told me you were coming."

"Do you know where I can find Mr. Rogers?"

"His office is right across the corridor," said Redmond. "You can tell it by the coffeepot."

"That's Chuck Rogers all right," said Jud. "He had the only

8

continually boiling coffeepot in Vietnam. I can't wait to see him again."

"'I saw him a few minutes ago on Male Receiving—carrying a bedpan," said John.

"What?"

"The chaplain is the most Christlike man I ever knew, Dr. Tyler." John Redmond's smile was gentle and warm. "But then you're his friend so I don't have to tell you that. One of the other orderlies was sick this morning, so Mr. Rogers took over."

The red-haired nurse appeared in the door of the Emergency Room, shouted a name as if daring the bearer to object, and turned back inside.

"That nurse in the operating gown just bawled me out for not being in line," Jud said.

"Miss Galloway's the seven-to-three supervisor; she must have mistaken you for a patient." John Redmond's voice had taken on a note of admiration. "Now there's a real nurse for you."

"Isn't anybody from the old days left besides you, John?"

"Dr. Wiley is still downstairs in the lab."

"But he was old enough to retire when I left ten years ago."

"So was I, if you count it by the years," said John. "But I guess the doc's just like me. He knows if he ever quits doing what the Lord intended him to do, he'll just wilt down and die. I've got to go up to Male Receiving, Dr. Tyler; I'll tell the chaplain you're here."

The orderly put his hand on Jud Tyler's arm again in what was almost a pleading gesture. "I've been praying a long time for somebody like you to take charge here, Doctor," he said. "Now that you're here, nobody can tell me prayer isn't answered and miracles don't happen."

CHAPTER II

The small room in the basement, its shelves lined with glass jars containing pathological specimens, had been the professional habitat of Dr. Jerome Wiley, the hospital pathologist, for at least twelve

9

of the twenty-four hours in every day during the two years Jud had spent at St. Luke's. The door was open now, but the older doctor was studying a slide under the microscope and, remembering Wiley's often irascible temper, Jud didn't indicate his presence until the pathologist looked up and swiveled the chair around to face him.

"You're thinner," he said. "Didn't the Army feed you?"

"Hospitals did that—almost ten months."

"What got you?" The sharp gray eyes had gone to Jud's scalp, where the hair still didn't quite cover the scars of surgery.

"A fragment of explosive shell casing."

"Russian made?"

"I imagine so. There wasn't time to look."

"Damn fool war!" The pathologist's bushy gray eyebrows bristled. "From the looks of that scar, it must have been in the neighborhood of Broca's convolution."

"Pretty close to it. My right side was paralyzed completely for a while."

"Any residual effects—besides the cane?"

"Considerable aphasia; I can't always be sure of my right hand and my right leg fails sometimes too. That's why I carry the cane."

"The left side okay?"

"Yes. I'm training the left hand to take the place of the right."

"The human brain has astounding powers of recovery if pushed hard enough," said Wiley. "The trouble is most people use less than one per cent of their capacity."

"I haven't been using very much of mine lately," Jud conceded.

"Except to feel sorry for yourself?"

Jud stiffened. "Ten months ago a section chief assignment was waiting for me at Walter Reed; now I'm a patient there in Rehabilitation, on leave until I decide whether to take this job. Would you expect me to go around singing 'Happy Days Are Here Again?'"

Wiley ignored the question. "What do you think of St. Luke's?"

"Anyone can see it's on the skids."

"When you were here, this was the best hospital in the city," said Wiley. "It's asking a lot of a plant that's nearly seventy years old to stay that way."

"In Vietnam we inflated our main hospital like a balloon; yet we gave better medical care than three-fourths of the hospitals in the States do."

"More like nine-tenths I'd say—at least in Framingham."

"And a soldier wounded on the battlefield still has a lot better chance of surviving than an automobile accident victim out there on the highway in front of the hospital."

"So it's the men who really make medicine efficient," Wiley agreed. "But you had two things going for you even on the battlefield that St. Luke's hasn't had for a long time—money and dedicated people."

"Chuck's letter mentioned that some of the house staff are Foreign Medical Graduates."

"*All* our residents are FMGs. Mostly they're fine young men but their education in medicine can't be compared with what a graduate from an American medical school gets. Besides, they're not getting the training here that could correct those deficiencies."

"Why?"

"It's like the gradual deterioration in victims of Parkinson's disease," said the pathologist. "From day to day you don't see much change, but let a month or two go by and you can tell that an entire body is falling apart. That's what's been happening to St. Luke's for quite a while now."

"And what they want me to change?"

Wiley shrugged. "If it isn't too late."

"If things are that bad, why was I welcomed so effusively by Mr. Ford just now?"

"Asa Ford needs you—but not necessarily to train FMGs."

"Is that a riddle?" Jud was beginning to be a little irritated, even with his old friend. "Or are you going to tell me what's it all about?"

"We'll both tell you," a familiar voice said from the doorway.

Chuck Rogers slapped Jud on the shoulder affectionately and pulled a stool from beneath a small table on which stood a microtome, wrapping his long legs around its base. He wore a black turtleneck instead of a clerical collar and was a little more stooped than when Jud had last seen him nearly two years before. His rather sparse hair was beginning to show a little gray too, although Jud knew that Chuck was still less than forty. But the blue eyes glowed with the same remembered fire and the smile was warm and encompassing, like a heavy cloak on a cold night.

"St. Luke's needs you—badly," said Chuck. "And I hope you need us."

"Why would I do that?" Jud's voice was still a bit sharp.

"I tried to get you on the phone one afternoon at Walter Reed

11

but you were out, so I talked to Colonel Standiford. He told me it's time you went back to work."

"In a charnel house?"

"All the more reason why it needs an expert—fast."

"Suppose you give me the nitty gritty, starting with my effusive welcome in the administrator's office." Jud's tone was a bit milder in the face of his friend's obvious delight at seeing him again.

"As usual, I've put my foot into it," Chuck admitted. "Charlie Gregg of the *Press-Bulletin* ran a series of articles a while ago exposing conditions here. We were hoping to arouse public indignation and get more money for the hospital, but the scheme backfired on us and the only people who really got indignant were the politicians we blamed for the mess here. Asa Ford and I rarely agree on anything but we do this time—having a medical hero take charge of St. Luke's is better than any public relations gimmick we could dream up."

"Colonel Standiford must have told you that I'm at best half a man; now you tell me I'm a gimmick," Jud's tone was acid. "Neither is very complimentary."

"Believe me, they're both meant to be," Chuck assured him. "The gimmick we need badly right now, but it's the long pull I'm really thinking about. You and I could start a revolution in medical care here, Jud—"

"Carrying bedpans?"

"Each must serve in his own way. I can carry bedpans but you've got the knowledge that could make St. Luke's a civilian MUST Unit like the one we had at An Tha."

"It would take Superman to do that."

"A superman named Jud Tyler, yes," Chuck agreed. "But please don't prejudge us, Jud; I've got too many hopes riding on you."

"There you go again," said Jud resignedly, "maneuvering me into a corner just like you were always doing at An Tha."

"But only because I knew you could work your way out of it," Chuck assured him. "We've got a small apartment in the OPD Wing for the Director of Emergency Services. Stay here a few days while you get a closer view of the situation, then make your final decision."

"That sounds reasonable," Jud admitted, then added suspiciously, "How long has this apartment been in use, by the way?"

"I had it fixed up right after you answered my first letter," Chuck confessed with a grin. Then his voice grew sober. "If St. Luke's is

12

dying, it's from heart trouble, Jud. Between us I know we can give it a new one."

II

The elevator that took Chuck and Jud back to the ground floor of the OPD Wing groaned like an arthritic patient on a wintry morning. As they stepped out into the crowded corridor, an ambulance siren wailed to a stop outside and both Jud and Chuck moved instinctively toward the Emergency Room. Almost immediately the doors leading to the unloading dock outside banged open and a wheeled stretcher was pushed hurriedly in by two attendants.

"Code Five! Code Five!" The man at the head of the stretcher shouted, and Jud needed nothing further to diagnose the nature of emergency. The cry of "Code Five" was almost universal, with a single meaning—cardiac arrest—a stopped heart creating the gravest of all emergency conditions.

The man who had shouted the alert held a portable respirator mask over the patient's face and obviously knew his business. But when Jud saw a dark-skinned doctor in whites appear beside the stretcher and start to adjust the tips of a stethoscope to his ears, intending to listen for a heartbeat and determine whether or not the patient was still alive, he found himself moving instinctively into the Emergency Room and taking charge.

"Did you attempt heart compression?" he asked the ambulance attendant, as he elbowed the dark-skinned doctor out of the way and pushed aside the blanket covering the patient's body.

"I'm not trained in that technique," said the attendant. "Besides, his pulse only stopped a few minutes ago."

Dropping his cane, Jud seized one of the carrying handles of the stretcher and lowered himself to the floor beside it. Kneeling there, he placed the heel of his crippled right hand on the lower third of the man's breastbone, or sternum, and used the heel of his good left hand to press firmly down upon it, forcing the pliant flat bone backward against the spine with his whole weight and compressing the heart between the sternum and the spinal column. Holding it there for an instant, he released the pressure of his weight as he straightened up, then leaned forward to press again.

"Inject ten c.c. of a ten per cent calcium chloride solution and a

13

half c.c. of Isuprel intravenously as a bolus," he told the dark-skinned doctor, who was now standing irresolutely beside the stretcher.

When the blank look in the resident's eyes told him the order had not been understood, whether from a language difficulty or lack of medical knowledge he had no time to determine, Jud spoke sharply to the group gathered around the stretcher—without, however, breaking the rhythm of compressing the heart.

"Doesn't anyone here know how to inject an intravenous bolus?" he demanded.

"I do," said a feminine voice.

"Then do it!"

Jud didn't attempt to identify the speaker; it was far more important to continue the rhythmic squeezing of the heart between sternum and spine, duplicating its action in life and keeping the blood of the patient flowing so it could absorb oxygen and carry that vital chemical to the brain cells in order to preserve life—if indeed life had not already fled.

"The veins are filling so the blood must be flowing already." It was the same feminine voice that had answered him and, when an efficient looking pair of feminine hands expertly placed a tourniquet around the patient's arm above the elbow, he saw that both voice and hands belonged to the red-haired nurse who had ordered him into the line of patients, when he'd first come into the OPD. She had changed from the shapeless and blood-spattered operating gown to a crisp white uniform. And perched upon her dark hair was the delicately fluted cap marking graduates of the Johns Hopkins School of Nursing the world over.

With a quick skilled movement, the nurse thrust the needle attached to a ten-cubic centimeter syringe through skin and vein wall, flipped the tourniquet loose when dark blood spurted back into the syringe, and injected the entire contents expertly with one quick movement, insuring that the full dose of the drug he had ordered—a bolus in medical terms—would reach the heart at the same instant, carried there by the artificial circulation he was creating by pressing upon the heart.

"Leave the needle in and start an I.V. of five per cent glucose," he directed her. "And we'll need another half c.c. of Isuprel, too—in five minutes."

The dusky tint of oxygen lack called cyanosis was already starting to fade from the patient's skin, proof that Jud's rhythmic pressure on the previously inert heart had taken over the function of driving blood through the lungs, where it could absorb vitally needed oxygen.

"Do you want to connect him to a cardiac monitor now, Doctor," the red-haired nurse asked, but Jud shook his head.

"At the moment it's more important to get the calcium and Isuprel directly into the heart where it can enhance the conductivity of nerve impulses."

Taking the glass connection of the intravenous set handed her by the tall resident, who had finally been galvanized into action, she deftly attached it to the needle, fixing the latter to the skin of the patient's forearm with adhesive so it wouldn't be pulled out while the glucose was flowing into the vein.

"You injected the bolus well," Jud complimented the nurse, as he continued to press upon the patient's chest in the rhythmic technique of cardiopulmonary resuscitation, shortened in hospital parlance to CPR.

"I had two years on a Coronary Intensive Care Ward at Hopkins," she said crisply. "Cardiac arrest wasn't exactly routine there, but we did see it quite often."

"Miss Galloway is the seven-to-three supervisor in the OPD and Emergency Room," said Chuck, who was looking over Jud's shoulder. "And this is Dr. Emilio Fernandez from Cuba, the Senior Resident."

As Jud nodded acknowledgment of the introductions, Chuck added: "Dr. Tyler and I worked together in Vietnam."

"You can listen to the heart now, Dr. Fernandez," Jud told the Cuban. "If it starts to beat spontaneously, you should be able to hear the sounds between my compressions."

Placing the bell of his stethoscope over the patient's heart, Fernandez listened intently for a moment, then shook his head.

"There is no sound," he reported.

"Think he'll make it, Doctor?" the ambulance attendant who was still handling the resuscitator asked.

"It's too soon to tell," said Jud. "What happened to him?"

"He works in the cardroom at Framingham Mills. Started having trouble breathing right after the shift began this morning, the foreman that called us said."

Jud remembered enough from his previous stay in Framingham to know the cardroom was the section of a textile mill in which the raw cotton was carded or combed to form a continuous strand

15

of fibers which could be twisted into thread, prior to being woven into cloth.

"The foreman said this is the worst case of 'Monday Morning Asthma' he's ever seen," the attendant volunteered, but Jud was too busy to question him about the meaning of the term.

"You can inject the second half c.c. of Isuprel now, Miss Galloway," he said. "The patient might have been in *status asthmaticus* before his heart stopped."

By the time Miss Galloway completed the second injection—as expertly as the first—Jud was conscious of a vast tiredness in his right arm. It had been a long time since he'd carried out the rather strenuous technique of cardiopulmonary resuscitation and he'd forgotten just how much energy it required. Almost as if she'd been reading his thoughts, Miss Galloway spoke.

"I can relieve you when you're tired, Dr. Tyler," she said.

"I'll go on for a little while, thank you," he told her.

For several more minutes Jud continued the rhythmic compression of the patient's heart. Although he could detect no evidence of a spontaneous resumption of its beat, the man's color grew steadily pinker as oxygen entered his blood and was transferred to his brain cells, the most vulnerable of all the millions making up the body.

Jud's muscles were leaden with fatigue and he was about ready to call on the nurse to take over, when Emilio Fernandez suddenly lifted the bell of the stethoscope from the man's chest. "It beats!" he cried.

Miss Galloway reached immediately for the patient's wrist. "I can feel the pulse," she reported. "It's regular too."

"Count it for fifteen seconds, please." Jud relinquished the pressure on the sternum, flexing and extending the fingers of his cramped right hand, while the nurse kept her eyes on her watch for the required period.

"Thirty for the quarter minute," she reported. "And getting stronger all the time."

"The blood pressure is eighty over sixty," Emilio Fernandez added.

"It's a miracle!" The voice of the attendant handling the resuscitator was awed. "A blooming miracle if I ever saw one."

"The miracle was that you got him here so soon after cessation," Jud corrected him. "We can start hearts with CPR, but if the brain cells are without oxygen too long, the patient still ends

16

up as a vegetable and is probably worse off than if it hadn't started at all."

The rhythmic clicking of the resuscitator valve suddenly changed to a spatter of short sounds, as air being expelled from the patient's lungs forced itself against the valve, interrupting the pattern.

"He's started breathing too." The attendant switched from "Resuscitation," with its automatic inflation of the patient's lungs, to "Inhalation," which allowed the patient to breathe oxygen directly from the rubber bag of the machine.

"You sure pulled him out of the grave, Doctor," he added admiringly.

"Did you say you have an Intensive Care Section?" Jud asked Miss Galloway.

"Only one cubicle. It's equipped with a monitoring system the County Medical Center gave us when they put in new equipment."

"Move him there and connect him to the hospital oxygen supply then. Coronary thrombosis is the most frequent cause of cardiac cessation, so you can put that down for the admission diagnosis. We'll find out for sure when we get a look at the electrocardiogram on the monitor."

Gripping the carrying handles on the sides of the ambulance stretcher by which he had lowered himself into a kneeling position, Jud started to straighten up. In the strenuous effort of starting the stopped heart, he'd forgotten his disability, however, as well as the fear that had dogged him for months, forcing him to carry the cane. That fear suddenly became a reality once more when he put weight on his right foot and the leg muscles, whether from failure of control by his will or the unaccustomed fatigue, went suddenly limp. He grabbed frantically for the carrying handle of the ambulance stretcher again but his right arm failed too, under the stress. And no longer able to support his own weight, he fell sprawling on the floor beside the stretcher.

He lay there for a moment looking up at the startled faces of those who had been watching, then the same strong pair of hands that had injected the bolus so expertly reached down to help him. Overcome by a sudden burst of shame, however, he struck her hand roughly aside like a child who had fallen instinctively lashes out at those trying to help it and managed to get himself painfully to his feet alone.

Instantly regretting his seeming ingratitude to the nurse who had

17

only been trying to help him, he turned to apologize but saw only her back, straight, uncompromising but quite graceful, leaving the room.

"In case you didn't notice, you dropped this," Chuck Rogers said when he handed Jud his cane.

"I seemed to have dropped a lot of things, including my manners," Jud admitted. "Do you think that coffeepot I saw in your office as we passed the door is still boiling, Chaplain?"

"If it isn't," said Chuck happily, "I'll outdo the Prophet Elijah and call down some fire from heaven to make it perk."

CHAPTER III

In Chuck Rogers' tiny office, Jud relaxed and let the warmth of the strong brew seep through his body, while the chaplain busied himself making another pot. The contrast between the two men was sharp: the minister stooped by the burden of his work, yet cheerful and hopeful nevertheless; Jud lean almost to the point of emaciation from his long illness, his face ravaged by the months of doubt concerning his ability ever to reach again the high goals he had set himself before An Tha. Six feet two, he was almost ugly, with his craggy profile and unruly mop of sandy hair. But when he had moved to take the cup of coffee, even though with his left hand, it was still with the instinctive grace of a born surgeon.

"I hope Dr. Fernandez thought to request an emergency consultation with the staff cardiologist," said Jud. "I'm no expert in treating coronary thrombosis."

"Dick Tubman will probably see him this afternoon," said Chuck.

"Probably?" Jud frowned. "Why not certainly?"

"Getting a quick consultation at St. Luke's isn't always easy."

"Don't you still have a visiting staff?"

"Yes. But not many of them visit any more."

"Ten years ago the top men in town were happy to be on the staff of St. Luke's," said Jud. "What happened?"

"I suppose I could quote the old saw about rats deserting sinking ships. Actually, ninety-five per cent of the professional side of the hospital—maybe even more—is now run by the FMGs."

"How many residents do you have?"

"Five in all. Emilio Fernandez is a Cuban, with several years of training in surgery before he came here from Miami. The others are Filipinos—and less well trained."

Foreign Medical Graduates, Jud knew, were much in demand by non-teaching hospitals in the United States because the graduates of most American medical schools were drawn for internship and residencies to teaching hospitals and other prestige institutions. Temporary visitors to America, bent upon improving the often inadequate training in medicine given by schools in their homelands and particularly hoping to profit at home from the éclat that a residency in a United States hospital gave them, the FMGs were far too often little more than glorified orderlies.

"How do you handle patients requiring specialized treatment?" Jud asked.

"As soon as they're able to be moved, most of them are transferred to other hospitals with better facilities."

"Are you sure you aren't being sentimental in keeping the hospital open at all?" Jud demanded bluntly.

"St. Luke's is mainly a thriving outpatient center serving a large ghetto area, where general practice is either a thing of the past or limited mainly to semi-quacks who aren't accepted elsewhere," said Chuck. "We keep only enough hospital beds in operation to handle charity patients on welfare, trauma cases that can't be transferred safely elsewhere at the moment and whatever else other hospitals don't want."

"How many beds are you operating?"

"About two hundred—most of them in the two receiving wards. They're filled as fast as they're emptied."

Jud shook his head slowly. "It took even more crust than you're usually capable of to invite me to become full-time Director of Emergency Services here, when you can't even make your budget and have to depend on what other hospitals throw away."

Chuck winced at his tone. "I had to do something and you seemed to be my only hope. Before Charlie Gregg ran the series

19

of articles on conditions at St. Luke's, Asa Ford was trying to hand the whole hospital over to a father and son team of industrial surgeons, who've been working hand in glove with insurance companies on automobile and industrial accident cases for years. Charlie and I foiled Asa's scheme, but the result has been that hardly anyone wants to work here any more."

"Why?"

Chuck shrugged. "I guess a lot of doctors figure it doesn't add to their professional standing with the public."

"You didn't hesitate to ask me," Jud reminded him. "Or were you just being kind to a crippled friend by giving him a job and hoping to cover up your own failure here by using my war record as a front?"

"I plead guilty—but in a good cause."

"What about that pigpen out there?" Jud nodded toward the OPD, from which the cacophony of human misery still continued to rise like the wailing of professional mourners.

"Actually, the picture's not as bad as you're painting it," Chuck protested.

"How in the hell can you say that?"

"I'm not talking about the present, but the future possibilities."

"If any."

"St. Luke's is the nearest hospital to some of the largest industrial plants in the city, Jud, and ambulances can reach us in minutes from the Interstate. Enough income to support this department and a full-time director could easily come from industrial compensation and insured accident cases alone, once we're able to continue expert treatment until the patients are well."

"What do you do with those cases now?"

"The residents give them emergency care and turn them over to private physicians."

"Who'll squawk if you employ a full-time surgeon to run your Emergency Department."

"Why should I worry about them when they do nothing for us—except make us hand over our patients because FMGs are supposed to work only under licensed physicians?"

"You've got a point there," Jud conceded. "With private doctors skimming off the cream and leaving you the rest—that nobody else wants—I can see why St. Luke's has gone down so fast."

"There's another factor too. Most people are naturally suspicious of foreigners so when patients discover that we only have FMGs on the staff, they're ready to leave as soon as it's safe for them to be transferred."

"Can you blame them?"

"Maybe not. But our residents are willing to learn, Jud—with somebody like you to teach them. And that could be good for you too."

"Mind telling me how?"

"Unless I'm wrong, you're searching for a way to be useful in medicine in spite of your own disability."

"What's wrong with that?"

"Nothing—as long as you don't let your anger at what you still lack endanger the function of what you already have."

Chuck had put his finger on a very sore spot, and Jud's temper, already stirred and never far beneath the surface since the tragedy at An 'I'ha, flared.

"After all, it's my life," he said sharply.

"To the extent that our lives really belong to any of us—yes. Mind telling me why you slapped Kathryn Galloway's hand aside just now when she was only trying to help you up?"

"Frustration, humiliation. It was an impulse."

"Weren't you really lashing out at her and the world because you think you got a raw deal?"

"Don't tell me you took a degree in psychiatry too."

Chuck smiled. "I didn't do too well in theology either but I can still recognize troubled people when I see them—and sometimes diagnose their needs. Poor as it is, this hospital is vital to the welfare of the Irontown people and a lot of others. Take it away and more babies will die in childbirth or shortly after, even though the infant mortality rate is far too high in Framingham already. If I can keep St. Luke's from dying on the vine by persuading you to stay, some of those will be saved."

"You always were too damned reasonable for anybody to be mad at you long," Jud grumbled. "All right, I'll give it a whirl for a few days at least."

II

The strain of the flight from Washington and the resuscitation of the stopped heart had exhausted Jud even more than he had realized. The apartment for the Director of Emergency Services adjoining the office was small, but the bed was new and comfortable. Five minutes after he lay down following lunch with Chuck and Dr. Wiley in the hospital cafeteria, he was asleep.

When he awoke, it was already dusk and the clock on the bedside table said a little after six. The cafeteria was almost deserted at that hour and he ate quickly so as not to keep the duty personnel waiting because of him. Noticing some activity in the Emergency Room, he went to the door, hoping Miss Galloway would still be there so he could apologize for his boorish behavior that morning. But a black nurse was helping one of the Filipino residents examine a small boy. The Filipino looked up and saw Jud standing in the door.

"I am Dr. Juan Valdese, Dr. Tyler," he said in a liquid Spanish accent. "And this is Miss Amanda Cates, the three-to-eleven supervisor."

The nurse acknowledged the introduction with a nod but her eyes were hostile, though for what reason Jud had no idea.

"This little boy complains of pain in the stomach but I can find nothing surgical," the Filipino doctor continued. "I was about to send him home."

"Freddie cries out a lot at night with cramps in his belly, Doctor," said the mother, a plump black woman who stood just inside the curtained-off space of the cubicle, where the boy was lying. "I been bringin' him here every few days for two weeks but nobody don't give him no medicine that helps."

"Would you care to examine him, Dr. Tyler?" Valdese asked. "The picture does not fit any syndrome with which I am familiar."

"Little boys get bellyaches for all sorts of reasons." Jud repressed a smile at the Filipino's somewhat tortured rhetoric and moved closer to the table. Leafing through the hospital record quickly, he saw that it contained records of two admissions, plus notations of several OPD visits. Like so many in the Irontown section, the doctors at St. Luke's were obviously the suppliers of medical care for the family.

"Fred W. Brown. Age four," was typed on the green sheet prepared by the Emergency Room secretary and attached to the front of the chart.

"Where does it hurt you, Freddie?" Jud asked the child.

"Down here, Doctor, but it's better now." The boy put his hand over his navel but just then a spasm struck him and he doubled up for a moment.

"The other attacks were less severe than this one, but the pain has always been spasmodic," said Valdese.

"Any fever?"

"None at all. The urine is negative and the white blood cell count normal—six thousand. The night laboratory technician is staining the slides for the differential but with a normal count I doubt if the slides will tell us anything."

Jud ran his fingers gently over the dark skin of the child's abdomen, pressing lightly upon the muscles as he sought to detect any increased resistance that would warn of an inflamed organ beneath, an appendix perhaps, or an acutely inflamed gall bladder in an older patient.

"Do you agree that he is not a surgical emergency, Doctor?" Valdese asked.

"No question about that," said Jud. "But I still get the impression that we're missing something here, something we should be seeing and aren't."

"Freddie's food don't seem to do him no good neither, Doctor," the mother volunteered. "He just gets weaker and weaker and can't hardly seem to stand up no more."

A faint warning bell rang in Jud's mind at her words. "What do you mean?" he asked.

"It's his legs—they just fold up on him sometimes."

"Do any of the other children have the same trouble?"

"A little. They look peaked most of the time. And they don't run and play like they used to."

"How long have you noticed this?"

"Since soon after we moved where we are now—more'n a year ago. I took 'em to the city Health Department clinic maybe six months ago and the doctors give 'em iron for 'nemia. They got some better too, but lately it's come back again. Seems like everything Freddie eats gives him cramps in the belly but he don't run off none from it."

"You'd better admit the child for observation, Dr. Valdese," said Jud, and held out his hand to the patient. "Okay, Freddie?"

"Okay, Doctor." Using his left hand, the boy reached across to raise his right and put it in Jud's outstretched palm. And with the action, Jud felt a sudden excitement stir within him.

23

"Say 'cheese,' Freddie," he said quickly. "You know—make with a smile like I was going to take your picture."

When the boy grinned, Jud saw what he had expected to see, a dark bluish line easily visible along the gums near the tooth margin. And seeing it, he knew what had worried him about the little patient from the start.

"Let's go down and take a look at the blood smears, Dr. Valdese," he said. "I've got an idea they'll make the diagnosis for us."

The technician was already examining the smears. She moved aside to let Jud look at the microscope and he adjusted the objective until the stained cells came into focus, sharply outlined by the light flooding up through the lens system. What Jud sought was immediately apparent, a sharply defined dark strippling in many otherwise normal white cells.

"Take a look," he told Valdese, and moved back from the scope.

The younger man studied the slides for a long moment but, when he looked up, the baffled expression was still on his face.

"I never saw anything like this before, Dr. Tyler," he confessed.

"Neither have I for a long time. Listen to this symptom picture, Doctor, and see how much differential diagnosis you can remember from medical school: wrist drop, a dark line around the gums, anemia, muscular weakness and strippling of the eosinophilic leucocytes of the blood—"

"Wrist drop, eosinophilic strippling, a dark line—" Valdese's face brightened suddenly. "Lead poisoning?"

"What else?"

"But how?"

"That's what we're going to find out—I hope. Let's start with the mother."

The major traditional source of lead poisoning, Jud knew, was occupational, largely limited to persons exposed to vapors high in lead compounds. Such conditions occurred primarily in smelters, solder or paint factories, and the like, but that source of the poisonous metal could hardly exist in the small patient they had been examining. Equally unlikely was poisoning by lead in paint used for applying a high glaze to ceramic containers or even the once frequent "painter's Colic," which no longer existed now that lead based paint had been largely outlawed.

Obviously the child was suffering from a chronic low grade form of poisoning due to long exposure to lead that had gradually saturated his body with the metal. And since that in itself ruled out any acute source, even an old-fashioned lead water pipe—also long forbidden—Jud knew they would have to look elsewhere.

"Does Freddie eat dirt?" Jud asked the mother, while the small patient was being taken to Pediatric Receiving.

"Oh no, Doctor. None of my children would do that."

"How about paint?"

"Ain't no paint 'roun' my house. It come off the walls a long time ago."

"The whole family still seems to be getting it from some place," he insisted. "Try to remember some other possible source."

"Ain't nothing I know of," the mother insisted.

"Should I not report the case to the health authorities?" Dr. Valdese asked, while Jud was making a note on Freddie's chart.

"First ask the mother to bring the rest of the children to the laboratory tomorrow morning for blood smears," said Jud. "I think we're going to find some other cases of lead poisoning."

"Does that mean you're taking the position of Director of Emergency Services, Dr. Tyler?" Miss Cates' voice was as hostile as her eyes had been.

Jud turned to her in surprise. "I haven't decided. Don't you approve?"

"What difference does it make?"

"I would still like to know the reason for your disapproval?"

She stiffened. "Is that an order?"

"Certainly not. I have no official status here."

"Don't you know they only want you so they can use your reputation to make people think St. Luke's will be improved?"

"I do know that," he told her. "Mr. Rogers was very frank about it."

"They'll use you as a front—and then not vote the money the hospital needs," she said hotly. "I grew up here in Irontown, so I know what it is to see babies die because their mothers had no prenatal care; to see old people fed tranquilizers so they'll sleep all the time and not clutter up the OPD; and sick people shuttled through here like hogs through a slaughtering pen, with no time for anybody to even try and find out what's really wrong."

"Do you think I'd be a front for all that?" he asked.

"What else can you do—when it's all so hopeless?"

She turned quickly and left the room, leaving Jud staring after her thoughtfully.

"Shall I report her behavior to the Nursing Office, Dr. Tyler?" the resident asked, but Jud shook his head.

"No, Doctor," he said. "You see she's right about everything—except that I've got to stay on now, or admit that I've been taken for a fool."

CHAPTER IV

Jud was enjoying a leisurely breakfast in the hospital cafeteria, when Chuck Rogers came in. The chaplain hurried through the serving line, stopping only for a couple of sweet rolls and some coffee.

"Have a good night's sleep?" he asked, as he pulled out a chair at the small table where Jud was eating.

"Perfect. I always sleep well when my mind's made up."

Chuck shot him a quick glance. "Don't keep me in suspense."

"I'm taking the job."

A smile broke over the chaplain's face. "Don't ever tell me prayers aren't answered. I spent half the night asking God to make up your mind the right way."

"It may have been God who settled the question—I'm not sure. But the direct cause was a little boy named Freddie Brown—with the bellyache."

"I know Freddie's family well," said Chuck. "St. Luke's has been their family doctor since they moved here from Mississippi—along with most of the other people in Irontown."

"Yesterday Asa Ford said something about St. Luke's having public support," said Jud. "What did he mean?"

"When the new County Medical Center was built, the administrator over there realized that, if St. Luke's were closed, his nice clean institution would be swamped by people from Irontown and the Mexican-American section called Chicanoville. So he talked the city fathers into keeping us open and giving us some support—

enough to keep us going, but not enough to decrease the appropriation for the county center."

"Is the OPD here always as crowded as it was yesterday?"

"From early morning to about six o'clock," said Chuck. "Then there's a break until ten, when automobile accident cases start pouring in. On Friday and Saturday nights the place is a madhouse, of course."

"Why?"

"We're only five minutes by ambulance from the Interstate. Private ambulance companies are paid by the trip, so we get the worst cases—plus shooting and cutting victims and kids who sniff too much glue or take off too fast on a trip with grass, acid, or speed."

"And this is what you want to hand over to me?"

"I'll handle my share of the burden."

"Start figuring how to get rid of some of it then," said Jud. "Why can't we send our overflow to the new hospital across the street?"

"Provident sends us the patients *they* don't want."

"Why?"

"It's a proprietary hospital built by a New York based corporation, with local doctors who want to practice there allowed to buy stock in the company. They're geared to yield a profit of something like twenty per cent."

"No hospital does that, Chuck."

"It's possible—by lopping off services that don't pay their own way, or failing to provide them at all."

"What for instance?"

"Emergency rooms to start with. Then pediatrics and obstetrics. But not gynecology; the uterus is still a gold mine for the general surgeon."

"But a hospital without those departments is less than half a hospital to start with," Jud protested.

"Maybe so, but it's the most profitable half, leaving the losing services for places like St. Luke's that have to struggle along so poor people can find the medical care they need to keep themselves alive."

"How about the County Medical Center?"

"They have to take everything that comes, of course—and they're busy. But it's a two-hour bus ride across town from Irontown and Chicanoville, with a change of busses and no transfers. How can a

27

mother on welfare with a half-dozen other kids take a sick one to the County, wait most of the day to be seen, and then haul the child all the way back?"

"I don't see the answer yet, but I do know where to start," said Jud. "First I'll fill out the application blank for the personnel office. Then I'm going to start planning a triage system for the OPD."

"Triage?" Chuck frowned. "I don't know the word."

"It's a military term that came into use during the Spanish revolution back in the thirties. Loosely interpreted, it means sorting cases out according to priority."

"We've always taken them as they come in the OPD for fear of incidents," Chuck said doubtfully.

"Separate medical from surgical conditions and your residents can handle twice as many patients per hour as you've been doing," said Jud. "I've used it in the field, and it worked."

"Make whatever changes you think are indicated then. I'll back you."

"I'm not giving you any choice," said Jud. "The minute I got here you went right to work on me knowing that no doctor with any social conscience at all could look at that line upstairs and not feel an obligation. The trouble is that in medicine, a conscience can be a millstone around your neck."

"Or the wings that will carry you to heaven," said Chuck. "Oh! Oh! Here comes Dr. Wiley. If those eyebrows of his bristle any more, he'll take off and fly right out the window. I wonder what's happened now?"

II

"What do you mean by sending five kids in this morning for blood smears?" The pathologist planted himself before Jud. "Don't you know I have only two technicians to handle all the laboratory work in the hospital?"

"Those must be the Brown children," said Jud mildly. "I think you'll find their slides challenging, sir."

"Why?"

"Well—it's not exactly an ordinary condition."

"Since when did surgeons get to be laboratory experts?" Wiley demanded with characteristic belligerence. "If you insist on being so damned mysterious, I'll go down and look at them now."

28

"What's going on here?" Chuck Rogers asked, as the crusty old pathologist charged back through the door to the cafeteria, the tails of his long laboratory coat flapping in the breeze created by his passing.

Jud glanced at his watch. "Let's see; it should take him about ten minutes to examine those slides and find the stippling characteristic of lead."

The pathologist stalked back into the dining room while Jud was finishing his second cup of coffee. Only eight minutes had passed since he had left.

"You think I'm too senile to recognize basophilic stippling?" he demanded.

"I just told Chuck you'd have the diagnosis in ten minutes and you're two under the wire," said Jud. "Sit down and pant while I get you a cup of coffee."

"I'll get it myself," said Wiley. "I haven't seen six children with lead poisoning altogether in nearly ten years."

"You know why, don't you?"

"Because we stopped looking, dammit! Just like we stopped doing a lot of other things since we started taking in FMGs to fill out the house staff and run the Outpatient Department. They're not trained to detect the symptoms of lead poisoning."

"Nine-tenths of today's U.S. medical school graduates wouldn't recognize it either," said Jud.

"Is this a very prevalent condition?" Chuck Rogers asked.

"Only in ghettos like Irontown," Jud explained. "About twenty years ago manufacturers were forced by the government to stop putting dangerous amounts of lead into paint for interior use. But when landlords paint—which isn't very often—they usually just splash on non-lead paint over the old without scraping the walls down to the plaster."

"If they did, the plaster would come off too," said Chuck. "I could show you plenty of that, a few blocks from the hospital."

"A lot of slum kids suffer from what pediatricians call 'pica' too," said Jud. "They eat dirt or anything else of a non-food nature they can get and for a kid crawling around in the average ghetto tenement, holes in the plaster are gold mines. He just claws it out and eats it, along with the scales of the old paint put on there when the house was built."

"And gets a dose of lead?"

"Exactly."

"But if it's so deadly, why don't the public health people do something about it?"

"They don't recognize it very often either."

"But you did?"

"Don't get the idea that I'm an expert," said Jud. "We saw a lot of lead poisoning in children when I was at Mass. General, because the Pediatric Department was on the lookout for it. Besides, after I saw Freddie last night, I spent some time in your medical library reading up on chronic lead poisoning. One of the journals I was reading said more than two hundred children die from it in the United States every year. About sixteen thousand are treated and half of these are left mentally retarded by the effects of the lead on their brain cells, so you can imagine how much retardation there is in the ones who aren't treated."

"That's criminal," said Chuck.

"Or worse," Jud agreed. "According to a public health report I discovered, only about one in twenty-five cases is ever diagnosed, which means that possibly four hundred thousand children a year are being poisoned with lead. And roughly half of those will wind up with some kind of mental handicap because of damage to their brain."

"A forgotten disease that strikes nearly a half million kids a year." Chuck shook his head. "It's unbelievable what havoc greedy humans manage to inflict upon other humans—and children at that."

"I could cite you a lot of other examples," Dr. Wiley assured him. "Such things as child beating for example."

"What's the next step?" Chuck asked. "Report these cases to the Health Department?"

"The Brown children were seen in a city public health clinic about six months ago but the diagnosis was missed. I want to see the place where they live and get some samples of paint from the wall."

"I'm busy this morning but I could take you there right after lunch." Chuck picked up his tray. "Okay?"

"Fine," Jud told him. "I'll go by the personnel office and fill in the application form. Then I want to see Freddie Brown and the coronary case we admitted yesterday."

"Don't spread yourself too thin at the start." Dr. Wiley's bushy eyebrows rose in a sardonic gesture. "It isn't very often we get to see a bona fide medical Man for All Seasons in action down here in the poor backward South—especially a surgeon. The most I ever expect of them is to know how to handle a knife and swing a golf club on Wednesday afternoon."

III

Male Receiving, where patients were held for observation if needed, was on the first floor of the Emergency Wing, the surgical ward being on the second where the operating rooms were located. When Jud came down the narrow aisle between the rows of beds to the Intensive Care cubicle at the far end of the ward, he saw a stocky man in a brown sports jacket and checked slacks examining the patient in the cubicle.

"I'm Jud Tyler," he said, when the other man looked up from listening to the patient's chest.

"Richard Tubman. I saw Aiken briefly last night and determined that he didn't have a coronary."

"Then why the cardiac arrest?"

"I couldn't figure that out either at first," said Tubman. "The EKG on the monitor showed a right ventricular preponderance, so I ordered a six-foot film of the chest to check the size of the heart. When Dr. Blanchard called me with the report, I decided to come by this morning and study Aiken some more."

"I feel fine, Doctor," said the patient. "Any reason why I can't go home today?"

"We've got to make some more studies that will probably take a few days." Tubman put his stethoscope back into his bag and closed it. "I'll see you tomorrow."

"What do you know about byssinosis?" The internist asked Jud as they were walking back to the chart desk.

"Never even heard of it."

"Not many people have, but I should have suspected it the minute Aiken told me he had 'Monday Morning Asthma.'"

"I wondered what that was when the ambulance attendant mentioned it," said Jud. "But I was pretty busy at the time."

"So I heard."

"It didn't look like the clinical picture of asthma to me either. But we were slugging him with Isuprel at the time so I couldn't be sure."

31

"Byssinosis is a fairly common disease among people who've worked very long in textile mills, particularly in cardrooms where there's a lot of cotton fiber dust," said Tubman. "The typical symptoms are a sense of tightening in the chest and difficulty in breathing when they return to work on Monday, after having been off over the weekend. I took my residency in internal medicine at Yale, where most of the work on the disease has been done."

"Monday Morning Asthma is descriptive all right," said Jud. "Could byssinosis be anything like the silicosis that mine workers get from breathing coal dust?"

"This is apparently more like an allergy. Aiken tells me half the men who've worked in the cardroom at Framingham Mills for a long time have the same symptoms he does. When the dust first hits them on Monday morning, after they've been breathing relatively clear air outside the plant for several days, the immediate reaction resembles asthma—hence the term."

At the chart desk for the ward, Tubman removed Aiken's X-ray film from an envelope and held it up to the light.

"Long-standing cases often show the sort of lung infiltration you can see here in Aiken's X ray, plus right-sided heart enlargement indicating that it's working against a back pressure," he said. "The older medical writers call that *cor pulmonale.*"

"Then you're dealing with an occupational hazard?"

"Unquestionably. But so little has been written about the disease in the United States, except by the Yale group, that its effects haven't become widely known. Most cases are simply diagnosed as asthma or chronic bronchitis, particularly in people who have smoked a lot."

"Does Aiken smoke?"

"Hasn't for over ten years," said Tubman. "He says the publicity about cigarettes causing cancer scared him off and he hasn't lit one since."

"Then how do you explain his heart stopping?"

"In long-standing cases of byssinosis, the functioning lung volume is markedly decreased and the acute attacks on Monday mornings only make it worse. Aiken's heart undoubtedly tried to keep an adequate flow of oxygen to the brain, even though his lungs weren't putting it into the bloodstream. The end result was that his cardiac muscle buckled under the strain."

"That still might be hard to prove in a court of law."

"The Yale group worked out a standard set of tests in a federal prison in Georgia where a cotton mill was being operated," said Tubman. "If I had a special kind of a spirometer with transistorized timers, I could check Aiken's Forced Expiratory Volume during the first second after he takes a deep breath and starts to expel it. In byssinosis, the pattern of the chart you get with one of those machines is pretty characteristic—and also diagnostic."

"I'm curious to know more about byssinosis," said Jud. "We'll pay for the machine, if you'll get it."

"I'll order one today—by telephone from Atlanta or Birmingham," said Tubman. "It should be here day after tomorrow."

"Mind if I kibitz when you do the tests?"

"Not at all. You did save Aiken's life yesterday—and you're paying for the machine."

"If half the men in the cardroom at Framingham Mills have symptoms of byssinosis, it must be an important occupational hazard," said Jud as they were leaving the ward. "Once we get the spirometer you need, why not work up a series of cases for presentation to the local medical society, so doctors can learn to recognize this disease and recommend measures to prevent it?"

"It's an idea." Tubman picked up his medical bag. There hadn't been much enthusiasm in his voice, however, and when several minutes later, Jud happened to glance out the window of his office, which overlooked the hospital parking lot, he saw the reason why.

Watching Tubman get into a Mark III and drive off, he was pretty sure the report on byssinosis wouldn't be ready any time soon; in Framingham, cotton mill workers wouldn't often visit the offices of doctors able to drive a Mark III.

IV

At midmorning, Jud was called to the front office to sign the application he'd made earlier which Asa Ford's secretary had typed up for him. On the way back to the OPD, he stopped in the Medical Receiving Ward to check on Freddie Brown and was surprised to see a man with a camera at the entrance to the Intensive Care cubicle where Jack Aiken was sitting propped up in bed.

"What the hell's going on here?" Jud asked a nurse when he saw the visitor raise his camera, aim it at Aiken, and fire a flashbulb.

"It's the newspaper, Dr. Tyler," said the nurse. "They're doing a story on Mr. Aiken."

"Who gave permission?"

"The chaplain, I suppose. That's Charlie Gregg of the *Press-Bulletin*. I saw him here before when he was doing the series of stories on the hospital."

The photographer finished taking the pictures and came up the narrow aisle between the beds, which were not only crowded together along the sides of the wall but were placed end to end down the center too, leaving barely room for one person to pass. He appeared to be about thirty, with a freckled face and a pleasant smile.

"You're Dr. Tyler, aren't you?" The reporter extended his hand. "I'm Charlie Gregg—with the *Press-Bulletin*. I was hoping you'd have a free moment for me after I finished photographing Aiken here."

"Aiken's the one who had the close shave," said Jud. "Not me."

"The way I heard it, except for you, Aiken wouldn't be here," said Gregg. "When Chuck called this morning to tell me you're the Major Tyler from An Tha, I knew I had a feature worth going after; the most decorated medical officer in Vietnam doesn't often turn up here. Mind if we go into Chuck's office? I could use a little of that java he keeps on tap there."

"All right, but you can play down the decorations as far as I'm concerned. I was only doing what any Army surgeon had to do in Vietnam."

"Taking a mobile surgical hospital practically into the Viet Cong back yard? I think not."

"The orders were cut in Saigon. I only obeyed them."

"You didn't have to look after the Montagnard tribesmen when you weren't swamped with casualties. Or train South Vietnamese doctors in war surgery for the ARVN."

"You seem to know a lot about our activities."

"I was with *Stars and Stripes* in Saigon for a while. We researched a story on you and your hospital from the records there but the brass decided not to publish it for fear the VC might use you as a target."

"They got around to that too—in time." Jud's voice was bitter.

"Mind telling me where you've been in the interim? Unless it's none of my business?"

"A Medevac plane flew me to Letterman General in San Francisco where I had brain surgery for a shrapnel wound. I've spent the time since then at Letterman and Walter Reed."

34

"Why would you come here to start all over again?"

"I interned at St. Luke's ten years ago and Chuck Rogers was chaplain of my unit until he got malaria. When he wrote me that St. Luke's needed somebody to take charge of Emergency Services, I took the job." Jud tapped his cane against Chuck's desk while Gregg was pouring himself a cup of coffee. "This—and a right hand that doesn't always behave—keeps me from doing much surgery myself but I can still tell people what to do."

"Do you think you can reverse the downward trend St. Luke's has been in for the past five years or so?"

"Most people I've talked to seem to think I can't—except Chuck. Which would appear to be a good reason for trying."

"Can I print that?"

"If you like. Why should it be important?"

"Some what you might call 'Interests' are quite content for St. Luke's to remain just what it is now, a dumping ground for people nobody else wants to bother with," the newspaperman told him. "They might not like the idea of your bringing the sort of knowhow here that gave such fine results in Vietnam."

"With accident cases on the expressway showing a higher mortality rate than the war wounds we treated, wouldn't you say some of what you call my knowhow is needed here?"

"No question about that. But Irontown and Chicanoville are enclaves of race and poverty in the midst of a highly industrialized southern city, Dr. Tyler. And with inflation pushing up the price of labor all the time, manufacturers are looking for new ways to keep it down."

"By employing blacks?"

"Not so much them as Mexican-Americans. It will take several generations before much of the black population can develop the skills needed in textile mills, but Mexico has always had a large reservoir of artisans, mostly employed in local industries. Lately, a steady stream of migrants has been pouring up from Mexico and Texas—legally or illegally—trying to find jobs in the mills. Naturally, the people who are already at the machines don't particularly like the idea."

"I can see how that would be an explosive issue economically."

"Economically—and racially," said Gregg. "We're sitting on a powder keg and with the relief rolls going up every day, a lot of people in this part of the country think bringing even good medical

35

care to poor folks is only going to encourage them to ask for more."

"What about you?"

"Anybody in his right mind knows people who are sick and undernourished can't have much incentive to work," said Gregg. "By the way, has Chuck talked to you about his dream of turning St. Luke's into something of a health center like the Mile Square Project in Chicago."

"No."

"You're familiar with that, aren't you?"

"I remember reading about the project in the journal of the AMA," said Jud. "But I haven't gone into it."

"Chuck flew to Chicago recently to study Mile Square. He was so much inspired by it that he came back by New York and tried to interest one of the foundations in sponsoring something like it with St. Luke's as the center. But with so many problems in northern ghettos and so much prejudice against the South, I don't know whether he'll ever get anywhere through the foundations."

"That won't stop Chuck from pushing," said Jud. "I just got steamrolled into taking a job I may not even be able to handle."

"My bet's on you but I wish the odds weren't so long." Charlie Gregg put down his coffee cup and picked up his camera. "I've got to get to the paper and have these films developed for the morning edition. This time tomorrow people will know St. Luke's is on the way up again."

CHAPTER V

It had been a long time since Jud had seen a slum area like Irontown at close range and the experience, as Chuck drove slowly through the cluttered, pothole-infested street, was depressing. Rutherford Street in particular was a gaping wound, revealing the decay and disease that was slowly destroying what had been the very

36

heart of Framingham's lower middle-class residential area no more than two decades ago.

When Jud had walked these streets as an externe—usually on what had been called "Outside OB" to make home deliveries of patients who'd borne children before and could therefore be expected to have an easy labor—the brownstone fronts of the row houses had been fresh and clean, the long lines of steps, white in the more prosperous section and brown in the less elegant, scrubbed every morning, the gutters cleaned of refuse, and the sidewalks clear, except for an occasional child's tricycle.

The mill workers who had lived there in Jud's day had long since moved out, however, and as rents had drifted lower from the general debilitation of the area, it had gradually been taken over by blacks. The congestion created by the slum clearance project west of Ventura Boulevard, Chuck explained, had caused the houses on the east side of the new traffic artery to literally swarm with people who had nowhere else to go. Sidewalks, streets and gutters were littered with trash and refuse while over the whole district hung the dank smell of rot. Rot which, Jud was sure, must inevitably affect the souls of people forced to live in such a neighborhood.

Number 723 Rutherford Street was clean compared to its neighbors, as was the inside of the house when Mrs. Brown let them in. But the plaster had crumbled and in places the wooden lathing showed through. Almost no paint was on the walls either, as Mrs. Brown had said, so Jud knew he would have to look farther for a source of the lead that was slowly poisoning the children.

A savory stew was bubbling on the stove, while Mrs. Brown ironed clothes in the kitchen. The children were gathered around the kitchen table with steaming bowls of the thick mixture in front of them, avidly wielding spoons or sopping up the fluid with slices of bread.

"Don't let us interfere with your children's lunch," Chuck told the mother. "We're just going to look around a little."

"Are the others poisoned like Freddie?" she asked anxiously.

"Yes," said Jud. "The tests we did this morning were positive, but none of them are quite as bad as Freddie is."

"Why would just Freddie get so sick, Doctor?"

"We haven't figured that out, unless he was more rundown than the others."

37

"All of us had what people 'round here call 'Green Death' last month," she volunteered. "Seems like Freddie had it worse'n the others."

"Green Death," Jud knew, was a popular term for a particularly vicious form of virus infection that attacked the digestive tract, leaving its victims weak and wrung out. It could easily have been the trigger that had set off a vicious cycle of acidosis, cramping pains, and failure to eat, bringing the four-year-old Freddie to the hospital. But it didn't explain where the lead had come from originally.

"Are you sure the children haven't been eating something you didn't give them?" Jud asked.

"We cain't 'ford no candy, Doctor; it's all my husband and me can do to pay the rent and feed the children. Most of the clothes they wears comes from the Salvation Army."

While the woman was speaking, Jud became conscious of a distant rumbling sound, that rapidly increased in loudness until he was barely able to hear her final words. The house, too, had begun to shake, at first only slightly but increasing rapidly to a crescendo in tune with the noise, while the air quickly filled with a fine dust that made him cough.

The children went on eating as if they were accustomed to the dust but, when Jud looked down at the tablecloth, he saw that it was covered with a grayish film, as was the surface of the bowls of stew in front of the children. Seeing the film, he looked up at the ceiling and knew he needed to seek no further for the source of the lead in the bodies of the children.

The ceiling had been painted a long time ago but the paint, cracked and peeling now, was flaking off in fragments of various sizes from the shaking caused by the passage of the train, filling the air and making the gray film on the bowls of stew. One chip of paint, half the size of Jud's fingernail, landed on the surface of the bowl from which a little boy was eating and, moving quickly, Jud picked up the spoon the boy had been using and skimmed off the small piece of plaster paint.

"Do you have something I can put this in, Mrs. Brown?" he asked. "I need to have it examined in the laboratory."

The mother found a small jelly jar in a drawer and he dropped the flake of painting into it.

"How long has paint been flaking off the ceiling?" he asked.

"Ever since we come here, Doctor. We told the landlord 'bout the dust, but he didn't do nothin'. Every time a train goes by, it's the same thing."

"How often does that happen?"

"They shakes the house a dozen times a day at least. I has to mop the floor every morning just to get rid of the dust. You think that might have somethin' to do with making the children sick?"

"It has everything to do with it," Jud assured her.

"We been wantin' to move but the rent's low here. And with six mouths to feed—" Her shrug was a gesture of hopelessness, much like the black nurse's cry last night, he thought.

"Did you say you reported the condition of the house to the landlord?" Chuck Rogers asked.

"Yes, sir."

"Didn't he do anything?"

"He come and looked at it. But he said if he did any paintin' he'd have to raise the rent, and we can just live on what we both make, so we told him to leave it like it is."

"Who is your landlord?" Jud asked.

The woman hesitated. "We don't want no trouble, Doctor. Now that we know what makes the children sick, we can always eat in another room of the house. Or watch the clock and be sure no train ain't comin' then."

"You can't stop them from breathing dust while they're asleep," said Jud. "My guess is that more paint goes into their lungs that way than through food."

"Ain't there nothin' we can do?"

"The landlord will have to scrape the ceiling down to the plaster and put on a new coat of paint without any lead in it."

"But he'll raise the rent."

"I don't think he will—after I've had a talk with him," Jud said grimly. "Give me his name, please."

"It's Mr. Angus Claiborne. "He's got an office on Front Street where we pay the rent."

"Will Charlie Gregg work with us on this?" Jud asked Chuck, who was staring at the ceiling as if he still couldn't believe what he was seeing.

"Sure." Chuck's face brightened. "This sort of thing is right up Charlie's alley."

39

"A friend of ours will come by this afternoon or tomorrow and take some pictures," Jud told the mother. "I want you to tell him just what you told us and don't worry—everything is going to be all right."

"I hope so, Doctor," the woman said doubtfully. "But landlords don't do much to places like this—not for poor folks like us."

II

"Angus Claiborne is one of the richest men in town—and the stingiest," Chuck said as they were driving back to St. Luke's. "He won't knuckle under easily."

"If we handle this thing right, we've got Claiborne in a bind. The only thing that worries me about it is whether he can strike at you because of your association with me."

"Claiborne can't do anything to me that hasn't been tried already," said Chuck. "Bishop Tanner will reprimand me publicly and commend me privately: that's the only way we've managed to get any social change accomplished in Framingham so far."

"Suppose the bishop is forced to fire you?"

"I've got plenty of other job offers."

"Any you'd like to take?"

"I guess not," Chuck admitted. "But a lot of the business leaders in the city know I've been able to persuade the people of Irontown and Chicanoville to cool it so far and avoid what happened in Watts, Hough, and a lot of other places."

"The question is—would they stand up for you in a showdown with slum landlords?"

"If things get real tough, I guess even they would stomp on me like a lot of people would already like to do," Chuck conceded. "And by the way, if you go through with this, you're going to put yourself right in my class."

"I'm in it already," said Jud. "What else do they have against you?"

"I've persuaded a big garage over by the river to run a vocational school for blacks and Chicano mechanics at night. We've turned an abandoned warehouse into an arts and crafts center too, and managed to sell quite a lot of what's produced. Now with you at St. Luke's I can assure both the blacks and the Chicanos that they'll get better medical care than they can get at the County

Medical Center, all of which is liable to give the ghetto people the courage to demand their rights."

"But I'm only starting," said Jud.

Chuck smiled. "Your way of starting is to jump in with both feet." Then his voice sobered. "But don't knock yourself out trying to change Angus Claiborne and people like him, Jud. I can always take a crew from the youth groups I've organized among the blacks and Chicanos into the Brown's apartment some night and scrape those ceilings and paint them."

"If we don't make a public example of this particular situation, a lot of other children who are gradually accumulating enough lead in their bodies to make them mental cripples will never be discovered," Jud said firmly. "That's where Charlie Gregg can help us—if it comes to stern measures. But first, I'm going to give Angus Claiborne a chance to practice a little pragmatic Christianity."

"You're poaching in my territory," Chuck said with a grin. "But I'll even pray for you—as long as you're not making your own condition worse."

"You said this is what the doctor—Colonel Standiford in this case—ordered for me. I wasn't quite sure of it at first, but now I know he was right."

At the hospital, Jud got Charlie Gregg on the phone at the office of the Framingham Press-Bulletin.

"I just finished writing my story on you and St. Luke's," the newspaperman said cheerfully. "Want to hear it?"

"And be accused of censorship? No thanks."

"Anyway I owe you for a good story."

"I'm ready to collect on that debt."

"Who do you want killed?"

"Possibly a guy named Angus Claiborne." When there was a sudden silence at the end of the line, Jud added, "Know him?"

"I know him." Greggs tone was grim. "He owns a lot of slum houses in your neighborhood and comes out from under the rocks every now and then to collect his rent—but not long enough for anybody to squash him. You going to try?"

"If necessary." Jud gave the newspaperman a quick rundown on the Brown children and what he and Chuck had discovered on Rutherford Street that morning.

"I thought lead paint was outlawed long ago," said Gregg.

41

"That didn't take it off walls where it already was—or ceilings in this case. Can you go to 723 Rutherford Street and get some pictures?"

"Sure. But I won't have a story unless some medical authority states unequivocally that the children are being poisoned."

"Don't break the story before I can practice a little judicious blackmail," Jud advised. "If it doesn't work, I'll be your medical authority and accuse Angus Claiborne of poisoning children."

"It'll make a hell of a story," Charlie Gregg sounded excited. "And probably cost me my job."

"Don't tell me Claiborne owns your paper too."

"No. But some of the city's leading citizens own a lot of those slum buildings in Irontown."

"If you don't want to go through with it, I'll understand."

"Hell, man! That's what newspapering is all about. When I can't take pictures of whatever I want to and write up whatever I want to, I'll go someplace else. When do you want the photos?"

"As soon as you can get them."

"I'll go over there right away and send you some prints by messenger as soon as they're developed, probably the first thing tomorrow morning. But move carefully, Doctor. From where I sit you look like the best thing that's happened to this town in a long time. I'd hate to lose you right here at the start."

III

It was a little after three that afternoon and time for the regular hospital personnel shift change, when Jud happened to look out a window of the corridor and saw Kathryn Galloway crossing the parking lot toward the rows of parked cars. All morning he had been trying to speak to her, but the visit to Rutherford Street had interfered. Now he hurried to where a door gave access from the corridor to the walkway leading to the lot. Opening it, he stepped down upon the asphalt.

"Miss Galloway," he called to her, "could I speak to you for a minute, please?"

She stopped, but for a moment he thought she was going to ignore his call. Then she turned but he saw that her expression was as disapproving as was the stiffness of her body—none of which, however, detracted from her beauty.

42

"Yes, Doctor?" she said coolly.

He had intended to apologize for the incident the previous morning, but her manner warded him off.

"I want to thank you for knowing how to inject the bolus of calcium chloride," he said. "It probably had as much to do with starting Aiken's heart as my clumsy attempt at CPR."

He turned and, as so often happened, almost fell over his cane, when his right leg responded slowly because of the anger in his brain. But he didn't look back as he limped across the concrete, although, not hearing footsteps or the slam of a car door, he was quite sure that she was still standing where he had left her.

"A patient is waiting to see you, Dr. Tyler," she called as he was opening the door to the corridor leading to the OPD—and he was sure her tone was mocking, not angry. "A private patient."

Two people were in Jud's office. One was a burly sergeant of police whose name—it was Tabor—he remembered from ten years ago. The other was a slender blond girl whose face seemed vaguely familiar.

"Hello, Dr. Tyler," she said brightly. "Remember me—Samantha Wright?"

"I'm sorry—"

"You fixed my elbow when I was thirteen," she said with a grimace. "I had braces on my teeth then so I don't blame you for not remembering me. But I've been in love with you ever since."

"Mrs. Fellowes is inclined to make extravagant statements, Doctor," said the sergeant dryly. "Especially when she's on a trip."

"You had to spoil that, Sergeant," said the girl. "I was on Cloud Nine—"

"Ninety would be closer to the facts," said the policeman. "On the expressway."

"I was still doing fine until you started blowing that siren." The girl seemed to harbor no resentment toward the policeman; obviously this wasn't her first experience with the law. "Then I looked back—"

"And crashed a Porsche through the fence," said the sergeant. "Anybody else would have been killed, Dr. Tyler, but I've been getting this young lady out of trouble since she started riding a tricycle. She seems to live a charmed life."

Jud remembered the girl now: at thirteen she'd been a frequent visitor to St. Luke's Emergency Room with various scratches, cuts,

43

and an occasional broken bone—like the one she had mentioned. He could even remember the X ray of her elbow, with the head of the radius completely dislocated and fragmented—a not uncommon injury in exceedingly active young people about that age.

The city's leading orthopedist had been called in to remove the head of the radius, an operation Jud could have done easily, even then. But interns at St. Luke's didn't operate on the daughter of Seth Wright, owner of the city's oldest and largest cotton processing mill and the richest man in Framingham.

"How's the elbow, Samantha?" he asked.

"You did remember!" The girl's face broke into a smile and, before he realized what she was doing, she leaped from the chair and gave him a resounding kiss. "My day is made!"

Only then did Jud notice that her left arm was bent sharply just above the wrist. His mind made the diagnosis immediately; only a "greenstick" fracture gave that appearance, so called because the bone didn't break completely through. Such breaks were rarely painful because the broken ends of the bone didn't actually separate; and they were easy to reduce, usually healing well in a few weeks.

"Nobody else in Framingham could have walked away from that accident with nothing but a broken arm, Doctor," said Sergeant Tabor.

"It's not broken," said the girl. "Only bent."

"You're both right," Jud agreed. "Who is your doctor, Samantha?"

"You," she said promptly—and happily. "Nobody else is going to look after me, now that you're back."

"How did you know?"

"Amanda Cates told me; her mother cooked for us a long time. Amanda's been going by in the morning to make Father take his medicine."

"I'm not a bone specialist," Jud reminded her.

She held out her injured wrist. "Did you ever fix one of these?"

"Lots of them."

"Then you can fix mine."

"All right—but I'll have to call your father first."

"What for? I'm twenty-three and I've been married and divorced." When she wrinkled her nose at him impishly, she was once again the thirteen year old he'd first known, a leggy kid with a penchant for accidents and unmistakable signs already of the stunning young woman she had become.

44

"Besides," she added, "Dad disinherited me when I divorced Horace Fellowes."

"Anybody who can smash up a Porsche isn't exactly penniless," Jud observed.

"Grandmother took care of that with a trust fund in her will," she confided. "She was independent, like me. Besides, I only married Horace to please my father—"

"The first time in history," Sergeant Tabor observed dryly.

"And the last." Samantha made a face at him. "Horace graduated from N. C. State as a textile engineer, so Dad figured he was gaining a vice president for the mill. He got the V.P. all right; but the daughter moved out. Are you going to put me to sleep, Doctor?"

"Probably not—considering what you've already had. What was it by the way?"

"I take the Fifth." Samantha smiled sweetly at Sergeant Tabor.

"I'll use novocain then," said Jud. "But it may hurt."

"I've been hurt before—and didn't cry."

There might be the seat of Samantha Wright's difficulties, Jud thought, but didn't voice it.

"We'll take an X ray first," he told her. "Then I'll straighten out that bend."

The fracture reduction, performed under novocain injected directly into the broken end of the bone in the X-ray room, took only a few minutes, as did the application of a light plaster splint to support the wrist. Actually, it could probably have gone without any support at all, since the fracture was not complete. But with Samantha's penchant for accidents, the splint seemed a logical precaution.

"Let me see this in a few days," he told her. "Can I call someone to take you home?"

"I'll take care of that, Doctor," said Sergeant Tabor. "Her car was being towed away when we left the scene of the accident."

"I'll give you a prescription for codeine in case you have any pain," Jud assured Samantha.

"If anything bothers me, I'll just call you," she said airily. "You're my doctor now, so you're responsible for me."

Jud couldn't repress a smile at her insouciant assurance that nobody could refuse her anything. "That's only true in the Orient, after you've saved somebody's life," he said.

45

"You saved mine," she assured him. "Before I heard you had come back to Framingham, I was dying slowly of an unrequited love, like the Browning sisters or somebody—I didn't get any further than that in college before they threw me out for smoking pot. So long, Doc; you'll be hearing from me."

And even as flip as she was, Jud couldn't find the idea anything but pleasant.

CHAPTER VI

The small office could barely accommodate the five residents and Jud, when they gathered there at his request that evening for a staff conference. Emilio Fernandez and Juan Valdese, he already knew; the others he'd been introduced to casually, while he and Chuck had been walking through the hospital yesterday. They were young, earnest, and with time could probably be made into capable doctors. But the language difficulty—though not so great as it might have been, since English was taught as a second language in the Philippines—plus deficiences in basic medical education, limited their capabilities and the nature of the duties Jud could safely delegate to them without supervision. In addition to Fernandez and Valdese, there were Dr. Ricardo Montez, Dr. Carlos Machave, and Dr. Raphael Gomez.

"I plan to institute a new routine for handling the Outpatient Department," Jud said when they were all seated. "It involves a military principle called triage."

Fernandez frowned. "I do not know the word, Doctor."

"It can be defined as sorting or classification," Jud explained. "In your present OPD routine medical and surgical patients are seen as they come. I understand that this procedure was instituted because the hospital authorities believed there might be objections, if the patients were seen by a doctor out of turn, but I think this fear has been exaggerated."

"It was Mr. Rogers' idea, Doctor," said Valdese.

46

"I've already explained what I plan to do to Mr. Rogers and he approves," Jud assured them. "If my plan doesn't work, we can always go back to the system you're using now—which can hardly be considered much better than chaos."

"It *is* very frustrating," Fernandez admitted. "Only Juan and I have had much surgical training, so when the others have patients with surgical conditions, they must send them to us. Which means more waiting if we happen to be examining a medical condition at the time."

"Starting tomorrow, I shall have a desk between the clinic secretary and the Emergency Room," said Jud. "I shall see each patient briefly and determine what seems to be the diagnosis. Surgical cases will go to Dr. Fernandez and Dr. Valdese in the Emergency Room, while those with medical conditions will be sent to a new department using several rooms in the Outpatient Wing. There, the women will be separated from the men and examinations made as rapidly as possible. By using nurses to record blood pressures and take the pertinent facts of the history, I believe we can reduce the time you spend in the Outpatient Department by one third, leaving you more time for the patients admitted to the ward."

"That will be good," said Fernandez. "We have almost none now."

"I will also make every effort to be available for consultation during the mornings while the Outpatient Department is the busiest," Jud assured them. "And I want each of you to feel free to call upon me when you're not sure of anything. Are there any questions?"

There were none, probably because the idea was so new in their experience at St. Luke's that questions had not yet formed in their minds. As the others were leaving, Emilio Fernandez held back.

"What is it, Emilio?" Jud asked.

"It is, how do you say, a very personal matter, Dr. Tyler. Are you to perform the operative surgery from now on?"

"I haven't operated since I was wounded," said Jud. "I shall assist you and Dr. Valdese whenever major surgery is necessary in accident cases or other emergencies, but I do not plan to operate myself."

II

Chuck Rogers was in the hospital cafeteria when Jud came in for breakfast after helping the residents take care of the victims from a three-car smashup on the expressway about 6:00 A.M. Fernandez

47

and Valdese had worked well under his direction and, although he was tired, he was satisfied that, with supervision, they could handle anything that was likely to be brought into the hospital for emergency treatment.

After filling his tray, Jud joined the chaplain at a table.

"You're famous!" said Chuck. "Seen the paper?"

"I've been tied up with those accident cases since six o'clock."

Chuck handed him a newspaper folded so the second section devoted to local news was on the top. Beneath photographs of Jud and of Jack Aiken in the Intensive Care cubicle was the caption:

SURGEON HERO TAKES OVER AT ST. LUKE'S
Promises Front Line Medical Care
to Accident Victims

The article that followed under Charlie Gregg's byline was a description of the dramatic resuscitation of Jack Aiken, plus what Jud had told the reporter about his conviction that the same principles used to care for wounded in Vietnam could save thousands injured in civilian life. The clincher, so to speak, as Jud's avowal that a soldier falling in battle had a better chance of surviving than an accident victim on the average Interstate Highway even within sight of a hospital.

"A lot of doctors are going to be at your throat," said Chuck.

"It's all true."

"That isn't going to change their reaction. And your association with me will only make it worse."

"When did you get to be such a pariah?"

"Ever since I started putting pressure on the union at Framingham Mills to let blacks and Chicanos work in skilled textile crafts like carding and spinning."

"What's wrong with that?"

"A lot of cotton mill workers are hillbilly migrants from Appalachia. They'll fight the idea because they're afraid it means fewer jobs for them and the millowners will do almost anything to avoid trouble. All of which makes me sort of a black sheep as far as they're concerned for trying to change the status quo, and since doctors are part of the Establishment, they'll fall in line."

Jud didn't doubt the truth of Chuck's words. Doctors as a whole were political conservatives. And since the major source of their income was the monied class, they tended strongly toward support of the Establishment at all levels.

48

"Don't your activities actually threaten the jobs of the present textile workers?" Jud asked.

"The more people that are working in Framingham, the less will be on relief," said Chuck. "And the more business there'll be in general."

"What about militant black elements?"

"This is the South—remember? Most blacks in Framingham know the only solution for them is literally to pull themselves up by their bootstraps. Their spokesman is Eric Cates, Amanda's brother; we work closely together."

"If he's as intelligent as she is, he should be a natural leader."

"Eric is a fine musician. He had two years of college and was going to make it a career, until he dropped out and went into the Army. But when he came back from Vietnam and saw that conditions here hadn't changed much for his people, in spite of all the talk about civil rights, he started trying to change things."

"Violently?"

"So far, no. But it's hard to convince young people that change can ever be achieved gradually—whether they're black or white—especially when they see so much injustice and neglect on every side."

"Speaking of neglect," said Jud. "I'm going to see Angus Claiborne as soon as I can get the photos Charlie Gregg was supposed to take yesterday."

"They're probably on your desk now," said Chuck. "The door was open when I came through the corridor to breakfast and I saw a large envelope lying on it."

Jud stopped by his office when he left the cafeteria. Chuck had been correct; the sheaf of photographs had been delivered at 9:00 P.M. the night before according to the notation on the routing sheet, probably just after he had gone to bed.

"Sorry to be late with these," Charlie had written on the note accompanying them. "I had to use a special developing technique to make those dust particles stand out the way they do. Let me know when to fire. You can keep these; I made extra prints."

The photos told a graphic story; the crumbling ceiling with the Brown children seated beneath it and the dancing particles of paint caught in a beam of sunlight shining through a window as a train was passing.

Charlie had also photographed the walls with the plaster worn down to the laths in places during the years since there had been

49

any repairs. And to make the indictment complete, he'd managed to get photographs of tax records at City Hall, proving that Angus Claiborne was the owner of the property.

III

The new system in the OPD worked very well that morning, but not without some difficulty. Many patients resented Jud's arbitrarily shuttling them in different directions according to the symptoms they gave. Several times, too, he was wrong in his snap diagnosis for purposes of classification and patients sent to the medical examining line had to be rerouted into the Emergency Room. But for the most part there was a perceptible speeding up of the long line that had started to form shortly after eight o'clock, when the OPD opened.

More than once during the day he had cause to be grateful for the masterly way Kathryn Galloway directed the human traffic crowding the corridors and coped with minor crises that kept arising from time to time among the discordant elements of the OPD population. He had intended to thank her for her help, but a child brought in just before three required a delicate job of suturing to prevent an ugly scar from a face wound inflicted by an angry parent, and he was kept busy showing Juan Valdese how to infiltrate the wound with novocain and close it with many tiny sutures to prevent scarring—the technique used by plastic surgeons.

It was three-thirty when he finally left the remaining patients to the care of the residents; by that time Kathryn Galloway had gone off duty.

In his office, he looked up Angus Claiborne's number and dialed it.

"Mr. Claiborne?" he asked, when a voice with a rough Scottish brogue answered.

"I'll see if he's in. Who's calling, please?"

"Dr. Judson Tyler at St. Luke's Hospital." Jud was pretty sure he was talking to Claiborne himself.

"What did you want to talk to Mr. Claiborne about, Doctor?"

"I'm new in the city and wanted to ask about some real estate." It wasn't exactly a lie, though not quite the truth; but it was the most tempting bait he could think of to dangle before a Scotsman.

"Mr. Claiborne will be here in another half hour, Doctor. He can see you then."

"I'll be there," Jud promised.

The Claiborne building appeared to be even older than the tenement on Rutherford Street, but much better kept. Angus Claiborne's office was on the second floor; only a fierce-looking old man with the cold eyes of a loan shark was inside.

"I'm Dr. Tyler," said Jud.

"My clerk told me he talked to you." Angus Claiborne waved Jud to a chair which, like the rest of the office, was hard and sparse. "What kind of property did you want to talk about, Doctor?"

"Rental property—at 723 Rutherford Street."

Claiborne's eyes narrowed. "You want to buy that?"

"Hardly," said Jud. "In the past forty-eight hours I have examined six children suffering from lead poisoning caused by paint flaking off the ceiling of the first floor apartment."

"Did you say poisoning?" Claiborne's voice was considerably colder than at the start of the conversation.

"Without question. The diagnosis is a matter of record at St. Luke's Hospital."

"You have no proof that they were poisoned at home, Doctor." The voice was barely a growl.

"You're mistaken, Mr. Claiborne," Jud said patiently. "We discovered lead in the blood of the children, and some paint scrapings examined in our laboratory also revealed lead. I came here to give you an opportunity to replaster and paint the apartment and whatever others you own like it, where lead poisoning is probably already present in the occupants."

"Such things cost money, Doctor."

"Burying children costs money too, Mr. Claiborne." Jud's short fuse caught fire. "And the state pays even more to care for those who become mentally retarded because of lead poisoning."

"That's not my responsibility."

"The building is."

"They don't have to live there."

"With six children, the Brown family doesn't have much choice."

The old man pushed back his chair and stood up. He was very tall and solidly built, more powerful, Jud suspected, than he—especially when, if it came to resisting ejection from the office, the use of his right arm and leg might be seriously hampered by his aphasia.

"Have you finished, Doctor?" Claiborne's tone was icy.

"Not unless you are going to do something about the property."

51

"I am not," said Claiborne. "In the future, I would suggest that you stick to your business, Doctor, and let me take care of mine."

Jud was keeping his temper under control with an effort; after all he hadn't really expected anything from the first moment he'd seen Angus Claiborne.

"My business is saving lives through medical measures, Mr. Claiborne," he said quietly. "But there are other ways."

"Are you threatening me, sir?" The old man was shaking with rage.

"I'm giving you a chance to turn that apartment and others around it into places fit for human beings to live in."

"I warn you that the law is on my side."

"And I warn *you* that other measures can be taken. Good day, Mr. Claiborne."

From a corner drugstore phone booth, Jud rang Charlie Gregg at the offices of the *Press-Bulletin*. "I just came from Angus Claiborne's office," he said.

"In one piece? Last year the old bastard threw out a tenant who complained about his houses. Broke two of the fellow's ribs."

"He threw me out too—but only verbally. I'm ready for you to turn your dogs loose, Charlie."

"Fine. The odds were so much in favor of Claiborne turning you down that I ordered cuts made from those photos. And I've been thinking about a lead for the story too. What would you think of this?"

The reporter's voice was brisk and efficient as, in a few brief sentences, he sketched the line his story would take. When he finished, Jud drew a deep breath.

"That should do it," he said.

"You wanted a bomb. Just don't get hit by another fragment."

"I'll be careful—and thanks, Charlie."

"You've done me a favor by restoring my faith in your profession," Gregg assured him. "I hardly ever see a crusading doctor any more; they're all too busy making money so they can buy their first Mark III."

CHAPTER VII

Jud was reading in his room after dinner when the phone rang about nine o'clock.

"Do you make house calls, Doctor?" A familiar voice asked.

"No, Samantha."

"But I need help."

"What's the trouble?"

"My wrist is throbbing like crazy and my fingers are changing color. The splint must have slipped or something."

"Did you take one of the codeine tablets I prescribed?"

"I was so excited over seeing you again that I didn't think to tell you the stuff always makes me sick."

"I'll phone another prescription to your druggist."

"Suppose the circulation gets cut off? That could be serious, couldn't it?"

"Call a taxi and come over here then," he said resignedly. "I'll meet you in the Emergency Room."

"I'm not dressed to go out and I don't feel like dressing again," she said plaintively. "Besides, a girl isn't safe even in a taxi at night any more. Why, just a few nights ago a secretary was raped when she called a taxi to take her home after working late."

Jud was pretty certain he was being given a snow job, but with any fracture there was always a possibility of circulatory obstruction and damage to fingers or toes beyond the cast. Besides, when he remembered the lovely young woman Samantha Wright had become, he found the idea of the house call less and less distasteful.

"Where do you live?" he asked.

"The Miramar Apartments; it's the high-rise you can see from the front of the hospital. I have one of the penthouses."

"Sounds like your grandmother was liberal."

She giggled. "Horace pays. After all, the only daughter of Seth Wright couldn't live in poverty in Framingham."

"I guess you're right," he agreed. "I'll be there in ten minutes or so."

Amanda Cates answered when he rang the Emergency Room telephone. "I'll need a medical bag with an elastic bandage, some cotton batting and a couple of rolls of plaster," he told her. "A fracture case I reduced is having some pain and I've got to make a house call."

53

"Yes, Dr. Tyler."

"Call me a taxi as soon as it's ready, please, Miss Cates. I'll be in my office."

There was a knock on the door about five minutes later. "The taxi's at the ambulance ramp," said the nurse. "I gave the medical bag to the driver."

The cab deposited him in front of the Miramar Apartments and a uniformed doorman opened the door.

"Mrs. Fellowes is expecting you, Doctor," he said. "It's Penthouse 'C'; the elevator's at the back of the lobby."

Samantha herself opened the door at his knock. She had told the truth when she said she wasn't dressed for going out, he saw. A blue robe was belted snugly at the waist and the froth of a nightgown was visible just below its hem. The fabric was quite filmy, in keeping with the blue satin mules she wore, and Jud didn't try to quell the quickening of his pulse at her proximity and the intimacy of the situation.

"You were a darling to come," she greeted him.

Her eyes were overly bright and, when he crossed the threshold, he recognized the sweetish odor of marijuana in the apartment. By that time, he was certain it had been a mistake to let her talk him into coming—and equally certain, when she closed the door behind him, that he didn't want to retreat.

"See?" She held out the injured arm. "My hand's all red and swollen just like I told you."

The skin was red; in fact it looked almost as if it had been burned by the sun. Swelling was less in evidence, however, nor did the picture exactly fit that of an extremity whose circulation was obstructed by a too tight splint, since in such a condition it would tend to be bluish in color and cool, instead of red and hot, as her hand was when he touched it.

"I brought an elastic bandage and some extra padding to make it feel better," he told her. "Suppose we take a look."

"Let's sit on the sofa. You can put your bag on the coffee table."

It took only a few moments to cut the bandage with a pair of scissors from the medical bag and remove the splint. He could see no sign of undue pressure, but the redness of her hand did extend exactly to the end of the splint, as would have been the case if the circulation were affected.

"It feels wonderful to have the splint off." She flexed and extended her fingers. "That means it had to be pressing, doesn't it?"

54

"Perhaps. I'll pad it more thickly this time."

Samantha leaned close to watch as he unrolled the length of cotton batting, cutting it into strips just longer than the splint, so it could be turned over the ends to form a soft cuff which could not possibly press into the tissue. Her shoulder touched his, reminding him that she was soft and desirable under the filmy nightdress—all of which made the job of padding the splint more difficult for fingers whose tendency to fumble was increased by excitement or emotion.

"Were you hurt very bad in Vietnam?" Her fingers touched the scar on his head and lingered there.

"I was paralyzed for several months after the operation; the same thing that's going to happen to you one of these days if you don't stop driving fast when you've been smoking pot."

She made a face at him but didn't draw away. "Everybody else tells me what I ought not to do," she said somewhat plaintively. "Don't you do it too, Jud."

"Did anyone tell you what you *ought* to do?" he asked as he applied the padded splint to her wrist and began to wrap the brown elastic bandage around her lower arm to hold it in place.

"Such as?"

"Finishing college instead of breaking rules to get tossed out. And maybe working at making a marriage succeed, instead of running away when everything wasn't exactly what you wanted it to be."

"Don't be so old fashioned, darling—that's Establishment and square."

"You said yesterday that I was responsible for you," he reminded her. "So I have to tell you what's best for you."

"Who gave you—?" She started to flare but he cut her off.

"Are you going to welsh on that like you have on everything else?"

The thrust went home—and hurt. He saw her lips quiver and, when tears started to form in the too brilliant eyes, pressed on while he had the advantage.

"Have you gone beyond pot yet?"

"What do you mean?"

"Heroin?"

"I've got better sense than that!" she said indignantly.

"What about LSD?"

"I've been considering that. Some people I know—"

"Don't consider it any more—unless you want to get your sex chromosomes loused up and give birth to a monster or two."

"You're exaggerating. I—"

"Don't you believe it. Studies of pregnancies in women who used LSD show a much higher incidence of abnormal births and miscarriages than should ordinarily occur."

"I love you when you're being severe—and pontifical." She moved closer. "Warn me some more."

"Really, Samantha—"

"I'd love to bear your child, darling. It would have your eyes and your strong jaw." Her fingers touched the corner of his mouth. "But I hope it would have my sense of humor."

The conversation had suddenly taken a turn in what, as a doctor, Jud recognized to be a dangerous direction. And yet, as a man who hadn't been this close to anyone so desirable for over a year, he couldn't help being excited—or fail to feel an urge to explore the situation further.

"I think I'd better go." Conscience made at least a token stand. "After all, I'm a doctor making a house call."

"You've finished taking care of me medically and we're just getting to know each other again after all those years we've wasted." Her fingers touched his scalp gently again, then moved exploringly across his face to touch his lips. "If you tell me you don't want to kiss me, I'll be crushed."

"Of course I want to kiss you." He heard the words but couldn't believe he'd spoken them himself. "But it's not ethical for a doc—"

She moved away quickly and, before he realized what she was doing, picked up his medical bag, opened the apartment door, and set it outside in the hall.

"Now you're not on a house call any more," she said, closing the door. "You're visiting me in my apartment and you're going to make love to me."

She was in his arms before he could protest—if he had intended to—which he wasn't at all sure he did. Her lips were soft and eager against his own and the touch of her warm flesh when, without volition, his fingers moved beneath the hem of her robe and the froth of the nightgown was like living satin.

He heard her moan softly as his hands roamed over her body, but only when he felt her move away a little and start to unbutton his shirt did he experience a sudden upsurge of the fear that had kept him from any intimacy with the Army nurses who had more than once evinced an interest in him as a man rather than as a patient. Even if he could, however, he wouldn't have removed Samantha's hand, when it slipped inside his shirt and along his body, for things had gone much too far for retreat.

He was trapped, trapped by his starved desires into a situation infinitely more dangerous and fraught with humiliation for him than when he'd fallen to the floor of the Emergency Room that first day, the most humiliating circumstances in which a man could possibly find himself—that of holding an eager and utterly desirable woman in his arms and finding himself unable to assert his manhood.

"Please love me," she whispered against his lips as her seeking hand caressed him—but brought no response.

Even then, he dared to hope and held her close, his touch savoring the intimacies of her body in a way that made her gasp and cling to him. But when his own body refused to answer the frantic demands of his throbbing brain, he knew that his daring to hope for a miracle under the stimulus of warm flesh, eager lips and caressing, even demanding, hands had been a tragic error.

With a tremendous effort of will, he released her then and pushed her away.

"I can't, Samantha," he said hoarsely. "Don't you see "

For an instant she was as rigid in his arms as if he had struck her in the face. Then she left his embrace and the couch in a single lithe movement and turned upon him like a jungle cat.

"You!" Anger bereft her of words momentarily before the torrent began to flow. "After I damn near burned my hand off with a sunlamp just to get you here."

"You don't understand!"

"What are you? A eunuch or something?"

Unable to stand the humiliation any longer, Jud took the only course open to him—flight. There was no point in trying to explain; in her anger at being spurned—as she understood it—Samantha couldn't possibly be expected to understand that, however much his will had urged his body to respond to hers, the nerve impulses necessary to prepare for sexual contact had simply not been able to penetrate the barrier of scar tissue in his brain, to say nothing of the even higher barrier of fear that just this might happen.

"Get out!" She screamed at his retreating back as he fled not

57

even realizing that he'd left the medical bag where she had placed it in the hallway beside the apartment door until he was out of the building and a half block away, walking blindly toward St. Luke's.

II

Two blocks from the hospital on a dark street, Jud was beginning to wonder about the wisdom of the route he had chosen as he had rushed blindly from Samantha's apartment, when a car pulled to the curb beside him at the corner. He hardly dared look until a familiar voice called his name and, in the light from a street lamp, he saw that the driver was Kathryn Galloway.

"What in the world are you doing out on foot?" she demanded. "Don't you know you could get rolled and maybe killed in this neighborhood at night?"

"I was looking for a bar called Tony's." Jud gave the first explanation that popped into his mind—anything but the truth. "We used to go there when I was an intern."

"Tony's went by the board years ago, like most of this part of Framingham. Hop in. If you're that much in need of a beer, I know a nice place."

He got into the car without further invitation and she drove on when the light changed.

"I'm glad you came along," Jud said gratefully. "I was beginning to be scared."

"You're lucky nobody mugged you before you got this far." In a spring dress she was considerably more feminine than in uniform. "There's a nice tavern at the top of Spring Hill that caters to young people, which sort of leaves us out. But the beer's good and so is the music—if you stay far enough away from the bandstand."

"I want to apologize for being rude to you that first day," said Jud. "I never know when my right leg may give away and, if I don't happen to have my cane handy when the aphasia blocks that leg, down I go. It was pretty embarrassing and I guess I acted like a child."

"Forget it," she said. "I've been hurt enough times myself to know that it's sometimes instinctive to lash out, even at those who want to help you."

"Do you remember speaking to me earlier that morning?"

"No. When was that?"

58

"About a half hour before the Code Five. I was wandering around the OPD and you told me to get back in line."

She laughed. "Was that you? All I saw was somebody with a cane. I guess I'm pretty rough on the patients sometimes when I'm in a hurry. But with so little order in the OPD, somebody has to be."

"What do you think of the new routine?"

"If it works every day as well as it did this morning, I think you've got something. We'll just have to see."

At the foot of the mountain she turned off Ventura Boulevard on a winding road that led upward past the gushing spring near the base of the height that gave it the name. Climbing gradually in a series of looping curves, they came to the top of the mountain.

Perhaps a quarter of a mile away, Jud could see the lights of the most exclusive club in Framingham, but Kathryn swung the car into the parking lot behind what appeared to be a rambling old house on a cliff overlooking the city.

"Not many people come here on Monday night, so maybe we can get a table on the porch," she said. "It projects out over the edge of the cliff and the view is absolutely fantastic."

The hostess who took them to a table addressed Kathryn by name and gave Jud an appraising glance, by which he judged that his companion often came here with someone else. They ordered tall steins of beer and were served a basket of pretzels.

From their table on the porch they could down on the city from a height of perhaps a thousand feet. In the distance the fiery torches of the blast furnaces cast a red glow against the sky and, in the nearer foreground, ribbons of light marked the boulevards that knifed through the city. Mercifully, the squalor and misery of Irontown, so apparent by day, was blotted out by the night, leaving only beauty.

Out of uniform, Kathryn Galloway proved to be much less brisk and efficient than she was in the hospital and considerably more feminine.

"How do you feel after your first days at St. Luke's?" she asked, when their order had been brought and the first urgency of thirst quenched.

"Challenged—and not quite certain I can handle it."

"I wouldn't think you'd be uncertain about many things."

"Somewhere along the line, the time will come when a person's life is going to hang on my ability to do the necessary thing at the critical moment with my right hand, or even my right leg," he explained. "Never knowing when one or both of them may fail and I'll be the cause of a patient's death can be a little unnerving."

"With conditions what they were before you came to St. Luke's, the case you're talking about wouldn't have had much of a chance anyway," she said cryptically.

"I suppose in the final analysis, I took the job for that reason— that and because Chuck Rogers went out on a limb to get it for me."

"Chuck's a remarkable person—but the way things are piling up on him these days, I wonder if he can cope with them."

"What do you mean?"

"He already had all he could do with his various projects in the ghetto and the hospital. Now he's working on the textile union to let blacks and Chicanos into the mills, and that's where he's bound to run into real trouble someday."

"Chuck knows that—he's even spoken to me about it."

"The trouble is that the millowners are beginning to consider him a troublemaker for pressing the cause of the minorities. And some of the richest are on the board of both the cathedral and St. Luke's."

"The Chuck Rogerses of this world seem destined for conflict," he said. "Anyone who tries to correct an injustice eventually gets in hot water one way or the other."

"But it still isn't right, especially when they're usually such gentle people."

"Maybe their very gentleness makes them unselfish and willing to sacrifice themselves for others," he said. "That reminds me: do you mind if I ask you a question?"

She gave him a probing look. "I won't know until you ask it, will I?"

"Why is someone with your ability and training working at St. Luke's?"

She smiled. "I could ask you the same thing."

"I'm crippled and St. Luke's is a refuge for me. Obviously you are not."

"There are different ways of being crippled." Almost it had seemed as if she were speaking to herself and not to him, then she added briskly: "I came back because of my father. He had an advanced case of Parkinson's disease and didn't want to leave Framingham, so I figured the least I could do was to take a few years out of my life and look after him during the last years of his."

"You said was?"

"He died three months ago."

"I'm sorry."

"Don't be. Dad's last years were miserable—until Dick Tubman started giving him L-Dopa."

"Is that the same Dr. Tubman who's consultant on internal medicine for the hospital?"

She nodded. "I had known Dick in Baltimore before he went to Yale, so I contacted him when I came here." Her eyes took on a warm glow. "It was miraculous what the drug did for Dad. His last six months were the most comfortable he'd had for years and he even started sitting on the front porch watching the girls go by. Those miniskirts really gave him a charge."

"I've heard that L-Dopa affects those taking it that way."

"It gave Dad the will to live. When the end came, it was sudden— a massive stroke. I don't think he ever knew what hit him."

"He was lucky. My right side was paralyzed for three months after the injury and there were times when I thought it would never come back."

"I'm sorry." She was suddenly contrite. "I shouldn't have mentioned this to you."

"I've got to live with it. The neurosurgeons at Walter Reed think I may regain my surgical skill in the right hand one day—if I keep on pushing it."

"I've seen some pretty miraculous recoveries from serious brain damage at Hopkins."

"Sometimes I think that's what it will take—a miracle," said Jud. "But I'm not going to wait around for one to happen. I hope you're going to stay on at St. Luke's."

"I've always thought I might go into pediatric anesthesia later on, so I'm taking some courses in child psychology at the university here at night," she said. "That's where I'd been tonight when I happened to see you walking along the street."

"If we're going to build up St. Luke's again, we'll need all the dedicated help we can get—especially people like you."

"Chuck has been using that argument on me, but I'm not convinced that he can develop his health center idea successfully," she said. "Meanwhile, I like it here in Framingham and there are some nice people, so I might just stay."

The waitress brought fresh steins of beer and took away their empty ones. Under its mellowing influence and the pleasure of being with a woman who obviously expected nothing of him except his company, Jud was feeling more relaxed.

"Sorry I can't ask you to dance," he said. "If you had to help me up in the middle of the floor, I'm afraid people would think I was loaded."

"I'm happy to sit and talk to someone who speaks the same language I do," she said. "Dick Tubman has a paging service, one of those radio things he carries with him. When we come here, I'm always waiting to hear it beep."

She had identified one of the reasons why she had stayed on at Framingham after her father's death. But though he experienced a normal sense of disappointment at knowing a woman he enjoyed being with was perhaps spoken for, the knowledge didn't depress Jud. It had been a long time since he'd thought about any woman romantically before tonight—and tonight had been a disaster. He had no desire to risk a repetition of it.

"Did you hear about the lead poisoning cases—the Brown children?" he asked.

She shook her head. "Most of my work, outside the OPD, is with Surgical Receiving and the Operating Room. What happened?"

"I found six cases in one family—all poisoned by paint flaking off the ceiling of a ghetto apartment. Charlie Gregg is doing a story on it."

"We saw quite a bit of lead poisoning at Hopkins, particularly after they worked out the mass survey technique," she told him. "When you see how many children have been mentally damaged by lead, it makes you want to go out and shoot a few slum landlords."

"You spoke of a survey. What kind was it?"

"Somebody discovered they could take a specimen of hair and identify lead in the tissues with the spectrophotometer. After that, every kid that came through the Pediatric OPD had a snippet of his hair cut off for analysis. I believe the whole thing was written up in a medical journal a year or so ago."

She glanced at her watch and reached for her bag which was lying on the seat of the booth where they were sitting. "Dick is coming by around ten-thirty after a medical meeting to talk about a house party we're supposed to go on in Mobile next weekend," she said. "This is nice, but I expect we'd better be going."

"I've imposed on your generosity too long," Jud said quickly. "Why don't you let me take a cab back to the hospital? The hostess can call one."

"Nonsense," said Kathryn firmly as they left the booth. "I have to meet Dick at my apartment and the hospital's right on the way. I enjoyed the beer and conversation tremendously, Jud."

"We'll have to do it again," he said, then added pointedly, "when you're free."

"Except for the hospital and the university, my time's my own."

He understood that she was telling him she was not committed to Dr. Richard Tubman and the thought filled him with a warm glow of pleasure—in spite of the near disastrous way the evening had begun.

CHAPTER VIII

When he made rounds the next morning, Jud stopped by the Surgical Receiving Ward to check on two fracture cases from the expressway pile-up the morning before. Both had been in deep shock when brought to the Emergency Room and he had thought best to treat them conservatively with traction splints, transfusion and anti-shock measures before definitive surgery to reduce the fractures and hold the bones in place.

The most severe case was a Mr. Gonzalez, with a shaft fracture of the upper thigh and considerable hemorrhage from other wounds, necessitating several transfusions to combat shock. It was Jud's intention to assist Emilio Fernandez and Juan Valdese the next morning in an open reduction and fixation of the broken bone with a plate made of Vitallium, a hard metal alloy that was both chemically and physically inert when placed in tissues.

As he moved down the ward through the narrow aisle between the crowded beds, stopping to speak to patients along the way, Jud saw that Gonzalez had a visitor, whom he judged to be a relative. But as he approached the bed, the man took a paper from an attaché case and handed it to the patient, holding the case for Gonzalez to sign the paper with a ballpoint pen.

Quickening his own pace, Jud came up to the bed before

Gonzalez could sign. "Are you a relative of Mr. Gonzalez?" he asked.

"I'm Henry Anders, claims adjuster for Great Southern Insurance." The visitor was a breezy looking man in his early thirties. "We represent the owner of the car that struck Mr. Gonzalez."

"I don't recall giving you permission to talk to this patient, Mr. Anders," said Jud.

"Mr. Ford always—"

"Mr. Ford is not in charge of this case."

"Who are you?" Ander's eyes narrowed at Jud's tone.

"Dr. Judson Tyler, Director of Emergency Services."

"That's a very impressive title for a new resident." Mr. Anders was jovial now. "Naturally you wouldn't understand—"

"Understand what, Mr. Anders?"

"Since St. Luke's no longer has a professional staff capable of treating serious accident cases, they're transferred elsewhere as they're able to be moved."

"May I see the document you wanted Mr. Gonzalez to sign?"

Anders hesitated, then handed it over. It was a request for transfer to Provident Hospital, to the care of a Dr. Clyde Trent.

"Dr. Trent is an industrial surgeon," Anders explained. "He handles all our accident cases."

"*All*, Mr. Anders?" Jud's eyebrows rose. "In most cities, the ethical code of the local medical society frowns on any such arrangement."

"Well—" For the first time the urbane Mr. Anders was on the defensive.

"You mean all the patients you can persuade to go to Dr. Trent, don't you?"

"Look here!" The insurance man started to bluster, but Jud had turned to the patient.

"This gentleman represents the company insuring the person whose car hit yours, Mr. Gonzalez," he said. "When you were brought in yesterday, you were in such deep shock and bleeding so badly from the wounds in your leg that we had to give you some blood transfusions. Do you wish to be transferred to another hospital now?"

"Not me, Doctor," said Gonzalez. "You and Dr. Fernandez save my life when I was bleeding. But this man, he say they don't pay—"

"That's not true," Anders protested, but before he could say more Jud turned on him with controlled fury.

64

"I'll give you one minute to get out of this ward, Anders," he said. "Or would you rather I reported this to the State Insurance Commission?"

"Look here," Anders blustered. "We've got an arrangement with Mr. Ford—"

"That arrangement is terminated as of this moment. Do you understand?"

"You'll hear more about this," Anders threatened, but he wasted no time in going.

"You're doing fine, Mr. Gonzalez," Jud assured the patient. "In the morning, we'll operate and fix up that leg of yours."

"Whatever you say, Doctor. Like I tell the insurance man, you and Dr. Fernandez save my life."

Jud was waiting for Chuck when he came into his office a little before nine.

"You look like Elijah bringing down fire to consume the priests of Baal," said the chaplain. "What's wrong now?"

"I just threw an insurance adjuster out of the hospital for trying to con one of the accident cases I admitted yesterday into requesting transfer to Provident, to the care of a Dr. Trent. Know him?"

"Trent's an industrial surgeon. He's got one of the biggest practices in the city and is also one of the incorporators of Provident. Unless I'm mistaken, he's on the national board of directors of Hospitals Incorporated too, which means he owns a lot of their stock."

"Working closely with insurance companies instead of attending to the welfare of patients is a pretty common practice among so-called industrial surgeons," said Jud. "But this is so open and flagrant that I'm surprised someone hasn't raised a stink about it before."

"There was some talk once of an investigation by the Academy of Medicine, but it never materialized."

"How long do you suppose this cozy little arrangement between Asa Ford and Provident Hospital has been going on?"

"Ever since Asa came here, I imagine," said Chuck. "But then nobody could really deny that, as recently as the day before yesterday, a patient was better off somewhere else than at St. Luke's."

"That's changed now."

"And nobody could be happier about it than I am, but go slow Jud. Even for you it will be an uphill fight all the way. How did you come out with Claiborne?"

65

"Just as you'd expect. He's not going to do anything."

"And Charlie Gregg?"

"I imagine the story will break tomorrow morning."

"And all hell with it, I suspect." Chuck's tone was sober. "You know, there have been times in the past forty-eight hours when I've almost wished I hadn't gotten you into this."

"Why?"

"I've never known anybody else with such a capacity for jumping feet first into controversy—sometimes it scares me."

"Losing your nerve?"

"No," said Chuck. "It's just that all of us like you so much, we don't want to have the guilt on our consciences of seeing you knocked down and not having helped you. It's a lot easier to say, 'I told him he was a damn fool to try,' instead of, 'If I'd done everything I should to help him, maybe he would have succeeded.'"

Then Chuck grinned. "But one thing I *am* sure of: if you do fall, the ground is going to shake wherever you land."

II

Jud telephoned Dr. Clyde Trent's office about ten o'clock.

"This is Dr. Judson Tyler," he told the secretary who answered. "I'd like to speak to Dr. Trent, please."

"He just got in a few minutes ago, from a medical meeting in Atlanta. Is it important, Doctor?"

"Very important," Jud said firmly.

"I'll get him on the phone then. Just a moment."

"Hello, Dr. Tyler." Dr. Trent had a booming voice, the tone, Jud recognized, of authority and power. "I don't seem to remember the name; are you from out of town?"

"I'm the new Director of Emergency Services at St. Luke's."

"Oh, a new resident." Dr. Trent's voice had become patronizing. "Well I'm pretty busy—"

"I'll only take a moment of your time, Doctor. This morning I found a Mr. Anders, who said he represents an insurance company, arranging to have a patient of mine at St. Luke's transferred to your service at Provident Hospital."

"That happens quite often since activities at St. Luke's have been so restricted, Doctor. We'll be glad to take the patient, of course."

"This patient has no wish to be transferred, Doctor."

"That's understandable," said Trent, still in the tone of explaining

66

something to a child. "Naturally he has no way of knowing that a trained professional staff is no longer available at St. Luke's."

"How well trained a staff do you think St. Luke's should have, Doctor?"

"Well, I don't like to boast. But, for an example, I'm a Fellow of the American College of Surgeons."

"So am I, Dr. Trent."

There was a pause, then Trent said somewhat lamely; "But you said you were a resident—"

"*You* jumped to that conclusion, Doctor. I'm not only a Fellow, but I also hold the diploma of the American Board of Surgery and was Chief Surgeon and Commanding Officer of my own mobile surgical hospital in Vietnam for over three years."

"Well, in that case—"

"In that case, Dr. Trent, I think you'd better warn the insurance adjusters who've been touting for you here at St. Luke's to lay off my patients. Good-by, Doctor."

Breathing hard with anger, Jud reached out to put the telephone on its cradle but, as so often happened under the stress of emotion, it dropped from his hand. Trembling, not only with anger but with frustration at the way his hand had betrayed him again, the bravado of indignation which had filled him at the patronizing tone of the older doctor's voice was suddenly deflated like a pricked balloon.

A sound at the door attracted his attention and he turned to see Kathryn Galloway standing there, looking concerned.

"Are you all right?" she asked.

"Just angry. Would you pick up the telephone for me, please?"

"Of course." She put it back on the cradle. "I ordered the Vitallium plates you wanted for the fracture reduction tomorrow, but Mr. Ford canceled the order."

"Did he give any reason?"

"He said St. Luke's can't afford new instruments, but I think he's really trying to drive you away. I wouldn't blame you for quitting right now either."

"I'd blame myself, though," Jud said quietly. "Can you still get the plates and have them billed to me?"

"Of course."

"Please do. And Kathryn."

"Yes."

"Do you know much about John Paul Jones?"

67

She smiled. "Wasn't he the one who said 'Damn the torpedoes?' "

"I believe that was David Farragut. The man I'm thinking about said: 'I've just begun to fight.' "

III

The OPD ran considerably more smoothly during the second morning of the new routine, but Jud was still kept busy. When he was finally able to get away to his apartment and lie down for a nap, his leg was hurting from the unaccustomed effort and his right hand felt stiff. He was generally pleased, however, with the way he'd been able to handle his duties as triage officer. Knowing he was backing them up, the residents—particularly the two who were surgically trained—had used their own judgment more often too, reducing the calls upon him.

When the phone rang, he was tempted not to answer it but, afraid it might be one of the residents with a real emergency, finally lifted the receiver from the cradle.

"Jud?" The voice was familiar—and not male.

"Yes, Samantha."

"Can you ever forgive me?"

"There's nothing to forgive—"

"I'm so ashamed!" She wailed. "I was high on grass last night. And when I am, I'm not really responsible."

"I just said I didn't hold anything against you."

"When I think how embarrassing it all was for you—me throwing myself at you like a hussy—I could die."

"Please don't go that far."

"Then I read the story about you in yesterday's paper again— about how you were wounded and all. And I remembered how it was with Tyrone Power and Ava Gardner in that picture, *The Sun Also Rises*—"

"I'm not Tyrone Power, Samantha."

"But you were wounded—"

"*My* wound was in the brain."

"I know all about that; I've been reading a book by those people who run a clinic in St. Louis. You know the ones who took all the pictures in color of people, when they were—"

"I'm familiar with the book, Samantha."

68

"Maybe I could be one of those women who helps out men—what do they call them?"

"I believe the scientific term is 'partner-surrogate.'"

"We could go to St. Louis together to that clinic."

"Did it ever occur to you that I might not want to become a seducer?"

"Last night you certainly acted as if you wanted to—"

"Samantha!"

"All right—if you want to be an old maid about it. But if you can't, you can't, can you?"

Jud couldn't help laughing. "You sound like Gertrude Stein."

"Now you're making fun of me. I'm not a child any more, you know."

"I do know—now. And any man would be flattered to know you wanted him to make love to you."

"Why Jud! That's the nicest thing anybody ever said to me."

"Surely Horace—"

"Horace was always in a hurry. And always thinking about that damn mill."

"Tell me this—didn't you really divorce him to get back at your father?"

"I certainly did not!" she said indignantly. "Why, all my life, I've been trying to get away from Framingham and everything it stands for."

"Even though Framingham is responsible for your income?"

"That's different. Anyway I want you to know I'm willing to help you any way I can."

"This is something I'll have to work out, Samantha."

"But you can't—without a woman helping you. Am I that repulsive to you, Jud?"

"You're not repulsive at all, quite the opposite. But my problems are my problems and I'll have to work them out in my own way."

"When will I see you again?"

"In about a week—when you come in for me to check that fracture."

"A whole week!"

"Spend the time looking for a theater that's showing *The Sun Also Rises*. I think you'll find that the girl ended up going from man to man and growing unhappier with each episode."

"That was because she couldn't have Tyrone."

69

"Maybe you'd better start looking for your own Tyrone then."

"I found him—last night."

"A Tyrone without the power? You can do better than that, Samantha. Good-by."

"You're not going to get rid of me that easy," she warned him. "If nothing else, I'll put on one of those pink uniforms the auxiliary wears and go around the hospital bringing sunshine to all the sick."

"Just be sure you don't run anybody down with the cart you'll be pushing," he said. "Good-by."

IV

The call from Samantha had dispelled any desire Jud had for an afternoon nap, so he crossed the corridor to Chuck's niche and poured himself a cup of coffee. As he was stirring in the sugar, he saw John Redmond in the hall.

"You're supposed to be off duty, John," he said.

"One of the other men was late, Dr. Tyler. I was just going to get my bicycle."

"Do you have time for a little chat? I've barely seen you since that first day."

Redmond's white teeth showed in a broad smile; as far as Jud could tell, they were all there in spite of his eighty years.

"The way you've been moving, Doctor," he said as he drew a mug of coffee from the percolator, "hardly anybody gets more'n a glimpse of you."

"But am I just stirring up a lot of dust that's going to make it hard for other people to see what they're doing?"

"You're getting somewhere," Redmond assured him. "This hospital has changed more in the three days since you've been here than in three years before that. It's beginning to be a little like the old days."

"Do you think we can ever bring them back, John?"

"Nobody really wants that, Dr. Tyler. When I first came here, people were still arguin' about whether or not germs caused disease."

"I know," said Jud. "The architect who designed this hospital put those double doors in the corridor because people thought they could keep contagion from spreading through the air, but that theory was dispelled a long time. Now we have the problem of staphylococcus infection carried by dust, which isn't really too

70

much different from the old contagion theory. It seems that you only cope with one difficulty before another one pops up."

"That's what keeps us alive and healthy," said Redmond. "I figure the good Lord only gives us the burdens he knows we can bear, if we really work at it. That's his way of testing us."

"He gave me a heavy one when he let that rocket shell explode in my hospital."

"Maybe that was just his way of sending you here, where you're so badly needed."

"I wish I had your faith, John."

"You do, but in a different way. The Bible says, 'Shew me thy faith without thy works and I will shew thee my faith by my works.' One's as good as the other."

"But you and Mr. Rogers have both, John. How can the lame keep up?"

John Redmond smiled. "You're the most active lame man I ever saw, Dr. Tyler. Everybody in the hospital's moving a little faster already because of you. If you ever throw down that cane, the rest of us won't be able to keep up."

CHAPTER IX

The operation on Mr. Gonzalez's fractured leg went very well. With Jud and Juan Valdese assisting, Emilio Fernandez capably incised the skin over the thigh and exposed the jagged ends of the broken femur. It was frustrating to Jud to see hands less expert than his own had once been fumbling at times, but a few quick working directions here and there gave Emilio Fernandez the confidence he needed and the bone shaft was secured with screws and a Vitallium plate.

Kathryn Galloway had proved to be quite as efficient in supervising the Operating Room as she did the Outpatient Department. "I had an orderly put a copy of the morning paper in the Doctors' dressing room," she said, as she was untying the strings of Jud's gown at the end of the operation. "Your friend Gregg really did things up brown."

The story Jud had given Charlie Gregg after his fruitless visit to Angus Claiborne was headed "I ACCUSE." Using Émile Zola's famous challenge in the Dreyfus case as a theme, it was a detailed account of how Jud had discovered lead in the Brown children's bodies and followed up his own diagnosis by identifying the source.

Charlie Gregg's photographs had printed up beautifully too, with bright silvery flakes of paint falling from the ceiling caught up in the slanting beam of sunlight through the kitchen window of the apartment. And he had even managed to capture the anguished look on the face of Jeff Brown, the children's father, as he told how he had begged Angus Claiborne to do something about the ceiling and walls of the flat and had been summarily turned down.

In the newspaper's morgue, Gregg had dug up a photo of Jud delivering a paper before a medical meeting, with a finger leveled, seemingly in accusation. Actually, he had been pointing to a slide being projected on the screen at that moment but, with Angus Claiborne's dour visage in the next column, he seemed to be denouncing the crusty landlord for his neglect.

The exposé ended with Jud's promise to provide the Brown family with the factual proof of physical damage to the children necessary for bringing suit against the landlord, unless something was done immediately to alleviate the situation.

When he came into his office, Jud found Chuck Rogers waiting for him. "Asa Ford wants to see you right away," said the chaplain.

"For what?"

"Who can tell what kind of mischief Asa has dreamed up? But it was bound to come as soon as a few of Framingham's leading citizens read the morning paper."

"That photo of the paint scales falling in the shaft of sunlight ought to win Charlie a Pulitzer prize," said Jud.

"I'll be satisfied if it doesn't cost you your head. Mind if I go along when you face Ford in his den?"

"I wish you would," said Jud. "The operation wore me out and, when I'm tired, I don't always think fast or control my temper very well."

What the administrator had cooked up was an alleged return by the city personnel department of Jud's application for the position of Director of Emergency Services, although Ford failed to produce the rejected application.

"Just what is in question?" Jud asked.

"Your professional credentials, Doctor." The effusive welcome which had characterized Ford's greeting of Jud upon his arrival at the hospital was gone now. "You failed to give any proof of them."

"That's easy." Opening his wallet, Jud selected a card from it and placed it on the desk blotter in front of Ford. "Here's my AMA membership card showing that I'm in good standing through my service in the Army."

Placing another card on the blotter, he added, "This certifies my Fellowship in the American College of Surgeons. I also hold the diploma of the American Board of Surgery, in case the personnel department is interested."

Ford was taken aback only momentarily. "We'll still need a transcript of these credentials—and references, of course."

Chuck Rogers had been building up steam throughout the questioning; now he exploded.

"You know Dr. Tyler commanded a mobile surgical hospital in Vietnam until he was wounded, Asa. He was a Major in the Army Medical Corps."

"Was a Major?" Ford pounced on the word. "Why did you leave the service, Dr. Tyler?"

"As a matter of fact, I'm still a Major in the Reserve, Mr. Ford." Jud drew a plastic sandwich card from his wallet and added it to those already on the blotter of the administrator's desk.

"This is a Geneva Pass, in case you're not familiar with it," he added, "establishing that I'm a member of the Armed Forces of the United States and giving my rank and serial number. Do you have any further questions?"

"You still need references." Asa Ford obviously knew he was fighting a losing battle and it made him even more stubborn.

"When I told you Dr. Tyler was coming, you were as anxious as I was to find somebody to take over the Emergency Department," Chuck Rogers said angrily. "What happened since then to change your mind?"

"I don't like what you're insinuating, Mr. Rogers." Asa Ford sat rigid in his chair.

"Could it possibly be that the corporation across the street doesn't want to see any better medicine practiced over here?" Chuck demanded.

A surge of color into the administrator's hitherto sallow cheeks

73

indicated that the thrust had gone home. "This is my office," he blustered. "I'll not be insulted—"

"Don't forget that the cathedral holds the majority of seats on the Board of Trustees of this hospital," Chuck warned. "You can be sure we'll look into this."

"I've already had two calls from trustees this morning, demanding a meeting of the board to investigate Dr. Tyler's action," Ford said on a note of triumph.

"If it's references you're concerned about, Mr. Ford," Jud interposed himself between the two angry men, "I can settle the question very quickly. May I use your phone?"

"Why—yes."

"I'd like to make a long distance call to Washington," Jud told the hospital operator. You can charge it to my personal account here at the hospital."

"Certainly, Dr. Tyler."

"Please call Colonel Joel Taylor in the office of the Surgeon General of the Army, the Personnel Department."

"Joel?" Jud said, when the call was put through. "This is Jud Tyler."

"Jud! Where are you?"

"I've taken a job as Director of Emergency Services in the hospital where I interned in Framingham. The administrator would like to talk to you about my qualifications."

"Certainly," said Taylor. "Put him on."

"Ask Colonel Taylor anything you like." Jud handed the phone to Asa Ford. "He's Chief of Personnel in the office of the Surgeon General in Washington."

"But—"

"You said you wanted references," Jud reminded Ford. "My whole record is in Colonel Taylor's files with all the references you'll need."

Asa Ford took the phone, though with obvious reluctance. "There's no question in *my* mind about Dr. Tyler's qualification, Colonel," he said. "It's just that the city personnel office—"

"A Telex detailing Major Tyler's medical qualifications and his Army record will be in your hands before the day is out." Both Jud and Chuck could hear Taylor's brisk voice in the receiver. "It will also state that Major Tyler is the most decorated medical officer in the Vietnam War."

74

"Thank you, Colonel." Looking a little shaken, Asa Ford handed the telephone back to Jud.

"That should do it, Jud," said Taylor. "Anything else?"

"No. And thanks, Joel."

"Any time I can put a petty bureaucrat in his place, it makes my day," said the personnel officer. "Good-by, Jud. And good luck."

II

"And so we come to the end of another chapter in the deterioriating relationship between the chaplain and the administrator," Chuck Rogers said wryly as they were walking back to the OPD. "Be sure and tune in for tomorrow's blowup."

"Don't tell me this happens every day."

"Except weekends. Asa's a city employee, so he only works five days a week."

"You mentioned Provident Hospital just now, but they don't have an Emergency Department," said Jud. "Why would anyone over there want to cripple St. Luke's?"

"The crack I made about Provident was a shot in the dark."

"But it obviously hit a target. Why?"

"I can't prove anything, but I do know that Asa's real thick with Jack Myers, the administrator over there. They could just be working together to keep St. Luke's a filter to weed out cases the other hospitals don't want—particularly Provident."

"Did it ever occur to you that you've conned me into buying a can of worms?" Jud demanded somewhat tartly.

"You could look at it that way," Chuck conceded. "But you have to admit that it's in a good cause. With you running this show, we'll soon have a magnet that will attract the finest young doctors in the country as well as among the FMGs."

"To a dying hospital?"

"A rejuvenated hospital," Chuck corrected him. "And you just might find yourself rejuvenated in the process."

The telephone in Jud's office was ringing when they reached it and Jud picked up the receiver.

"This is Joseph Morgan III, Dr. Tyler," said a pleasant masculine voice. "Of the firm of Morgan, Morgan, Morgan, and Taliaferro."

"What can I do for you, Mr. Morgan?" Jud remembered enough from his two years in Framingham to know the law firm was one of the most prominent in the city.

"Call me Joe; I'm the third Morgan—two years out of Harvard Law School and still not dry behind the ears, according to my father and grandfather. I called to congratulate you on that nice piece of hatchet work you did on old Angus Claiborne. If you'll let me, I'd like to help make Angus and the other slum landlords clean up the Irontown area."

"By razing it and building high-rise apartments poor people can't afford?"

"That concept went by the board long ago, Dr. Tyler," said Morgan cheerfully.

"But they're still being built."

"And will be, as long as there's a rake-off for all concerned, from the politician who introduces the bill to the contractor who uses shoddy material and the city building inspector who gets payola for not seeing it."

"You seems to know the answers."

"While I was studying law in Cambridge, I did some work at the Center for Urban Studies," said Morgan. "Jane Jacobs exploded the urban-renewal-by-bulldozer myth ten years ago in *The Death and Life of Great American Cities*."

"Can I ask you a question, Mr. Morgan?"

"Sure. But call me Joe."

"What's a Framingham Brahmin doing in that field?"

Morgan chuckled. "When I got my law degree at Harvard, I wanted to go to work for HEW implementing some of the new rulings by the Supreme Court. But welfare is still a dirty word in the South and I was afraid my father would have a heart attack, so we finally compromised. I came back to work with the firm, writing wills for rich people, who want to keep their children from throwing away what they work so hard to accumulate, and briefs for U. S. Steel—but only part time. The rest of the time I try to bring social and legal justice to people who've never had it before through the law—pretty much the same sort of thing you're doing with medicine at St. Luke's."

"Are you getting anywhere?"

"Chuck Rogers can tell you we've made some headway," said Morgan. "We got a particularly sadistic guard drummed out of the county jail a few months ago."

"More power to you."

"You gave us more power when you discovered lead in those Brown children," Morgan assured him. "We've never had a real

76

cause we could get our teeth into handed to us before, and I'd like to do something about it before it gets away from us."

"What do you have in mind?" Jud asked.

"For openers I could bring a suit in the name of the Brown family for damages under the landlord property responsibility law. Angus is a real scrooge but by threatening to make it a class action, we might scare a lot of other slum landlords into doing something."

"The more, the better," said Jud.

"It will take a few days to see which way Angus will jump," said Morgan. "Meanwhile I'd like to visit the Brown family and get all the information I can."

"By all means do."

"Why don't you and Chuck have lunch with me some day soon, so we can plan our strategy? I'm free day after tomorrow."

"Just a moment, I'll have to call Chuck," said Jud and stepped to the door. From it, he could see that the chaplain was in his office across the hall.

"Can you have lunch with Joe Morgan III and myself day after tomorrow?" he asked.

"Sure," said Chuck. "But tell Joe I refuse to go to the Spring Hill Club. It might compromise my position as the defender of the poor."

III

When Jud went to the cafeteria for lunch, Kathryn Galloway was ahead of him in the line. As she was getting a glass of water from the fountain, after selecting her lunch, he stopped beside her.

"Mind if I sit with you?" he asked.

"Not at all."

They chose a table for two in a secluded corner where they could talk without being overheard and placed their trays upon it.

"This time next week you'll probably not want to be seen in my company," he told her. "Did you hear that the Board of Trustees is calling a special meeting to claim my pelt?"

"It was on the grapevine this morning."

"How's the betting?"

"Male or female?"

"Both."

"Men are more realistic than women, so the odds there are against

77

you. But the women are all for you, so my guess is you'll come out okay."

"Why would anybody in the hospital be against me—except Asa Ford?"

"Hospitals are part of the medical profession and therefore citadels of the status quo," she reminded him. "You've lived in them long enough to know that anybody who stirs up things is automatically taboo."

"I never thought about it that way, but I guess you're right."

"You're the kind of doctor who goes around uprooting people from their little niches of incompetence. Naturally you have to be destroyed before you can knock somebody in the administration out of his comfortable spot by showing how incompetent he is. Mind you I'm not calling any names."

"When did you get to be such a philosopher?" he asked.

"I was a ward supervisor at Hopkins for a couple of years. Riding herd on a bunch of nurses will either make you a philosopher or send you to the booby hatch."

"How do you figure Miss Cates?"

"What do you mean?"

"She seems antagonistic toward me, yet I've never done anything to her."

"Amanda carries a chip on her shoulder where most white people are concerned. She's a better nurse than nine-tenths of those at St. Luke's, yet she's always conscious of being black."

"Why would that make any difference—as long as she's a good nurse?"

"It probably doesn't to you or me. But being black in the South pretty well rules out her marrying a doctor—unless he's black too—and we don't get any black residents here. The big teaching hospitals are all scrambling for them to prove they don't discriminate. Besides, Amanda worries that some redneck will take a shot at Eric."

"Chucks says he's brilliant."

"Both of them are and they're very devoted to each other. Their mother is dead so Amanda sort of feels that she has to look after Eric."

They were halfway through lunch when Jud said, "Is it asking too much to inquire what's between you and Tubman?"

She gave him a startled look. "That's pretty personal."

"You don't have to answer if you'd rather not."

"Let's just say I'm fond of Dick."

78

"Are you in love?"

She shrugged. "When you get to be my age—and still a spinster—you don't make fine distinctions."

"Engaged then?"

"He hasn't asked me. Why?"

"I enjoyed the other night on Spring Hill very much and was hoping we could do it again."

She studied him for a moment with those level gray eyes which, he realized again, were quite beautiful.

"You don't waste any time, do you?" she said at last.

"I guess I'm the kind of a guy who's constitutionally incapable of beating around the bush."

"That being the case, you ought to know that I didn't come back to Framingham just because of Dad," she told him. "It seems to be my fate to attract men who need someone to lean on—"

"Is that why you gave me the brush-off in the beginning?"

"Partly. But you didn't exactly do anything to endear yourself to me that first morning, remember?"

"For which I've already apologized."

"And the slate's clean. But I was hurt badly once and I don't want to be hurt again."

"Why not tell me to shove off then?"

"Maybe because I'm attracted to you—any woman would be, you know. But maybe because no one can be around you very long without knowing you're not the kind of person who leans on anyone."

"Except my cane."

"And you even fight that."

He smiled. "You just explained why I'm so awkward with it."

"You've been frank with me, Jud, so I'm going to be frank with you," she said. "I was in love with a doctor at Hopkins. He was weak—I know that now, but I was too much in love to see very closely, until he married the daughter of a department head and was very suddenly made an associate professor. Dad's illness gave me an excuse to leave Baltimore and St. Luke's gave me a job nearby; while Dad was living they even let me work broken shifts whenever he needed me."

"Are you over that particular disappointment now?"

"Except that it cured me of taking up with weak men."

"Even one who can't ask anything of you except companionship?"

She gave him a startled look. "I wonder if a relationship between

79

a strong man and a strong woman can ever be simply that for very long."

"You've been frank with me, so I'm going to be the same with you," he told her. "Did you miss a medical bag from the supply room?"

"A taxicab driver brought it back. He said you left it when you made a house call."

"I left the bag at Samantha Fellowes' apartment, the night you picked me up on the street. The splint I put on her wrist was painful and she asked me to make a house call and loosen it."

"I doubt if the splint was tight enough to interfere with the circulation thirty-six hours after it was put on," she said casually.

"It wasn't. The real reason I left in such a hurry was because I was running away."

"She's very beautiful. Most men wouldn't have been that strong."

"It wasn't a question of strength but the lack of it—that condition often follows damage to the brain centers."

A sudden look of understanding—and compassion—in her eyes told him she had grasped his meaning.

"I thought you were quite disturbed when I picked you up that night. No wonder."

"Now that I've confessed my weakness, are you still willing to be friends?"

"Of course." She smiled. "Every woman likes to have handsome men pursuing her—whatever the cause. That's the name of the game, isn't it?"

CHAPTER X

The new routine of clinic procedure was functioning more smoothly every day; by four o'clock the bulk of the OPD cases had been taken care of. When Jud came into his office, he found Chuck Rogers waiting.

"You look tired," said the chaplain. "Sure you're not overdoing?"

"I'm carrying out the treatment Colonel Standiford prescribed—work." Jud dropped into his chair and put his feet on the desk.

"I had a call right after lunch you might be interested in," said Chuck casually. "From Mrs. Fellowes."

"Samantha? What did she want?"

"To work here as a volunteer nurse's aide. She said you suggested it."

"I guess I did while I was giving her a lecture on getting some purpose in her life before she killed herself in an automobile. But I'd never thought she'd do it. Why did she call you?"

"I'm in charge of recruiting volunteers, but not many women in Framingham are willing to work here. Do you think Mrs. Fellowes could stand up under conditions at St. Luke's?"

"I'm sure Samantha can do anything she sets her mind to."

"What about the fractured wrist?"

"In a few days I'll mold her a splint of Lightcast and she'll hardly know she has one on." Seeing that Chuck's expression was still doubtful, he added. "What else is bothering you?"

"Will it trouble you to have Samantha Fellowes around?"

"Why would you ask that?"

"Several people heard her pledge undying affection for you the day you fixed her broken wrist. Besides, you did make a house call at her apartment the other night and leave your medical bag."

"St. Luke's may be on the skids but the grapevine certainly isn't," said Jud with some asperity. "The undying affection you speak of is merely Samantha's way of expressing herself—extravagantly. The other—" He stopped.

"Forgive me for probing, Jud. I was only trying to protect you."

"You might as well know the truth. The night I made the house call, Samantha expected certain things of me and I failed to measure up." His voice became bitter. "That's another aftermath of severe brain injury."

Chuck nodded slowly. "You've had enough, without having her around all the time to remind you of—"

"Let her work, Chuck."

"But—"

"Samantha's never had to face reality—or thought she was really needed. The experience here could save her."

"If that's what you want, but—"

"I don't know of a better place for her to learn what life is all about."

"You're a tough case but I wonder if even you are tough enough to stand all the slings and arrows that will be thrown at you," said Chuck. "Plus being reminded of one of your few failings by seeing Samantha Fellowes every day."

Jud shrugged. "If one faction of your trustees gets its way, I won't be here much longer than next week anyway."

"Don't be too sure of that," said Chuck. "We Christers are hard to bring down; I guess it's one of the compensations for getting your head bloodied regularly. But if your enemies ever find a weak spot in your armor, do you have any idea what it might be?"

"Not unless it's my disability."

"If you insist on doing surgery yourself then, for God's sake don't lose a case. By the way; what about Jack Aiken?"

"Tubman is supposed to do a special vital capacity test on him. If I can prove that byssinosis is an industrial hazard, the burden of responsibility will be in the millowners to protect the workers against it."

"I'm more concerned about the trustees' meeting," Chuck confessed. "Several members of the board are cronies of Angus Claiborne, so they'll try to stymie anything that could be counted in your favor."

"They can't keep us from showing the Brown children and the results of the tests we ran on them for lead. How could anybody combat that sort of truth?"

"Don't underestimate Angus Claiborne, Jud. If he risked getting his friends to call a special meeting of the board, after what you and Charlie Gregg revealed about his houses, he must have an ace up his sleeve somewhere."

II

Jud was about to leave his office a little after five, when the telephone rang. He was tired and his right leg was cramping, as it so often did when he had been on it more than usual, so he'd hoped he was through for the day. Resignedly, he picked up the phone.

"This is Dr. Tubman's office, Dr. Tyler," a feminine voice said. "The doctor has just received the Pulmonary Function Recorder he ordered from Atlanta and wonders if you can join him on the Medical Receiving Ward at the hospital tomorrow morning at ten. He'd like to do the test on Mr. Aiken then."

"I'll be there," said Jud. "Thank you for calling."

Before leaving the office, Jud called Joe Morgan; fortunately the lawyer was in his office.

"Any chance of your coming over here tomorrow morning at ten?" he asked.

"Sure," said Morgan. "What's up?"

"Dr. Tubman is doing an important test on a case and I think you should see it."

"More litigation?"

"Possibly."

"I haven't talked to the Brown family yet. How's the boy?"

"We're getting the lead out of his system. But if that house isn't fixed before he goes home, he'll be back in the same shape he was in."

"I'll go by there when I leave the hospital tomorrow morning," Morgan promised. "Old Angus and the other landlords have had time to stew for a while; I guess it's about time to turn on more heat now. See you at ten in the morning."

"The Emergency Room entrance; I'll be on the lookout for you."

At five minutes to ten, a tall young man with heavy horn-rimmed glasses came into the hospital and spoke to the reception clerk who nodded toward Jud's office where he was waiting in the doorway.

"Joe Morgan," said the newcomer, shaking hands. "I recognized your picture, Dr. Tyler."

"Glad you could come," Jud told him. "I think Dr. Tubman is about ready. Do you know him?"

"Dick and I play golf together occasionally," said Morgan. "Mind telling me what's so important about this case?"

While they were going to the Medical Receiving Ward, Jud gave the lawyer a quick summary of Jack Aiken's physical findings.

"What did you say this is he's got?" Morgan asked with a frown.

"Byssinosis."

"Never heard of it."

"I didn't know anything about it myself," Jud admitted, "until I asked Tubman to see this patient and he recognized the symptoms of Monday Morning Asthma."

"I've had a few Monday morning symptoms myself, but never asthma."

In the ward, Morgan shook hands with Tubman, who looked surprised at his presence, and was introduced to Aiken. The sick man was eyeing rather apprehensively the apparatus on a small table

83

beside the bed—a metal case with an electric cord and a flexible hose attached.

Tubman plugged the cord into an outlet and opened the top of the case, revealing a strip of recording paper driven by toothed wheels attached to an electric motor somewhere inside the cabinet. A ballpoint pen was so designed that, as the paper moved across the top of the machine, the volume of air expired during the test would be recorded in the form of a graph. From inside the case, Tubman took a paper mouthpiece, which he attached to the end of the hose.

"This instrument is essentially a spirometer for measuring respiratory volume," he said. "But it differs from ordinary spirometers in having a transistorized timer, which records time while the volume of air exhaled is also being recorded. Actually, we're most interested in the first second of expiration after a deep breath, called the Forced Expiratory Volume or FEV. But as a matter of record, we also graph the total lung volume too."

Picking up a round blue case that was lying at the foot of Aiken's bed, Tubman zipped it open to reveal a portable hair dryer.

"In this type of spirometer, the flow signal comes from the pressure during forced exhalation against a piece of filter paper placed between the mouthpiece and the main tank of the spirometer," he said. "I borrowed the hair dryer from a friend to dry the paper between blows."

Jud had a pretty good idea who the friend was but didn't mention it.

"Ingenious," said Joe Morgan admiringly. "I love gadgets."

"You can be the guinea pig this morning, Joe," said the internist. "We'll need a normal curve against which to compare Mr. Aiken's test."

"What do I have to do?"

"Take the deepest breath you can, hold your nose with your left thumb and forefinger, put the mouthpiece in your mouth, and close your lips around it snugly," Tubman directed. "Then, when I say 'breathe,' blow into the mouthpiece and empty your lungs as much as you can. We'll use the average of two test blows as a normal for the Forced Expiratory Volume. Understand?"

Morgan nodded and took the mouthpiece in his right hand.

"Inhale," Tubman commanded, and the lawyer took a deep

84

breath, pressed his nostrils together, and placed the mouthpiece in his mouth.

"Breathe!"

The motor inside the small cabinet hummed and the paper recording strip moved across the top of the machine while the pen touching it drew a curving line, rising rapidly with the first part of expiration, then falling off toward the end.

"Fine," said Tubman. "Give me a minute to dry the filter paper and we'll run the next one."

The hair dryer operated briefly, then Tubman handed Joe Morgan the mouthpiece again. The second blow was also satisfactory and he tore the two sheets off the recording section at the top of the machine.

"How old are you, Joe?" he asked.

"Twenty-eight, six feet two, one hundred and eighty pounds."

Tubman studied the table printed on the lid of the machine and made some calculations on the record sheet. "Looks like you'll live—if you don't start smoking," he reported.

Picking up the hair dryer, Tubman dried the filter paper again. Then discarding the mouthpiece Morgan used, he attached another to the hose.

"All right, Mr. Aiken," he said. "Please do exactly as you saw Mr. Morgan do."

As Aiken performed the two runs of the test, Jud didn't need to look at the pen tracing the curve of Forced Expiratory Volume to know the mill worker's vital capacity was far less than Joe Morgan's had been.

"How did I do, Doc?" Aiken asked anxiously, while Tubman was making the calculations from the table printed on the sheet attached to the inside cover of the machine. "Not so hot, I guess?"

"It could be better," the internist told him. "But if you were a smoker, it would probably be a lot worse."

"Are you telling me that breathing cotton dust all these years has done that to me?" Aiken asked.

"I'm afraid so." Tubman was closing the machine.

"Can I go back to work soon?"

"You'd be better off doing something else."

"Being a carder is all I know how to do, Doctor. I've been one for twenty years; when Ed Grogan retires, I'm going to be foreman in the carding room."

"When will that be?" Jud asked.

"Maybe a few months. Ed's got heart trouble; he can't climb more than half a dozen steps without panting."

"Does he cough much?"

"All the time. Why, some Mondays he can't hardly breathe for asth—" Aiken's eyes widened. "Hey, I wonder why his heart didn't stop instead of mine."

"Maybe you got lucky," said Jud. "Yours was warning you to change jobs before it's too late."

"I've got to keep on, Doc," Aiken insisted. "That girl of mine has two more years of college before she can get a teacher's certificate. She ain't gonna be no cotton mill worker if I can help it."

Outside the ward, the three men stopped in the chart room.

"What was Aiken's final result?" Jud asked Tubman.

"Less than thirty per cent of Joe's normal average on the two blows," said the internist. "Which means that he has an advanced case of byssinosis."

"Irreversible?"

"I'm afraid so. He's also got typical right-sided enlargement of the heart and a chest that looks like a light snow storm."

"All that from breathing cotton dust?" Joe Morgan asked incredulously.

"Plus a couple of other factors," said Tubman. "In recent years, the speed of carding has been increased considerably by new machines, which means considerably more dust is produced. Mechanical cotton pickers leave a lot more trash in raw cotton even with the best of gins—what's called 'bracts' from the husks around the center of the boll where the cotton is. The New Haven group that did most of the work on byssinosis found that bracts contain agents which release histamine in the body."

"And histamine constricts the bronchi," said Jud. "That could account for Monday Morning Asthma, couldn't it?"

"Apparently an allergic factor is involved too," said Tubman. "When cotton dust first hits the lungs on Monday morning, both agents give a pretty severe jolt to the lining membrane of the air sacs. In Aiken's case, that put a strain on an already weak heart and it suddenly quit."

"Is byssinosis recognized as an occupation hazard by the State Industrial Commission, Dick?" Joe Morgan asked.

"I don't believe so," said Tubman.

"What about other states?"

86

"I've never heard of it being legally established as a cause of disease anywhere."

"Do you think a suit for damages would hold up?" Jud asked the lawyer.

"It's worth a try—if Dick will testify to his findings."

Tubman flushed with annoyance. "Do you want to put me out of business? Half of my patients are connected with textiles one way or another, mostly in management. They're bound to fight any attempt to make byssinosis a compensable disease."

"You're the only expert on it anywhere around here, I imagine," Joe Morgan reminded him. "How many people would you say suffer from it in southern cotton mills?"

"The studies made at New Haven showed there are roughly two hundred thousand textile workers in the United States and the incidence of the disease among those who have worked in the mills for any long period may be as high as twenty-five per cent."

Joe Morgan whistled softly. "That means the lives of fifty thousand people could already have been shortened and will be even more, if they keep on working in mills where dust isn't controlled."

"I guess that's a fair estimate," Tubman conceded, somewhat reluctantly.

"What about prevention?" Jud asked.

"Filter systems are being manufactured now that can keep down the amount of dust, but they're pretty expensive," said Tubman. "Moving workers from one part of the mill to another helps too; there's a lot less dust in the spinning room than where the carders work."

"Thanks for the lesson in industrial medicine, Dick," said Joe Morgan. "If Aiken will let me, I'm going to file a claim before the State Industrial Commission, using him as a test case. That way we can get a hearing immediately where a suit would be delayed for months or even years. In fact, I might even make this a class action on behalf of other textile workers as well."

Tubman had to move on to his office and Jud escorted Morgan to the outside door through the crowd that already filled the OPD.

"It's looks like I could use a good lawyer myself soon," he said.

"At the trustees' meeting?"

"Is it that well advertised already?"

"The whole town's buzzing with it. You and Charlie Gregg really stirred up a hornet's nest."

"Do you have any objection to advising me?" Jud asked.

87

Joe Morgan grinned. "I thought you'd never ask. Now I can go back to the office and write a half-dozen wills without feeling I'm nothing but a legal lackey for the Establishment."

III

Jud was busy in the OPD until the tide of patients ebbed in midafternoon. He didn't even know Samantha was working in the hospital until a sleek convertible with the top down pulled to a stop beside him as he was coming back from the drugstore across the street, where he had been buying shaving cream—and wishing he had a car and could feel safe driving it on such a gorgeous spring day. Samantha was behind the wheel.

"Get in," she said ominously. "I've got a bone to pick with you."

Jud got in and the car moved into the traffic on Ventura Boulevard. The pink checkered uniform she was wearing, emblem of the St. Luke's volunteers, was short, revealing long and very lovely legs, quite in keeping with what he already knew about the rest of her. And even though his body might not respond, his brain quite certainly did.

"I'll have to leave word that I'll be out for a while," he told her. "Pull your skirt down and drive by the Emergency Room."

"Why should I bother about the skirt if it doesn't give you a charge?"

"I've still got a brain. And you're a remarkably pretty girl."

"Why Jud, darling, I didn't know you cared." Her irritation vanished in a warm smile. "My place or yours?"

"Neither. Are you sure you should be driving with that broken wrist?"

"I've got such a good doctor, it doesn't bother me at all."

"Not even the sunburn?" He could see that the fingers of her left hand below the splint were considerably browner than the right.

"So I'm a conniving brat and used the sunlamp to make my hand look red. But you must admit I'm a lovable one." Then her eyes took fire again. "Do you know what Miss Galloway had me doing today?"

"Handling bedpans?"

"I wouldn't have been surprised. It's all over the hospital that she's carrying a small torch for you."

"Only a small one? I must be slipping." But he was pleased at the idea and Samantha realized it.

"I put my brand on you when I was thirteen," she warned him darkly. "Besides, she's been playing house with Dick Tubman."

"You really learned a lot today, didn't you?"

"I keep my eyes and ears open. But she's betting on the wrong horse if she expects to nail Dick Tubman with a marriage license. He's got his sights set on a rich wife who won't mind if he makes out with a nurse or a secretary every now and then, just so he gets to be president of the State Medical Association and she can queen it over the rest of the wives at the convention."

"Did anybody ever tell you that you're a shrew?"

She shrugged. "Every woman is—when she's after a man. And I'm after you, my friend."

"At least you're honest. What did Kath—"

"So it's first names you're using already? When are you going to sleep with her?"

Jud ignored the question. "What did Miss Galloway do that stirred you up so much?"

Samantha didn't reply but swung the car into a turn slot and shot across the opposite lane ten feet in front of an oncoming car, leaving the driver white and shaken.

"That will teach him not to crowd other people," she said triumphantly. "What did you say?"

"I asked what you were doing that set you off?"

"Looking after babies. If they didn't spit at me from one end they wet me with the other."

"Going back tomorrow?"

"Of course I'm going back." She turned to give him an indignant look and almost rammed a station wagon in front of them. "They're so cute and lovable, especially the little Chicanos." Her tone became wistful. "Maybe if Horace and I had—"

"Turn in here at the Ambulance Entrance," he told her. "I've got to leave word that I'll be away for a while."

Everything was running smoothly in the OPD, so Jud went back to where Samantha was waiting. The car, he saw now, was an Alfa Romeo, sleek, fast, and continental in styling.

"I haven't been to the mountains since I came back," he said. "Do you suppose we could make it to Round Top and back in, say, three hours—unless you have something else to do?"

"My sole purpose in life at the moment is to nail you," she

89

assured him as she meshed the gears and whirled out of the driveway into the traffic on Mountain Avenue.

"Take it easy," he admonished her. "I'm too young to die."

"You don't have to worry. This car is new and I have to go slow while I break it in. The manual says not over seventy for five hundred miles."

"See that you follow instructions then," he said as she swung expertly into the UP ramp for the expressway. "How did you get a new car so quickly? They usually have to order these things."

"I was planning to trade before I cracked up the Porsche, so the insurance company decided to pay for part of this car instead of trying to fix up the old one."

"You mean any company will insure you?"

She wrinkled her nose at him. "I'm in the pool. Whoever draws my name just pays up."

"How do you manage to keep your driver's license?"

"The kind of accidents I have happen only to *me*. Nobody else has ever been hurt."

"That's a comforting thought. I was put together once on an operating table at Letterman General and the results weren't too good. Don't make me repeat the experience."

"Oh Jud, I forgot." She was suddenly a contrite little girl. "Was it really so bad?"

"Imagine what it's like to black out in the middle of an operation you're performing and wake up ten thousand miles away with one side of your body paralyzed—apparently forever."

"I get all shivery just thinking about it."

"Just keep the shivers out of that foot on the accelerator." They were on the Interstate now, headed west toward the low mountain range at the southern tip of the Appalachian. The Alfa Romeo had settled down to a throaty growl that held the odometer needle steady.

"I imagine the sort of experience you had in Vietnam does something to your soul too," she said, to his surprise.

"Wondering whether you're going to stay paralyzed isn't exactly the most comfortable thought to occupy your mind."

"Poor darling. If I'd known what you were going through, I would have been right there beside you in the hospital holding your hand."

"Tell me about yourself," he said. "What have you been doing since we fixed that elbow of yours?"

"The usual things: finishing school, a year of college. Then I made my debut—as if everyone in Framingham didn't know who I was. It was all pretty stupid."

"No love affairs?"

"None that amounted to much—even the marriage to Horace."

"How long did that last?"

"Less than a year. Horace is a nice guy but he was married to the plant before he was to me. Imagine going to bed with a man knowing that all the time he's making love, he's thinking about what he's got to do the next day—and hurrying to get it over with."

"I can't imagine that in your case."

"I guess I wasn't really fair to Horace, though. You might not believe it from the way I talk, but I'm a pretty romantic sort of a girl. You know, hearts and flowers and all that."

"You do manage to hide the sentiment from casual scrutiny."

"Now you're being sarcastic and I don't like it," she said. "Actually I've been in love with you for so long that poor Horace—or anybody else for that matter—didn't have a chance."

"Isn't that carrying a girlhood crush pretty far? Letting it break up your marriage?"

"It's not a girlhood crush and, besides, I'm not a child any longer, Jud Tyler." The gamin smile appeared suddenly. "You ought to know from the other night, the way you were squeezing my—"

"You don't have to be so anatomical."

"You know what?" She turned to face him but the car swerved a little and she had to give her attention to the road again. "I think your trouble is you're so afraid you may not make out that you won't let yourself go. Horace was that way. Why the first night he didn't even—"

"Please. I'm not preparing a Kinsey report."

"I'll bet if you really let yourself go, you wouldn't have to squeeze and run any more."

"Let's change to another subject," he begged. "What do you think of St. Luke's after working there a day?"

"It's a lovely old place and Chuck Rogers has worked so hard to keep it going—it's a shame he doesn't really have a chance to save it. Or does he?"

"With any sort of a break, I think Chuck and I can make St. Luke's into a health center for the people of Irontown."

91

"You know I never realized what it must be like to live there until I was caring for those cute little babies today."

"The death rate for newborns in the ghetto is nearly twice what it is in your part of town."

"But so many of the people are apathetic. They have to be shoved around like the cattle on a dude ranch I spent a summer on when I was in high school."

"If you could only get menial jobs and then be paid lower wages than a white man doing the same work, you might be apathetic too. Particularly if you couldn't feed your children the kind of food they need to develop healthy bodies and throw off disease."

"But you can't change all that through St. Luke's."

"We can make a start by giving poor people something they can't get without going all the way across town to the County Medical Center—good medical care. We can pick up things like lead poisoning before minds are destroyed beyond repair, or rickets, which distorts the bones of growing children. And we can catch the complications of pregnancy before it's too late to save both the mother and the child."

They were in the foothills now and the road had begun to wind upward, demanding her total attention. Finally it ended on the flattened crest of the peak called Round Top, overlooking the entire valley to the east with smoke from the chimneys of Framingham visible in the distance.

When Samantha opened the door and got out Jud followed, using his cane to steady himself on the rough gravel covering the parking space. Standing at the edge of the overlook itself, a lovely picture with the wind molding the uniform to her body, Samantha looked down at the valley for a while without speaking, then turned to face him.

"I guess you think I'm pretty much of a parasite, don't you?" she said.

"A butterfly would be more apt. You toil not, neither do you spin."

"I was spinning today—"

"Yes. And I'm proud of you."

"Are you really, Jud? I mean you're just not saying that?"

"I'm not in the habit of just saying things, Samantha. Even a butterfly is part of nature's plan for keeping life on earth; it flies but only to pass life on to its offspring. You're important to

St. Luke's, not just because you're intelligent and healthy and strong and able to work, but also because if you keep on helping us, others will come to help too. And we need all of you."

"I guess I've always been the way I am—without purpose until today—because nobody ever needed me before. Or almost nobody."

"Surely Horace—"

"Oh, I guess he loved me—still does. But marrying the boss's daughter was just another step up the ladder for Horace. He's determined to be a very important man in the textile field and I was a means of getting there faster—until I rebelled."

"You might be wrong. After all, your father did keep him on in charge of the mill after your divorce."

"Oh, Horace is tops in textile engineering; everybody says that. Besides, Dad doesn't think much of me. Mother died when I was born and I guess he always held that against me. He never told me in so many words, but he didn't want to be bothered with me when I was small. Come to think of it, I guess I was never really a child; even when I was little I always played with older children. At Miss Parham's I went with college boys while I was still in high school. In college, I simply couldn't stand all that sorority crap, so I just dropped out."

"Do you think you're any happier for rebelling?"

"Than when?"

"Any time."

"I guess the happiest I ever was must have been when Dad had his heart attack." Her tone was wistful. "It was at the end of my first year in college and, after he left the hospital, Dad had to stay in the house for two months. He wrote me that he needed me, so I came right home."

"Was that the first time he ever said he needed you?"

"The very first—and the last. I was happy looking after him too. But when he got better and realized he wasn't going to die, he started ordering me around again, so I knew he didn't need me any more and moved out. I didn't realize how much Horace was like Dad, until we were married."

"Girls often marry men like their fathers. It's a recognized psychological principle."

"So I left Horace just like I left Dad? Is that what you're saying?" She sat on the low stone wall guarding the edge of the overlook and swung her legs across it, letting them hang over the edge, with a precipitous drop of perhaps a hundred feet below her.

The movement was so characteristic of her that he couldn't help smiling.

"What's so funny?" she asked, a trifle sharply.

"The way you always rebel—even against the wall when you sat down just now. Ninety-nine people out of a hundred—maybe more—would sit with their feet on the safe side."

"A lot of right you have to talk," she retorted. "You've been in rebellion against the situation at St. Luke's since the minute you arrived."

"Touché. But I don't look for situations where I'll be exposed to personal danger."

"Maybe the kind of danger you look for is more of a threat to you than this drop below my feet is to me. Every time you use your right hand in treating a patient, you're making yourself liable for anything that goes wrong."

Once again he was amazed by the acuity of her perception. But then, by her own admission, she had never really been a child.

"That's a chance I took when I came back," he said.

"Deliberately?"

"Yes."

"That took a lot of courage."

"In anything worth doing, there's always a point of no return. I had reached it, so I had only one way to go."

"And I almost wrecked your whole future by throwing myself at you the other night," she said contritely. "Can you ever forgive me?"

"There's nothing to forgive, Samantha. You offered me the greatest gift any woman can give a man as proof of her love and I failed you."

She leaned across the slight space between them to kiss him and instinctively his left arm went around her waist, holding her close—until she pushed him away.

"Part of you may not be functioning yet, but all of me is," she said a little breathlessly. "Maybe we'd better go."

Halfway down the mountain, she said: "There's a lovely inn at the foot of Round Hill and it's still early. You won't be disgraced if you take a girl in a hospital uniform there for dinner—or do you have something else in mind?"

"I'd love to have dinner with you, but I'd better call the hospital from the inn and see if things are under control. I told them I'd only be away about three hours."

94

When the operator rang the Emergency Room for him, he was surprised to hear Kathryn Galloway's voice answer.

"What are you doing on duty after the three o'clock shift went off?" he asked.

"Amanda had to be off until seven. Where are you?"

"At the Valley Inn, near the foot of Round Hill."

"I know the place; Dick and I go there for dinner sometimes. Don't worry about the OPD; we've got the situation well in hand."

"Thanks, Kathryn. I should be back by ten o'clock."

"Enjoy yourself—you're entitled to it. And tell Mrs. Fellowes she did fine her first day on duty."

The phoned clicked in his ear, leaving him momentarily speechless in the face of that most remarkable of communication systems, the hospital grapevine.

CHAPTER XI

The Valley Inn specialized in Gulf Coast sea food, brought there each night in refrigerated trucks. They dined on shrimp cocktails, broiled red snapper and hearts of palm salad, then lingered over a bottle of Lancer's crackling rosé. It was nine o'clock when they left and Samantha drove slowly for a change.

The expressway connecting the city's traffic system with the Interstate passed almost over Framingham Mills. When they came to the exit for the mills, Jud was surprised to see that the street in front of the main gate was crowded with people. The usual pale blue light shone from every window of the several long brick buildings that housed the textile factory, but in addition floodlights had turned the half block in front of the building complex into a blaze of illumination.

"I wonder what could be happening at the mill?" said Samantha, then added quickly: "I see Horace down there. Something must be wrong."

95

Before Jud could object, she had guided the car into the exit lane marked "Framingham Mills—All Employee Traffic."

Perhaps a hundred blacks and Mexican-Americans were gathered around the main gate near the foot of the curving ramp, facing a cordon of security guards and police reinforcements at the gate. A tall man, whom Jud judged to be Horace Fellowes, was talking to a captain of police.

Across the street from the entrance, the crowd of blacks and Mexican-Americans was marching slowly in a circle, many of them carrying signs bearing legends such as: "FRAMINGHAM MILLS UNFAIR TO BLACK WORKERS," "NO DISCRIMINATION IN HIRING," "NUTS TO AFL-CIO," and the like.

"Your ex seems to be okay but trouble could flare up at any moment," Jud told Samantha. "You'd better turn around and let's get out of here."

She didn't argue but braked the car to a stop and started backing into a corner niche of the high fence surrounding the complex of buildings that made up the textile plant.

"What do you suppose is happening?" she asked as she shifted gears.

"Chuck Rogers has been trying to get the mill union to let blacks and Chicanos be employed in skilled categories. I know Chuck has been worried that a militant faction might try to take things into their own hands and it looks like they're staging some kind of a demonstration."

"Then there's going to be a fight?"

"Not necessarily—but all hell could break loose when the three-to-eleven shift goes off the job."

Samantha had almost finished turning the car when it was surrounded by a jeering group of blacks, forcing her to halt or run them down. One of them, a tall man with a badly scarred face who must have weighed two hundred and fifty pounds, most of it muscles, ran his hand across the hood of the car.

"Made in Italy, ain't it?" he asked.

"Yes," said Jud.

"What's the name of it?"

"An Alfa Romeo."

"That's the new doctor at St. Luke's, Al," a voice called from the crowd. "He's okay."

"Doctor, eh?" said the one called Al. "This your car?"

"No. If you will excuse us—"

"Man, ain't you polite. What about that chick you got in there? This her car?"

"Yes. Will you move back, please, and let us go through?"

"Why be in such a hurry, Doc?" said the big man. "Them union bastards inside that mill won't let us have no jobs. Soon's they come off shift, there's goin' to be one hell of a fight here and maybe we'll be need'n a doctor—a nurse too. That chick is a nurse, ain't she?"

Al put his hands on top of the car and lowered his head until it was opposite the open window on Samantha's side. Jud saw that she was like a statue, rigid from fear and with all color gone from her cheeks. He was reaching for his cane, the only weapon he had, ready to do his puny best to poke Al with it, when Samantha suddenly cried: "Eric! Eric Cates!"

A tall, light colored Negro man who had been arguing with the guards at the gate turned quickly at Samantha's cry. Moving with the grace and speed of a tiger, he was at the car window before she could call again and seized the one called Al by the shirt collar, spinning him around and away from the car in spite of his weight.

"What's the trouble?" Eric Cates asked.

"That man stopped us." Jud answered for Samantha when her mouth worked only soundlessly. "He was being insulting to Mrs. Fellowes."

"I'm sorry, Samantha." Eric Cates' voice was gentle. "You see, Al doesn't have much sense."

"This is Dr. Tyler." Samantha found her voice at last.

"Recognized you from your picture, Doctor," said Cates. "My sister, Amanda, has been telling me about what you're doing at St. Luke's."

"Mrs. Fellowes is pretty upset by all this," said Jud. "Can you get us out of here?"

"Make room!" Eric Cates' voice was sharp as he spoke to the crowd surrounding the car. "Get lost!"

The others turned and moved away obediently. Only Al took a step toward Eric Cates, but when the labor leader turned quickly, poised in the stance of the professional boxer, Al shambled off with the others.

"Does Chuck Rogers know about this?" Jud asked Cates.

97

"He does by now. Chuck was at a meeting, but I just heard he's on his way over here."

"Is there likely to be trouble?"

"Who wants trouble?" Eric Cates' grin was sardonic and also very wise. "This is a demonstration, Doctor—just enough to put the fear of God into the mill management so they'll pressure the union to take in blacks and Chicanos. When Chuck gets here, we'll let him argue us out of staying until eleven o'clock and having a confrontation."

"You mean Chuck engineered this scheme?"

Cates shook his head. "Chuck's square when it comes to things like this. He believes people will eventually do what's right. But after Vietnam, you and I know differently, don't we, Doctor?"

"I guess so," said Jud. "We'd better be going, Samantha. Do you feel like driving?"

She nodded, although she was still quite pale. "Thanks, Eric," she said gratefully.

"Think nothing of it," said the demonstration leader. "I'm glad of the chance to repay your family for old times."

"Drive on to your apartment," Jud told Samantha as they were approaching St. Luke's. "I'm going to pour you a stiff drink and put you to bed."

"You can't walk back to the hospital."

"The doorman will get me a taxi. I want to be sure you're okay first."

"I was scared stiff when that big one stuck his face in the window," she admitted. "I guess I would have just died, if I hadn't seen Eric."

"Where did you know him?"

"Eric and I are about the same age. When we were both small, his mother—she was our cook—used to bring him to the house to play with me. Dad helped Eric get a scholarship to college."

"What about Amanda?"

"She was older, but I knew her very well too. She's been helping look after Dad."

At Samantha's apartment house, she drove into the basement garage and parked her car. But she held his arm closely, as they took the elevator up to the apartment floor, and he could feel her trembling. At the door she fumbled with the key, so he took it from her and unlocked it with his left hand, letting them in.

98

"Get into your night clothes while I pour you a drink," he directed. "Where's the liquor?"

"In the cabinet under the bookcase."

When she came back into the living room, wearing silk pajamas and a matching robe, he had poured a double bourbon for her and filled the glass with ginger ale.

"This will help you sleep." He handed her the glass. "You've had quite an experience tonight."

She shivered but took the glass obediently. "Where's yours?"

"I'll take a rain check. If Chuck and Eric Cates don't stop that demonstration before the eleven o'clock change of shift, I'm liable to be busy tonight. By the way, you don't need to come on duty in the morning; I'll explain to Kathryn Galloway."

"Don't, please. I'll be there."

"But—"

"That's the least I can do." She had half emptied the glass. "When I remember how you faced up to that Al—"

"With my trusty cane as a weapon? He could have broken me across his knee and not even felt a bone crack."

"But you didn't back down." She came over to where he was standing. "Kiss me good night and then go—fast. That bourbon's about to reach my brain."

Her lips were soft but without passion. Jud released her quickly, when he felt a warmth begin to spread downward through his body from his brain.

"Good night, darling." Her voice was already a little slurred from the bourbon. "Next time bring your pajamas; I think this surrogate business just might work a miracle, if we go at it right."

II

Two notes were on Jud's desk when he came into his office the next morning, both to call Joe Morgan. The last call had been at nine-thirty the night before.

"I tried to get you last night," said the lawyer, when Jud rang him. "Samantha Wright and I had dinner at the Valley Inn."

"Fine girl, but a little nuts. She's lots of fun."

"We found ourselves in the middle of that demonstration at Framingham Mills. I thought for a while I'd have to fight my way out with my trusty cane."

99

"Saw it on film on the eleven o'clock news," said Morgan. "Fortunately Chuck Rogers arrived in time to cool things off."

"We left before that," said Jud, but he was remembering Eric Cates' mocking words: "When Chuck gets here, we'll let him argue us out of staying until eleven o'clock and having a confrontation." And he wondered how Chuck would feel if he knew the truth.

"I called to tell you that I stopped by 723 Rutherford Street late yesterday afternoon," said the lawyer. "Did you know the Browns have flown the coop?"

"What?"

"They're gone—vamoosed."

"But Freddie was still in the hospital yesterday when I made rounds. Wait a minute and I'll check."

Jud reached for a pile of hospital charts that had been placed on his desk that morning, representing the cases discharged in the last twenty-four hours. The chart he sought was third in the pile. Stamped across it was the cryptic words: "Discharged against advice." The time had been 3:00 P.M.

"Freddie was taken out yesterday afternoon," he told the lawyer. "Any idea where the family went?"

"In Irontown, blacks don't tell a white man much. But I did learn that the husband lost his job."

"Why?"

"He worked at Framingham Mills unloading cotton bales. Seth Wright and Angus Claiborne are old friends, and it would be easy for the management, to say nothing of the hillbillies who don't want to see blacks working in the cotton mills anyway, to put so much pressure on Brown that he'd get scared and leave town."

"At least the kids are better off out of the city than being slowly poisoned with lead," said Jud. "Fortunately, we still have their medical records as evidence against Claiborne, when I come up before the trustees next week."

"The rumors are all over town that they're going to gang up on you."

"It does look like I'm the lamb who's to be sacrificed for the maintenance of the status quo," Jud agreed. "I'm afraid you chose the wrong horse to bet on, Joe."

"The race hasn't even started," said Morgan cheerfully. "I'm on the board of the local ETV station. They usually cover school board and council meetings live and the manager tells me he's had an invitation to cover the entire trustees' meeting with television."

"With the victim limping in to be slaughtered?" Jud said somewhat bitterly.

"Come off it—you're worth any two of us, cane and all," said Morgan. "Do you have any idea how you're going to fight it, now that we don't have the Brown children?"

"Not yet. How about you?"

"Nothing here either," Joe Morgan admitted. "I've been tearing my hair—"

"Hair!" Jud exclaimed. "That's it?"

"What?"

"I can't tell you now; we don't know who might be listening in on the hospital switchboard. But we've got a chance to sink the enemy; just be in my corner when the fight starts."

"With towel and smelling salts," said the lawyer. "Let me know if you need a delaying action before the meeting, something like an injunction against Framingham Mills for endangering workers' health by promoting that disease—what's the name of it again?"

"Byssinosis."

"I'll have to practice pronouncing it. Right now I sound like a punctured tire."

III

Noting that Chuck Rogers was in his office, Jud crossed to it.

"I see you stopped the trouble at Framingham Mills last night," he said.

"Don't kid yourself," said Chuck morosely. "It stopped because Eric Cates didn't want it to go any further. I was the patsy."

"The important thing is that it did stop."

"Only because Eric doesn't believe he's strong enough yet to put the real squeeze on management and the union. What worries me is the carnage that may result when he finally decides to make a try."

"Don't you think Eric is capable of making that decision? I was very much impressed by what I saw of him last night."

"He's playing this thing too close to his chest," said Chuck. "Even Eric can't always be sure of controlling the people he's using as pawns."

"One of them almost tackled him last night. They called him Al."

"That was Al Porter," said Chuck. "I wouldn't trust him as far as I could throw him. Did you know the Brown family has flown the coop?"

"I was talking to Joe Morgan about it just now. Claiborne didn't lose any time."

"There was never any doubt about his striking back—only the target—and he finally found the weakest link. Some of the biggest fortunes in Framingham are partially built on slum rentals in Irontown and landlords can't have tenants suing them. Just be thankful the Brown family helped us identify another health hazard; with the evidence we've got, we can still force the city government to do something about it."

"I plan to use the lead poisoning records as part of my defense when I'm attacked at the meeting of the board next week," said Jud. "But it would have still been a lot better if we could have had the children themselves there and shown the lead line along little Freddie's gums."

"I agree," said Chuck. "Now the Claiborne faction can claim that the tests were in error and, without the children to repeat them on, they might still cut your defenses from under you."

"I've got still another barrel to fire. Kathryn Galloway gave me the answer to it the other night—"

Chuck looked surprised. "You've been seeing her?"

"Kathryn picked me up as I was walking back to the hospital the night I went to Samantha Fellowes' apartment to loosen the bandage on her splint."

"Don't ever walk the streets of Irontown again at night," Chuck warned. "Or we'll be dragging you out of the gutter dead."

"Kathryn told me about a mass survey that was conducted at Johns Hopkins for lead poisoning in a ghetto area. Do you think you could get your youth groups to canvas Irontown in the next few days and give some children haircuts?"

"What sort of a joke is that?"

"I'm serious." Jud explained his plans for a quick survey by means of the spectrophotometer to determine the occurrence of lead poisoning among children in the area.

"I suppose you want us to concentrate on the houses owned by Angus Claiborne," said Chuck.

"Those, of course. But I'd also like to get as many others as we can. Joe tells me the meeting is to be open and televised."

"I didn't know that." Chuck frowned. "They must think they've got enough evidence to deny approval of your appointment and make a public example of you."

"That can work both ways," said Jud. "If we produce a list of houses owned by some of Framingham's best families—all slowly poisoning children because the landlords have been criminally negligent—some people are going to be in for an unpleasant surprise."

"That I would like to see." Chuck's face brightened. "Tomorrow's a school holiday, so I'll get some crews out early in the morning. How much hair do you need?"

"Just a snip. Each specimen should be put into a small envelope and labeled with the names of the child and the parents, the address and, if possible, the name of the landlord."

"The enemy is liable to get suspicious if we require all that information without saying why."

"Tell your haircutting crews we're looking for evidence of air pollution," said Jud. "Everyone's on an ecology kick these days anyway and you'll really be telling the truth. Meanwhile we'll check all the children who come through the OPD; I'll go down now and see Dr. Wiley about the lab work."

The old pathologist was in his office; his bushy eyebrows bristling as always. Jud gave him a quick rundown on his plan for a mass survey of the children of Irontown, both in the hospital and out.

"I remember reading that article," said Wiley. "But I'll look it up again, just to bring myself up-to-date on the technique."

"Will the chief of laboratories at the County Medical Center co-operate with us?"

"He'd better; I trained Ed McLean myself. When do you want to start?"

"Today with clinic and hospital patients; Chuck's task forces will go into action tomorrow. If doing the test runs into overtime because of the weekend, tell Dr. McLean I'll pay the technicians myself."

"No need for that," said the pathologist. "I'll be running a lot of them after I leave here in the afternoon."

"I don't remember the exact figures of the lead concentration in the blood of the Brown children," said Jud. "But we're certain to need that for the board meeting too."

"I can find that out easily enough." Wiley pressed a button

on his desk and a technician appeared in the door almost immediately.

"Get me the records of those lead determinations we did on the Brown children the other day, Ethel," Wiley directed. "I told you to make copies for the lab's files."

"Right away, Doctor," said the technician, but it was quite a while before she came back. And then there was a look of distress on her face.

"They're gone, Dr. Wiley," she reported.

"What do you mean—gone?"

"The records of the lab work on the Brown children aren't in the files."

"Well find out where they are."

"Miss Jernigan." Jud read her name from the printed name plate all hospital personnel wore pinned on their uniforms.

"Yes, Doctor."

"If you'll go up to my office and look on my desk, you'll find Freddie Brown's chart there. Please bring it down here."

She was gone only a few minutes, but even before he leafed through the chart, Jud was quite sure what he would find—or rather would not.

The laboratory report sheet had been removed, also the record of the physical examination by Juan Valdese. Nowhere on the chart was there anything to prove that the diagnosis of "chronic lead poisoning" written on the space left for the final diagnosis was supported by either physical examination or laboratory findings.

"It seems like the enemy has spiked our main battery, Dr. Wiley," Jud said soberly. "Somebody removed everything from the hospital records that would verify the diagnosis."

"Who do you suppose it was?"

"I have my suspicions but I can't prove anything. All this means is that I'll have to work harder on that survey."

"*We'll* have to work harder," Wiley corrected him. "No son-of-a-bitch can steal my laboratory records and not get a kick in the tail—if I can just figure out some way to deliver it."

IV

Jud and Chuck met Joe Morgan for lunch at the downtown Holiday Inn the next day—at Jud's request.

"We lost another battle," the lawyer reported glumly when they were seated and had given their orders.

"Aiken?" Jud asked.

"Yes. He won't let me bring an action before the Industrial Commission."

"I imagine he's afraid of losing his job."

"He says half the men in the cardroom where he works have the same symptoms he does. If he loses the case, Seth Wright would probably fire him and the others too."

"Wouldn't the state industrial laws protect him?"

"Theoretically, yes. But practically, no," said Morgan. "The whole question is pretty confused."

"But Aiken's future is medically predictable," Jud protested. "With only about thirty per cent of his lung volume left, he's bound to get into real trouble sooner or later. And this time it will probably be fatal."

"A few years ago there was a test case in North Carolina," said Joe Morgan. "The worker who brought it lost."

"Why?"

"His lawyers sued on the grounds of chronic bronchitis and emphysema—byssinosis hadn't even been heard of then, except by the people Dick Tubman spoke of at Yale. The worker happened to be a heavy smoker too, and the court ruled that he hadn't proved cotton dust caused the symptoms. With a ruling against byssinosis as an industrial disease already on the statutes, lawyers have hesitated to take any cases on a contingency basis."

"How about you?"

Morgan shrugged. "I only do this sort of thing so I can live with myself, while I'm doing what I have to do to make a living. Aiken was a perfect test case because he almost lost his life and that alone would have carried a lot of weight with a jury. Get me another clean-cut test case and I'll do battle for you, but you may have a hard time finding another one like Jack Aiken."

"Maybe we'd better take stock and see exactly what weapons we do have available for the battle next week before the trustees," said Chuck. "With the Browns gone and the hospital records stolen, we can't make much of a case against the landlords for poisoning ghetto children with lead."

"Don't write that off until the results are in on the survey," said Jud. "Do you have any idea how many hair specimens the task forces have collected since they started the campaign?"

"Just before I left to come here, they had corralled fifty in Iron-town."

"We've been clipping kids in the OPD for a day and a half," said Jud. "Samantha's been busy all morning at it."

"Is she really working at St. Luke's?" Morgan asked.

"Like a beaver."

"I guess Horace Fellowes and Seth Wright will bust a gut when they hear of it."

"Samantha tells me she doesn't have to depend on either of them."

"That's true," said Morgan. "My firm represents the bank that handles the trust set up by her grandmother. The old girl was pretty much of an individualist in her own right and Samantha's named after her."

"Do you think Seth Wright really cares what happens to Samantha?" Jud asked.

"With the old man, it's hard to tell," said the lawyer.

"What about Fellowes?"

"Horace is a very capable textile engineer, but he's probably a prime example of the engineer type who understands machines but can't understand his wife. One thing is certain—by keeping Samantha off the highway for eight hours a day, you're doing the rest of us travelers a favor."

Morgan turned to the chaplain. "How do you figure the voting is liable to go at the trustees' meeting, Chuck?"

"Bishop Tanner's worried, which means it will probably be close. Depending on how many members of the board show up, we could win or lose by a vote or two. One thing you can be sure of, the Claiborne faction will be out in force."

"Any ideas about strategy, Joe?" Jud asked.

"I think we'd better start out by letting Chuck make a motion, as a member of the Board of Trustees and the Selection Committee, for approval of your employment as Director of Emergency Services. The ETV station is going to broadcast the proceedings live starting at six o'clock, so they can be sure of the biggest audience while people are having dinner. And that means the Claiborne faction will have to make their move early, before people decide this is going to be just another long-winded board meeting and switch channels."

"The Romans used the same principles when they were throwing Christians to the lions," Chuck observed.

"At least Jud will have the satisfaction of either losing or winning in a blaze of publicity," said Morgan. "And if it works out the way we hope it will, that blaze will also cook Angus Claiborne's goose."

CHAPTER XII

Driving back to the hospital from lunch, Chuck turned off on a street that bisected Irontown east of Ventura Boulevard. Since his return to Framingham, Jud had seen only that part of the ghetto on Rutherford Street which, it turned out now, had been almost a showplace compared to the less attractive section they were in.

Black children, their potbellies—in Africa called *kwashiorkor*—eloquent testimony of protein lack in a diet composed largely of carbohydrates like cornmeal and pork fat, played listlessly in the streets. Here and there, women gathered in knots to talk, often with children hanging on their skirts. On a street corner bench, several old men like the one Jud had seen dozing near the statue of St. Luke's in front of the hospital the day he had arrived argued or played checkers. And from a corner bar came a burst of loud male voices, as the door was opened and a man staggered out.

"Even the unemployable can still drink beer," said Chuck.

"And the employables who are too lazy to work."

"Take a look around you and tell me what living in a place like this would do to build a man's pride."

"It might stimulate him to get out of it."

"You and I, yes," the chaplain conceded. "But if you had come into this world stunted from malnutrition in your mother's body and with your mind already crippled because of it, you might be content to let others feed and clothe you."

Chuck pulled the car to the curb before a weatherboarded old

church set back from the street under the trees. A sign beside the
door said:

ST. SIMON OF CYRENE CHAPEL
REV. CHARLES A. ROGERS, PASTOR

"Simon of Cyrene?" said Jud. "I don't seem to remember him."

"On the way to the Place of the Skull, where Jesus was crucified,
he fell under the weight of the crossbeam called the patibulum
that condemned men were forced to carry to their execution. The
New Testament says a man of Cyrene called Simon took the beam
upon his shoulders and carried it the rest of the way; legend made
him an important figure in the early church."

"Wasn't Cyrene a city in Africa?"

"Yes. Many biblical scholars believe Simon was black."

Inside the church the pews were plain, though adorned here and
there with a name carved into the back by some restless youngster
with a pocket knife. A large Bible was open on the pulpit lectern
and on both sides were rather unusually large choir stalls for a
church of that size.

"My congregation is theoretically integrated but ninety per cent
black," said Chuck. "They like to 'Make a joyful noise unto God'—
in the words of the psalmist. Sometimes we have twice as many
people in the choir as we do in the rest of the church, but
it's a way of getting them inside."

"How large is your congregation?"

"Maybe a hundred or a hundred and fifty. I stay so busy at
the hospital I don't have much time to keep up with the church
records."

"Is it growing?"

"Lately it is, especially among young people where growth
really counts. We stage a Rock Mass here once a month and
pack the church on a Sunday night so we have to put loud
speakers outside in the street."

"Does the cathedral vestry approve?"

"They didn't, until I reminded them that I have twice as many
people in the chapel here for a Rock Mass as they have in the
whole cathedral for the average Sunday morning service."

"Why not stage one downtown then and fill the cathedral?"

"That will be the day," said Chuck as he opened the door at
the back of the spartan chancel. "We can go out this way. I want
you to see a gravestone."

The cemetery behind the church was quite small, the stones very old and in many places so covered with lichens that the inscriptions were undecipherable. At the back of the cemetery, where a rusted iron fence was almost hidden by honeysuckle vines, Chuck paused before a family plot.

A large headstone identified the occupants as Abijah Ferron and his wife, Rebecca. Beside the large stone, on the side of Abijah, was a smaller one whose inscription was so old and weatherworn that Jud had to kneel to read it:

> Henry, faithful and beloved servant of Abijah and Rebecca Ferron. He gave his life protecting the honor of his mistress. Greater love hath no man than this, that a man lay down his life for his friend.

"Abijah Ferron was a Colonel in the Confederate Army," said Chuck. "His plantation was located near this church and, when Sherman moved south to Atlanta before the famous march through Georgia, a Yankee raiding band visited the house. Henry was the only house servant who had remained with Rebecca Ferron; when one of the raiders tried to rape her, he shot the man dead, although he was dying himself from Yankee bullets. Henry was buried in the plantation slave plot but, when Abijah Ferron returned at the end of the war, he had Henry's body exhumed and reburied in the family plot."

"With no repercussions?"

"The church split apart over it and more than half of the congregation left, but Abijah Ferron didn't give in," said Chuck. "He had freed his slaves even before the war and, when he built the first new textile mill in Framingham, he insisted that white and black alike be employed in it. So you can see just how far Framingham has really come in a hundred years."

"I tell my congregation to follow Henry's example of loyalty and devotion," Chuck continued as he opened the gate and let Jud through into what appeared to be a warehouse yard behind the church. "But Eric Cates keeps reminding me that even though Henry has been dead over a century, a lot of blacks still can't claim to be emancipated, so you can understand why it's hard to convince them."

The area in which they found themselves appeared to be the back loading yard of a large warehouse building, which had long since been abandoned, judging by the growth of weeds around it.

"This warehouse lies almost in the center of Irontown and most of the inhabitants can reach it easily by walking, so it's an ideal spot for a community center." Chuck's voice deepened and took on a new timbre. "Here at the back we'll build a swimming pool one day for the kids and, when we get the money, we'll enclose it so it can be used the year round. I see a well baby clinic here and one for expectant mothers too, plus classrooms where everything from weaving to skilled trades can be taught."

"It's an ambitious project."

"Soul food may be good for the spirit, but it's bad for the body, so one of the greatest needs in the ghetto is for an expert nutritionist to teach mothers how to buy and prepare the right kind of food for their families. We'll concentrate on that too, plus a medical clinic here that can take much of the routine load off the staff at St. Luke's and leave more time for hospital patients."

"That means expanding St. Luke's when practically everybody thinks it's dying."

"Don't you think it can be done?"

"When I'm with you, yes. But then I look at the OPD, especially when I'm tired and it's crowded, and I see how little we're really doing—"

"You've saved one man's life and reorganized the whole clinic operation in less than a week," Chuck reminded him.

"But I'm still only one man—and little more than half a one at that."

"Half of you still adds up to a medical John Bunyan."

Jud laughed. "You're obviously building me up for something; go on and break the news to me."

"I'm hoping to interest one of the national foundations in your idea for a traumatic surgery clinic at St. Luke's modeled after the work you did in Vietnam," said Chuck. "Will you have time to prepare a presentation on it before the Board of Trustees meeting next week?"

"I may not be Director of Emergency Services after that."

"I'll take the chance. Can you do it?"

"Sure. But aren't the foundation people liable to boggle when they see that you're depending on a cripple?"

"Not with your war record as a drawing card for young doctors to staff the clinic."

"There's that gimmick again," Jud warned.

"And it's working," said Chuck. "Besides, if the law to make

110

automobile liability insurance compulsory goes through, most of the St. Luke's accident cases will be paying patients."

"Provided we can keep them in the hospital."

"You kept Mr. Gonzalez and he's doing well. With that as a start, we'll soon be able to get enough support to put the hospital back on its feet."

Jud's enthusiasm was building in spite of his misgivings. "If we could manage to start a rehabilitation clinic, a lot of traumatic cases might be sent to St. Luke's by insurance company pressure because we could get them back to work considerably earlier than they're getting now. Several of the big insurance companies are working on this sort of a thing, and Framingham would certainly be a fine place to have such a clinic in operation."

"Now you can see why it's important for your presentation to be ready," said Chuck.

"And even more important that I win in the hearing before the Board of Trustees. We'd better stop dreaming—and see how the hair snipping campaign is going."

II

Chuck dropped Jud off at the hospital before checking on the activities of the survey teams in Irontown. As Jud was passing through the OPD, he saw Samantha working in one of the cubicles to which a stream of small patients was being directed, sometimes with considerable vocal objections.

She looked up and smiled wearily, as she reached for an envelope in which to drop a lock of hair she had just cropped from the woolly head of a small black boy, who was howling at the top of his voice. The splint on her left wrist obviously made the movement awkward, for she dropped the envelope and was forced to stoop to pick it up as the small patient was being led out of the cubicle.

"Miss Galloway," Jud called to Kathryn, who was watching Emilio Fernandez suture a wound in an adjoining cubicle.

"Yes, Doctor." She looked as fresh and crisp in her uniform as Samantha was mussed in her pink checked uniform.

"Did the Lightcast material I ordered yesterday come?"

"I believe so."

"I'd like to put a new splint on Mrs. Fellowes' wrist; the plaster one gets in her way. Would you bring the material to my office?"

"Right away. It should be in the stockroom."

"You look like you could use a cup of coffee," Jud told Samantha. "Wait in my office and I'll bring you one. Black?"

Her eyes suddenly sparkled and some of the weariness went out of them. "You remembered!"

"Is that so unusual?"

"Horace never did."

"And look what he lost."

Samantha giggled. "Careful, Doctor."

Jud brought the coffee. "How did you feel this morning?"

"Lousy. When you get a girl drunk, you get a girl drunk."

"I told you not to come on duty, if you didn't feel like it."

"Unh! Unh! I've started a lot of things in my life and didn't finish them—too many I guess. But I'm staying with this one." She finished the coffee and put down the cup. "It's all over the hospital that Mr. Ford and some of the trustees are sharpening the ax for you. Have they got a chance to cut you down?"

"From the looks of things, the odds are on their side."

"Why?"

"They can argue that I'm not much more than half a man."

"A lot *they* know," she said. "I'll admit that I didn't get very far seducing you the other night, but I did learn you're not quite as dead as you think you are. I'm pretty sure what's holding you back, not just from sex but from doing the kind of surgery you're capable of doing, is fear of failure."

"You're a very acute observer."

"Every woman's an acute observer where men are concerned; it's part of the feminine intuition."

"Or mystique?"

"There's nothing mysterious about me. I'm after you." Then to his surprise, she raised her voice and changed the subject abruptly. "We're getting a lot of hair specimens, Doctor. Any idea how many of them will show lead?"

Before he could answer, Kathryn Galloway appeared at the open door, carrying a tray with material for the new type of cast and a special lamp used in hardening it. Jud had no way of knowing how long Kathryn had been within earshot or how much she'd overheard, but he'd just been given a striking example of what Samantha had called intuition—which only meant that, with the heightened sense of perception women naturally possessed, she'd heard Kathryn in the hall outside before he had.

"I think I've got everything." Kathryn put the tray on his desk. "We've never used one of these casts before at St. Luke's."

"It's a new process." Jud snipped a piece of adhesive with which he had secured the elastic bandage he'd applied in Samantha's apartment to hold the splint in place and removed it. "Once the cast is hard, you can even take a shower with it on."

"That will be a relief," said Samantha.

The bones were straight, as the checkup X ray had shown, and only a few pressure marks showed on her skin where the plaster strip used to make the splint had become wrinkled. The difference in skin tone between her sun-bronzed hand and the wrist he covered with a splint was quite noticeable, however.

"It sure feels good to get that off." Samantha flexed and extended her fingers gingerly.

"You'll hardly know you have this one on." Jud was working expertly, molding a support for the wrist from the plastic material called Lightcast. When it was completed, he turned on the special heat lamp and positioned Samantha's wrist beneath the cone of brilliance it cast on the surface of the desk.

"The material hardens under the lamp in about three minutes," he told her. "You'll only have to stay quiet a little while."

"I'd better put a towel over your hand so it won't get burned any more." Kathryn Galloway draped a cloth across Samantha's fingers. "The skin looks like it might blister next time."

Samantha laughed airily. "I'm always doing dumb things—like trying to apply heat to my wrist with a sunlamp when it was hurting so much. But it only turned my fingers red and I still had to bother Dr. Tyler to make a house call and loosen the splint."

Jud turned back to his desk to hide a smile at the thrust and parry that had just occurred. Feminine intuition—as Samantha had called it—was no sharper, he suspected, than the impulse to compete where the attention of a male was concerned. But it did hearten his spirits a little to realize that two beautiful women had crossed lances, however briefly, for his benefit.

"Thank you for your help, Miss Galloway," he said formally. "The new splint should be hard enough by the time Mrs. Fellowes goes off duty at three."

"I'll tell Miss Cates to put the lamp away later," said Kathryn. "Right now I'd better get back to the Emergency Room and finish clipping the hair specimens to send to the laboratory."

"She hates me," said Samantha complacently when Kathryn had gone.

"Nonsense. She's very efficient and believes in being professional —as a nurse should."

"There's a lot of woman under that starched uniform and she doesn't have that red hair for nothing. You know why she came back to Framingham, don't you?"

"To be with her father."

"Looking after her father was only an excuse. The man she was in love with in Baltimore—he was a doctor—married a society girl and she came here to get away."

"How do you learn all these things?"

"I heard that at the morning coffee break the first day I came on duty. The aides say she was in a deep funk the first two months she was here—until she started going out with Dick Tubman. And particularly since you two went to that beer joint on Spring Hill the other night."

"How did you know about that?"

Samantha shrugged. "The night orderly saw her letting you out of the car at the Emergency Room entrance and it was all over the hospital by the coffee break the next morning. It won't do her any good though. I'm after you and Dick's got his sights set on a big house on Spring Hill."

"Don't tell me you've been out with him?"

"I'm a divorcee. I'm rich. And I'm supposed to be a hot number—"

"Supposed?"

"You ought to know." She wrinkled her nose at him in the gamin fashion he found so delightful. "Every loose male in town— and a lot who think they want to be loose—are on the make for a divorcee."

"Maybe men figure that, having failed once, you're anxious to prove it wasn't your fault by being good in bed."

"Why, Dr. Tyler!" Her eyes crinkled mischievously. "How you do understand women."

Then she sobered. "A lot of times it's the truth though. Deep down inside her, every woman who's divorced knows that some of it was her fault."

"But not many admit it."

"Those are the ones who wind up as alcoholics or on a couch— psychoanalytic or otherwise. It's a lot better to admit it and vow to do better next time."

"That's a rather remarkable admission."

"I've been in love with you for years, so I don't have to hide anything from you," she said. "Come to think of it, I couldn't anyway—after the other night."

Outside, a buzzer sounded, marking the change of shifts. Jud lifted her left hand and examined the cast. It was already hard and smooth, so he switched off the lamp.

"Be a little careful driving home and don't lean on the hand for a while," he advised. "This splint should be a lot lighter than the old one—and easier to handle."

"It doesn't feel much heavier than an evening glove," she told him and, with a quick glance into the corridor to see that it was empty, raised herself on tiptoes and kissed him.

"That's for the new cast, and for the other afternoon," she said. "I had a wonderful time—until we got to the millyard. But don't ever get me drunk again and walk away. You'd never believe what alcohol does to my libido."

III

Late that afternoon, Jud received a call from Dr. Richard Tubman. "I thought I should tell you that Mr. Aiken is no longer under my care," said the internist.

"Did he pay his bill?"

"It was paid by Framingham Mills. Aiken has gone back to his family doctor."

"Mind telling me who that is? I'd like to keep up with him."

"Dr. Harold McTavish, a G.P. in North Framingham. He's treated Aiken before for asthma."

"What with? Burning leaves?"

"I don't set myself up as a judge of a fellow physician's capability," said Tubman frostily.

"You're still the only doctor in this part of the country who can be considered an expert on byssinosis."

"That reminds me," said Tubman. "If Aiken does petition the Industrial Commission for a hearing, I'm afraid I can't be a witness for you."

"Joe Morgan could have you subpoenaed."

"I doubt if the court would consider me an unbiased witness."

"Why not?"

"I've become the family physician of Mr. Seth Wright, the owner of Framingham Mills."

"When did this happen?"

"Mr. Wright's family doctor died last year and he hadn't been examined since. Mr. Fellowes called me yesterday and asked me to see Mr. Wright."

"Didn't you suspect you were being bought off?"

"I don't like your insinuation, Doctor."

"And I don't like your weaseling out where a man's life may be involved." Jud slammed the phone into its cradle and, as so often happened when he was angry, missed it and hit the desk instead.

"Is anything wrong, Dr. Tyler?" A cool voice asked from the door and he looked up to see Amanda Cates, with a sheaf of papers in her hand.

"No, thank you, Miss Cates." Jud retrieved the telephone with his left hand and put it carefully in place. "What do you have there?"

"The charts of patients discharged this morning."

Jud put the charts on his desk. "I just had a call from Dr. Tubman. He's no longer looking after Mr. Aiken and has become the family physician of Mr. Seth Wright."

"I know," she said. "I was so impressed with the way Dr. Tubman diagnosed Mr. Aiken's condition that I recommended him to Mr. Wright."

When Jud looked surprised, she added: "My mother was the Wright family cook for nearly forty years. Eric and I practically grew up in their back yard."

"I remember Samantha telling me that now. Please thank him for getting us out safely the other night."

"He was glad to do it, Dr. Tyler. There really wasn't any danger."

"You make me feel pretty small," Jud said wryly. "I was getting ready to defend us when your brother intervened. Did Dr. Tubman tell you what Mr. Wright's trouble is?"

"Gout—also diabetes, but I've suspected that for a long time. I've been going by the house mornings before I come on duty, putting hot packs on Mr. Wright's toe. He thought it was rheumatism but I suspected gout. When he heard that Mr. Aiken had almost died and asked me about him, I recommended Dr. Tubman."

"Did you tell Mr. Wright that Aiken has byssinosis?"

"Yes."

"Anyone else?"

"Mr. Fellowes was there at the time."

Jud nodded slowly. The whole picture was quite clear now.

"Let me pose you a theoretical question, Miss Cates," he said. "What would you think of a doctor who diagnosed a dangerous industrial hazard and then refused to follow it up because he'd become employed by the owner of the mill that caused the hazard?"

"I'd say he was on the way to becoming very successful in his profession."

"And what about one who lets himself be conned into thinking he could revitalize a dying hospital?"

She smiled, one of the first times she had appeared really relaxed in his presence. "I think he deserves the name they've given him in the hospital—Dr. Galahad."

"That's a tough one to live down."

"Or live up to. Is there anything else, Dr. Tyler? I usually go to dinner early on Friday before the rush starts in the Emergency Room."

"I'll be in my quarters this evening working on a plan Mr. Rogers wants me to develop for St. Luke's as a traumatic center," Jud told her. "Come to think of it, you said you were trained at Cook County in Chicago, didn't you?"

"Yes."

"You must have seen a lot of trauma there."

"Friday and Saturday nights were like war. But it really isn't much different here."

"Would you be offended if I asked you why you came back to Framingham?"

"Not at all. It was mainly because of Eric, but also because Mr. Wright needed me."

"Did he tell you that?"

Again she smiled. "Mr. Wright isn't the kind of man who tells anybody he needs them."

"He did in Samantha's case—when she was in college and he had the heart attack."

"I was in training then so I wouldn't know about that." She started for the door but he spoke before she could leave.

"Are you familiar with the Mile Square project in Chicago, Miss Cates?"

"I worked there for a few weeks." She turned back to face him. "It was part of our training."

117

"I'm thinking of starting such a project here. You could help me with the plans."

"Who's going to furnish the money?"

"The chaplain hopes to interest one of the foundations in it. And we can earn enough fees from insurance cases to bear a lot of the expense."

"Why knock yourself out, when you know they'll cut you down the moment you start making any progress?" Her tone was very much as it had been the night when he had examined Freddie Brown.

"Who are 'they,' Miss Cates?"

"The millowners, the people who own houses in the ghetto, those who exploit black people as cheap labor. When the County Medical Center was built we were told it would make the best medical care available to the people in Irontown and Chicanoville —then they located it so far away that nobody who doesn't own a car can get there. If you're able to make any real progress toward turning St. Luke's into a center for blacks and Chicanos, they'll move in and cut you down."

"How does the black community feel about my chances next week with the Board of Trustees?" he asked.

"They're not taking sides."

"Don't they at least give me credit for wanting to do something?" he asked sharply.

"My people have been disappointed too often, Dr. Tyler. When the houses were torn down west of Ventura, we were told that new houses would be built, ones black people could afford. But look what went in there: hotels, apartment houses with uniformed doormen, a shopping center where poor people can't even afford to buy, a private hospital they can't get into. When you revealed what slum houses are doing to black children by discovering lead in their blood, you wrote your own death warrant as far as succeeding here in Framingham is concerned, Dr. Tyler. The landlords of Irontown will get you one way or the other."

"What about Mr. Rogers?"

"He's learned how to give when he's hit and not be knocked down. But he's supporting you and that means he'll eventually go down with you."

"Is that why you dislike me?" he asked.

"I have great respect for you as a doctor," she said coolly. "But

118

as an effective force to change conditions here, I know you can't last."

"What will happen then?"

"Things will go on as they are, until there's a real explosion."

"With your brother directing it?"

"Eric doesn't tell me his plans any more, Dr. Tyler."

"Because you're so close to the Wright family?"

"Partly that, I suppose. But I'm a nurse and I've seen my share of what violence can do, so I want no part of it." Her voice suddenly took on a note of fervor. "Why don't you leave before your crippled right hand causes you to make a mistake that can ruin your career? Plenty of clinics and hospitals need trained men to direct the younger ones and teach them, places where you can be effective."

Jud shook his head. "The only time I ever quit in the midst of a battle was at An Tha—and then I was carried out unconscious. Maybe as you say that's how it will end up here. But I don't know any other way."

"*Ich kann nicht anders*, I can do no other." Chuck's voice sounded from the doorway. "A man named Martin Luther said much the same thing over four hundred years ago—and *he* changed the faith of the world."

CHAPTER XIII

Friday night at St. Luke's was everything Jud had been warned it would be. Starting before dark, when the workers going off shift had gotten down to the serious business of drinking for the week-end, a constant stream of battered humanity began to pass through the Emergency Room. Knife slashes, jagged wounds left by broken bottles and rocks, children battered by drunken parents, bodies torn by smashed automobiles—they formed a steady procession.

Some were patched up and sent out to fight again, some admitted to the hospital for more definitive surgery. A few were wheeled into the morgue in the basement, from which what was left of them would be transferred the next morning to the County Medical Center, whose pathologist was also the medical examiner.

The carnage began to slacken around midnight and Jud fell into his bed, still in the scrub suit in which he'd guided Emilio Fernandez through the task of controlling a slashed femoral artery in the groin of a man whose blood volume would have been drained away, if the ambulance had tried to take him across town to the Medical Center.

He awakened about eight Saturday morning and was making ward rounds, when the pager he carried in the breast pocket of his white coat beeped. "Mr. Horace Fellowes is waiting in your office, Dr. Tyler," said the operator, when he made the connection.

Jud was tempted to keep Fellowes waiting until after he finished making rounds, but decided against it. For one thing, he was curious to see at close range the man Samantha had married—his only previous view of Fellowes had been when they'd driven into the factory yard the night of the demonstration. For another, he was wondering why the mill superintendent had sought him out.

"You look tired, Dr. Tyler." Fellowes was tanned, athletic—and very sure of himself.

"Friday night around here is worse than the battlefield," said Jud. "What can I do for you, Mr. Fellowes?"

"I dropped by on the way to play golf to talk to you about one of our employees named Aiken. I believe he was discharged from the hospital recently."

"I'm familiar with the case."

"Before we discuss Aiken, though, I believe my former wife is working in the hospital as a nurse's aide."

"She's a member of our Volunteer Aide group."

"At your suggestion?"

"Yes."

"Might I ask why?"

"I knew Samantha ten years ago, when her elbow was operated on here. She broke her wrist right after I came to St. Luke's again and I took care of that. It seemed to me that if she were busy in some worthwhile activity, she'd at least be less liable to break her neck wrapping another automobile around a power pole."

"I can see your point but her father isn't happy with the idea."

"Samantha tells me he's disowned her."

Horace Fellowes laughed and Jud found some of his distrust for the other man begin to lessen.

"Surely as a physician you can understand a man with a gouty toe being irritable, Dr. Tyler," he said. "Seth is really quite fond of Samantha, but they're both stubborn and sometimes communication between them is difficult. Maybe you're right at that, though; Samantha could be better off working here—for the time being anyway."

"And after that?"

"I've always assumed that we'd be married again—once she gets over this freedom kick. Come to think of it, you prescribed a good treatment for that too. This is the only time she's ever worked in her life and the experience might be valuable."

"I'm sure it will be."

"Now about Aiken." Horace Fellowes' voice became incisive, where before it had been warm and understanding. "His hospital expenses will be taken care of under our group contract with Blue Cross and Blue Shield, of course. But I believe you also gave him some professional treatment when he was brought in—saved his life in fact."

"I'll submit a bill to the insurance company for my services—in the hospital's name, of course, since I'm an employee."

"Please do. I'm on the Board of Trustees of St. Luke's and I know how much the hospital needs the money."

"Actually, Mr. Aiken is an industrial compensation case."

"How do you figure that?" Horace Fellowes' manner was wary by now.

"Byssinosis is recognized in England and some other countries as an industrial hazard—"

"But not in the States."

"Perhaps not—yet," Jud conceded. "I haven't made a study of that aspect of it but I'm sure Mr. Morgan will."

"Has Aiken engaged Joe Morgan?" Fellowes' voice was suddenly tense.

"I have advised him to. Does that trouble you, Mr. Fellowes?"

"A little," the engineer admitted. "Joe is one of the brightest lawyers to come out of the Harvard Law School in a long time—and also one of the most dedicated. He's sort of hipped on battling for lost causes."

"From what I hear, a lot of them aren't lost, once Joe starts working on them. But anyway I'm glad you think he's capable."

"Joe will have a hard time proving any connection between Aiken's heart stopping and this disease—what did you call it?"

"Byssinosis—and I don't think we'll have much trouble. Medical literature has been full of papers lately on the relationship between cotton dust and lung disturbances."

"We installed dust removers just after I came to Wright Mills and air-conditioned the entire plant too," Fellowes protested. "I don't know what else we could have been expected to do."

"Why did you install them?"

"With the high-speed cards we put in at the same time, as much of the dust as possible has to be removed or the men wouldn't be able to work around the machines."

"Which is the same thing as saying it's an industrial hazard?"

"Save your trap questions for the courtroom, if we ever get there, Dr. Tyler," said Fellowes. "I don't remember the exact reference—and I wouldn't give it to you anyway—but I believe a similar case to this was decided against a worker some years ago."

"Joe has already looked that one up—and byssinosis as a disease wasn't the complaint. Can I help you in any other way, Mr. Fellowes?"

"No." The other man stood up. "By the way. What are you planning to do with St. Luke's?"

"Keep it going—as long as I can."

"And if you fail?"

Jud shrugged and didn't answer, since none seemed to be indicated.

"You could always go back on active duty, couldn't you?" Fellowes asked, but Jud shook his head.

"Not any more, I resigned my commission."

"Might I ask why?"

"I've decided to fight it out on this line if it takes all summer. Having an Army commission to fall back on might have made me less diligent."

The engineer shook his head slowly, as he might have at a foolish child. "I can admire your courage, Doctor," he said, and Jud was convinced that he was sincere. "But, believe me, you're fighting for a lost cause."

"One thing about lost causes—any progress you do make has to be upward," said Jud. "Good day, Mr. Fellowes. I'll tell Joe Morgan you're worried; it's sure to make him happy."

II

"Didn't I see Horace in here just now?" Jud looked up from the chart he was completing to see Samantha standing in the doorway of his office.

"Yes," he said. "What are you doing working on Saturday?"

"We need all the hair clippings we can get for your survey, so I volunteered to help out." She dropped into the chair beside his desk and lit a cigarette. "What was Horace doing here?"

"One of his men was a patient—"

"Mr Aiken?"

"Yes."

"Did Horace tell you that's why he came?"

"He asked about Aiken—but he also talked about you."

"Of all the nerve! Going behind my back."

"He's concerned about you, Samantha."

"Concerned, hell! He just thinks it beneath the dignity of his divorced wife to be working as an aide in the hospital."

"By the way, how are you making out?"

"Lousy." She rubbed the back of her hand across her forehead, which was damp from perspiration, leaving a smudge. "I never had any idea there was so much misery in the world."

"You're helping to reduce some of it," he assured her. "If we can find enough lead in those hair specimens from ghetto children, public opinion will force the landlords to scrape off the old paint in those houses and put on new."

"At least I'm worth something to somebody then." Samantha relaxed in the chair with a sigh.

"Did you know that Mr. Wright has both gout and diabetes?"

She sat up straight and he saw that she was really concerned. "Did Horace tell you that?"

"I knew it already. Amanda Cates has been stopping by the house before she comes on duty and putting wet dressings on his toe."

"I know, Dad paid her tuition in nursing school and I guess she's grateful, but Amanda's not the same since she went to

123

Chicago. Come to think of it, you're not like you were when I was in the hospital with my elbow either."

"How am I different?"

"You were fun then. Always making jokes, pretending you were in love with me, stuff like that."

"Ten years have passed—"

"It isn't just the years; you're much more serious now and more reserved. I guess with your wound, you couldn't help changing some, could you?"

"You've changed, too—just in the few days I've been here."

"Which me do you like best? The harum-scarum one or the tired one?"

"I like both and they're both you," he told her. "The serious you was there all the time but you went around emphasizing what you call the harum-scarum part just to keep people from realizing it."

"Why would I do that?"

"Maybe because you were afraid of being hurt by people who would refuse to take you seriously."

"So I kept on doing screwy things?" She shook her head in mocked bewilderment. "You ought to be a psychiatrist, Doctor."

"Are you really getting anything out of being at St. Luke's, Samantha?" he asked.

"Yes—and no."

"What do you mean by that?"

"Well, I'm getting nowhere with you, which is why I came in the first place. But even though I go home every afternoon so grubby that I have to take two showers in succession before I feel clean, I'm eating like a horse."

"And sleeping?"

"Alone—thanks to you," she flared, then was instantly contrite. "I didn't mean—"

"I know. I should have asked, 'How do you sleep?'"

"Raw—if that's any temptation to you." She giggled. "Horace comes from a straight-laced Presbyterian family in central Carolina; his bloodline goes all the way back to Flora McDonald. Once a year he goes back to the family reunion so he can wear kilts for a day or two, but he never got used to me sleeping in the raw."

"And you wouldn't change, just to spite him."

Her eyes suddenly sparkled with anger. "What's this, an inquisition?"

"You didn't answer my question. Do you sleep better since you started working here?"

"Sleep better? I'm out cold for ten hours. And why wouldn't I be—after working in this hole like a slave all day?"

"You haven't torn up a single car this week," he reminded her.

"Hell, how could I? I'm too pooped even to go out to eat." She regarded him darkly. "So you've made me a square in less than a week. I hope you're pleased with your handiwork?"

"Very pleased."

"You didn't ask me whether I liked it or not?"

"I did in a way."

"Well I do—and that's the worst part of it all. I'm too young to shrivel up and die from hard work."

Jud smiled. "I don't see any signs of shriveling. In fact you've gained a few pounds, haven't you?"

"Five."

"But well distributed," he said, and saw her break into a smile again.

"So you noticed! Maybe there's hope for you yet, Doc."

She got to her feet. "Thanks for the rest and for the analysis. But I'd still rather have had it on a couch—in my apartment."

III

Chuck Rogers came into Jud's office just before noon. "The bishop asked me to drop by this morning," he said.

"So the heat's on?"

"With all burners going. Several members of our vestry are also on the Hospital Board of Trustees. They've told the bishop they have no choice except to vote with Angus Claiborne's group."

"That's going to put you in a bad light."

"I'm not worried about myself; they need me too much as a buffer to dump me. But I do worry about what a vote of censure will do to you—or even a revocation of your contract. The rumor's out that you resigned your Army commission."

"I did."

"Why?"

"Horace Fellowes asked me the same question and I'll give you the answer I gave him—that I couldn't be sure of giving St. Luke's my full loyalty as long as I had an ace in the hole, so to speak."

"But did it make sense to burn your bridges behind you?" Chuck demanded in a tone of exasperation. "Every prudent commander keeps the route open for retreat."

"I guess I never was much of a soldier, even when I was in uniform. My adjutant was always griping because I didn't demand more spit and polish from the hospital complement, but it would have looked pretty stupid, when two-thirds of the time we were taking care of people who were only one step above the aboriginal." Then he sobered. "I guess what really happened was I realized that St. Luke's is my Thermopylae, even if I'm a poor excuse for a Leonidas."

"You certainly couldn't have chosen a less suitable battleground to make your stand," Chuck agreed.

"I'm hoping that's exactly what I need," Jud admitted.

"Why?"

"Colonel Standiford believes the nerve impulses headed for my right hand and leg might find a way through, or around, the scar tissue in my brain—if the need ever becomes great enough."

"And when that happens, you'll be as good as new?"

"*If* that happens," Jud corrected him. "We don't have any certainty that it ever will."

"But you're counting on it?"

"Betting would be the better word, I suppose. The point is that the more I demand of myself, the more likelihood that the miracle of the synapses might happen."

"Miracles I understand—synapses I don't."

"Nerve cells have fibers growing out from them: several on one side act as receivers, and a single neuron on the other passes the impulse on, sometimes all the way from the gray matter in the spinal cord or the brain to the muscles that move one's fingertips. Between the end of the single fiber from one cell and what you might call the antennae fibers from the other there's an ultra-microscopic gap called a synapse."

"Like the cat's whisker touching the crystal in a radio I built when I was a boy?"

"That's a close enough analogy. We don't know exactly how it works but the resistance at the synapses to passage of a particular nerve impulse determines the pattern of an action. Right now, the resistance in some of my synapses is too great to allow a new impulse from the brain center for motor activity located in the left temple near where the shell hit me to get through to the muscles of my right hand and leg. But if the pressure at the synapses becomes strong enough, Colonel Standiford thinks the gap might open."

"Any way to build it up?"

"That's the mystery of the ages. Right now I'm doing it the only way I can think of, by burning those bridges you spoke of, but there's always the chance that may be the wrong way. What worries me most is whether, when the moment of truth happens and something turns up here that Emilio and the others can't handle simply under my directions—"

"Like that first morning when we had the Code Five?"

"It will have to be more of a crisis than that," said Jud. "After all, Kathryn Galloway could have given CPR to Aiken."

"There were two Code Fives that morning—one for Aiken and one for St. Luke's," said Chuck soberly. "Maybe Kathryn could have started Aiken's heart but only you could have handled the second emergency. And every night I thank God in my prayers for sending you to us."

"We'll see how good a *pray-er* you are next week when the board tries to boot me out of here," said Jud. "Meanwhile, I don't have to remind you that the Lord also promises to help those who help themselves. How's the haircutting program going?"

"I have six teams working in Irontown this morning," said Chuck. "It took a little digging yesterday afternoon at the City Hall to turn up a list of Angus Claiborne's rental units, but I think we got them all. After they finish with Claiborne's property, the haircutters will visit houses owned by a few other members of the board, whose names I discovered while going through the tax lists of Irontown property. You'll be surprised to find out how many WASPs from the upper level of society are included there."

"I'm glad we'll be televised in color then," said Jud. "Red faces show up very well on TV screens."

IV

Chuck crossed over to his office and poured himself a mug of coffee, but almost immediately returned.

"I forgot to ask you something," he said. "What in the world were you and Samantha doing at Wright Mills the night of the demonstration?"

"We were on the way back to town from Round Top and stopped for dinner at Valley Inn. On the way home Samantha saw the floodlights on in the millyard and recognized Horace Fellowes. My private conviction is she thought he was in trouble and instinctively went to help."

"That could mean she still loves him."

"I'm sure she does, if she'll ever admit it. And I'm equally sure that he loves her."

"Which could make him vote against you next week. Does he suspect—?"

"That I'm impotent?" Jud faced the word unflinchingly.

"Yes."

"It isn't exactly something you go around boasting about."

"Horace would still be more likely to vote in your favor, if he knew you weren't on the make for his ex-wife. But I can see how letting him know would pose some difficulty."

"Getting back to the demonstration." Jud changed the subject pointedly. "As soon as we came off the ramp into the millyard, the car was surrounded by toughs led by one they called Al—"

"Al Porter—he's a real troublemaker."

"I was wishing my cane was the old-fashioned variety with a sword in it, but fortunately Eric Cates came along and broke it up."

"What did you think of Eric?"

"He gave me an impression of intelligence—and of controlled power."

"Eric has the potential of becoming a major leader of his people in the arena where they've got to win their final battle for equality—politics," said Chuck. "But like so many educated blacks, he's caught up now by an ambivalency that's hard to shake off."

"Ambivalency is an odd word to use in describing him. He seemed quite sure of where he was going the other night."

"I think Eric is troubled by a conflict between the natural resentment of a black over the way his people are treated, particularly the lack of jobs that can give men a feeling of self-respect, and his sense of obligation to Seth Wright for making it possible for him and Amanda to get the education they have."

"That's a pretty involved set of emotional factors."

"In Eric's case, I think it's even more complex than that," said Chuck. "Come to St. Simon of Cyrene Chapel tomorrow night and you'll see something interesting; we're staging our monthly Rock Mass."

Jud was surprised to see Kathryn Galloway in the cafeteria at lunch, since it was Saturday and she was supposed to be off duty. As he was leaving he stopped by her table.

"Thought you were off this weekend?" he said.

"Amanda wanted me to change with her. She's singing in the choir Sunday night at Chuck Rogers' church."

"Chuck just invited me. Could I persuade you to come along? Or will you have to work tomorrow evening too?"

"One of the other nurses is filling in tomorrow. I'd love to go, Jud. I've never been to one of those services."

"If I'm not too inquisitive, what happened to the house party on the Gulf?"

"*You* ruined that."

"How?"

"I'll tell you about it Sunday night," she promised. "Shall I stop by for you about seven-thirty?"

"That will be fine."

"Can't have you running around after dark alone like you were the other night. Those of us who want to see St. Luke's stay alive have too many hopes invested in you."

CHAPTER XIV

Although it was still fifteen minutes to eight when Jud and Kathryn reached the chapel, the church itself was already packed. The crowd had filled the small churchyard too, and spilled out into the street, which had been roped off at each end of the block, with loud-speakers placed at strategic points so all could hear the service inside.

A large number of young white people were among the audience, students from the university and other colleges in the area, Jud supposed. As they were looking for a place to sit, John Redmond touched him on the arm.

"Mr. Rogers has reserved seats for you inside, Doctor," he said. "Good evening, Miss Galloway."

"Hello, John," said Kathryn. "Is it always like this?"

"These services are getting more popular all the time." John led them through the crowd to the entrance of the church. "But this is something special: the premiere of a Folk Mass by Eric Cates."

"Eric?" Jud said in amazement.

"He had two years in music at the university here," John explained, "before he dropped out and joined the Army."

"Has anyone ever found out why he left college, John?" Kathryn asked.

"I've known Eric since he was a boy playing in Mr. Wright's back yard while his mother was in the kitchen, Miss Galloway," said Redmond. "He's a proud young man and I think he just got tired of feeling that he was beholden to anyone."

"I can understand that," said Jud.

"I know, Doctor," said the gray-haired orderly. "You're a proud man yourself."

Inside the chapel, John ushered them to a pew at the back. No one appeared to resent the special treatment being given them, a tribute to John Redmond's standing among his own people.

The programs John handed them were titled simply:

A JOYFUL NOISE
Folk Mass by Eric Cates
Rev. Charles Rogers, Narrator
Peter Jamison, Organist

The choir stalls were already filled. About a fourth of the singers were white, most of them young, and two rows of chairs had been placed before the choir stalls for the musicians. Guitars predominated but banjos, a single flautist and two trumpeters, one on either side, were also included. Beneath the pulpit, a drummer sat upon an elevated platform.

Eric Cates occupied a chair beside the pulpit. He was robed as were the others, but the pulpit itself was empty.

At the stroke of eight, Chuck's voice sounded at the door leading from the chancel to the small cemetery. But it was a Chuck Jud had never seen before who moved slowly into the chancel itself.

The weekday chaplain of St. Luke's was a slightly stooped, partially bald, and somewhat harried man, while the minister of St. Simon of Cyrene Chapel was a tall commanding figure in his priestly vestment. When he spoke, his voice was sonorous, filling the small church and silencing the buzz of conversation from the audience, as much with the authority of his presence as with the words of the Psalm:

130

Be still and know that I am God.
I will be exalted among the nations.
I am exalted in the earth!
The Lord of hosts is with us:
The God of Jacob is our refuge.
Clap your hands, all peoples,
Shout to God with loud songs of joy.

Still speaking the words of the Psalmist, Chuck moved into the pulpit and, at a signal from Eric Cates, the choir rose with the musicians. The organ tones, muted while Chuck was speaking, now swelled in the beautiful harmony of the *Kyrie eleison,* and the choir took up the refrain, at first softly, then swelling in the ritual of the ancient prayer:

Lord, have mercy upon us.
Christ, have mercy upon us.
Lord, have mercy upon us.

As the words of the prayer died away in whispered repetition, Chuck spoke from the pulpit and once again Jud was struck by the change, the air of confidence, even of power, he radiated as he sounded the stirring call:

Praise the Lord!
Praise God in his sanctuary:
Praise him for his mighty firmament!
Praise him for his mighty deeds.
Praise him according to his excellent greatness!
Praise him with trumpet sound.

The trumpets sounded high and sweet in the summons, like the ancient ram's-horn shofar calling men of old to worship their God.

Praise him with lute and harp.

The strings, much amplified by electronic means, joined in.

Praise him with timbrel and dance.

The clash of tambourines came from the back of the choir.

Praise him with strings and pipes.

The high sweet notes of flute and guitars in the upper register filled the chapel.

Praise him with sounding cymbals.

The drummer began a low rhythmic beat upon the throbbing drumheads.

Praise him with loud clashing cymbals.

The crash of brass plates together filled the room, as the choir broke into the final exhortation!

Let everything that breathes praise the Lord!
Praise the Lord!

Eric brought his hands down sharply and every instrument, every voice, was instantly stilled, while all eyes were fastened upon the tall figure in the pulpit as the song of praise came to an end.

Kathryn Galloway, too, had been caught up by the magnificence of the invocation and her hand groped its way into Jud's as they sat pressed close together in the jammed pew. He was sure she had no consciousness of the action, however, but was merely yielding to the instinct to share with another the sense of joy that had seized her.

Chuck stepped back from the lectern now and Eric Cates took his place, his back to the congregation, his hands uplifted once more. They swept downward and the organ with the musicians began a strange almost barbaric rhythm which, while still innately religious in tone, nevertheless had much the same effect as the throbbing drums to which the ancestors of many in the choir and the audience had danced long ago in another land far to the east.

The printed program identified the selection only as: "Kol Nidre, adapted from the Sixty-fourth Psalm."

The very intensity of the singers, however, the cadence of the drums, and the wild crashing tones of the guitars transformed it into a lament of the persecuted, the cry of David himself, hunted so long ago by a vengeful Saul in the wild mountain country between the Jordan and the sea:

Hear my voice, O God, in my complaint;
Hide me from the secret plots of the wicked,
From the scheming of evil doers.
Who whet their tongues like swords,
Who aim bitter words like arrows,
Shooting from ambush at the blameless,
Shooting at him suddenly and without fear.
They hold fast to their evil purpose;

They talk of laying snares secretly,
Thinking, "Who can see us?"
"Who can search out our crimes?"
"We have thought out a cunningly conceived plot."
For the inward mind and the heart of man are deep.

Standing tall in his white robe, Eric Cates literally molded the instruments, the organ and the choir into a single voice. Always under perfect control, they responded like the strings of a plucked harp to the movement of his facile hands and to his will.

Now, he brought the whole to a sudden cessation, creating a moment of silence which, in its effect upon the hushed listeners, was itself a promise of change.

Poised, holding choir musicians and audience literally in his grasp, Eric's hands swept down once again and the trumpets sounded a paean of victory, followed by the guitars, the clash of tambourines, the soaring notes of the organ and, above it all, the high-pitched wailing of the flute—until all were drawn into a joyous hymn of faith in God's willingness to lift his people even from the depths of adversity:

But God will shoot his arrow at them;
They will be wounded suddenly.
Because of their tongues, he will bring them to ruin;
All who see them will wag their heads.
Then all men will fear;
They will tell what God has wrought,
And ponder what he has done.
Let the righteous rejoice in the Lord,
And take refuge in him!
Let all the upright in heart glory!
Amen.

"I feel like I've been put through a wringer," Kathryn whispered as the choir took their seats.

"It was magnificent," Jud agreed. "I can see now why Chuck says Eric is a great musician."

II

Coming after the stirring phrases of David, the sweet singer of Israel, and the music Eric Cates had created as a frame for it in

133

his version of the ancient Kol Nidre, Chuck had obviously realized that any message of his must be simple and short.

"The Kol Nidre," he told the congregation, "is the ancient song for the Day of Atonement of the Children of Israel. It was sung on this holiest of all their religious days as a prayer of forgiveness for the sins of the people in straying from the way God had set for them. The Kol Nidre is old beyond the memory of men, harking back to a day when Israel was not yet a nation but merely a group of tribes wandering wherever their flocks and herds could find grass to sustain them.

"Time and again, in their history, the Israelites were forced under the iron hands of foreign conquerors to stray from the principles set down by God to guide them—and us, whose religious heritage is the same. But though a conqueror may put a man's body in chains, he cannot imprison his soul, which constantly cries out to God, even under the burden of his own transgressions. The Kol Nidre is such a cry, a prayer of the heart for forgiveness, when men have erred under the pressure of adversity, oppression and their own sins. And our brother Eric Cates has given it the most modern of musical frames, while retaining the ancient words of David, the Psalmist.

"You will remember that when yet a young man, David was annointed King of Israel by the prophet Samuel but was hounded by his enemies and forced to flee into the wilderness, where he and his followers lived in caves. With his soul in torment, David cried out in protest, using the words of the Psalm you have just heard sung by the choir. Yet in the end, his faith in God could let him say:

'Let the righteous rejoice in the Lord,
And take refuge in him!
Let all the upright glory.'

"Many of you know what oppression means. Some of you have seen your children sick and hungry and have wondered whether God had not forsaken you. Others feel old and useless, or are crippled by disease, until sometimes you can see no place for you in God's plan for the world and the people in it. Yet you have only to remember the words of the beautiful prayer you have heard sung here tonight to know that God does indeed hear the cries of his children when they pray. That God does indeed have a purpose for all who believe in him and try to follow him—even

134

though you may be weak at times and fall by the wayside. And knowing this, you, too, like David, can rejoice in the Lord's mercy and be sure he will give you the strength to go on."

III

Chuck moved to the back of the chancel and Eric Cates took his place once more before the choir and the musicians. To a stirring rhythm that still retained the sounds and feel of their African heritage, they chanted the words of the confessional, following it with the impassioned plea of "Our Father, Our King."

On a softer note, they sang the "Adoration" and closed with the beautiful spiritual hymn in which the audience joined, the lament of an enslaved people: "Nobody Knows the Trouble I've Seen."

Chuck gave the benediction then, and the congregation filed from the church almost in silence, still a little awed by a spiritual experience which could not have failed to move even the most callous among them.

"Let's speak to Eric," said Kathryn as they were coming down the steps. "I think he would appreciate knowing what his music meant to us."

"If I can talk," said Jud. "I've still got a lump in my throat."

"Mine too."

They waited until Eric's tall form emerged from the basement, where the choir robed in the Sunday-school room.

"We couldn't leave without telling you how much we were moved by your music," said Jud.

"And how lovely the whole service was," Kathryn added.

For a moment Jud was sure that real glow of appreciation showed in the eyes of the young black, then it was replaced by a mocking light.

"Don't thank me, Doctor," he said. "I merely took a little Handel, a smidgen of Brother Gregor, a dash of Berlioz and a whiff of Offenbach—"

"Plus a considerable amount of Cates," said Jud. "I'm no musician, but I could recognize the individuality."

"Why not? After all my ancestors were dancing around jungle campfires to such rhythms hardly three hundred years ago."

"But not everybody can make it speak to people today with

135

the voice of God," said Jud. "And no mask of cynicism is going to hide that, or what doing it meant to you."

"I bow to your wisdom," said Eric, but the note of mockery was gone from his voice. "Now, if you'll excuse me, I think my sister is ready to go home."

"You're a strange person, Jud Tyler," said Kathryn, as they were walking to the car.

"Why do you say that?"

"Doctors aren't always the most perceptive people in the world, outside of medicine, but you just spoke a great artistic truth without any apparent effort. I'm sure Eric was impressed and I know I was."

"Isn't there a place somewhere nearby that we could go for coffee and maybe a waffle?" he asked. "All this adulation is going to my head."

"There's a Pancake House between here and Spring Mountain."

"Would you like that?"

"I'd love it. When I'm emotionally washed out from something as beautiful as Eric's music, I'm always hungry."

The Pancake House was brightly lit and crowded; they found a booth in the back and ordered waffles and coffee.

"I've often wondered what gives Chuck such an appeal to the blacks of Irontown," said Kathryn while they were waiting for their order. "Tonight I found the answer. It's his basic sincerity and honesty—and decency too. Nobody could know him long and not feel it."

"Eric Cates has some of that same charisma," said Jud. "The trouble is that knowing you have power to move people sometimes makes you want to use that power to control them."

"You have it too," she assured him. "The way you fired up the staff at St. Luke's, just by being there, is hard to believe—unless you're in the middle of it as I am."

"I'm afraid I've been so busy feeling frustrated over my own inadequacies, that I haven't been able to see anything else very clearly," he admitted. "Sometimes when I'm assisting Emilio and Juan with an operation, it takes all my will power not to reach out and take the instruments they're trying to use. But since I can't, I suppose I've been sublimating that impulse in fighting things like lead poisoning and byssinosis."

"You've done something else too, though I'm sure you're not

136

conscious of it. You may even have saved me from going off the deep end—and I don't mean a pier."

"Is that why you're in town this weekend?"

"Yes. I guess I've been seeing too much of Dick Tubman to really see him, just as you're so close to your work that you can't see your own progress."

"But he's a very capable doctor."

"And headed for success—come hell or high water."

"There's nothing wrong with ambition."

"Not the right kind. But would you deliberately organize your life so as to accumulate a lot of money?"

"No. But then there's not much likelihood of my achieving that kind of success."

"After you came, I guess I started measuring Dick against you, and maybe that wasn't fair to him. Anyway, I told him he should have gone along with you and helped persuade Mr. Aiken to take the test case before the Industrial Commission."

"Then I *was* responsible for your breaking with him?"

"Not entirely. An uncle I was very fond of when I was growing up worked in the cotton mills all his life. He died when he was fifty of what they called asthma but I'm sure now it was the same thing Mr. Aiken had. I guess that influenced me too, but anyway Dick and I quarreled, so that was that."

"Any regrets?"

She shook her head. "At Hopkins I saw too many wives of successful society doctors become victims of alcoholism, narcotics— or just plain boredom."

"It's a well-recognized clinical entity, though I can't really see it happening to you. I hope you're going to stay on at St. Luke's. I need you."

She smiled suddenly and put her hand across the table to squeeze his. "I guess that's the most any woman wants from a man she admires—to be needed. I'll stay as long as you do—or until we have a fight."

"I can't conceive of that happening."

"Even after the way I shoved you around that first morning?"

"That may even have influenced me to stay at St. Luke's," he assured her. "My first thought that morning was that you were Juno in a nurse's uniform."

"That does it!" She laughed and pushed her plate away. "Now I will have to go on a diet." She glanced up at a clock on the wall.

137

"Goodness! It's after eleven, and six o'clock comes mighty early these mornings. I'll drop you by the hospital."

"Will you be okay the rest of the way? I can always defend you with my cane."

"One day you're going to throw away that cane," she said firmly. "And I'm going to be there to help you do it."

When the car pulled to a stop at the curb in the shadows of the trees along Ventura near the hospital entrance, Kathryn didn't cut the motor.

"Thanks for a lovely evening, Jud." She leaned forward to kiss him, a warm kiss of friendship with just a hint of passion in it. "And good luck with the trustees Tuesday. I'll be rooting for you."

"How about having dinner with me Tuesday night to celebrate my victory?"

"Are you that confident?"

"Frankly, no. But I'd love having dinner with you—even in defeat."

"Win, lose, or draw we'll celebrate—I've got a bottle of Cold Duck in the refrigerator."

Jud stood at the foot of the steps leading up to the main hospital entrance until Kathryn's car was out of sight around the corner. Only when he came into the lobby, with its empty shadows, where once had been the teeming life of a great hospital, did the crushing burden of truth suddenly descend upon him.

He was romantically attracted to two women, and physically incapable of pursuing either or both of those attractions to its logical conclusion.

IV

Joe Morgan III telephoned Jud Monday morning. "I was wondering if you've had any report from those lead tests they've been running," he said. "The board meets tomorrow and we've got to organize an attack."

"I thought it was going to be a defense."

"General Patton demolished that theory a long time ago. If you attack at the outset and throw the other fellow off guard, you can often convince him you're stronger than you really are."

"I don't have the data in the lead tests," said Jud.

"Can you get them?"

"I made Dr. Wiley promise not to let me know the results until they're presented to the board."

"Isn't that taking a chance?"

"Maybe. But that way, even my opponents can't claim we didn't start the race even."

"It's still a hell of a way to treat your lawyer—withholding evidence that could mean we have nothing to base our defense on."

"What do you think our chances are anyway—with a loaded board against us?"

"We won't know until the votes are in Tuesday afternoon," said Morgan. "You know Horace Fellowes is one of the trustees, don't you?"

"Chuck told me."

"I hear he's burned up about Samantha working at the hospital as an aide. Couldn't you persuade her to stop?"

"I'd rather not. She's doing a good job and enjoying it. Besides it's good therapy for her."

"The therapy Samantha needs most is for Horace to take her over his knee and paddle her cute little behind—or hadn't you noticed that?"

"I've noticed."

"The scuttlebutt is that you were seen leaving her apartment at night—twice."

"The first time I rebandaged the splint I had put on her wrist. The other time we had almost been attacked by a group of blacks during a demonstration at Wright Mills. Samantha was pretty upset so I took her home and gave her a sedative."

"That doesn't alter the fact that Horace is still in love with her," said Morgan. "And if he thinks you're trying to muscle in, he'll be sure to clobber you when the board meets on Tuesday, no matter what the evidence says."

"You don't sound very optimistic."

"How could I be when you've just ruined my day? Ask the hospital operator to transfer this call to Dr. Wiley, will you? You may be too high minded to put the squeeze on somebody who's trying to knife you, but I'm certainly not."

When Jud hung up the phone, after transferring the call, he looked up to see Kathryn Galloway standing in the doorway of the office.

"I have the invoice for those Vitallium plates you ordered the

139

other day," she said. "But there's something about it I don't understand."

"What seems to be wrong?"

"I ordered two of each of the three sizes of Vitallium plates you might need for a femoral shaft fracture." She spread the invoice out upon his desk. "But this invoice is for a dozen of each size."

"Are they billed to me?"

"No, to the hospital. But we didn't get a dozen each of the plates; just the two of each size I ordered."

The invoice appeared to be in order, except for the discrepancy in numbers. The price, Jud saw, was for the lot of a dozen stated on its face.

"How did you happen to get this?" he asked.

"It was in the package with the plates," she said. "Ordinarily the invoices are supposed to go to Mr. Ford's office immediately, but I ordered the plates charged to you and we were pretty busy when they came out, so I put the invoice aside until I could give it to you later. I only found it just now when I was getting ready to throw the carton out while I was cleaning the OR supply room."

"Has anything like this ever happened before?"

"Once or twice that I remember, when we had to order something special. I always marked the invoices as being in error and sent them along to Mr. Ford like we do all the rest."

"Who ordinarily does the ordering?"

"Mr. Ford. We just send him a list of what we need."

"What about the invoices when the supplies are delivered?"

"They go directly to him; that's a routine he instituted when he first came here. Do you think—"

"I think we may have stumbled on one of the big reasons St. Luke's stays so much in the red," said Jud. "Do you happen to remember the name of the salesman who handled the order at the surgical supply house?"

"It was Mr. Moore. He has the St. Luke's account."

Jud dialed the number she gave him for the surgical supply house. "Moore, here," a masculine voice said. "Can I help you?"

"This is Dr. Tyler at St. Luke's, Mr. Moore. I'm checking on an order for Vitallium plates we placed with you last week."

"What about them, Doctor?"

"You billed us for twelve of each size, but we only ordered two. And they were supposed to be billed directly to me."

"Have you talked to Mr. Ford about this, Doctor?" Moore asked. "He usually handles the ordering."

"Ford refused to order the plates originally, so I asked Miss Galloway to have them billed to me."

"I'll check into it, Doctor. We usually deliver such items in dozen lots; the others are probably around the supply room somewhere."

"Who checks in surgical supplies when they're delivered?" Jud asked, when he hung up the telephone.

"John Redmond," said Kathryn. "He's been doing it for years."

"Would you ask John to come down here as soon as he's free?"

"Of course."

"And, Kathryn?"

"Yes."

"You have a duplicating machine in the Nursing Office, don't you?"

She nodded. "We use it to get out the nurses' assignments for the ward bulletin boards; the dietician duplicates the menus with it too."

"Please have this invoice duplicated in a half-dozen copies. Then turn the original in to Mr. Ford's office, just as if you hadn't found anything wrong with it, but bring the copies to me."

"You don't waste any time, do you?" Her voice had taken on a note of admiration.

"Not when my neck's on the block. And don't mention this to anyone else, please."

John Redmond knocked on the office door about five minutes later. "Did you want to see me, Dr. Tyler?" he asked.

"Close the door and have a seat, please, John. I understand that you check in the surgical supplies as they're received."

"That's right."

"Did you ever notice any discrepancy between what's on the invoices and what's delivered to the hospital?"

"I don't see the invoices, Dr. Tyler; they're usually in sealed envelopes. When he first became administrator, Mr. Ford instructed me to deliver the envelopes directly to his office. Is anything wrong?"

"Not with you, John, but I suspect with somebody else. When will you be getting in another batch of supplies?"

"This morning," said the orderly. "We send the requisitions to Mr. Ford's office on Thursday and they're delivered here on Monday, except for special orders."

141

"Do you think you could locate an electric hotplate and a kettle to make some steam?"

John Redmond grinned. "My boys taught me a word they use in the Navy for that sort of thing—scrounging," he said. "I'll have what you want, Doctor."

"Good. Let me know as soon as the supplies arrive and we'll do a little checking. And don't telephone me, John; give Miss Galloway the word when you're ready."

v

By noon, Jud's suspicions were confirmed. In a secluded corner of the hospital supply room, he, Kathryn, and John Redmond had opened the cartons in which the surgical supplies for the week had been delivered, removing the invoices in their sealed envelopes. Jud himself steamed the envelopes open and made a quick check against the contents of each carton, noting the amounts of the various supplies that were actually delivered. Then he gave Kathryn the invoices to be duplicated in the Nursing Office, after which the originals were once again sealed in the envelopes.

The evidence was damning; the hospital was being charged for roughly a third more of each item than was actually received. And every one of them contained the name Moore.

"I guess I was pretty dumb not to realize what's been going on before," said Kathryn, when they had finished checking that Monday's shipment.

"I suspected it once or twice, Doctor," said John Redmond. "But I had no proof and—"

He didn't say more but both of them knew what he meant, that in Framingham even the word of so respected a black man as John Redmond would hardly stand up against the testimony of a white man before a jury.

"Neither of you know anything about this," Jud told Kathryn and the orderly, when they had finished with the load of supplies delivered that morning. "Leave everything to me."

"Won't we have to testify?" she asked.

"In medical school I was considered a fair to middling poker player," he told her. "Poker's at least a third bluff and this time I've got a pat hand, so I don't think I'll have to show more than a few of the copies you made. Go ahead and deliver the original invoices to Mr. Ford just as you usually do, John. The envelopes ought to be dry by now. I'll follow up a little later."

It was shortly after eleven when Jud came into Asa Ford's outer office and told the secretary to notify the superintendent that he wished to see him.

"Mr. Ford says he can't see you today, Doctor," she reported. "He's busy getting ready for the meeting of the trustees tomorrow afternoon."

"So am I." Jud took one of the duplicate invoices from an envelope he'd brought and handed it to her. "Just show him this. I think he'll change his mind."

She was gone only a moment. "Mr. Ford will see you, Dr. Tyler," she said, and held open the door for Jud to enter the superintendent's office.

Asa Ford was sweating, Jud noted, although the room was cool. And the look in his eyes was that of a cornered animal.

"What the hell is this, Tyler?" he blustered, but Jud cut him short.

"You know perfectly well what it is, Mr. Ford."

"How did you—"

"We won't go into that. The important thing is what are you going to do?"

"You can't prove—" Ford stopped when Jud took a half-dozen more invoice copies from the envelope he carried and dropped them on his desk.

"I've got several other sets—for the Auditor and the County Prosecutor," he said.

"This is blackmail."

"I prefer to call it justice."

"What is it you want?" Ford summoned up enough strength to ask.

"Under the circumstances, I think you will be requesting immediate transfer back to the City Finance Department—or wherever you were before you came to St. Luke's."

"You mean you're—"

"Giving you a chance to escape prosecution? Yes—with some qualifications."

"What?" Ford asked warily.

"That you have second thoughts about making charges against me before the Board of Trustees tomorrow."

143

"I had already decided not to bring them." Ford's expression was that of a man hearing word of a reprieve from his death sentence at the last moment.

"I thought you would see things my way," said Jud. "Good day, Mr. Ford."

CHAPTER XV

The meeting of the Board of Trustees was being held in the hospital teaching theater where, as an intern, Jud had often presented cases for consideration at the weekly clinical pathological conferences. The members of the board, a half-dozen in number, were seated at a large table with TV cameras from the ETV station beaming down upon them from two angles. An empty chair stood at one end of the table.

The auditorium was already filled with hospital personnel off duty and visitors when Jud and Joe Morgan came in a few minutes before six and took their places on the front of the tiered rows of seats. As in most older medical classrooms, these were arranged so students could look down upon a patient being presented for study and see the physical features being described.

Dr. Wiley was in the second row of seats with a man Jud didn't know. Charlie Gregg was there too, with his camera, as well as representatives from several of the commercial television stations with their portable cameras. Obviously, word of a dramatic meeting had been well disseminated by Asa Ford prior to Jud's conference with him the day before, but Ford himself was nowhere to be seen.

Chuck Rogers sat beside the chairman, a stern-faced man who appeared to be in his seventies. When Jud appeared, the chaplain held up thumb and forefinger touched in the traditional circle of assurance. But when he looked at the faces of the men making up the board, Jud himself could feel no particular assurance of victory.

"The chairman is Joseph Neslor, a retired banker," Joe Morgan whispered. "He'll be fair, but he thinks only in terms of money.

The one beside Chuck is a lawyer named Farleigh Grossett; he's Angus Claiborne's attorney and his main stooge on the board. He owns some of the houses in Irontown too, so he has a lot to lose if you win here today."

"Not as much as I have," said Jud.

"The fat guy next to Grossett is Dexter Johns. Dexter's going to run for Mayor, so he'll jump whichever way looks politically best for him. The one next to Dexter is another Claiborne stooge, and the guy on the end, beyond Chuck, is named Alvarez. He represents the Mexican-American faction and will go along with you, if Neslor gives you a chance to tell what you have in mind for St. Luke's."

The chair next to Alvarez was vacant but, ten seconds before six, Horace Fellowes hurried in and took it. Exactly upon the hour, Joseph Neslor banged on the table with his gavel.

"This special meeting of the Board of Trustees of St. Luke's Hospital is now in session," he announced. "Mr. Ford sent word that he was suddenly taken ill—a virus, I believe—and will not be able to attend. In his absence, the Reverend Charles Rogers will act as secretary. Do I hear a motion that we dispense with the reading of the minutes of the last meeting?"

"So moved," said Horace Fellowes, and the second came from Dexter Johns. The vote was unanimous and Neslor reached for a sheet lying on the table before him.

"The only business on the agenda today is the employment of Dr. Judson Tyler as Director of Emergency Services for this hospital, at a salary of twelve thousand dollars a year, with meals and lodging to be furnished by the hospital. May I have the report of the Selection Committee?"

Chuck Rogers got to his feet and opened a folder before him.

"The members of this board know that we have been trying for about a year to employ a qualified surgeon as Director of Emergency Services," he began. "A Selection Committee composed of myself, Mr. Johns, and Mr. Alvarez has been charged by the board with this task but, for various reasons, particularly the meager salary we're able to offer, we had not been able until recently to find a man we felt was qualified for this position. Frankly, we had about given up hope until I wrote Dr. Judson Tyler, at that time a Major in the Medical Corps of the United States Army and a patient at Walter Reed Hospital, recovering from wounds sustained at An Tha in Vietnam.

145

"Dr. Tyler's credentials are impeccable, gentlemen," Chuck continued. "He was educated at Harvard College and Medical School. He served an internship here at St. Luke's about ten years ago, completed his surgical training at the Massachusetts General Hospital and is licensed in this state. At the completion of his surgical residency in Boston, Dr. Tyler joined the U. S. Army Medical Corps and rose to the rank of Major, commanding a forward surgical hospital. He was working with the Montagnard tribesmen in the mountains of Vietnam about a year ago when a rocket struck the hospital, exploding a shell he was removing from a North Vietnamese prisoner and sending Dr. Tyler to the hospital."

Chuck paused and looked around the board. When there were no questions at the moment, he continued:

"Dr. Tyler is a Fellow of the American College of Surgeons, a Diplomate of the American Board of Surgery, and is, therefore, eminently qualified professionally to fill this position. Gentlemen, I move that the employment of Dr. Judson Tyler as Director of Emergency Services for St. Luke's Hospital be approved by the board, at a salary of twelve thousand dollars a year, plus meals and lodgings."

The motion was seconded by Arturo Alvarez.

"Is there any discussion?" Joseph Neslor asked.

"Mr. Chairman." Farleigh Grossett opened the attack. "I should like to ask Dr. Tyler some questions, if I may?"

"Certainly," said Neslor. "Unless the doctor objects."

"I have no objections," said Jud.

"Would you take the chair at the end of the table, Doctor?" Grossett requested.

The move placed Jud in full view of the TV cameras. He was painfully conscious of his cane as he walked to the chair but dared not risk falling, if his leg should give way at this moment of tension—as it often did.

"Dr. Tyler," said Grossett. "Please tell the board why you accepted this position."

"The neurosurgeon in charge of my case at Walter Reed felt that I would have a better chance of recovering full use of my surgical skills, if I were actually at work where they could be used."

"Were you not paralyzed at one time?"

"For about a month after definitive surgery was performed at Letterman General Hospital."

146

"And are you not now partially paralyzed to the point where you have to walk with a cane?"

"I suffer from aphasia—"

"Please explain the term, Doctor," Joseph Neslor requested.

"My right hand and right leg do not always obey immediately the commands of my brain," said Jud.

"A rather dangerous disability for a surgeon, wouldn't you say, Doctor?" Farleigh Grossett's tone was sharp and probing.

"Admitted—if I worked alone. But St. Luke's already has two surgically trained residents, Dr. Emilio Fernandez and Dr. Juan Valdese. I always operate with one or both of them and he performs the actual surgery."

"Then you're not really needed here at all, are you, Doctor?"

Chuck started to protest, but Jud raised his hand and the chaplain sat back in his chair.

"Dr. Fernandez and Dr. Valdese lack experience and often require direction, Mr. Grossett. In teaching hospitals young surgeons frequently operate but a more experienced surgeon always assists them in important cases, in order to give them confidence and direction."

"Wouldn't you say, nevertheless, that St. Luke's is your last straw, Doctor?" Grossett bored in. "Surely no other hospital would employ a cripple—"

"Mr. Chairman, this is unpardonable!" Chuck Rogers broke in angrily. "Mr. Grossett is deliberately trying to humiliate Dr. Tyler and create doubts about his ability, for reasons which I plan to make clear later on."

"I have no objection to answering the question," said Jud quietly. "It so happens that I had not made application elsewhere before Mr. Rogers wrote me about St. Luke's. But while I was still at Walter Reed, I was assured of employment with the Veterans Administration, if I wished it."

"But you still jumped at the chance to come to St. Luke's, didn't you?" Grossett insisted.

"I welcomed Mr. Rogers' invitation," Jud conceded. "After all I spent two years here as an intern, so the hospital has a sentimental attraction for me."

"Do you think any other hospital would employ a crip—a handicapped surgeon?"

"I haven't been looking for a position, Mr. Grossett, so I don't know." Jud kept his temper, knowing that the lawyer was using an old courtroom trick in trying to make him lose it and become rattled. "But I'm sure many teaching and research positions would be open to me because of my training and experience."

"Anything else, Mr. Grossett?" the chairman asked.

"I yield to Mr. Johns," said Grossett. "But I shall have more questions of Dr. Tyler later on another matter."

"Mr. Johns?" said Neslor.

Dexter Johns looked uncomfortable; he had obviously been caught off guard by Farleigh Grossett's sudden change of action.

"Mr. Ford had spoken to me of a matter, Mr. Chairman," he said. "I was relying on him to give the details."

"What kind of a matter?" the chairman asked.

"I hate to bring this up, especially publicly. But Mr. Ford seemed to think Dr. Tyler had shown poor judgment in attending a so called rock festival in the Neg—, in the Irontown district."

"Is this to be the platform of your next political campaign, Mr. Johns?" Chuck Rogers snapped. "If so, I suggest that you name names here and now and not try to smear a fine surgeon with lies and innuendo."

"Well, I—" Dexter Johns was squirming.

"I believe Mr. Ford left the hospital shortly before this meeting, Mr. Chairman, so I imagine he's had time to get home," said Jud. "Perhaps if you called him on the telephone, he might give you the details about this charge."

"An excellent idea." Neslor rapped on the table with his gavel. "I declare a recess of five minutes."

II

"What's up?" Charlie Gregg had moved to a seat in the row just behind Jud and Joe Morgan.

"Dexter Johns was making a political ploy for TV," said Joe Morgan. "They need time for Farleigh Grossett to prepare the rest of the attack."

"But Johns must have something?"

"Last Sunday night I took Kathryn Galloway to the Rock Mass at Chuck's chapel," Jud explained.

"Hell!" said Charlie. "Our music critic reviewed it in yesterday's paper. He said it was out of this world."

"Neslor should be back in a minute or two from talking to Asa

148

Ford," said Jud. "Unless I miss my guess, you're going to see Dexter Johns with egg on his face."

Charlie Gregg gave him a swift appraising look. "For somebody on trial you're pretty damned confident. What did you do to Asa anyway? Poison him?"

When Jud didn't answer, the newspaperman turned to Morgan. "What's up here, Joe?"

"Let's just say it looks like Asa Ford had his fangs pulled?" said Joe Morgan with a chuckle. "I don't have the least idea how it was done and I don't want to know."

"The story doesn't go out either," said Jud pointedly. "Unless Asa changes his mind while he's talking to Neslor."

"Changes his mind about what?"

"Requesting transfer back to the County Finance Department."

Gregg whistled softly to himself. "Where's the corpse buried?" he asked, but just then the chairman returned to the room and gaveled the meeting into session, so Jud had no opportunity to answer.

"I am happy to report that Mr. Ford denies the allegation made by Mr. Johns," Neslor said. "Dr. Tyler attended what was called a 'Rock Mass' at Mr. Rogers' church Sunday night. Incidentally," he added frostily, "my daughter was one of the participants. In the future, I would appreciate it if no trustee would attempt to use this forum as a political sounding board. Anything else, Mr. Johns?"

"No, Your Hon— No, Mr. Chairman."

"All right, Mr. Grossett." Neslor turned to Jud's first inquisitor. "I believe you said you had some more questions."

"Before we move to any other subject," Chuck Rogers broke in, "I feel that the board should know something about Dr. Tyler's record since he has been at St. Luke's. The day of his arrival, he restored a case of cardiac arrest to life. And he has also completely reorganized the operation of the Outpatient Department, making it at least fifty per cent more efficient than before."

"Is that all, Mr. Rogers?" Neslor asked.

"I was on the point of explaining about Dr. Tyler's presence at the Rock Mass, when he suggested calling Mr. Ford. But since the whole thing was obviously a trumped up political ploy, I decided to give Mr. Johns the rope with which to hang himself— and he has done it very effectively."

"What else did you wish to bring up, Mr. Grossett?" The chairman turned to the lawyer, as laughter swept through the room.

149

As for Dexter Johns, he looked as if he would have been happy to disappear through the floor.

Grossett rose to his feet once more and opened a folder.

"Last week, Dr. Tyler made a vicious attack through the newspapers upon a respected citizen of this city, Mr. Angus Claiborne," he said. "In this attack, he alleged that Mr. Claiborne had neglected a house at 723 Rutherford Street, rented by a family named Brown. And that as a result of his neglect, several children became seriously ill at a later date from lead poisoning. It is Mr. Claiborne's intention to bring suit against Dr. Tyler and the newspaper that printed this libelous attack, but he thought the matter should also be brought before this board prior to Dr. Tyler's appointment being considered by it."

"Do you have anything to say to this charge, Dr. Tyler?" the chairman asked.

Jud told the story of his diagnosis of lead poisoning in Freddie Brown and later in the other Brown children, of his visit with Chuck Rogers to 723 Rutherford Street, and his subsequent visit to Claiborne's office.

"Tell me, Doctor," said Grossett. "Did you make a medical record of your alleged findings in the case of the Brown children?"

"Yes, I did." Jud could see what was coming but had no way of heading it off.

"Mr. Chairman," Grossett turned to Neslor. "I have requested that the hospital records of Freddie Brown and the Outpatient records of the other Brown children be produced as evidence to support Dr. Tyler's allegation in the article which appeared in the newspapers."

"Dr. Tyler?" the chairman asked.

"All records of the Brown family involving lead poisoning are missing from the hospital record room," Jud admitted. "They were removed almost a week ago."

"By whom were they removed, Doctor?" Grossett asked.

"I don't know."

"Perhaps by yourself—because they did not support your allegations?"

Jud clamped a tight rein on his temper. "The records would have proved my claim that Mr. Claiborne's houses are deathtraps, so I had nothing to gain by removing them, Mr. Grossett."

"Then who else besides you could have profited by their removal?" Grossett asked.

"Since you seem to be prosecuting a case against me on behalf of Mr. Claiborne, I would say that both you and your client would have profited by the loss of the records, Mr. Grossett."

The implication was plain and Grossett got it, as did the audience and the TV cameras.

"Are you accusing Mr. Claiborne or myself of tampering with hospital records to which we did not have access?" Grossett shouted angrily.

"With the television cameras you and the faction that wants to drive me away from St. Luke's arranged to have trained on me here, I'd be a fool to make any such claims." Jud's voice was icy with contempt. "But the fact remains that those records did prove the children were poisoned by lead and that the records have been removed from the hospital files."

"Mr. Chairman!" Farleigh Grossett spoke to Neslor. "The way Dr. Tyler has used completely unfounded charges in an attempt to discredit a prominent citizen of this community fully supports the contention that he is not fitted for the post under consideration. I, therefore, make a substitute motion that his appointment not be approved by this board and that Dr. Tyler's connection with St. Luke's Hospital be terminated immediately."

"Is there a second?" Neslor asked, and Dexter Johns mumbled his assent.

"Any discussion?"

Chuck started to speak, but before he could, Horace Fellowes asked, "Isn't Dr. Tyler to be given an opportunity to refute the allegations made by Mr. Grossett and Mr. Johns?"

"Dr. Tyler?" said the chairman, but Jud could see from his manner that whatever good will Neslor might have felt toward him at the start of the hearing had largely been dissipated by the failure to produce the incriminating records.

"I have asked Mr. Joseph Morgan to represent me," said Jud.

"This is not court of law!" Grossett protested at once.

"Maybe not," Joe Morgan snapped. "But you have threatened Dr. Tyler publicly before this board with an action for libel. Mr. Chairman, I submit that since Mr. Grossett has made a public attack upon Dr. Tyler, the doctor has every right to answer with the advice of counsel."

"The chair so rules," said Neslor. "Proceed please, Mr. Morgan."

"I call Dr. McLean, Chief of Laboratories at the County Medical Center and medical examiner for the county. He will testify concerning the results of certain laboratory determinations performed there during the past several days."

As Jud moved back to his seat on the front row, the man who had been sitting with Dr. Wiley took the chair he had vacated at the end of the table and placed a small folder he carried upon it.

"Let the record show that Dr. McLean is Chief of Laboratories at the County Medical Center," said Joe Morgan.

"It is so recorded," said Joseph Neslor. "Proceed, Mr. Morgan."

"Do you have in your laboratory an instrument called a spectrophotometer, Doctor?" Joe Morgan asked.

"I do."

"Can it be used to discover the presence of lead in body tissues?"

"It can."

"Please explain, Doctor."

"The level of lead content in the body can be determined by examining with the spectrophotometer a small amount of hair clipped from the head of a person."

"Would you say that this instrument is useful in carrying out a mass survey for lead poisoning, Doctor?"

"Unquestionably. It has been so used in Baltimore and a number of other cities around the country."

"Was such a survey, to your knowledge, conducted recently in the part of Framingham called Irontown?"

"On Thursday of the past week," said McLean, "Dr. Wiley at St. Luke's called me. He said Dr. Tyler had found serious poisoning in several children from lead in old paint and wished to make a survey by clipping hair from a number of other children in order to determine how frequently this condition occurs in the city. I promised to have all specimens examined and did in fact examine most of them myself."

"How many specimens of hair were examined in your laboratory, Dr. McLean?"

"Two hundred and fifty in all. One hundred were identified as having been taken at St. Luke's from the outpatient and inpatient population under six years of age. One hundred and fifty were collected in Irontown."

Farleigh Grossett appeared stunned by the unexpected turn of events, but now he broke in with a question.

"How is this survey done, Doctor?"

"Dr. McLean only examined specimens brought to him in the laboratory," Chuck Rogers interposed. "When we learned that the hospital records of the Brown children had been stolen, Dr. Tyler decided that a survey should be made to determine just how many other children in Irontown were being poisoned by old paint left on the walls by ghetto landlords. At his request, I assigned teams from the youth clubs I have organized in the area and they were busy until yesterday afternoon, snipping hair from children in Irontown. They also," he added with some emphasis, "made a record of the addresses where the children lived from whom the specimens were obtained."

As if he could see what was coming, Farleigh Grossett started to rise from his chair to leave the room, but Joseph Neslor banged on the table with his gavel.

"You started this line of questioning, Mr. Grossett," he said severely. "Unless you are ill, I would suggest that you remain to hear the results."

Grossett subsided in his chair and Joe Morgan continued to question the laboratory expert.

"Please give us the results of your examination, Dr. McLean," he said, and the pathologist took a sheaf of reports from the portfolio he had placed upon the table.

"Specimens were taken only from children between the ages of one and six, where the incidence of lead poisoning is known to bo highcot," ho explained. "Among those in the hospital or the Outpatient Department, significant amounts of lead in the hair were found in six per cent of the children examined. In Irontown itself, the incidence was seven per cent but, where more than one child was living at the same address, the incidence of significant lead poisoning in that family rose sharply, in some places to fifty per cent."

Farleigh Grossett looked as if he had been bludgeoned but his humbling was not yet complete. From his brief case, Joe Morgan took a sheaf of papers similar to that held by Dr. McLean.

"I have here the names and addresses of all children in whose bodies lead was determined, listed according to the owners of the houses in which these children lived, Mr. Chairman," he said. "It is very interesting that the name of the landowner having the most rental property on this list is Mr. Angus Claiborne. Next in frequency, is Mr. Farleigh Grossett."

The cameras were trained on Grossett, who seemed incapable of speech.

"Mr. Chairman." Chuck Rogers spoke in a decisive voice. "I call for the question on the substitute motion."

Horace Fellowes seconded, and the vote that followed produced only one "Aye," from Grossett himself. On Chuck's motion to confirm Jud in the position, the vote carried, again with only one "Nay" —and that from Grossett.

"Mr. Chairman," Chuck said, before any of the opposition could move an adjournment. "I would like for the members of this board to hear some plans Dr. Tyler has for the future of St. Luke's, since this is a matter of vital concern to all of us."

CHAPTER XVI

"As most of you know, I'm sure," Jud addressed the board, "a revitalized St. Luke's has long been the personal dream of Chuck Rogers. If I have contributed anything to this dream, it is the possibility that we may now be able to make it a reality."

"How do you propose to make a going concern out of a business that now operates at a considerable deficit?" Horace Fellowes asked.

"We have a plus factor here that most hospitals in the area don't possess," said Jud, "a staff that is on duty at all times to handle emergencies and follow them through to a final outcome. At the moment, it can be statistically proved that a soldier wounded on the battlefield has a considerably better chance of survival than the average automobile accident victim on a thruway in sight of most hospitals."

"Why is this, Doctor?" Joseph Neslor asked.

"Emergency patients in teaching hospitals are treated by interns or residents under the direction of the medical faculty, most of whom are full time and are therefore immediately available. But since only a few hospitals fall in the teaching class, the average patient reaching an Emergency Room today is handled by Foreign Medical Graduates, whose training is often not adequate, or by full-time physicians employed by the hospital. Anyone requiring major surgery must still go through a waiting period while a hospital staff surgeon is called, often from his home in the middle of the night and an operating room is prepared."

"How do you propose to change this?" Fellowes asked.

"By instituting here the same sort of system of emergency care that we had in my hospital at An Tha in Vietnam. Accident cases reaching the hospital will be seen at once by one of the resident staff. Unless the condition is a simple one which can be taken care of in the Emergency Room, I will be called or Dr. Emilio Fernandez, who is my deputy."

"Is Dr. Fernandez capable of handling any emergency?"

"Not any emergency; only a surgeon specially trained in traumatology can do that. But he has had several years of surgical training and does have excellent judgment. Where a case needs major attention, I will be called, of course."

"Does that mean you will always be on duty?" Fellowes asked.

"Not necessarily in the hospital. Our paging system reaches most of the city, so I can be called by means of the pager at almost any time."

"You admitted earlier that your right hand doesn't always work, Doctor," Dexter Johns reminded him.

"I will always be operating with one of the residents and can direct him in whatever procedure has to be carried out. In the case of special conditions, such as brain surgery, we will, of course, call upon one of the specialists on the staff of the hospital."

"Let's get down to the nitty gritty," said Horace Fellowes. "How do you propose to finance all this, Dr. Tyler?"

"Most automobile drivers today carry some form of liability insurance and I understand that a bill will soon be presented to the legislature requiring insurance by all who own automobiles," said Jud. "This means that every patient admitted from an automobile accident, for example, will be an insurance case, with the insurer responsible for the cost. And since Framingham is essentially an industrial city, most in-plant accidents are covered by insurance under the State Industrial Commission, which means that they, too, will be prepaid."

"If what you said is already true in many cases admitted to St. Luke's," said Fellowes, "why is it that the hospital has operated at such a deficit through the past several years?"

"For the simple reason that a concerted effort has been made to transfer patients with insurance, or those able to pay their own way, out of St. Luke's to the other hospitals."

There was a stir among the spectactors and Jud noticed that several of the newsmen were busy making notes.

"Surely you aren't implying that some sort of a plot has been in existence to downgrade this hospital, Doctor?" said Fellowes.

"If you examine the records, Mr. Fellowes, I think you will discover that cases which would be financially profitable to a hospital, a surgeon, or an internist, have consistently been transferred from St. Luke's to other institutions very soon after admission. Charity patients on the other hand, have been allowed to remain in the hospital, so in that sense, St. Luke's has been acting as a filter to prevent other hospitals in the community from being saddled with patients they didn't want."

"In other words it's a dumping ground?"

"You might say that. Yes."

"Incredible," said Fellowes, and Jud's estimation of him went up another notch.

"These are very serious charges, Dr. Tyler," said Joseph Neslor. "Are you prepared to substantiate them?"

"If the board will give me an opportunity to study hospital admissions for the past several years and examine the financial records, I shall be glad to prepare a report and present it at a future meeting."

"Please do that," said Neslor. "Is this the extent of your plans for St. Luke's?"

"No," said Jud. "This hospital has long served as the family doctor for a large section of the city which has almost no practicing physicians in it and no prospect of gaining any more. The new County Medical Center is located so far from Irontown that it is almost impossible for most of the residents to obtain medical care there. Mr. Rogers and I envision St. Luke's as the nucleus of a major community health center, not only devoted to the treatment of outpatients and those requiring hospitalization, but also for the eradication of chronic ills which arise because of ghetto life."

"Such as lead poisoning?" Horace Fellowes asked.

"Exactly," said Jud. "Where lead poisoning occurs because landlords are not forced to remove lead-bearing paint from the walls of the houses they rent to poor people, severe mental retardation occurs and the victims must be cared for in special institutions. A study made recently in Washington, D.C. indicated that by the time such a retarded person reaches the age of nineteen, the community and state will have expended more than forty thousand dollars for his care—all because landlords are too stingy to spend a few dollars scraping and repainting the walls of old tenements."

"Mr. Fellowes is right," said Joseph Neslor. "What you are telling us is completely incredible."

"But true, nonetheless, Mr. Neslor," Jud insisted. "I will be glad to present you with the proof."

"I'm not doubting you, Doctor," said Neslor. "I'm just wondering how all of us could have been so blind."

"Mr. Rogers and I plan to lay before the city government a list of the houses from which the children came who were definitely diagnosed as having lead poisoning," Jud continued. "In all probability this is only a fraction of the total number in the city, but it does indicate the areas where houses have been neglected to a point where they pose grave risks for children living in them."

"Perhaps Irontown should be razed," said Horace Fellowes.

"Experience in northern cities has shown that nothing is gained by razing areas of neglected housing, Mr. Fellowes. What's needed is a thorough renovation of the Irontown area to remove health hazards, particularly lead-containing paint upon the walls. If Mr. Rogers and I are successful in demonstrating to the city government the necessity for this move, I am sure dramatic results will be forthcoming."

II

"I couldn't have described our plans for St. Luke's better, Jud," Chuck said exultantly when the meeting was over. "And I've been dreaming about them for over a year."

"We're going to need money to get started."

"The TV station will let us use the tape of what you just said to convince one of the national foundations that they should help us. As for the rest, the Lord will provide."

"I wish I had your faith."

"We've just had a demonstration of it," said Chuck. "When I had given up hope of getting the kind of doctor we need, the Lord sent you to us. I've got a committee meeting tonight, or I would invite you to have dinner with me and celebrate."

"I've already been invited—by Kathryn Galloway."

"Fine. You two could be good for each other."

157

"What's the committee meeting about?" Jud asked.

"Framingham Mills—as usual. Horace Fellowes has been trying to talk Seth Wright out of hiring blacks to break the union but he's having a hard time of it. My job is to convince the union leaders that blacks have the same right to membership they have, so I can help Eric Cates hold the militant faction among them in line."

"Then Eric is with you?"

"He's about the only moderating force among the blacks, but he's caught in a classical impasse. Unless Eric goes along to a certain degree with the militants, he'll lose his leadership over the group as a whole."

"Who would step in then?"

"Al Porter, from the looks of it. You've met him before so you have some idea of what his approach would be."

"I can see that you and Eric are walking a tightrope."

"With pitfalls on either side," Chuck agreed. "Where jobs are at stake, passions are liable to be strong. And speaking of jobs, don't let the vote this afternoon delude you into thinking Asa Ford won't still be after your head, once he gets over the bug that kept him away today."

"I think you'll find Asa's illness will keep him from coming back here at all."

Chuck looked startled. "Rather sudden wasn't it—and convenient for you?"

"An acute attack," Jud said with a grin. "I saw Asa yesterday and advised him of the danger to his future. After all, being in jail isn't exactly good for the body or the mind."

They had been walking back through the corridors of the hospital from the teaching amphitheater. At his office, Jud beckoned Chuck inside and closed the door. Going to his desk, he unlocked the top drawer and took out the photostatic copies of the invoices he, Kathryn, and John Redmond had steamed open the day before.

"The pencil marks opposite each item show the actual amount received by the hospital," he explained. "You can see that there is a considerable discrepancy between the number billed and the number actually received."

Chuck studied the invoices for a moment, then looked up. "When you get riled, you play for keeps, don't you?" he said on a note of admiration.

"I learned a few things at An Tha besides medicine." Jud

158

gathered the papers together and locked them again in the drawer of his desk. "We've finished regrouping our forces; now we can attack some of the problems I spoke about this afternoon."

"You're already attacking yours," said Chuck. "Did you know that you locked the drawer just now with no hesitation whatsoever, using the right hand?"

III

"You're famous!" Kathryn Galloway cried when she opened her door to his ring about seven-thirty. "I watched the live ETV broadcast; it was so exciting, I could hardly breathe."

She was flushed with pleasure and very lovely; impulsively, he took her in his arms and kissed her. Her body was vibrant with life in his embrace and her lips eagerly responsive beneath his own. But after a moment, she pushed him away a little breathlessly.

"If winning a battle does *that* for you, I'm sure no woman in Vietnam was safe."

"No woman in Vietnam was like you. What have you been using to hide your real self? Camouflage?"

"It's all that starch we put in nurse's uniforms, to hide ourselves so we won't be pursued by doctors all over the hospital."

Still breathing quickly, she started removing the cork from the bottle of Cold Duck which had been cooling in a bucket of crushed ice. It came out with a loud pop and she poured the heady mixture of champagne and sparkling burgundy, a favorite drink in the South, into two glasses.

"To your triumph." She lifted her glass to touch his. "May it be the first of many."

After the tension of the afternoon, Jud was glad of the opportunity to unwind, stimulated by the wine and the presence of the woman beside him. Almost he dared to believe a warmth which had been dormant for so long was beginning to stir in his loins, but he put the thought away at once, lest it be a false alarm and the spell of the moment be broken.

"They were pretty rough on you at that meeting," she said. "Asa Ford had been boasting all over the hospital that today would be your last at St. Luke's. I wish he had turned up so you could have clobbered him."

"After what we discovered about those invoices, I'm sure yesterday was Asa's last day at St. Luke's," said Jud. "And I owe it all to you."

159

She drew a deep breath. "It scares me when I think what might have happened, if I had overlooked the figures on that invoice for Vitallium plates the way I'd done several others."

"Asa would have been caught eventually. He must have been skimming since the day he came to St. Luke's."

"Skimming?"

"It's a gambling term—in this case taking the gravy off the top by getting a rake-off on the purchase of supplies. I understand that it's a pretty common practice with purchasing agents in a lot of companies, but I never would have suspected it, if you hadn't become suspicious first."

"I'm a pretty tough character; you learned that your first day."

"And I guess I'm a babe in the woods." Jud held out his glass for a refill and she lifted the bottle from the bucket of ice. Already he could feel the bubbles floating to his brain, washing away the dregs of doubt and fear of failure that had dogged him since he'd awakened in Letterman General almost a year ago.

"That's the end of the bottle." She poured the last drop into his glass. "Shall we go to dinner while we can still walk?"

"I'm so happy, I didn't even know I was hungry—but now that you remind me of it, I am."

She stood up in a froth of chiffon skirt and lovely nylon-clad legs and touched her glass to his again. "To Dr. Galahad, and St. Luke's."

"And to us."

"To us." A sudden warm glow showed in her eyes. "Does the Spring Mountain Inn suit you?"

"Whatever you like, I like." Taking her hands, he drew her to him and looked down into the lovely gray eyes lifted up to his. When he bent his head to kiss her, she put her arms around him, holding him tightly against her while their lips were joined eagerly.

IV

It was almost ten, when Jud opened the door to Kathryn's apartment with the key she took from her purse. He hesitated at the door, but she took his arm firmly and drew him in.

"After the wonderful evening we've had, you must finish it off with a nightcap. I refuse to let you go without one."

"I was afraid you wouldn't ask me," he confessed.

It *had* been a lovely evening, he thought, while she was fixing

160

drinks for them in the small kitchen of the apartment. The dinner at the restaurant atop Spring Mountain had been perfect, with the lights of the city spread out before them like a net of glowing jewels cast across a dark sea. Afterward they had driven for a while through the night, stopping to watch the moonlight shimmer on a small lake in one of the many parks, while they talked of things they'd enjoyed in Framingham and elsewhere.

More than once, Jud had been sure Kathryn would have let him make love to her, as they sat in the car watching the play of lights upon the lake. But always the fear of failure and of repeating the ignominious admission of incapability that had sent him fleeing into the night from Samantha's apartment held him back. Now he was wondering whether it hadn't been a mistake to have come into her apartment at all.

When she came back carrying the drinks, they sat close together on the sofa, watching television and not knowing what was being done or said in the increasing awareness of each other—until Kathryn reached over and shut it off.

"Do you mind if I ask you a question?" she asked.

"Of course not—if I can answer it."

"You don't have to answer, if you'd rather not. But did your injury remove your capacity for sexual desire?"

"Not desire." Oddly enough, he found that he could talk easily to her about the fear that had been with him so long.

"The capability then?"

"I don't know. There's been no sign of physical response since the injury."

"You weren't—"

"Physically damaged in that respect? No."

"I thought not. Earlier this evening, when you held me in your arms, I was sure there was—an awakening."

"I think you're wrong." It was hard for him to say it but it wasn't fair to let things go much further between them without her knowing the full truth. "It's more than—"

"Hear me out, please Jud," she said. "I think I'm falling in love with you and you may think me a hussy for admitting it, but I have to know the truth."

"I've called myself half a man, but I'm not even that," he said with some bitterness. "Perhaps it will be better if we don't see each other again outside of work."

"I'm not sure, darling, and I have to be. From what I've read,

161

impotence in cases like yours is usually in the mind; you avoid trying to make love because you're afraid you'll fail—"

"Can you imagine anything more embarrassing?"

"For a man, I suppose not. But what may really be holding you back is the fear of failure and it would be tragic to wreck your chances of happiness with any woman—if she loves you—by letting fear rob you of your real manhood."

"Don't you think I want to be sure?" he cried. "It's plagued me ever since I first saw you."

"Then I'm right in believing I'm the only woman, at the moment at least, who can help you," she said calmly. "I want you to spend the night here, Jud."

"But—"

"We're friends, whether we ever become lovers or not—and we ought to know the answer to that question one way or another before morning. Do you have the courage to make the try?"

He smiled wryly. "When you put it in the form of a challenge, how could anyone refuse?"

v

The bedroom was exquisitely decorated and completely feminine. When Kathryn came out of the adjoining bath, Jud was lying under the sheet. She didn't turn out the bathroom light but left the door partially ajar so the room was filled with a soft glow. She was wearing a silken robe as she came over to the bed, but when she slipped beneath the sheet beside him and he reached out to touch her, he discovered that she had dropped it beside the bed.

"One thing more," she said. "This is my experiment, so I make the rules."

"Agreed. What are they?"

"We'll just lie here together learning about each other. If nothing happens, it will have been only a pleasurable experience for us both, like the kiss we had earlier. But we have the whole night before us, darling, so there's no need to rush."

The warmth of her body touched his gently, but with no urgency, as their lips met in the warm glow that filled the room. Her mouth was soft, fragrant, and infinitely pleasurable as they lay there. After a moment, when his tongue touched her lips, they parted and he was able to explore the warm cavity of her mouth. When he drew back, she responded and he shifted position a little until

162

his arm was beneath her neck and he could reach her mouth more easily.

Gently, tenderly, he moved his other hand down the warm satiny surface of her back, exploring the hollow along her spine and the firm roundness of her hips. Her hands had been upon his chest, caressing his ribs with gentle fingers. But she moved a little closer against him and the pressure of his hand upon her back brought their loins together.

He could feel the silky ringlets of the hair over her pubis touch him with a separate caress of their own now. And when he shifted his right hand down beneath her waist, she lifted herself until one hand could rest beneath her hip, while the other was above. By spreading his fingers then, he was able to encompass the soft roundness of a hip in each hand and knead them gently, opening and closing the crevice between.

Pressing her soft intimate flesh against his own, he moved it gently until the cleft beneath the crest of the pubis opened to form a warm moist trough in which his own manhood lay—though as yet unaroused. They lay there for a while, savoring the exquisite pleasure of bodily contact with no urgency for any deeper intimacy. But when Jud continued to knead the softness gently between his hands, she suddenly caught her breath and pushed him away.

"Remember, I make the rules," she said breathlessly. "I'm way ahead of you, darling."

"I told you—"

"Turn on your back," she whispered, and he obeyed almost reluctantly. Momentarily, as the crevice of her most intimate flesh had encompassed his, he'd dared to hope there was a beginning of response. But she had made the rules and he had agreed to submit to them.

He felt her move beside him but, disturbed by the thought that he had already failed in the challenge, didn't realize what she was doing until he felt her legs pressing against the side of his chest and realized that she was kneeling astride his body, with her knees near the level of his own nipples.

She had thrown back the sheet too, and he could see her lovely body above him now, the breasts thrust forward so challengingly that he instinctively reached up to caress them, pulling her gently down until he could take first one nipple and then the other between his lips, caressing it with his tongue while it swelled and grew hard under the pressure.

163

"Darling! Darling!" she whispered, and he felt her hands upon him where for so long had been only the assuredness of living death, the hopelessness of despair that he would never again be a man in the real sense of the word.

"You almost made it just now but I was too far ahead of you," she said.

"If you want to—"

"But I don't—not yet. I'm going to give you back the one thing that can free you from the unhappiness of the past year. When that happens, we'll go on together."

His hands slipped from her breasts down to the slenderness of her waist, the round cup of her navel, the swelling fullness of her belly just beneath it and the curly ringlets of soft hair upon the mound that rose there. Her own fingers were caressing him with the coaxing gentleness of love, now stroking, now folding the membranous layers guarding her own intimacy about him, until the rising tide of her passion made her draw back to wait for him.

At first there was nothing, nothing save the helplessness of despair. But then somewhere deep inside his body, where the network of veins carried blood from the lower part of his torso back to the heart, he felt a slowly gathering constriction, as the return flow of blood from that part of his body was shut off by the psychological stimulus of desire. The arteries continued to pump, however, pouring in blood with each throbbing beat. And the tissues from which its escape had now been shut away by the psychophysical mechanism that prepares the male for procreation began to engorge, to swell, and take on life once again.

Seized with a rising sense of triumph and accomplishment, of power within him, Jud reached down and took Kathryn's fingers which encompassed him so tenderly, pushing her hand gently backward, past the sensitive tender shaft called the clitoris until there was no more resistance to the throbbing pressure that now demanded entry.

His hands moved across her back as he laced his fingers together behind it, drawing her gently down to engulf him. Locked together there as she leaned forward to kiss him, they were caught up by instinct alone in a rhythm as old as time, until at last the urgency of a shared need lifted them to the crest of a final wave of desire, carrying them together until it broke and they collapsed in each other's arms, exhausted from their lovemaking, and were almost immediately engulfed in sleep.

Around four o'clock, Jud was awakened by the pressure of Kathryn's head upon his arm. When he moved it gingerly, she stirred and opened her eyes.

"Happy?" she asked.

"Yes—and all because of you."

"I'm glad I was the one. What time is it?"

"Four o'clock."

"You don't have to go yet, do you?"

"Not necessarily."

"Good." She put her arms about his neck and, when he leaned down to kiss her again, he felt a surge of passion at the touch of her warm naked flesh against his own.

"Are you still all right—with the precautions, I mean?" he whispered against her lips.

When she nodded assent, he moved deeper into her embrace and then into her body until they were caught up again on the crest of desire and let it sweep them along as it would.

"You gave me something I was needing badly, Jud," she said as he kissed her good-by shortly after five-thirty. "Since Father died I've been drifting without purpose, but tonight you made me feel like a woman again, with something worthwhile to give."

Walking back to the hospital in the dawn, Jud felt a new confidence flooding through him. Only for a moment did he experience a spasm of jealousy, when he wondered how many times Dick Tubman had driven away from Kathryn's apartment at about this same hour. But before he could dwell upon the thought, the first rays of the sun broke across the rise of Mountain Avenue to the east with its promise of a new day and he put it from him.

CHAPTER XVII

Jud was in his office, when the morning shift changed to afternoon the day after the hearing before the trustees and its dramatic conclusion, working on the plan Chuck had asked him to develop for presentation to one of the national foundations. When Samantha came into his office unannounced, he saw that her eyes were smoky with indignation.

"So you made out," she said in a voice tense with the gathering storm of anger as she closed the door.

"My appointment as Director was approved, yes."

"I'm not talking about that—and you damn well know it."

"What are you talking about?"

"You and Kathryn Galloway! You slept with her last night!"

"What makes you think that?"

"Think, hunnh! I know! You were seen coming in a little before six looking like the cat that stole the cream. And she's been going around all day like she was floating on air." Samantha momentarily choked with anger and had to stop before going on. "She even spoke kindly to me. To me, mind you—when she's been riding me because of you ever since I came here."

"I suppose this is another example of what goes over the hospital grapevine—and about as accurate."

"It's accurate all right. You came in at six and the night shift told it to the day shift an hour later." Suddenly she jumped to her feet and, reaching up, began to unzip the back of the uniform she was wearing. She had it down to her waist and was unbuttoning her blouse to reveal that she eschewed a brassiere, when he realized what she was doing and said sharply:

"Stop it, Samantha! Have you gone out of your mind?"

"I've been insulted, that's what!" The blouse was down to her waist now and she threw back her shoulders, thrusting two lovely breasts at him.

"What's wrong with these?" she demanded, half crying.

"Put your blouse and pinafore back on and sit down," he said. "You're acting like a child."

"I bet you never saw any child with tits like these," she raged, but she did start buttoning the blouse again. And when it was finished, she pulled up the pinafore and zipped it up in the back.

"There's nothing wrong with you," he said.

"Then why did you turn me down when I offered to sleep with you—a long time before she did?"

"Samantha, you're married to a man I'm beginning to admire and respect."

"We're divorced. You know that."

"He's confident that you'll be married again."

166

"What makes you think that?" Some of the anger had gone out of her voice now.

"He told me so."

"You mean he warned you not to—"

"Nothing so melodramatic as that. But he still loves you and I'm sure you still love him."

"You're only guessing," she said, but her voice was definitely softer.

"Actually, I'm sure you broke with Fellowes as a way of rebelling against your father."

"There you go again with your analysis," she exclaimed. "The next thing you'll be telling me that every time I went to bed with Horace, my unconscious mind was accusing me of incest. For your information, it wasn't me that always went off as soon as the fuse was lit; it was him."

"And you didn't try to help?"

"Damn you! When I come in here mad, why do you make me go out feeling guilty?"

"Because you already felt that way and got mad trying to hide it. I don't think you'll have to worry about Horace, though. He's a very handsome man and can always find what you call a surrogate."

"Over my dead body he will!"

"You live body would do better. Why don't you make up with your husband, Samantha?"

"And have him lord it over me the rest of our lives, like my father did Mother and me? Oh no. He's got to want me—"

"I'm sure he does."

"Then let him come and tell me."

"I know he's very much impressed by your sticking to what is a pretty unpleasant job here." Jud stretched the truth a little. "Maybe he's just begun to realize what the real you is like, the one that isn't always smashing automobiles. I hope you're going to stay on, now that the hair snipping is finished. You've helped a lot there."

"Did I, Jud? I'm glad."

"And not mad any more?"

"Put out is the better word, I guess. I've never in my life done anything I could say was really worthwhile."

"Working here is."

"I know that now. After taking care of those cute little babies,

I can't wait to have some of my own. Where did I go wrong with you, Jud?" she asked a little wistfully. "Did I push too hard?"

"Push! You scared the hell out of me." They both began to laugh and the faint remnants of tension between them evaporated.

"Why don't you go by to see your father?" he said as he opened the door for her. "He may even be worried enough about himself to admit that he needs you."

"I might."

"Amanda Cates can tell you when Horace comes to see him."

"Who's pushing now?" Samantha made a face at him, but there was no rancor in her voice.

II

It was a little after 5:00 P.M. when the whine of a siren at the ambulance unloading platform sounded its strident summons. By the time Jud reached the Emergency Room, a Fire Department ambulance was being wheeled in. What startled him, however, wasn't the fact that the scene was almost a direct repeat of the one he'd faced the first morning he came to St. Luke's, it was the identity of the blanket-covered figure upon the stretcher, a man whose purplish ear lobes and fingertips betrayed a dangerous oxygen lack.

He was Jack Aiken, the byssinosis patient who had played the leading role in that earlier drama.

This time Aiken was still breathing. And when Jud took the stethoscope Amanda Cates handed him, he could hear the heart sounds plainly, even through the background noise of Aiken's labored respiration. The distended veins in the mill worker's neck, his struggling attempt to breathe, all added up to the same picture—severe congestive heart failure.

"Get him on the examining table," Jud directed Emilio Fernandez, who had also appeared, and an orderly. "Miss Cates."

"Yes, Doctor."

"Get me the largest sterile needle you can find. I won't need a syringe, just a measuring cup to catch the blood. I'm going to bleed him to reduce the congestion."

"Give him an ampoule of Isoproterenol intravenously in the left arm," Jud told Fernandez as the nurse moved away. "I'll be using the right—and while you're at it, Emilio, you'd better give him an ampoule of Digitoxin."

168

While Jud was cutting Jack Aiken's sleeve to allow room to work, Amanda Cates appeared at his elbow with a large needle wrapped in a sterile cloth cover, a measuring cup and a sponge moistened in alcohol. She applied the tourniquet while he scrubbed the space in front of Aiken's elbow where the veins bulged ominously.

"Better stand back," Jud warned her as he took the needle. "The venous pressure is quite high."

Jud thrust the large needle through both skin and vein wall in one movement, allowing blood to spurt several feet and spatter on the tile floor. Then holding the needle in his left hand, he directed the arching stream into the measuring cup Amanda Cates held to catch it. On the other side of the patient, Emilio Fernandez was injecting the drugs into a vein.

"Is this congestive heart failure, Dr. Tyler?" the Cuban asked.

"It has all the appearances of it."

"A coronary attack?"

"I'm no cardiologist but to cause heart failure to this degree, the block to his coronary arteries would have to be massive," said Jud. "I don't think he would have survived to reach the hospital."

While Jud was talking, blood had been pouring from the needle he was holding. Already signs of change in the patient's condition were perceptible: the bulging veins in his neck, first indication that the right side of the heart was unable to pump the blood passing through it from the entire body—except the lungs which had a circulation of their own—had lessened noticeably. Aiken's labored breathing was easier too, partly from the effect of the Isoproterenol in dilating constricted small bronchial passages and allowing freer exchange of oxygen in the lungs. The powerful heart drug, Digitoxin, was also exerting its traditional effect upon the cardiac muscle, slowing the beat and giving it a chance to cope with the strain which had been put upon it.

"Two hundred and fifty c.c. out." Amanda Cates' eyes were on the level of dark red blood rising steadily in the measuring cup.

"Take the pressure, please, Emilio," Jud directed, and the Cuban bent over the blood pressure cuff he had wrapped around Jack Aiken's arm.

"One hundred over seventy and rising," he reported a moment later. "But how could it rise when you're *removing* blood, Doctor?"

169

"We're dealing with right-sided failure, due to an overly strong resistance to the flow of blood through the lungs from congestion," Jud explained. "Old textbooks call this type of heart *cor pulmonale*. The heart is pumping more freely now, so additional blood is being forced through the lungs—you can tell that by the decrease of cyanosis in his ear lobes and fingertips. And with more blood coming from the lungs to be pumped to the rest of the body, the left side of the heart is able to increase the pressure in the arterial circulation, and the blood pressure rises."

"Three hundred and fifty c.c.," Amanda Cates reported.

"Blood pressure one-ten over seventy-five," said Emilio Fernandez.

"I'm going to stop at four hundred c.c." said Jud.

When the level in the cup reached that mark, he withdrew the needle and strapped a gauze sponge tightly over the puncture wound with a piece of adhesive. By that time, the improvement in Jack Aiken's condition was truly remarkable; his color was almost normal and his breathing far easier.

"Put him in the Intensive Care cubicle and have the lab take an EKG, Miss Cates," Jud directed. "I'll call Dr. Tubman so he can leave orders for further treatment."

"A man from the mill where Mr. Aiken works is outside, Doctor," she said. "I asked him to have a seat in your office."

III

"Andy Green, Doctor." The gray-haired man in work clothes stood up when Jud came into the office and shook hands. "I'm seven-to-three foreman in the cardroom where Jack works and secretary of the union at the mills. Does he have a chance?"

"A good one, I'd say. Sit down, Mr. Green. Maybe you can give me some information."

"I'll help any way I can, Doctor."

"Why did Jack go back to work so early?"

"I guess that's my fault," Green admitted. "He planned to come back Monday but right after lunch today, Ed Grogan—he's the three-to-eleven foreman in the cardroom—called in and said he had food poisoning. Jack is coming up for Ed's job as soon as Ed retires, so I called Jack and he said he'd be happy to take Ed's shift."

"Did Aiken seem to be all right when he came to work?"

"Just like always. I had to stay at the mill on some union business; national headquarters is pushing us to let niggers work on the machines. The first I knew anything was wrong was when I saw the ambulance and they told me Jack had had another heart attack. That's what it is, isn't it?"

"This time it's heart *failure*," said Jud. "But I'm sure the cause is the same as the attack he had the other day."

"Monday Morning Asthma?"

"Yes. Do you know how his symptoms began today?"

"The men in the cardroom say Jack came to work feeling fine. But about a half hour after the shift took over, he began to choke up the way we all do—"

"*All*, Mr. Green?"

"Well, all the old-timers—like me and Jack. Sometimes on Monday morning, it's like you had a vise around your chest for a couple of hours. You just can't seem to get enough air in your lungs no matter how hard you try."

"You know what this trouble is, don't you?"

"Jack was telling me you and Dr. Tubman say it's a new disease of mill workers."

"Not a new disease—an old one workers haven't been protected against."

"But when Mr. Fellowes took over a couple of years ago, the whole mill was air-conditioned. He even had new filters put on the machines."

"Did they cut down the amount of dust?"

"I can't tell about that," Green admitted.

"Why?"

"High-speed cards were put in at the same time and the new fast machines always increase the dust."

"Then the two sort of cancel each other out—is that it?"

"I wouldn't have any way of knowing." Andy Green hedged.

"Do the men have as much trouble with their breathing now as they did before?"

"I can't see much difference. They certainly complain about it as much."

"How about yourself?"

"I don't have to stand right over the carding machines and part of the time I stay in the office on union business. But it's still pretty rough on me Monday mornings just like it is on most of the other old-timers."

171

An idea had suddenly begun to take form in Jud's mind. "Did you say you were secretary of the union, Mr. Green?" he asked.

"The local, yes."

"Has the question of protecting workers against cotton dust ever come up in your negotiations with Framingham Mills?"

"Not to my knowledge."

"How about other textile plants?"

"They're not organized—at least not around Framingham—but I've never heard of any trouble. You sure this asthma is from the dust, Doctor?"

"Just think about it a minute," Jud told him. "You're free from it on weekends until you go back to work on Monday. When we tested Jack Aiken recently his lung capacity was only thirty per cent of normal and he doesn't smoke. What would you say?"

"Jack could have something else." Green hedged again.

"On top of the drop in lung capacity, Aiken has almost died twice after inhaling cotton dust. The whole picture fits a severe case of byssinosis, Mr. Green."

"I never could understand medical terms very well," said the union secretary doubtfully.

"Would it help if I demonstrated exactly what's happening to you and the workers?"

"Well—yes."

"When is your next union meeting?"

"Thursday night."

"I'd like to bring a machine to that meeting and test anyone in your membership who's willing. I think I can show you some things that will startle you."

"I don't know," said Green doubtfully.

"One of your members already is a cripple for the rest of his life because of the dust that comes out of those machines," said Jud sharply. "Aren't you interested in keeping your men alive, Mr. Green? Or do you want to have that on your conscience the rest of your life?"

"When you put it that way, I guess I don't have any choice," Green admitted reluctantly.

"Don't mention this before the meeting," Jud warned. "I don't want news of it to get around in advance."

"Neither do I," said Green. "You know how Mr. Wright is."

"Mr. Wright won't have anything to say about what happens

172

in the future," Jud promised. "The state will see that you and your men are protected. Where do you meet?"

"Mr. Fellowes lets us use the cafeteria in the evening when we need it. They don't serve nothing there but sandwiches at midnight anyway, so there ain't much going on in the evening."

"I'll be there Thursday night," Jud told him. "What time?"

"Eight o'clock." Green hesitated then spoke again: "You figurin' on bringin' Reverend Rogers with you?"

"I hadn't thought about it."

"I wouldn't if I were you, Doctor."

"Why?"

"Well he's got that little church down in the nigger district and he's always trying to get 'em into the union. A lot of our men feel like he's too much of a nigger lover for us."

"I won't bring Mr. Rogers," Jud promised. "But you're wrong about him; all he wants is to see the blacks get an even chance with the whites. There've been laws on the books requiring that for quite a while."

IV

When Green left, Jud picked up the telephone and dialed Dr. Richard Tubman's office. The secretary was a little reluctant about letting him talk to Tubman but, at his insistence, finally connected him.

"Jack Aiken was admitted again just now," he told the internist.

"What happened?"

"Advanced right-sided heart failure. He went back to work this afternoon on the three-to-eleven shift and started having trouble breathing as soon as he inhaled a lungful of cotton dust. About a half hour later they had to call the ambulance. I bled him—"

"That was quick thinking."

"The native witch doctors among the Montagnard tribes still use bloodletting. I saw some rather dramatic effects at An Tha and decided it might help Jack."

"Does it look like he's going to pull through?"

"He's coming around; we gave him Isoproterenol and Digitoxin. But treating heart failure is beyond my capabilities except in an emergency. You can order whatever you wish when you see him."

173

There was a moment of hesitation, then Tubman said, "I'm pretty busy."

"Too busy to stop by on your way home and leave the order for whatever he needs?"

"I told you Aiken had gone back to his family doctor."

"Would he know how to handle something like this?"

"Well—no."

"You're still a consultant on the staff of this hospital, aren't you?"

"Yes."

"Was your appointment made before you became Seth Wright's physician?"

"Well—yes."

"Then from where I sit it looks like you've got a clear choice, Doctor—either take care of Aiken's case or resign your staff appointment."

There was still silence at the other end of the telephone, so Jud added the clincher: "And it wouldn't sound good in Framingham for the newspapers to report that you refused to treat a seriously ill man, would it?"

"You don't give me much choice," Tubman protested.

"You're damn right, I don't," Jud snapped. "Your oath as a physician takes precedence over any fee Seth Wright paid you so you wouldn't investigate the incidence of byssinosis in the mills here. But I'm going to investigate it anyway and you're going to be involved whether you like it or not. Think about that, Doctor."

He slammed up the telephone but, in his anger, didn't even notice that this time he placed the receiver squarely on the cradle —and with his right hand.

As Jud went in to dinner, he saw Tubman's Mark III in the parking lot. When he came out it was gone, but a call to the ward revealed that the internist had left the necessary orders for treating a case of heart failure.

Aiken was already much improved the next morning; his heart was functioning considerably more efficiently—though the X-ray report showed a great deal of enlargement, notably on the right side.

The mill worker was sitting up in bed eating breakfast when Jud came by making rounds.

174

"I guess I was a fool not to listen when you told me I shouldn't start work in the cardroom again, Doctor," he said.

"How do you feel about going back now?"

"You couldn't drag me in there with a team of horses. I'm going to ask Mr. Fellowes to put me in the spinning room or on an outside job, even though it'll mean less money and givin' up my shot at bein' foreman in the cardroom to boot. But at least I can live awhile longer."

"You can still help those who have to work there," said Jud. "All we need is a test case to get this condition included in the State Industrial Commission protection laws and make the mill-owners take the precautions they should have taken a long time ago. That way, you'll not only be doing your friends among the workers a favor, but you'll be paid for the damage cotton dust has already done to your lungs."

"I don't know," said Aiken doubtfully. "They've been pretty good to me at the plant."

"Framingham Mills has taken away more than two-thirds of your lung capacity and weakened your heart by at least fifty per cent," said Jud bluntly. "I wouldn't call that treating you particularly well."

"Is it really that bad, Dr. Tyler?" Jack Aiken looked scared.

"It's that bad." Knowing this was the time to press hard if he was going to get anywhere at all, Jud kept boring in. "You've gotten into trouble twice in one week when exposure to dust decreased your lung capacity to where you weren't able to get enough air to keep your body functioning normally. Because your heart is also enlarged, the extra strain put on it trying to pump the blood to absorb more oxygen caused the stoppage last week and heart failure yesterday."

"Does that mean I may have more trouble later on, no matter where I work?"

"I'm no heart specialist. Didn't Dr. Tubman tell you how serious your condition is?"

Aiken shook his head. "I think he was glad to get rid of me the other time—when he sent me back to my family doctor. They were saying at the mill that, since he's become Mr. Wright's family doctor, he don't pay no more attention to mill people."

"Dr. Tubman is a specialist in heart trouble and also an expert on the effects of cotton dust on the lungs," said Jud. "It's true that he's Mr. Wright's doctor too, but in the final analysis, that won't affect the way he treats you."

"I'd rather depend on you, Dr. Tyler; after all you saved my life twice. What are my real chances with the future?"

"I'm going to give it to you straight, Mr. Aiken. With only about a third of your lung capacity at work, you've got two-thirds less lung to fight with, in case you get pneumonia or some other infection—and only about half of your heart. Take care of yourself and you could live a long time. But go back inside the cardroom and you'll be signing your own death warrant."

Aiken nodded slowly. "Coming as close as I did to dying twice has made me realize I can't go on like I've been. But my wife's afraid that if we fight this case the way Mr. Morgan wants us to, the mill will fire me and then we won't have anything."

"I can't guarantee that you're going to be able to work much longer anyway," Jud told him. "If Mr. Morgan wins a test case before the Industrial Commission, you'll have a lifetime disability pension that you wouldn't otherwise have."

"I guess I'd better go along with you then," said Aiken. "Dying twice is enough for anybody—the next time I might not be so lucky."

CHAPTER XVIII

Jud met Kathryn in a deserted section of the main corridor the morning after Jack Aiken was admitted the second time. She'd been away from the OPD all the previous day and he'd wondered if she'd learned that his spending the night at her apartment after the board meeting was now general knowledge in the hospital and was angry about it.

"Where've you been?" he asked casually.

"I had to substitute in the Nursing Office. Did you miss me?"

"Very much."

Her eyes twinkled. "The way I heard it, you didn't exactly lack for female companionship yesterday. The system of communication at St. Luke's is very thorough."

176

"Samantha was pretty angry."

"Everybody in the hospital knew she was after you—I can understand how she felt."

"She's not after me any more; I talked her into making up with her husband."

"Not many men would have had the courage to turn down something that young and eager."

"And not many men are lucky enough to find someone as understanding as you are. There's an easy way to stop that talk on the grapevine, Kathryn. We can be at the marriage license bureau at City Hall in fifteen minutes and I hear you can get blood tests in an hour."

"No wonder the hospital calls you Dr. Galahad." Her voice was tender. "But you don't have to make an honest woman of me, Jud. We're consenting adults—of different sexes—so there's no valid reason why we shouldn't have slept together when we both wanted to."

"None at all," he agreed. "And I'm grateful to you."

"That's a poor basis for marriage. Besides, there's still a stumbling block—"

"We got rid of that the other night."

"The purely sexual one, yes. But you're not the kind of man who would settle for less than using his full capability—you've proved that since you came here, even with your handicap. If we were married now, I'm sure I would try to convince you to make the best of your situation, as far as surgery is concerned. And I'm not at all convinced that it would be the best thing for you and your self-respect."

"That doesn't mean we can't see each other outside the hospital, does it?"

"Of course not. I enjoy being with you and there's no reason why we can't have a perfectly friendly relationship—"

"When can I see you again?"

"You see me every day."

He laughed. "In that starched armor? Even Sir Galahad couldn't cope with that."

"I've got an idea you'd find a way somehow," she assured him.

"I'm speaking to the local union at Framingham Mills Thursday night on byssinosis, but I'd like to come by afterward if I may, provided it won't be too late for you."

"We'll watch the eleven o'clock news and the movie," she promised. "That way you'll get home about one-thirty and the grapevine won't have much to talk about."

II

Joe Morgan was waiting in Jud's office when he finished setting a particularly difficult fracture in the Emergency Room a little after six. It was the first time Jud had talked to the young lawyer since the climactic session of the Board of Trustees.

"I just finished talking to Jack Aiken," said Morgan. "You certainly put the fear of God into him this time."

"That's what he needed. Even a moderately severe respiratory infection could reduce his lung capacity sharply and leave him no way to get oxygen. If that happens, nothing anybody can do is going to help him."

"That bad, eh?"

"About as bad as it could be—and let him still live. From what he and the foreman of the cardroom told me, plenty of others working at Framingham Mills are just as bad, to say nothing of the other textile plants in the area. Is Aiken willing to go through with a class action?"

"It's all set. I'm going to file for a hearing before the Industrial Commission in the morning."

"How long will that take?"

"They always have a backlog of cases, so it will be a couple of months at least. Then Framingham Mills is sure to plead for a continuance, which might make it three more."

"Five months!"

"In addition to being blind, justice is also slow as hell."

"But let a tough epidemic of Asian flu come along in the meantime and a lot of those fellows won't be around any more."

"The way you talk, one would think you've got a personal vendetta against disease," said Morgan.

"I do. That's my job."

"Most doctors don't look at it that way."

"Maybe I'm a throwback—to the age of microbe hunters Paul de Kruif used to write about."

"One thing's certain," said Morgan admiringly. "Once you get your right hand back to where you can use it, you could make a fortune practicing surgery."

Jud shook his head. "That's not for me. I haven't told this to many people, Joe, but in the first thirty-six hours after I was wounded, my heart stopped twice. Once was in the hospital I was flown to in Japan. Fortunately, they had a highly trained CPR team—"

"CPR?"

"Cardio Pulmonary Resuscitation—the technique of starting the heart by pressing it between the breastbone and the spine. Those fellows got to me in a hurry and I wasn't out for more than maybe a minute. The other time was on an ambulance plane taking me to Letterman General. A real smart lieutenant in the Nursing Corps and an enlisted corpsman started it that time. I was all the way out, of course, and didn't know what had happened until I read the medical record at Letterman before I was transferred to Walter Reed for rehabilitation. But I figured then that, if the Lord had taken the trouble to start me up again after I'd stopped living, it must be for some other purpose than getting rich from the practice of medicine."

"You and Chuck Rogers." Morgan shook his head admiringly. "The only thing an ordinary guy like me can do is stand in awe of you."

"You're making a sacrifice too."

"But after I make a comfortable living doing something else —and then, I guess, only as a hobby to ease my conscience. You and Chuck go about this business of helping other people like it was your main purpose in life—and I guess it is."

"Getting back to Jack Aiken's case," said Jud. "Are you sure we can't use any legal short cuts to speed this thing up?"

"None that I know of."

"Then I'll have to go at it another way."

"How?"

"I may have it already." Jud described the conversation with Andy Green and the way he had maneuvered the union secretary into letting him offer free spirometer tests to the union members.

"Neat," said Morgan when he'd finished. "You're tricky enough to be a successful lawyer."

"If I can just get enough of those men scared, the way I did Jack Aiken, I can really get some force behind this movement to make byssinosis a legal industrial hazard."

"Seth Wright's sure to get his back up when he hears of what you're doing," Morgan warned.

"How about Horace Fellowes?"

"Horace is smart enough to recognize the handwriting on the wall. He's already pushing the old man to employ some blacks in skilled positions at the same salary as whites, but he hasn't gotten far in that direction yet. Jared Heath was superintendent of the mill before Horace came along and he's always stayed in good with Seth Wright, besides hating Horace's guts. Between them, they'd fight what you propose, if for no other reason than because it's something they never heard of before."

"What about the lead poisoning situation?" Jud asked. "Isn't there any way we can force Angus Claiborne into fixing those houses—short of arousing public opinion?"

"Angus and his ilk don't give a damn about public opinion. They know the blacks haven't got anywhere else to live even though their houses are deathtraps."

"Why can't the Health Department act?"

"It's so mired in politics, they can hardly examine a specimen of urine without an act of the City Council."

"The courts then?"

"County judges are elected, so they're too closely tied in with the county political machine for us to get anywhere."

"That's a hell of a situation."

"It's a fact of life all over the country." Morgan shrugged. "Lawyers have to get used to it."

"That's like saying a doctor would treat a Republican differently from the way he would a Democrat."

"Maybe the patient's politics doesn't have anything to do with the way most doctors treat him but the size of his pocketbook certainly does. If it happens to be empty, a lot of doctors won't spend enough time to really find out what the trouble is."

"I know," Jud agreed soberly. "We're always finding cancer of the rectum that's gone undiagnosed to where it's inoperable because the family physician didn't take the trouble to put in a finger and find out. So who do we go to now—the City Council?"

Joe Morgan shook his head. "Angus and the president of the City Council are cronies. We could get a bill introduced to eradicate health hazards from rented homes, of course. But by the time the president got through burying the bill in several committees, it would take a year to get the ordinance out. By then public indignation will have subsided so they could quietly scuttle it."

"Are you saying we went to all that trouble proving that ghetto children are being poisoned for nothing?"

"Not at all—merely that what we do has to be done at the federal level. If we get knocked down here in the Federal District Court, we can always make a fast appeal to the Fifth Circuit with a good chance of winning."

"On what grounds?"

"That's taking some doing, but I think I've found the answer," said the lawyer. "First, we have to determine the chemical level of lead in the blood of those kids who showed it on the survey. Chuck has been bringing them in for blood samples in his own car but only about half so far have been willing to come to the laboratory. Those already in the hospital don't have much to say about whether we get blood from them or not, so it still looks like we'll have enough to make a case."

"What good will that do, if the landlords simply refuse to remove the hazard? You said yourself you can't make them do it under the existing city ordinances."

"I've dug up one they may not have thought about." Joe Morgan lowered his voice. "Most ghetto families stay a month or two behind in their rent. When Angus and Farleigh Grossett discover that the children are being tested again, they're pretty sure to start wholesale evictions, figuring to get rid of incriminating evidence—in this case the lead in the bodies of the kids. But state law forbids putting a sick person out of a rented house so, as soon as a few are evicted, we'll make our move in the courts, on the grounds that the landlords are endangering the lives of the children by evicting the families."

"But you said the courts are—"

"Once a few of the families are evicted, we can slap a federal injunction on Grossett and Claiborne under the Fourteenth Amendment—interpreted pretty broadly, I'll admit—and keep them from renting the houses again until the hazard is removed."

"It's a hell of a comment on civilization, when you have to squeeze a man's pocketbook to make him do something he wouldn't have done because of his conscience," Jud said bitterly.

"If we lawyers had to depend on people's consciences to right wrong," Joe Morgan said with a grin, "the profession would soon be out of business."

III

Jud hadn't seen much of Chuck Rogers during the early part of the week, but late Thursday afternoon, the chaplain came into the supply room where he was checking over the spirometer he planned to use at the union meeting that evening.

"You're really sticking out your neck going to a meeting of those rednecks," said Chuck, when Jud told him what he was planning to do. "Sure you don't need some help?"

"You've got all you can do getting those blood samples."

"It isn't easy," Chuck admitted. "Kids who didn't object at all to having some hair snipped off are very much afraid of a needle."

"Will you have enough specimens to really make a good case?"

"We think so. Eric has been helping me; he has a lot more influence over the people in Irontown than I do." Chuck looked at his watch. "I've got a staff meeting at the cathedral, but I'll be through by seven-thirty. Sure I can't help you tonight?"

Jud decided to tell the truth, since it wasn't in his nature to equivocate anyway.

"Andy Green asked me not to bring you," he said, and Chuck nodded soberly.

"The nigger-lover theme again, I suppose. They condemned Christ for eating with publicans and sinners, so maybe I should feel honored."

"I think you should."

"You're beginning to be tarred with the same brush, you know. Don't you mind?"

Jud smiled. "What I mind most is not being half the man you are. Do me a favor and hang around the pearly gates for a while after you get to heaven. The way I've been hating my fellow men for poisoning children with lead and lack of proteins in the diet, I'm going to need a helping hand to pull me through."

"Right now I'm tired myself." It was the first Jud had ever known his friend to be depressed. "Tired of being my brother's keeper and having him kick me in the face."

"What you need is a home and children to come to at night. I seem to remember a nurse at An Tha that you were pretty fond of."

"Eleanor and I were going to be married as soon as her hitch was up; she didn't feel right about quitting in the middle of a fight. We almost made it too. She was at Fort Dix waiting for discharge and we were going to be married the next month, but her physical showed a far advanced cancer of the uterus."

"Surely she must have had symptoms."

"She didn't want to report sick; said there was too much to do, so she didn't bother anyone. The Army sent her to Walter Reed as soon as they discovered what was the trouble, but they opened and closed her there without being able to do anything. Later they used radiation therapy but it was too late for that too. She died six months after I came back to the States and I haven't felt like looking at another woman since."

"I wish I'd known, Chuck—"

"You were busy with your own troubles—it must have been while you were at Letterman. I was pretty well broken up—almost went off the deep end for a while and gave up the ministry. Then Bishop Tanner offered me this job and I've been too busy ever since to do more than remember Eleanor occasionally when I'm low—like tonight."

Chuck stood up. "If you won't take me with you, at least take a nurse. She can help you run the machine."

"That's a good idea," said Jud. "I'll call Kathryn and see if she's free. I was going to call a taxi but if she'll go, we can use her car."

Kathryn answered when he rang the phone. "How about working awhile tonight?" he asked.

"Do you pay overtime?"

"Scrambled eggs and sausage afterwards—"

"That's the best offer I've had in days. What do you want me to do?"

"Help me with some spirometer tests at Framingham Mills. We'll need your hair dryer too."

"How do you know it'll work?"

"A friend of yours used it once before in the same test."

"Oh!" There was a brief pause, then she said, "Shall I wear a uniform?"

"It will be more impressive if you do. Wear one of those starched ones—you know, the armor. We'll be testing some men—"

"In that case I'll wear a new nylon job I just bought—very seductive. What time shall I pick you up?"

"The meeting's at eight. A quarter to will be okay—at the Emergency Room unloading platform."

"Fine. I won't forget to bring the hair dryer."

CHAPTER XIX

The rows of chairs at one end of the mill cafeteria were half filled when Jud and Kathryn came in carrying the spirometer in its case and the hair dryer. Her new uniform elicited a few wolf whistles as, with the help of Andy Green they set up a table at one side of the lectern and plugged in the machine.

"I figured it was only fair to let Mr. Fellowes know you were coming tonight, Doctor," said the union secretary. "He said he'd try to make it."

"Good. We'll use him as a dog."

"A dog?"

"That's a medical school term for the subject of an experiment," Jud explained.

Horace Fellowes hadn't appeared when the meeting was called to order five minutes after eight, so it was opened without him.

"You all know Jack Aiken came near losing his life twice in the past week," said Andy Green. "Dr. Tyler is the new head doctor at St. Luke's. He saved Jack's life both times so, when he asked me if he could talk to you a few minutes tonight at the start of the meeting, I told him he could. Go ahead, Doctor."

"I believe a lot of you are suffering from the same trouble that came near to killing Jack Aiken," said Jud. "You call it Monday Morning Asthma and I call it byssinosis—the medical name for the disease. But whatever you call it, the trouble is a gradual involvement of your lungs from the cotton dust you inhale all the time while you're at work, particularly those of you whose jobs keep you around the carding machines."

"How come it only bothers us on Mondays, Doctor?" a burly man with a barrel chest asked.

"Byssinosis isn't simply an accumulation of dust in the lungs, the way coal miners or people in rock quarries get what we call silicosis," Jud explained. "Cotton dust sets up an irritation in the lungs that tends to shut down the small air passages. You become sensitive to it too, just like some people have asthma from ragweed or goldenrod. That's why, when you've been out of the mill and away from the dust over the weekend, it hits you so hard on Monday morning when you start back to work."

"Seems like there's more of it lately, even though the mill's been air-conditioned," said another man. "Why would that be, Doctor?"

"Air conditioning and new filters make it a lot easier for you to breathe as long as the cards are run at the same speed that they were before the new protection devices were put in. But high-speed cards put out more dust, so one usually tends to cancel out the other. Another reason for the increase in byssinosis is that mechanical cotton pickers often mix parts of the hulls from the cotton bolls in with the fibers—"

"You can say that again," said the burly man who had asked the first question.

"Unfortunately the bracts—that's what the pieces of boll husks are called—contain a substance that triggers asthma-like attacks in people who are liable to them."

"So what can be done?" the same man asked.

"We'll talk about protective measures later," said Jud. "Right now, I want to show some of you what cotton dust has already done to your lungs. We're ready for volunteers."

When there were no immediate takers, he had an inspiration.

"I'm going to ask my nurse to take a spirometer test, so you men can see how it operates," he announced. "Do you mind, Miss Galloway?"

"Not at all," she said, although he hadn't mentioned it to her before.

Obeying his instructions, she inhaled deeply and blew into the mouthpiece, while the recording strip was drawn across the top of the machine and the pen marked a curve showing the Forced Expiratory Volume. Between the tests—which were excellent—she dried the filter paper with her hair dryer and, when both runs were completed, held them up to show the audience the curves that had been recorded. Then Jud handed the sheets to the man on the end of the first row so they could be passed around, while Kathryn was attaching a fresh paper mouthpiece to the hose.

"The important part of this test is the amount of air blown out in the first second," Jud explained. "In long-standing cases of byssinosis, the first second of what we call the Forced Expiratory Volume is sharply diminished, indicating the decrease in lung function."

As he finished speaking, Jud noticed that Horace Fellowes was standing at the back and was seized by a sudden inspiration.

"Perhaps Mr. Fellowes would be willing to take a spirometer test," he said. "We need a normal male reading to compare with the normal reading for a woman, which Miss Galloway has just given us."

While Horace Fellowes was making his way to the front of the room, the test sheets Kathryn had made were passed around. When they came to the burly man who had done most of the questioning, he looked at them and whistled with admiration.

"With them lungs she's got, it's a wonder she didn't bust the machine," he said, and a wave of laughter went over the room.

Jud introduced Horace to Kathryn Galloway, then showed him how to use the mouthpiece and conduct the test. Fellowes eyed the machine a bit warily but nevertheless took a deep breath, placed the mouthpiece in his mouth, held his nose, and blew mightily into it.

As the pen drew an impressive-looking curve upon the moving sheet, Jud saw that he had been right in assuming that an athlete like Fellowes would give an excellent test. The second curve was like the first and he removed the sheet from the machine, made the necessary calculations, and started passing them around.

"I think you can see that both Miss Galloway and Mr. Fellowes have an excellent output of air during the first second of the test," he told the audience. "Now we would like to have a volunteer from among you."

"How about you, sir?" he asked, when there was no immediate response, directing the question to the burly man who had questioned him earlier.

The man stood up and shambled forward. Jud had chosen him for two reasons: first, because, barrel-chested as he was, he might have emphysema, which would cause the test to show up poorly; and second, because, if he did have byssinosis, it would be a prime example of the dangers of the disease to an otherwise healthy-looking individual.

While Kathryn recorded the big man's name—James Baker—his address, age, and other personal data, Jud put a new mouthpiece on the end of the breathing tube and showed him how to use it.

"Where do you work in the mill, Mr. Baker?" he asked.

"I'm a spinner—used to be a carder."

"Why did you change?"

"My doctor said I was coughing too much. He made me stop smoking and that helped. But, when I noticed how the men in the cardroom were coughing all the time, I thought I'd better move."

"You may have saved your life," Jud assured him. "Ready?"

"Okay, Doc. I'll blow that thing off the table."

Horace Fellowes had started back to his place in the rear.

"I think you'll be interested to watch some of these tests, Mr. Fellowes," Jud called to him. "You can tell Mr. Wright about them later."

Fellowes came back to stand by the table, while Baker inflated his lungs for the first blow. Watching the pen describe a curve on the moving record slip, Jud knew he had made a wise choice in selecting Baker as the first example although, when Baker had said he was a spinner, the least affected by byssinosis, he had been afraid momentarily that the test might be useless. Now, he saw that there was a marked falling off of Baker's FEV in the first second of the test run, an abnormality that was repeated in the second run.

After making the calculations, Jud handed the test paper to Baker who studied it with growing concern; the difference between it and the other two was obvious, even to one unversed in medicine.

"Guess I didn't do so hot, eh Doc?" he said finally.

"Your lung function has been reduced about half," Jud told him. "Do you still have Monday Morning Asthma?"

"Not much since I changed to the spinning machines. But when I get a cold, it always settles in my chest."

Jud handed the test report to Horace Fellowes. "You can see the marked reduction of expiratory volume in the first second, and the total volume is reduced by half. Both are diagnostic for byssinosis."

Fellowes looked up from the sheet. "Baker's obviously got emphysema too—look at that chest on him. Do you think picking him as the first example was exactly cricket?"

"Suppose you choose a carder whose chest is normal in size," Jud challenged. "We'll see what the next chest shows."

Fellowes' eyes ranged over the crowd. "Sharkley," he called. "Do you mind taking the test?"

A slender, almost emaciated man in the second row looked startled when his name was called. But as those around him began to jeer when he hesitated, he finally rose from his seat and came forward.

"See what you can do with this one." Horace Fellowes challenged Jud *sotto voce*.

Jud wasn't too happy with Fellowes' choice either, until he asked the crucial question. "How often do you have Monday Morning Asthma, Mr. Sharkley?"

"Practically every week," was the answer. "Some days I have to leave the machine for a while before I can even get my breath."

"Looks like you backed the wrong horse," Jud told Horace Fellowes. "But just so you can't claim foul, I'll let Miss Galloway run this test alone."

Kathryn had learned the technique by now and the two blows were executed as faultlessly as if Jud had been supervising them himself. At the end, he showed Fellowes how to make the calculations from the table printed on the lid of the spirometer and stood by while they were being completed.

"Sixty per cent reduction of volume," Fellowes reported, and now his voice was sober. "Do you smoke, Sharkley?"

"Not any more, Mr. Fellowes. I quit because of the asthma."

"Convinced?" Jud asked the mill's vice president.

"It looks like you've got a pat hand," Horace Fellowes conceded. Then he did something Jud hadn't expected, but which elevated the other man considerably in his opinion.

"Men," he said, addressing the audience, "I'll admit I wasn't convinced that Dr. Tyler was right in his contention that our machines are damaging your bodies, but the early evidence is certainly impressive. I'm not going to tell you to take this test; that's not within the province of management. But I advise you strongly to take it, and if the results continue to show what they've demonstrated so far, I promise to go to Mr. Wright personally and request that additional filters be placed on the carding machines to cut down the amount of dust those of you who must work over them will be breathing into your lungs."

"That took a bit of courage," Jud said as the first of the men began to move forward for the FEV test. "Putting those filters in would cost the mills a lot of money."

"And a lot more if you initiate a test case for byssinosis and win it," said Horace Fellowes. "In case you didn't recognize it, I was raising your bet in the hope of forcing you out of the game."

II

The spirometer tests continued smoothly during the next hour and a half. When they were finished, the results were beyond argument: at least half the men, most of them carders, had lungs which were already seriously crippled by the daily intake of cotton dust, as evidenced by the sharp reduction in the first second of the Forced Expiratory Volume.

"Convinced?" Jud asked Horace Fellowes, who had stood by and watched every test being run.

"No question about it," the engineer admitted. "Will you give me the test sheets so I can have them Xeroxed? I'll send the originals back to you in the morning."

"Take them by all means." Though he'd lost the records of lead poisoning in the Brown children, when their hospital laboratory reports had been stolen, no doubt by Asa Ford, Jud was sure he need not have the same doubts with Horace Fellowes.

"Do you feel like joining Miss Galloway and me for a late supper?" Jud asked the mill superintendent.

"Give me a rain check," said Fellowes. "I want to show these to Seth Wright tonight before some stooge among the workers gives him another version of what happened here."

"By the way," said Jud casually. "I've asked Miss Galloway to marry me."

Horace Fellowes' startled look showed that the meaning of Jud's words had reached him. "Congratulations," he said.

"She hasn't accepted me—yet," said Jud. "But, thanks for coming tonight. I think you came to scoff but I'm glad you remained to pray."

Andy Green called the regular meeting to order again while Jud and Kathryn were packing up their equipment preparatory to leaving. But the effect of the revelation by the tests that more than half the men present had already been seriously damaged physically by the industrial hazard of cotton dust proved to be more than Jud had even hoped for.

"Mr. Chairman," said James Baker as soon as the meeting opened.

"I'd like to make a motion before Dr. Tyler and his assistant leave."

"You have the floor, Jim."

"I move that this union go on record as demanding that Framingham Mills proceed immediately to install the best filters available on the carding machines to protect us from the dust."

A chorus of seconds sounded.

"But you have Mr. Fellowes' word that he will take it up with Mr. Wright," Green protested.

"I've known Seth Wright ever since my father used to bring me to the mills to watch the machines run," said Baker. "He's not going to give up without a fight, but if we pass the resolution tonight demanding the protection we should have had a long time ago, it will strengthen Mr. Fellowes' hand."

"Question! Question!" Several people called, and Green had no choice except to put the motion to a vote, with a resounding chorus of 'Ayes.'"

"The motion is carried," Green conceded. "A resolution will be sent to Mr. Wright in the morning."

III

"Well, you won another battle," said Kathryn. They were sitting in the small brightly lit restaurant over scrambled eggs, sausage, toast and coffee. "How does it feel to win them all?"

"I could name one I haven't won yet—you."

She reached across the table and squeezed his hand. "Don't push me, Jud. I've been in love before, maybe more than I am with you at this moment."

"That isn't very complimentary."

"First love is always more intense for a woman than any other; I suppose because she hasn't learned yet how badly she can be hurt by someone she loves."

"Surely you don't think—"

"You're practically perfect, darling, so perfect it scares me sometimes. No woman could really measure up to you without occasionally feeling inferior."

"But—"

"I've seen this happen too often with people younger than we are. They marry before the boy finishes his education and she starts working to help support him. But she's in one world and he's in another, so they move on an entirely different level. The two don't have time to explore and understand each other and they drift apart gradually. One of the biggest jobs psychiatrists in medical schools have is counseling unhappy wives of medical students, residents, and even the faculty—if things haven't gone too far before the girl comes to counseling—"

"It should be a dual approach."

"It should be, but it rarely is. Everything in a doctor's education and training is geared toward making him able to assume authority and the further he goes, the more responsibility he has to take."

"Psychologists agree that no more authoritarian figures exist in society than doctors," Jud admitted. "But medical marriages do work—particularly at our age."

"I'm not arguing that. What scares me is the high divorce rate among medical families and even more, the separations. I don't want that to happen to me again, Jud."

"But you didn't marry the guy."

"We were going to be married—until he saw a chance to get a head start on a profitable partnership. I know nothing like that would ever happen with you, but if I keep on feeling about you the way I do, and something did happen to break us up, I'm afraid I'd become the sort of nurse you find in a lot of hospitals. She's known everywhere as a good scout and a good lay—you've seen the type, everybody has who works around a big hospital very long. The trouble is that she starts having affairs with younger and younger men as she grows older, until one day she's left high and dry."

"So where does that leave us?"

"Right where we are—for the time being. Unless those terms don't suit you."

"I want you on any terms, Kathryn," he said, and she reached over to squeeze his hand with a smile.

"Just for that, I'll let you stay awhile after we get home, even though tomorrow is another working day," she promised. "After all, we do have a victory to celebrate."

It was misty but warm when Jud came out of Kathryn's apartment house on the brightly lit thoroughfare of Ventura Boulevard shortly after three the next morning. She had insisted that he take a parasol—with her car in the adjoining garage, she wouldn't need its protection in getting to the hospital the next morning. Now, as he walked along the brightly lit boulevard, he suspected that anyone seeing him could easily deduce the circumstances of the past several hours. The gay parasol, so out of keeping for a man who also carried a cane, the warm light of satisfaction still glowing in his eyes at the way his body had responded without prompting or hesitation to the lure of her flesh against his own, all of it bespoke the lover who had just quit the arms of his beloved.

But then, the dark windows of the closed wards of St. Luke's visible across the street, as he waited on the corner for the lights to change in front of the entrance, the reality of the grime-covered walls, the pollutant stained-glass panes in the windows, even the faint glow of the light with one bulb missing above the entrance in the mist, reminded him that, although he had come far in the something like two weeks he had been at St. Luke's, much further indeed remained to be traveled if Chuck Rogers' dream for the hospital were to be realized.

What he could not foresee, however, was the speed at which the climactic series of events set in motion that evening by his testing the lungs of the workers at Framingham Mills would develop.

CHAPTER XX

The first knowledge Jud had of any repercussions, following his meeting with the company union of Framingham Mills the night before, was when Samantha came into his office the next morning.

"Where have you been keeping yourself?" he asked.

"On Pediatrics Receiving—helping Chuck Rogers bring the records up to date on the blood specimens from those lead poisoning cases," she said wearily. Then some of the old fire showed for a moment. "What were you and that you-know-in-white you've been shacking up with doing last night? Laying land mines?"

"We ran some spirometer tests on members of the company union at your father's plant. By the way, your ex was there—"

"I know. He called me just now."

"Horace is a pretty nice guy."

"With no job."

192

"What?"

"Dad fired him—and all because of you."

"Does Horace blame me?"

"No. He's even come to admire you—since you wouldn't let me seduce you."

"Doesn't that prove he still loves you?"

"Oh, he loves me all right; I've known that all along. But he needed taking down a peg or two."

"Now that it's happened, you two ought to get back together again."

"That's what Horace called about. Dad fired him because he threatened to resign if filters weren't put on the machines in the mills to protect the workers. Horace's idea is for us to take a plane to the Caribbean or somewhere on a second honeymoon while Dad comes to his senses."

"With or without another marriage certificate?"

"With—of course. Horace is the epitome of propriety; he even wears trunks under his kilts, when he goes to the Highland celebration at King's Mountain every year."

"Aren't you going to take him up on the proposition?"

"I'd like nothing better—especially after a grubby day here. But Horace doesn't know my father the way I do. Dad's too stubborn to give in, even when he knows he's wrong—which he'll never admit anyway."

"At least this crisis has brought you and your husband together again—if you're willing to admit that you'd like to go away with him."

"*You* brought us together again by making me see that somebody needs me."

"So what are you going to do?"

"I'd hate to see Father destroy the mills. Maybe when he cools down a little, I can talk some sense into him. Amanda told him I was working here and she says he's really proud of me—not that he'll ever admit it."

Samantha stood up and stubbed out the cigarette she'd lit when she sat down by Jud's desk. "Horace and I are having dinner tonight at the Spring Hill Club. I've got to have my hair and nails done as soon as I get off duty and take a shower."

"I still think you should take him up on that second honeymoon offer. It might do your father a lot of good to see that the old ways are dead."

She shook her head. "Facing the fact that he's wrong isn't going to be easy for him. If I'm around, I might be able to soften the blow, like I did when he was sure he was going to die after the heart attack."

When Samantha was gone, Jud rang the operator and asked her to page Amanda Cates.

"Miss Cates didn't come on duty this afternoon, Dr. Tyler," said the switchboard operator. "She said Mr. Wright needed her and asked the superintendent of nurses to get someone to relieve her."

"Do you know where Mr. Rogers is?"

"No, Doctor. He hasn't been in since lunchtime."

"Try the laboratory at the County Medical Center. He might be there."

A call to the County didn't turn up Chuck Rogers there either and Jud hung up. But almost immediately the telephone rang; this time it was Joe Morgan.

"What sort of a hornet's nest did you stir up last night at Framingham Mills?" the lawyer asked.

"We did some tests for byssinosis on the members of the union. Half the men there have lungs that are already severely damaged. Why?"

"Our firm handles Seth Wright's legal work. He called from the plant today and talked to my grandfather; they're old cronies. Did you know he fired Horace Fellowes?"

"Samantha told me that a few minutes ago."

"He's also going to fire every man that voted last night to demand new dust filters on the carding machines. Was that your idea?"

"The men voted it themselves after Horace left," said Jud. "All I did was give him the test sheets we ran so he could show them to Mr. Wright."

"He showed them all right—and the names on the sheets too. I talked to Horace a little while ago and he says the old man kept the sheets overnight, saying he wanted to study them. But this morning he fired Horace first and then ordered every man whose name was on one of those test sheets locked out of the plant. Some of them in the middle of the day's work too."

"The old bastard! Doesn't he know he can't do that?"

"Grandfather called my father in and the two of them tried

to sell old Seth on the fact that the NLRB wouldn't stand for it. But he's so stubborn, he wouldn't listen to reason."

"Samantha said the same thing."

"Seth even threatened to get another firm to represent him. Said he was going to fire the whole union and hire blacks and Chicanos."

"That would light the fuse of the powder keg this town has been sitting on for a long time," said Jud. "Can he be stopped?"

"The union could beat Seth to the draw there by striking," said Morgan. "Then the national headquarters of the AFL-CIO would send down some experienced labor lawyers to pin old Seth's ears back."

"Can he shut down the mill?"

"Maybe. But the government can slap some pretty heavy penalties against him for doing it the way he's doing it."

"I can't ask you to proceed with the hearing on byssinosis before the Industrial Commission, when your firm represents Mr. Wright," said Jud.

"We may not have to do that after all," said Joe Morgan. "The fight has moved into a different arena; Seth Wright saw to that when he fired the men. Oh! Oh! Something's just coming in on the radio. Wait a minute?"

Jud could hear a distant voice in the receiver, but could make out nothing about the details of the newscast. After a moment, Joe Morgan's voice sounded in his ear again.

"It's official," the lawyer reported. "Seth Wright has ordered a lockout of all union members and issued a public call for blacks and Chicanos to man the mill. Now there'll really be hell to pay. Good-by, Jud."

II

About an hour later, Jud was paged while he was finishing the plan he'd been working on for Chuck Rogers to turn St. Luke's into both a community health center and a hospital mainly for the treatment of trauma, both of which would probably be torpedoed now by the reluctance of any national foundation to put money into a community torn by industrial strife.

"I suppose you've heard what's been happening?" The voice on the phone was Chuck's; he sounded tired and tense.

"I should, since I seem to have started it."

"Don't blame yourself, Jud. Things have been coming to a

195

head for a long time; you only put the lance to the boil last night and let the poison erupt."

"Anything I can do?"

"A group of us are going to Seth Wright's house to beard the old lion in his den and try to get this matter settled," said Chuck. "Can you join us?"

"Of course. But I'm sure he doesn't have a very high opinion of me."

"The same goes for me, but I've got to do what I can. Eric is with me and Samantha can call for you there in a half hour. I'll call her."

"What about Horace?"

"He'll be there too. I only hope we can pound some sense into the old man's head."

Samantha picked Jud up in the Alfa Romeo at the ambulance entrance. Her hair was still damp and she wore a frilly cap to cover it.

"Isn't this some get up to wear when you're trying to lure your husband back to the marital bed?" she said. "I look a fright."

"If he's got any sense, he'll still jump into it," Jud assured her.

"This time things are going to be different. Horace has got to pay more attention to me and less to the mill—if there's any mill left."

"Are you going to be more considerate of him too?"

She wrinkled her nose at him. "Are you telling me to go slow?"

"Only to use your brain; it's a pretty good one, you know."

"I'll try to keep Horace from finding that out," she promised. "This time I'll even wear a nightgown—a very thin one."

The Wright mansion occupied the crest of a rise and, with its lawns and gardens, covered an entire block. The sleek car turned through the gate and along the curving driveway to a stop before the house. Four other cars were already there: one was Chuck Rogers' old Chevy, one a slick Jaguar, and the other a battered MG.

"The Jaguar belongs to Horace." Samantha took off the cap and patted the waves in her hair with the aid of the rearview mirror. "Eric owns the MG."

A grizzled black butler opened the door for them. "They're all in the library, Miss Samantha," he said.

"This is Arthur Redmond, John's brother," said Samantha. "Dr. Tyler, Arthur."

"Good evening, Doctor," said the butler.

Jud was able to see the resemblance now to the hospital's head orderly. "Your brother and I are very good friends," he told the houseman.

"He often speaks of you, Dr. Tyler," said Redmond. "And he prizes your friendship very much."

Jud followed Samantha into the library, a large room paneled in dark oak, with bookcases reaching to the ceiling. Normally a sunny and no doubt delightful room in which either to browse or engage in serious study, it had now taken on something of the air of an armed camp.

Seth Wright, heavy and almost completely bald, looked like a statue of Buddha in a big winged chair, but with none of the benignity of that oriental philosopher. His eyes, almost the only animated portion of his granite-carved face, glowed with anger. And the tortuous pattern of an artery Jud could see pulsating in his left temple betrayed the force of that emotion upon the million-aire's body. He was in shirt sleeves, for the room was warm.

"Hello, Dad." Samantha went to kiss his cheek but Seth Wright didn't betray, by so much as a smile, any sign of affection for his only daughter. "This is Dr. Jud Tyler."

"Damned Communist," Seth Wright snapped.

The charge was so absurd that Jud couldn't help laughing.

"What's so funny?" Wright demanded.

"It's just that I've spent the past several years fighting Communists in Vietnam, Mr. Wright." Jud raised his cane slightly. "This is what they did to me."

"We've been trying to explain to Mr. Wright that, once you discovered what cotton dust had done to Jack Aiken, you had no choice except to show the other workers where the danger lay," said Chuck Rogers.

"In the long run, Framingham Mills will save a lot of money by installing filters rather than by having a succession of damage suits and perhaps even death claims brought against you, Mr. Wright," Jud added. "In fact, I doubt if your insurance carrier will even want to continue your coverage after this."

"We're self-insured," said Horace Fellowes. "Which only makes it worse."

"Please listen to what Dr. Tyler is saying, Dad," Samantha begged. "He's already kept one claim from being brought against you by saving Jack Aiken's life."

"Shut up, Samantha!" Seth Wright's temporal artery throbbed

even more ominously and Jud glanced at Amanda Cates, who was standing beside his chair.

"Remember your blood pressure, Mr. Wright," she said softly. "Dr. Tubman told you to avoid stress."

"Who can avoid stress when your own get turned against you?" Seth Wright growled. "And people you trusted with responsibility betray you?"

Horace Fellowes started to speak—since the thrust had obviously been directed at him—then shrugged and remained silent.

Wright turned to Chuck Rogers and Eric Cates, who were standing together. "You've been training niggers—"

"Mr. Wright!" Amanda's tone was sharp.

"All right, Amanda—blacks. But I don't see any difference." He turned back to Chuck and Eric. "Like I said, you've been training blacks to do skilled jobs in the mills, haven't you?"

"Yes, we have," said Chuck.

"Well, now's your chance to let 'em show how good your training was. I've ordered Jared Heath to hire every one you send to him until the machines are manned again. We can spin thread without a bunch of cowards who are afraid a machine will hurt them."

Chuck looked at Eric and neither responded.

"You've been squawking about equal opportunites for blacks ever since they let you out of the Army, Eric," Wright snapped. "Do your people want the jobs or don't they? I can always bring in more Mexicans."

"We want jobs, Mr. Wright," said Eric quietly. "But we don't want them on these terms—as scabs to help you break a legitimate union whose members are only asking for the protection they're entitled to."

"The National Labor Relations Board wouldn't let you do it anyway, Seth," said Horace Fellowes.

The millowner turned on his former son-in-law fiercely. "When I want advice from you I'll ask for it. You've been fired, so shut up."

"Horace is my husband, Father," Samantha said quietly. "We're going to be married again as soon as this is all over. He has the same rights here as I do."

"I gave him his chance and he turned against me," Seth Wright raged.

"Only because I couldn't stand by and see the lives of at least a fourth of the men who work at the mills endangered any longer," said Horace.

"You didn't worry about that when I hired you."

"I didn't know about it then."

"And you took the word of a Communist doctor—"

"Before I brought those test reports to you last night, I went over every one of them with Dr. Tubman," said Horace. "If it comes to a suit, Dr. Tubman will have to testify in court that half the men tested last night already have byssinosis and the rest are in grave danger of getting it if they work longer without protection."

"There are other doctors," said Seth Wright stubbornly.

"When Tubman is subpoenaed as an expert witness, he'll give the names of a team of experts at Yale University who have done more work on this disease than everybody else in the world put together," said Horace. "You're licked, Seth, and you might as well admit it."

Jud would have stopped Horace, if he could, before the last sentence. But it was out now and his immediate concern was for the man to whom the words had been directed—in this case as a doctor.

Seth Wright had half risen in his chair at Horace Fellowes' words, his faced suffused with rage while the artery at his temple threatened to burst through the skin. Then he collapsed suddenly and his right hand went to his chest, pressing over the heart.

Realizing what was happening, Jud took a step forward as Amanda moved quickly from behind the chair to pick up the left wrist of the millowner, whose face was now contorted with agony.

"Do you have any amyl nitrite ampoules?" Jud asked Amanda.

She nodded and he took Seth Wright's wrist himself, while she went to get the medication. The pulse was full and bounding, confirming the pattern of threatened apoplexy indicated by the tortuous throbbing artery at his temple.

Amanda was back in a moment with a small fiber-covered ampoule and a bottle of tiny tablets which Jud judged to be nitroglycerin, the standby relief for all sufferers from angina pectoris. At his nod, she held the ampoule beneath Seth Wright's nostrils and crushed the glass within its fiber protective covering, releasing the potent vapor.

The millionaire gasped as it struck his nostrils and instinctively turned his head but she held the ampoule in place beneath his nose, forcing him to inhale the blood pressure reducing drug. With his fingers upon Seth Wright's pulse, Jud could feel the volume decrease as the drug took effect, sure evidence that the spasm of the arteries which had shot up the pressure, endangering not only his heart but also his brain, was being alleviated.

"Do you have a sphygmomanometer?" Jud asked Amanda Cates.

"Dr. Tubman ordered one so I could check his pressure every day," she said. "I'll get it. Shall I give him a nitroglycerin tablet too?"

"Let me check the pressure first," said Jud. "We don't want to drop it too fast."

Seth Wright made no objection as Amanda expertly rolled up his shirt sleeve and applied the blood pressure cuff. But when Jud started to take the pressure, he drew his arm aside.

"You take it," he told Amanda. "I don't want *him*."

Samantha started to object, but Jud shook his head at her and moved back beside Chuck and Eric Cates. Amanda took the pressure expertly but left the cuff in place on Seth Wright's arm so it could be taken again at intervals.

"One-ninety over a hundred," she reported. "It dropped ten points while I was taking it."

"What's it been running?" Jud asked.

"About one-sixty to eighty. The diastolic has been stabilized at around a hundred."

"I'm all right." Seth Wright straightened up in his chair, his pain relieved by the effect of the drug he had inhaled. "Damned doctors!"

"You might at least thank Dr. Tyler for being concerned, Father," Samantha said sharply.

"He can send me a bill," said Wright. "Now get out of here all of you—except Amanda. Let me run my business the way I want to run it."

"Mr. Wright—" Eric started to speak but the millowner cut him off.

"You had your chance, Eric—I promised your mother I'd give it to you. Now get out and leave Amanda and me alone."

"I think you'd better lie down, Mr. Wright," the nurse said firmly. "I'll call Dr. Tubman and ask him to stop by to see you."

"Don't need any more damned doctors," Seth Wright grumbled, but he did not object when Amanda helped him from the chair and from the room.

Those left in the library looked at each other like people who have just been through a tornado and are still struck dumb with wonder that any of them are alive. Samantha was the first to speak.

"Was he really in danger just now, Jud?" she asked.

"I think so. To drop to one-ninety after inhaling an ampoule of amyl nitrite, his pressure must have been well above two hundred when he was so angry."

"What's the danger?" Horace Fellowes asked. "A heart attack?"

"Angina is a warning signal that spasm of the coronary arteries is jeopardizing the circulation of the heart," said Jud. "But the same applies to practically all arteries in the body, particularly the brain."

"And this drug—what was it?"

"Amyl nitrite. It's only an emergency measure that can be inhaled and acts immediately to dilate the arteries. A nitroglycerin tablet under the tongue gives very much the same effect but goes into the body a little more slowly. Judging from the looks of that artery in Mr. Wright's temple, I'd say the greatest danger just now is rupture of an artery in the brain—in other words an apoplectic stroke."

"You probably saved his life this time," said Chuck.

"So where does that leave us?" Eric Cates asked.

"In serious trouble," said Horace. "Seth has already fired the union members and ordered Jared Heath to hire all the blacks and Chicanos he can to keep the mill running."

"Could Heath be persuaded to revoke the order?" Jud asked.

"Revoke?" Horace's laugh was more of a bark. "This is just what Jared has been waiting for, a chance to provoke a confrontation between whites and blacks in Framingham. His kind would love to see the sort of situation here that practically wrecked Birmingham some years ago."

"But surely he must realize that nobody really gains—"

"Jared was assistant superintendent when I was brought in and has hated my guts ever since," Horace explained. "Now that he's the super, he'll do his best to tear down everything I've managed to accomplish."

"When your people are offered the jobs you've been fighting for them to get, Eric," said Jud, "will they still hold off?"

"I don't know, but I think I'd better start finding out." Eric's voice was sober. "If Heath tries to run the mill with what blacks and Chicanos he can talk into taking jobs, there's going to be hell to pay."

"I was in favor of letting Seth stew in the mess he cooked up for a while," said Horace thoughtfully. "But this thing has become too explosive now to be left to chance."

"What else can you leave it to?" Samantha was looking at her ex-husband as if she were seeing him for the first time—and liking what she saw.

"Seth had no legal grounds for laying off the union, so the members can move for an injunction to close the mill."

"At least that would give things time to cool off," Chuck agreed.

. "Even Jared Heath couldn't go against a court order from a federal judge shutting down the mill," said Horace. "If we can establish that this is a case for the NLRB, the government will handle it for us and we'll get action a lot more quickly. Keep enough of your people from taking jobs to man the eleven-to-seven shift, Eric, and I may be able to head off trouble. Coming, Samantha?"

"I'll stay here," she said. "If Dad gets scared enough, he'll need me—and I want to be available."

CHAPTER XXI

Kathryn Galloway had come on duty at seven to fill in for Amanda Cates in the evening hours, when the Emergency Room was often most active. Jud had missed dinner in the hospital cafeteria because of the conference at the Wright mansion. After they finished patching up four teen-agers, injured when two sports cars engaged in a drag race on Ventura Boulevard with the inevitable conclusion—she fixed some sandwiches for him at a table in a corner of the empty cafeteria.

"The six o'clock news said there's liable to be a crisis in the next twenty-four hours if Framingham Mills tries to operate with black workers and Chicanos," she reported.

"I guess we stirred up a real hornet's nest at the union meeting last night."

"But the workers themselves voted to present Mr. Wright with the ultimatum."

"They wouldn't have, if I hadn't proved that most of them have byssinosis."

"We proved that. I was there too."

"I was the eager beaver who decided to run the tests in the first place. You can't be blamed."

"How many lives will be shortened, if the men go back to work without some change in the machines to protect them?" she asked.

"All whose tests were positive."

"So you were only doing your duty as a doctor in discovering the danger to them. Have you ever stopped to consider what you've accomplished in the few weeks you've been here?"

"I'm afraid there hasn't been time."

"Item One: you knocked Asa Ford out of a comfortable niche, where he had been able to steal thousands of dollars from the people of Framingham. Item Two. you revolutionized the operation of this hospital and gave the people who work here reason to be proud of it. Item Three: you showed how thousands of children in Framingham are being poisoned because they've got Scrooges for landlords."

"I haven't corrected that yet."

"You will. Item Four: you've identified an industrial hazard—"

"Your friend Tubman did that."

"Dick had been here over two years and wasn't doing anything about it until you came, so he can't take any of the credit. Item Five: you've got Horace and Samantha Fellowes back together and taught her what responsibility means."

"Yet I can't persuade you to marry me."

She smiled. "Rome wasn't built in a day either—or a night. Item Six: you put together a plan to save St. Luke's—"

"That will probably fail if the city explodes the way it well may." Jud started to pick up his coffee cup with his right hand, then unconsciously shifted to the left, as he'd taught himself to do during the long months of his recovery.

"Why not the right hand?" she asked. "Are you still afraid to use it?"

"Is that what you think?" He put the cup back on the saucer.

"Aren't you?" she challenged. "Fear crippled you once before, until you conquered it."

"*You* conquered that."

"You already know I'm a shameless hussy, so I can admit that I was as anxious for that experiment to turn out well as you were." Her eyes took on a warm light where before there had been only challenge. "This brings me to Item Seven: you're a perfect lover."

"All of which should make me a perfect husband."

"Except for one thing—the right hand. I could marry a man who wasn't afraid to help himself, Jud, but not one who lets fear of failure make him a cripple."

Challenged, he reached for the coffee cup with his right hand and felt the old familiar tension of fear start to grow within him. He could almost sense the strength of the impulses building up in the nerve tissue between the damaged portion of his brain and the muscles of his hand, battering themselves futilely against barriers that had held them back from normal functioning for so long. And so, when his fingers finally moved to touch the handle of the cup, they fumbled and sent it clattering to the floor, spilling the coffee in a brown puddle upon the freshly waxed linoleum tile.

"Darling! What have I done?" Kathryn seized his hands in hers, pressing them against her face, and he felt the warm flood of her tears upon his fingers. "I'll marry you, whether you can use your right hand or not."

"No, Darling; you're right," Jud said gently. "I could never come to you as less than a whole man; it wouldn't be fair to you—or to me."

II

The hospital was quiet when Jud switched on the small portable TV set in his bedroom and stretched out in the lounge chair to look at the late news. As he had expected, it was filled with accounts of the day's dramatic happening at Framingham Mills.

"The government has been asked to intervene in the impasse between Seth Wright, owner of Framingham Mills, the county's largest textile complex, and the company union," said the news reporter. "This afternoon, Horace Fellowes, ex-son-in-law of Mr.

204

Wright and former Executive Vice President of the textile manufacturing corporation, petitioned Judge Harold Cantor for a stay order preventing Mr. Wright from locking the workers out of the mill, following the ultimatum issued to them by him. This same group, viewers will remember, last evening took part in tests designed to determine the incidence of a new industrial hazard. The disease called byssinosis, according to Dr. Judson Tyler, the controversial new director of St. Luke's Hospital, causes serious lung damage in workers not properly protected from inhaling cotton dust while working in the mill."

A picture of Horace and a tall man with glasses appeared on the screen, leaving the downtown Federal Building. Even before they announced a continuance, Jud knew Horace had failed in his initial attempt to forestall disaster.

"Judge Cantor has taken the plea for a stop order under advisement and promises a decision within three days," the reporter continued.

"During which everything can explode," Jud muttered to himself.

The picture changed to the millyard of the textile plant. As on the occasion when Jud had visited it, in company with Samantha, the floodlights were on and the building was surrounded by armed guards.

"Meanwhile Jared Heath, appointed mill superintendent when Horace Fellowes was summarily fired along with other mill employees involved in the controversy, has announced that Framingham Mills will continue to operate under Mr. Wright's personal direction. Mr. Heath is seen here conferring with Reverend Charles Rogers, who seeks to act as mediator in the rapidly boiling dispute, and with Eric Cates, a leader of the black community who is trying to keep blacks and Mexican-Americans from accepting employment in the mill until the controversy is settled."

Chuck and Eric were seen arguing with Jared Heath, a spare, hard-faced man whose unyielding expression showed that he was not being affected by what they were saying.

"Meanwhile, a new element was added late this afternoon," the newscaster continued. "A faction of blacks headed by Al Porter, who claims to lead the militant organization in Framingham, has joined forces with Carlos Enriquez, a leader of the Mexican-Americans, to promise Framingham Mills a full supply of workers from the ranks of the new group. A confrontation is expected tomorrow if the mill management continues to lock out the union and the Porter-Enriquez faction attempts to take the place of union members at the machines."

Once again, the picture switched, this time to the Wright mansion upon its knoll overlooking the city.

"According to Mr. Seth Wright's physician, Dr. Richard Tubman, the millowner is ill and cannot receive reporters. Meanwhile, city officials are concerned over the fast-breaking development but admit they are powerless to intervene."

Jud switched off the TV and got into bed, but it was a long time before he slept. And when he did, he was no nearer solving the complex problem brought to a boil by his attempt, as a doctor, to protect men who were slowly being destroyed by a killer whose existence they had not even suspected before.

III

Nothing had really changed, Jud saw, when he switched on the TV for the early morning news, while shaving in the bathroom of his small suite. Seen reflected in the mirror, the events taking place upon the screen were distant and unreal, but no less a threat to his and Chuck's plan for St. Luke's, as well as the community as a whole, than they had been the night before.

Dr. Wiley was in his basement office when Jud sought him out a little after nine. The pathologist's dramatic eyebrows rose in a gesture of unbelief.

"No scars?" he asked. "After the statement Seth Wright gave the press yesterday about you, I expected to see your head bloody, if unbowed."

"It's bowed a little, even if it doesn't show," Jud admitted. "How are the lead poisoning determinations coming along?"

"Running quantitative blood levels is a lot more trouble than just looking at a few hairs with the spectrophotometer," said the pathologist. "Theoretically, a child shouldn't have any lead in his body at all, but we're using an arbitrary cutoff level of twelve, which rules out some with borderline poisoning."

"Will Joe still have enough to make a case?"

"More than enough, I would guess," said Wiley. "We've already confirmed the Washington, D.C., survey finding that, of all the abnormal conditions turned up in a ghetto district, lead poisoning is exceeded only by general malnutrition."

"That's a hell of a comment on the public's concern for its children's health."

"If we had a couple of germanium-lithium detectors, we could go around checking the plaster right on the walls of houses to show how much lead they contain. But those things cost about four thousand dollars each and the City Fathers would rather spend that on police dogs to help control the kind of riots we'll have if the landlords aren't made to keep lead away from small children. Has Joe Morgan been in touch with you?"

"There was a note to call him at the office when I got in from Seth Wright's yesterday afternoon," said Jud. "But he'd already left and I couldn't reach him at his apartment. I'm going to call him this morning. Do you have any idea what he wanted to talk to me about?"

"Angus Claiborne and Farleigh Grossett have started evicting tenants who let blood samples be taken from their children. Joe's about ready to lower the boom."

"With local Health Department inspectors?"

"Not a chance. Angus has too much muscle at City Hall, with Dexter Johns running for Mayor and everybody there wondering whether they'll keep their jobs if he's elected."

"How's Joe going to do it then?"

"He discovered that Angus and Farleigh borrowed some money on an FHA loan a few years ago, one of those very low-interest long-term things the government offered for renovating old tenement buildings. The money was supposed to replaster ghetto houses in Irontown but from the looks of a lot of the walls, all it lined was the pockets of the owners. Joe thinks he's got enough on Claiborne and Grossett to hail them into Federal Court, using the lead survey as grounds. I imagine that's what he wanted to tell you."

"Have you seen Chuck since yesterday?" Jud asked.

"He was in the dining room earlier for breakfast—on the run as usual. I think he was going out into Irontown to try and shore up Eric Cates a little."

"In keeping his people from taking jobs as strikebreakers, I suppose?"

"More like keeping Eric himself from going over to the enemy," said the pathologist.

"But that's unbelievable."

"Maybe—but Chuck is very close to Eric and I know he's

not entirely convinced that Eric won't weaken, if it looks like his following is about to desert him."

"Did Chuck say that was likely to happen?"

"No. But things are moving so rapidly toward a showdown between Eric and the militant faction led by Al Porter, that nobody can be sure one minute just what's going to happen the next."

IV

Oppressed with the sense of futility at his own ability to do anything to lessen the tragic potentialities of the swiftly moving sequence of events he had unwittingly set in motion at Framingham Mills the night he had run the spirometer tests, Jud started making ward rounds. Even before he reached the cubicle where Jack Aiken was sitting up in bed, listening to the radio while he ate breakfast, he could tell by the suddenly excited voice of the news announcer that something dramatic had happened.

"Hear about Mr. Wright, Doctor?" Aiken asked.

"No."

"The radio says he had a stroke about an hour ago and isn't expected to live. An ambulance took him to Provident Hospital."

Jud turned and hurried back to the chartroom, where Kathryn Galloway was checking the narcotics cabinet.

"Seth Wright has had a stroke," he told her. "The radio says he's dying."

"This could change everything, couldn't it?" she said quickly.

"If things break right, yes. I'm going over to Provident."

"Of course," she said. "We'll page you there if we need you."

"I'm Dr. Tyler," Jud told the receptionist at the hospital across the street. "I'd like to see Mr. and Mrs. Fellowes—they're with Mr. Wright."

"Mr. Wright is in 402, Intensive Care, Doctor. Please go right up."

The elevators at the back of the lobby—there was a bank of two—rose smoothly and swiftly, with none of the clanking and halting progress that characterized those at St. Luke's. Seth Wright's room adjoined a small parlor for visitors and relatives. There, Jud found Samantha, Horace Fellowes, and a distinguished-looking elderly man.

"I came as soon as I heard," he told Samantha.

"Mr. Joseph Morgan, Dr. Tyler," said Samantha, and Jud shook hands with Joe Morgan III's grandfather.

"The radio said Mr. Wright had a stroke," Jud said to Samantha. "When did it happen?"

"This morning. Amanda stayed with Father last night. She said he was restless but he ate breakfast this morning and talked to Jared Heath at the mill on the telephone. Soon afterward, she found him slumped in his chair unconscious."

"Dick Tubman is with him," said Horace. "Here he comes now."

As the internist came out of No. 402, Jud saw Amanda Cates through the partly opened door. She was in uniform, standing beside the bed.

"You can see him now, Mrs. Fellowes," said Tubman. "But he's still unconscious. Morning, Tyler."

"Hello," said Jud. "Has he been conscious at all?"

The internist shook his head. "He's had a massive stroke of the classic type; my guess would be the lenticulostriate artery on the left side. There's left-sided paralysis of the face and right-sided involvement of the body muscles. I've asked Dr. Ditler to see him as soon as he can."

Ditler, Jud knew, was the city's leading neurological surgeon, a man of great experience and impeccable reputation. But with things as Tubman had described them, especially the almost certain rupture of the particular artery most often involved in strokes deep within the brain, it wasn't likely that Ditler would operate. The ultimate prognosis would almost certainly depend on whether the ruptured portion of the blood vessel closed itself off with a clot, allowing the blood which had seeped into brain tissue to be absorbed gradually, or a new leak occurred at the point of rupture, steadily increasing the damage until nearby vital centers were involved and death resulted.

"Do you think he might regain consciousness any time soon?" Horace asked.

"Not likely," said the internist. "And even if he does, he probably wouldn't be able to speak intelligently for some time."

"Everything could go down the drain while Seth's lying there in a coma." Horace Fellowes threw up his hands in a gesture of despair.

"Couldn't you petition the court to declare Mr. Wright incompetent, at least for the moment?" Jud asked the lawyer. "Then the mill could be placed in trusteeship during the crisis."

Joseph Morgan I pursed his lips thoughtfully. "That might be possible," he said. "I must admit that it hadn't occurred to me."

"Then Mr. Fellowes could take charge and rescind the order firing members of the company union," said Jud.

"Mr. Fellowes was discharged by Mr. Wright—"

"But for no good reason. Horace only pointed out to Mr. Wright what I had already proved, that the carding machines in particular are a hazard to the lives of men working in the mills."

"Nevertheless, Doctor, both the mill and the machines are Mr. Wright's property," Joseph Morgan pointed out. "The men had not objected to working on the machines until you came along."

"Only because they were ignorant."

"My grandson tells me that in at least one case a claim such as you have encouraged the workers to make against Mr. Wright was disallowed by the court."

"Only because it was not properly presented," said Jud. "Once the danger of these machines has been established by medical authority, it is as reprehensible for a millowner to leave them without protection as it is for a tenement owner to leave lead paint on the walls of the buildings he rents."

"Do you claim to be such a medical authority, Doctor?" Joseph Morgan's tone was frosty. "I thought you were a surgeon—"

"I'm a doctor, Mr. Morgan, but you don't have to take my word. Dr. Tubman here is an expert in the field of byssinosis. Ask him."

Morgan turned to the internist. "Is this true, Dr. Tubman?"

"Dr. Tyler is correct." Tubman didn't hesitate. "I ordered the spirometer he used in making the tests myself."

"Why didn't you make them then?"

Tubman's shoulders sagged a little. "Because I let myself be bought off by becoming Mr. Wright's family physician. If I'd thought a little more about being a doctor and less about what having the richest man in Framingham as a patient could do for my practice, I would have been there that night running the tests myself."

"Then the carding machines do form a real hazard in your opinion?"

"I can furnish you with a whole library of published reports to prove it," said Tubman. "If you'll excuse me now, I'd better get back to Mr. Wright."

"My grandson admires you very much, Dr. Tyler," said Joseph Morgan I, when Tubman had gone back into room 402.

"The esteem is mutual, sir."

"I should know by now that the eyes of the young see with a

clarity that old fossils like me no longer possess," Morgan admitted. "All I saw was that you had disturbed the status quo in Framingham more than any ten men together have done in my memory. And since I've come to an age when I no longer relish seeing the still waters roiled, I naturally distrusted you. My apology—"

"None is needed, sir. Where human lives are concerned, I suppose I am a bit like a bull in a china shop."

"Mr. Morgan." It was Horace Fellowes. "Do you think there might be a chance that the court would appoint—say, your firm— as a temporary trustee for the mills, as Dr. Tyler has suggested?"

"Possibly," Morgan conceded. "But we know nothing about running a mill."

"Why couldn't you use Mr. Fellowes' knowledge of textile manufacturing?" Jud asked. "Unofficially, of course, if you feel that's best."

"An excellent suggestion, Doctor," said Morgan. "I'll go back to the office and draw up a petition for Judge Myers of the Circuit Court." The lawyer allowed himself to smile. "The fact that he's an old friend of both myself and Seth Wright should have some bearing on the case."

As Joseph Morgan was putting on his hat, a lean man with the bleak features of a pulpit exhorter came in. Jud didn't need to be told this was Jared Heath, acting superintendent of Framingham Mills since yesterday; he recognized the face from the TV picture the night before.

"How's Mr. Wright?" Heath's question was directed at no one in particular.

"Not very good, Jared," said Horace Fellowes. "He's had a stroke, a bad one."

"I heard it on the radio and came right over," said the mill superintendent. "Is Samantha here?"

"She's with her father. Do you know Dr. Tyler?"

"Don't know as I want to," said Heath. "Seein' as how he's the cause of everything that's happened."

Jud didn't reply, judging that nothing was to be gained by antagonizing Heath even more.

"I'm glad you came, Mr. Heath," said Joseph Morgan. "I was going to call you as soon as I got back to my office."

"So?" Jared Heath's expression didn't change; obviously he wasn't inclined to trust people easily.

"My firm has been Mr. Wright's legal advisers for many years."

"I know that, Mr. Morgan."

"We're also trustees under Mr. Wright's will—both for his daughter and for the foundations created by it."

"Mr. Wright ain't dead, is he?"

"He is paralyzed and unconscious. Even if he regains consciousness, Dr. Tubman doesn't believe he will be able to speak for some time."

"I'm sorry to hear that. Mr. Wright was my friend until—" Heath didn't finish the sentence but the look he directed at Horace Fellowes was bitter.

"Obviously this is no time for a crisis at Framingham Mills," Joseph Morgan continued.

"There ain't goin' be no crisis, Mr. Morgan."

"Then you're rehiring the discharged workers?" Horace asked.

"I ain't rehirin' nobody, includin' you," Jared Heath snapped. "Mr. Wright gave me his orders and I'm carryin' 'em out just like he said—until he tells me to stop."

"Where are you going to find workers?" Jud asked.

"If you looked at the newspaper this morning, Doctor, you saw an advertisement inviting anybody that wants to work to apply to the employment office at the mill. The same offer has been broadcast on the radio all morning too."

"Do you know what you're doing, Jared?" Horace Fellowes demanded angrily.

"I'm doin' exactly what Mr. Wright ordered me to do yesterday mornin'—right after he fired you," said Heath. "And if you ask me, *that* was long overdue."

Samantha came back into the room just then. Her eyes were red and, when Horace held out his handkerchief to her, she dried them and moved close to him for support.

"Excuse me, Jared," she said. "When I see Father lying there helpless and remember how strong he was—"

"Don't you worry none, Miss Samantha," said Heath. "Everything at the mill will be run just the way your father wanted it to run."

"Jared has just refused our request to rehire the discharged workers," Horace explained. "He's going to hire anyone who comes to the mill instead."

"But that could mean—"

"There's still a chance that Chuck and Eric Cates can keep

212

things under control," said Jud. "We'll just have to rely on that until Mr. Morgan can act."

"Ain't nothin' Mr. Morgan can do either," said Jared Heath. "Mr. Wright put me in charge and I'm goin' to stay in charge until he stops me."

"You'd really risk destroying the mill just to get back at me, wouldn't you?" Horace Fellowes asked incredulously.

"I'm doin' what I have to do," said Heath stolidly. "Sorry about your Father, Miss Samantha. Me 'n' him always got along fine until Fellowes come along with all of them new ideas that didn't work. If Mr. Wright wakes up, be sure and tell him I was here. I've got to get back to the mill now."

"I know you think you're doing what's right, Jared," said Samantha. "But I'm going to fight you every way I can to save the mill."

Heath left and Horace turned urgently to the lawyer.

"We've got to get the mill out of his hands, Mr. Morgan," he said. "If he brings blacks and Chicanos in to take the place of union members now, there's bound to be trouble."

"We ought to have a decision from Judge Myers this afternoon," Morgan assured him.

"Pray that it comes in time to head off trouble before the eleven-to-seven shift goes to work then," said Horace. "That's when the whole thing could blow apart."

CHAPTER XXII

Since there was nothing else Jud could do, he started to leave, but turned back when a thought struck him.

"Would you stay with your father for a minute, Samantha, and ask Amanda Cates to come out here?" he asked.

"Certainly."

Amanda looked tired and Jud was sure she hadn't slept much in the past twenty-four hours.

"I need to talk to Mr. Rogers and Eric as soon as I can,"

he told her. "Do you have any idea where I could reach them at this time of day?"

"Are you trying to help them convince black people not to take jobs at the mills?"

"Yes."

"Even though you know that means tearing down everything Eric and Mr. Rogers have worked more than a year to accomplish?"

"If Mr. Wright dies, the mill will be run by Mr. Fellowes again. He will see that your people get an equal chance for employment."

"He didn't before."

Horace Fellowes spoke before Jud could reply. "I guess I didn't do a lot of things I should have done, Amanda, which is one of the main reasons why Samantha left me. But Dr. Tyler has shown me the error of my ways and I promise to make it up."

"Eric hangs around Mama Lona's," she said. "He's able to talk to a lot of people that way."

"Mama Lona's?"

"It's a soul food restaurant—on Rutherford Street."

"Thanks," said Jud. "I'll try to catch them there."

Outside the hospital, Jud asked the uniformed doorman to call him a taxi.

"Where to, Doctor?" the doorman asked. "The way things are now, the cab companies always want to know."

"A restaurant," said Jud as the doorman picked up the telephone beside the door and started to dial. "Mama Lona's."

With his finger still in one of the dialing slots, the attendant stopped and hung up the phone.

"I don't think it would be best for you to go there with things like they are, Doctor," he said.

"I have to see Mr. Rogers and Eric Cates immediately," Jud explained. "To head off more trouble than has already occurred."

"No white taxi would take you to Mama Lona's today. I'll call my brother-in-law; he has a private cab in Irontown."

It was nearly ten minutes before a somewhat battered cab with *New Deal* printed on the door in fading letters coughed its way up the circular drive to the marquee in front of the hospital.

"Dr. Tyler wants to go to Mama Lona's to see Mr. Rogers and Eric Cates, Joe," said the doorman. "Can you get him there okay?"

"We'll make it," said the driver. "Things ain't so bad—yet. But jes' wait 'til tonight."

Mama Lona's was located in a battered old building on the

corner of Rutherford and an arterial cross street. Its glass front was clean and the lettering on it was fresh. Inside, a dozen or so blacks were eating but Jud couldn't tell whether the sullen silence that greeted his entry represented hostility or merely curiosity. A plump woman in a light green dress with a turban of the same material wrapped about her head stood behind the cash register.

"I'm looking for Eric Cates and the Reverend Charles Rogers," said Jud. "It's very important."

"You're Dr. Tyler, aren't you?" Mama Lona asked.

"Yes."

"The one that found out about those kids being poisoned?"

"Yes."

"Did you know a lot of people that let their children be tested have been put out of their houses?" The woman's voice was still hostile.

"We expected that to happen," Jud explained.

"Have you and Mr. Morgan figured out what those people are going to do, Doctor?"

"I'm sure Mr. Rogers plans to care for them," said Jud. "And I assure you that nobody else will move into those houses until they are fixed."

Mama Lona nodded. "I guess you found those landlords' weakest spot after all, Doctor—their pocketbooks. The Reverend and Eric are in the back room." She nodded toward a door at the rear of the restaurant. "They're holdin' what you might call a council of war."

When Jud knocked on the door Mama Lona had indicated, Eric Cates opened it. He looked startled, as did Chuck, but let Jud into the room. Besides the two, there was a short, dark Mexican-American, several blacks, and Al Porter.

The latter looked up at Jud and grinned, showing white teeth in his scarred face.

"Where's your nurse, Doc?" he asked. "I didn't know you went out by yourself."

"Shut up, Al," said Eric. "Dr. Tyler has done more for the black people of Framingham in a few weeks than you and I have done in our whole lives."

"How many walls has he scraped and painted in them houses where they found lead?" Al demanded angrily. "You know damned well Whitey ain't gonna do nothin' for us, unless we got a gun at his head. When we take them jobs that's bein' advertised in

215

the paper and on the radio, we're gonna be inside the mill. Then all the pigs in town ain't gonna get us out."

"Why did you come here, Jud?" Chuck Rogers asked.

"I just left the hospital. Seth Wright is critically ill."

"The radio said he had a stroke."

"He did—a severe one," said Jud. "Dr. Tubman says even if he becomes conscious, he won't be able to speak."

"That's fine," said Al Porter. "Now the old man can't change his mind about them jobs. The advertisement said first come first served and that means black or white. Let's stop foolin' around, Eric."

"Are you going to let your people become scabs?" Jud spoke directly to Eric. "You know it can't come to anything else except that."

"Let it come then," said Al Porter. "We're ready for it."

"Shut up, Al." Eric's tone was mild and, when Jud glanced quickly at Chuck Rogers, he saw by the frown on the chaplain's face that he, too, realized Eric was inclined to agree with the considerably more militant attitude taken by Porter.

"What you say is probably true, Doctor," Eric admitted. "But we've gone a long time without jobs on the machines in textile plants where a man can make a decent wage. Now they're being offered to us."

"But only to cause trouble between blacks and whites. Surely you can see that."

"We're ready for it," Al bragged.

"How long do you think those jobs will last if Heath can provoke a race riot?" Jud demanded. "Then everything Mr. Rogers and Eric have accomplished in Framingham would be destroyed."

"Are you accusing Jared Heath of deliberately trying to provoke a riot, Jud?" Chuck Rogers asked.

"What else can you believe? Just now Samantha Fellowes asked Heath to revoke the order firing union members—"

"And do away with our jobs?" Porter demanded ominously.

"I just finished telling you they won't do you any good if the police have to move in," Jud said sharply.

"What did Heath say?" Chuck asked.

"He refused to revoke the order. Which proves what I'm saying."

"You could be right, Doctor." Eric's tone was thoughtful. "Heath is known to be a racist."

"Why not put off any action for a day or two then, until you

216

know what's going to happen to Mr. Wright?" Jud suggested. "A riot now would be a disaster for everybody."

"Specially for the pigs." Al Porter got to his feet and kicked his chair back so hard that it crashed against the wall. "You may be chicken, Eric, but I ain't—and a lot of others are with me."

"Judge Myers is being petitioned to declare Mr. Wright incompetent and put the Morgan law firm in charge of the mill as trustees," said Jud. "If that petition is granted, the Morgan firm will remove Jared Heath and the men who were fired will be hired again."

"You tricky white son-of-a-bitch!" For an instant Jud was sure Al Porter was going to knock him down, until Eric Cates moved up close beside the black man with the scarred angry face.

"Tryin' to talk us into layin' off 'til you can get a court order and leave us out," Porter raged. "Come on, Enrique. You and me and whoever else we can find are gonna sign on for the three o'clock shift at the mill so we can get inside. Then nobody cain't put us out 'til we get what's coming to us. Coming, Eric?"

"Not today, Al." There was no hesitation in Eric Cates' voice now. "If Jared Heath hires you and he's turned out tomorrow, you're going to be turned out with him and all of you are going to look like a bunch of damn fools."

"That's what we get for listenin' to somebody that's half white." Al Porter swaggered from the room, elbowing Jud out of the way and almost knocking him down.

"Let it go, Eric; I'm not hurt," Jud said quickly when Eric started to move, and the young black dropped his hand to his side.

"How much of a following does Porter have?" Jud asked, when the door had closed behind the two militants.

"Not much—until today," said Eric soberly. "He's always accused me of being soft where whites are concerned because Mr. Wright arranged scholarships for Amanda and me. Now with the mill advertising for people to fill jobs and me advising people not to accept, a lot of people are saying he's right."

"They'll still listen to you—and to me," Chuck assured him.

"Maybe," said Eric. "But what troubles me is that Al may be right. Once blacks and Chicanos get into the mills, the management will have a hard time getting them out, especially those we've trained to operate the machines."

"We won't get anywhere sitting here talking," said Chuck. "Eric

217

and I had better keep moving around so we'll be ready to cope with whatever comes up. I'll drop you by the hospital, Jud."

At the hospital, Jud found enough work waiting to keep him busy and was thankful for it. The number of patients in the OPD that morning was sharply less than usual, and the backlog was finished well before Kathryn was ready to go off duty shortly after three.

"Amanda phoned a little while ago to say she was staying on duty with Mr. Wright," she told him, when he met her in the corridor near the door to the hospital parking lot shortly after three. "She must be dead on her feet."

"I doubt that she's slept since sometime yesterday," he agreed.

"She said Samantha wants her there, in case Mr. Wright becomes conscious. Apparently Amanda can do more with him than anybody else."

"Did she say anything about his condition?"

"Only that he seems to be losing ground steadily."

"I thought that would happen from what Tubman said this morning. Did you notice anything different about the patients today?"

"They're scared. These are mostly the women and children and the old. They always worry when there's talk of war—and suffer most when it happens."

"I'm still praying that it can be avoided."

"If it hadn't been for Chuck Rogers and Eric Cates, Framingham would have exploded in a race riot a long time ago," she said. "I heard some of the patients talking while they were waiting and they're convinced now, that it has to come."

"They may be right at that. Jared Heath is doing everything he can to provoke a confrontation between blacks and whites at the mill. He'd like nothing better than to see dogs turned loose on blacks here the way they once were in Birmingham."

II

Joe Morgan III called at five o'clock. "I thought you'd like to know that Judge Myers has just approved grandfather's petition to declare Seth Wright incompetent to handle his own affairs because of a grave illness and appointed our firm as trustees. A copy of the petition and an order naming Horace Fellowes acting superintendent of Framingham Mills will be served on Jared Heath in a few minutes. Horace is going on television during the six o'clock news to ask the workers to return to their old jobs."

"What about the houses in Irontown?"

"As soon as Amos and Farleigh Grossett evict a few more families whose children have lead poisoning, we'll lower the boom with a court order."

"Are you sure you can get one?"

"As sure as grandfather was that he could persuade Judge Myers to co-operate." Joe chuckled. "This is where being an established blue blood helps; there've been Morgan lawyers in Framingham since before the Civil War. I've got to run; it looks like we've got the crisis under control."

But there, as it happened, Joe Morgan was wrong.

CHAPTER XXIII

Horace Fellowes appeared at the beginning of the six o'clock television news. His voice was calm, his manner sober, as he read a prepared statement:

"By order of Judge Myers, control of Framingham Mills during the illness of the owner, Mr. Seth Wright, has been assigned to the legal firm of Morgan, Morgan, Morgan, and Taliaferro, as trustees. The trustees have placed me in full charge of the mill and I am asking all workers to return to their regular shifts, starting with the eleven o'clock shift tonight. I can further assure all Framingham Mill employees that every effort will be made to alleviate the conditions which we learned only a few days ago pose a hazard to the health of workers in the mills. I have just finished talking to the president of a firm in Charlotte, North Carolina, which specializes in the manufacture of protective filters for carding and other textile manufacturing machinery. Their engineer will be here tomorrow to make a survey of Framingham Mills and, as soon as their report is completed, I will meet with the company union to go over the measures which need to be taken."

When the news was over, Jud walked across the street to Provident Hospital. He found Samantha alone in the sitting room adjoining Seth Wright's room.

"I was hoping you'd come," she said. "All this medical mumbo jumbo sort of scares me but I know I can depend on you to make it simple. Did you see Horace on TV?"

"Yes. I thought he did fine."

"I guess you could say Horace always operated before under Dad's shadow—he had to get what he could done and still not set Dad off. But now that he's in charge, he can do what's been needing to be done at the mill for a long time."

"How's your father?"

"Not very good, I'm afraid. Dick Tubman is in there now with Dr. Lewis Ditler. This is the second time Dr. Ditler has seen Dad today but he doesn't offer us any hope from surgery."

Tubman and Dr. Ditler came out of Seth Wright's room about ten minutes after Jud reached the hospital.

"Glad to meet you, Dr. Tyler," said Ditler. "We must have lunch together sometime. I'd be interested to hear more about how you handled brain and nerve injuries in Vietnam."

"I'd like that," said Jud. "Right now I'm busy trying to help Chuck Rogers and Eric Cates keep the mill situation from exploding."

"Mr. Fellowes seems to have it under control," said Ditler confidently.

"For the moment at least."

"You don't sound too optimistic, Dr. Tyler."

"Let's say I'm hopeful."

"Things will work out, as long as Fellowes and the police keep the upper hand." Ditler turned to Samantha. "I'm afraid there's no real change in your father's condition, Mrs. Fellowes. If anything, the degree of paralysis may be increasing."

"Meaning what, Doctor?"

"Probably that the artery where the rupture occurred—that's actually what a stroke is—has not been completely shut off and there's still some leakage."

"Then he's liable to get progressively worse?"

"I'm afraid so," said Ditler. "Though of course, as his blood pressure falls, the degree of hemorrhage tends to decrease."

"I'll be going, Samantha," said Jud after the other doctors had left. "But if you need me, I'll be right across the street."

He was glad to get out of the new hospital and back to the shabbiness and decay of St. Luke's. Ditler's bland confidence that a firm hand by the police would solve all of Framingham's racial and economic problems was infinitely depressing. But then he knew that the same sort of Neanderthal outlook was common in his profession and the greatest barrier to any real progress in solving the problem of making high quality medical care available to all the people.

II

Chuck Rogers was in his cubbyhole of an office in the OPD when Jud returned, drinking coffee from a mug. The chaplain's shoulders drooped and his face was gray with fatigue.

"Did you have any dinner?" Jud asked him.

"I ate something—I don't remember what—at Mama Lona's. You were there."

"That was lunch. I'll have a tray fixed for you."

"No time; I'm meeting Eric in a few minutes. He went to see how Mr. Wright is."

"I just missed him then."

"Is Dr. Ditler going to operate?"

"The artery that's leaking is deep inside the brain, which means a surgeon couldn't possibly get to it. From the way things look, Mr. Wright can't last much longer."

" 'One generation passeth away, and another generation cometh': says Ecclesiastes, 'but the earth abideth forever.' Not much more than two hours ago I would have given you odds that a large part of Framingham would be a smoking ruin by morning; now it looks like we've got a chance to achieve an orderly change."

Chuck got to his feet and once again, Jud was impressed with his obvious weariness—plus something else, an air of discouragement that was foreign to the chaplain.

"What's worrying you?" Jud asked.

"Whether I can keep Eric with me."

"Do you think there's any real doubt about it?"

"Considerable—now that Seth Wright is dying."

"Why would that change things—with Horace in full control at the mill?"

"Eric and Amanda both feel a strong sense of obligation to Seth Wright, in spite of the way he's treated the rest of the black community. Except for Mr. Wright, neither of them would have had an education."

"Are you saying that if Seth Wright dies, Eric might not feel that obligation any more?"

"I don't know," said Chuck. "When your emotions are as ambivalent as Eric's are about this situation, a little weight can tip the scales either way."

"Surely Eric would be impressed by the way Horace Fellowes has met the situation head on."

"I'm sure he is. I've always had an idea that Horace would do that, given the opportunity to act independently of Seth Wright. Do you think he and Samantha are safely back together again?"

"They're okay."

"For which they both have you to thank. For a while there, she was ready to go off the deep end for you—"

"But only in a rebound from her disappointment in Horace." Jud gave his friend a probing look; once again he couldn't escape the conviction that something else was on Chuck's mind.

"Was that coffeepot of yours the only thing that brought you back here tonight?" he asked.

Chuck shook his head. "We brought in a head wound; Emilio's sewing him up now. Two sets of pickets got into a scuffle in front of the mill—"

"Two sets?"

"Jared Heath's followers are out waiting for a chance to make trouble. And some blacks Eric hasn't been able to control are out there too, in front of the mill gates, demanding jobs they claim were promised them by the management."

"That could create an impasse, if the former workers try to go back to their old jobs."

"Right now it's a standoff, and, if we can keep it that way for another twenty-four hours or so, we might avoid any real trouble. Horace Fellowes has promised to force the company union into a showdown on employment, so Eric and I just might be able to get everything we've been fighting for without any actual violence. The trouble is that Jared Heath and his crowd don't want that to happen, so they're trying to provoke the blacks into some sort of a disturbance. If they do, we may never get as far toward equal employment again as we are now."

"It's a tight situation," Jud agreed.

"Tighter than anything you ever saw, even in Vietnam. If one black can be provoked into attacking one of Jared's crowd tonight, all hell could break loose."

Jud put his hand on his friend's arm. "Don't get caught in the middle when you try to stop them, Chuck," he warned. "You're still primarily a minister—even in a turtleneck."

" 'No man, having put his hand to the plough, and looking back, is fit for the Kingdom of God,' " said Chuck. "Jesus didn't have to go to Jerusalem that last Passover, when he knew those who hated him were plotting to destroy him, but he went just the same. I can hardly do less and be faithful to my vows."

Kathryn Galloway called shortly after nine o'clock. "Have you been watching TV?" she asked.

"I've only got a small portable and it's been acting up. What's new?"

"They've been interrupting the regular programs with spots on the Framingham Mills situation. Just now Channel 19 announced that they're going to start continuous coverage at ten-thirty."

"When I saw Chuck a couple of hours ago, he thought things were under control."

"Not any more, apparently. Why don't you come over here and watch mine? The operator can get you on the beeper if you're needed."

"I've got the whole hospital staff on emergency alert," said Jud. "It wouldn't look good if I left the building."

"I'd better come over there then," she said. "The way things are beginning to look, I'll probably be needed anyway. There's a color set in what used to be Asa Ford's office. Go turn it on and I'll be there in a few minutes."

As soon as the TV screen was illuminated, Jud saw why Kathryn had been concerned. The millyard had all the appearance of an armed camp, with a small army of security guards and police inside the tall fence surrounding the entire factory, and two sets of pickets glaring at each other across the open street leading to the gate. They were separated by still another contingent of police but, if ever the stage was set for a confrontation, this was obviously it. Nor was there any doubt when that would happen; the changing of shifts at eleven made it practically inevitable.

"We interrupt the regularly scheduled program"—the voice was that of Pendleton Crews, director of Channel 19's news division— "in order to bring you up-to-date on the rapidly developing crisis at Framingham Mills. This crisis is particularly dramatic, since Seth

Wright, sole owner of the mills, is reportedly dying at Provident Hospital.

"Viewers of Channel 19 will recall that yesterday the company union of Wright employees issued an ultimatum to the owner that protective devices must be placed upon carding machines to prevent the occurrence of byssinosis. This hazard had been dramatically demonstrated during a union meeting the night before by Dr. Judson Tyler, himself a controversial figure by virtue of his having identified a high incidence of lead poisoning in slum children, allegedly from lead-containing paint on the plastered walls of ghetto houses owned by some of the most prominent families in the city.

"Following discharge by Mr. Wright of workers belonging to the company union, as well as the firing of his son-in-law, Horace Fellowes, then Executive Vice President of the mill, employment was offered to all by Jared Heath, appointed mill superintendent by Mr. Wright before he was suddenly felled this morning by an apoplectic stroke. A number of black workers belonging to a militant organization led by one Al Porter are now inside the mill, and more have indicated their intention to join the shift due to start work at eleven this evening.

"In another dramatic development this afternoon," Crews continued, "Judge Eli Myers declared Mr. Wright incompetent to handle his own affairs because of his grave illness, and placed them in care of one of the city's most prestigious legal firms—and Mr. Wright's personal attorneys—Morgan, Morgan, Morgan, and Taliaferro. The attorneys promptly placed Mr. Fellowes once again in charge of the mill and he offered employment again to the members of the company union. This offer has been accepted by them with Mr. Fellowes' promise that protective devices will be installed upon the machines in question as quickly as possible.

"The situation appeared to be under control, until a Channel 19 reporter was able to interview Al Porter inside the mill about eight this evening. It was discovered then that members of Porter's faction are fully armed and determined to keep control of the mill until their demands for preferential employment of blacks and Mexican-Americans at increased wages are met. Police are waiting until the eleven o'clock deadline, when workers in the mill would normally come off duty, to see whether Porter and the faction he represents—already denounced by leaders of the black community —will make good their threat to seize the mill.

"Keep tuned to this station for continuous coverage of the Framingham Mills crisis, starting at ten-thirty. If further developments occur before that time, we will keep you informed."

Kathryn came in as the regular program was resumed. She was in uniform.

"I was listening to the car radio coming over," she said. "Things look bad, don't they?"

"And all because of me," Jud said morosely. "I guess the old saying that fools rush in is still true."

"Nonsense!" she said briskly. "I'll get some sandwiches and coffee from the cafeteria; then if trouble does start, we'll at least have something in our stomachs to go on."

The telephone rang and she picked it up. "It's for you—Joe Morgan III."

"Congratulations!" said the lawyer. "You made the news."

"I know—and I'd rather not be in it. Where are you?"

"At the front—Horace Fellowes' office in the mill. The firm had to have someone on duty and both Dad and Granddad are too old to fight."

"The TV picture looks pretty grim."

"It's just as grim inside. Some of the men are already starting to leave the machines."

"Where are Chuck and Eric?"

"Outside, trying to pacify the blacks out there. Nothing would please the Jared Heath group more than to crush a few black skulls, so there's no point in arguing with them."

"What about strategy? Has Horace thought of anything?"

"He's going to give Al Porter and the militants a chance to walk out peacefully at eleven, with the assurance that their demands will be discussed in the presence of a mediator."

"Who?"

"Probably someone from the Department of Labor in Washington. That will give time for things to cool off a little."

"What if they don't accept?"

"As soon as everybody except Porter and his group are out of the mill, the main switch will be thrown and the current will be cut off. The place is already surrounded and the authorities will just wait them out."

"You said when you finished law school you wanted to do something of an activist nature," Jud reminded the lawyer. "At least you're getting your wish."

"Am I ever," said Joe. "Until you came along, I'd just about given up hope of doing anything except guard the trust funds of little old ladies. But when this is over, I'm going back to Cambridge and get me an MBA from the Business School."

"Anything new?" Kathryn asked when Jud hung up.

"The same old story. I started the whole thing—when all I wanted to do was keep people from dying before their time."

"I didn't give you back your manhood so you could come sniveling around every time some wrong you tried to right backfires on you," she said sharply.

The accusation—plus the fact that she was really angry—shook him up enough to throw off the feeling of guilt that had tortured him for the past forty-eight hours.

"Thanks for pushing me into line again, like you did that first day." He managed to smile. "I guess even Sir Galahad sometimes got scorched by the hot breath of the dragon he was fighting."

"That was St. George, silly." Her voice had softened and she leaned down to kiss him. "I really wouldn't want you to be anything except the way you are; one thing I could never stand about Dick Tubman was that he was always so damned sure of himself. I'd better get the sandwiches; from the looks of things we may not have another chance to eat tonight."

III

By the time continuous TV coverage began at ten-thirty the voluntary exodus of workers on the three-to-eleven shift from Framingham Mills was already well under way. Obviously none of them wanted any part of the expected crisis at eleven, especially when the faction led by Jared Heath was waiting with bludgeons taken from a nearby lumber yard, eager to attack any black man who tried to enter the mills to work.

The size of the militant faction facing them had shrunken considerably, Jud saw. Only about a dozen blacks now milled around uncertainly across the street in front of the main gates, which had been thrown open to let those departing leave without any difficulty. And not many of these were remaining to support the Heath group.

On the TV screen, Jud could see Chuck Rogers and Eric Cates talking to those who remained. And though he couldn't hear their voices, he was sure they were urging them to depart too, decreasing the possibility of trouble.

By eleven, the flow of workers from the mill had slowed to a

226

trickle. Equally small was the number of union members waiting to enter the brick structure with its rows of blue lighted windows, a common sight in any southern textile city. Nor did any of the militant faction of blacks and Mexican-Americans waiting across from Jared Heath's group seem inclined to try to enter the mill and begin work on the graveyard shift.

"It appears that the mill will have to be shut down," said Pendleton Crews. "We switch now to Mr. Fellowes' office and Elbert Jarvis of Channel 19."

The scene changed to an office half filled with men. Jud recognized Joe Morgan and Horace Fellowes; the others appeared to be administrative and supervisory personnel of the mill, since they were somewhat better dressed than the workers usually were.

Elbert Jarvis, a slim man with Lincolnesque features, held out an interview microphone to Horace Fellowes. When the camera zoomed into a close-up, Jud saw that Horace looked worn and tense.

"I certainly wouldn't want to be in his spot right now," said Kathryn. "Even though his wife will probably inherit a few million by morning."

"It's like walking on eggs," Jud agreed.

"Mr. Fellowes." Jarvis' voice came from the TV set. "Would you tell us roughly what the situation is here at the moment?"

"We're waiting for Porter and his group to come out peacefully," said Horace.

"Any indication that he intends to do so?"

"I'm afraid not. Porter's men are armed and they're holding the foreman of the carding room as a prisoner."

"What are your plans now, sir?"

"We'll wait them out. There's nothing else to do."

"There's a rumor that you plan to shut down the power, if Porter and his group seize the mill, as they have threatened to do."

"We can't do anything that might make them hurt Mr. Green," said Horace. "We've been notified that they are holding him as hostage."

"Thank you, Mr. Fellowes," said Jarvis. "And now back to Pendleton Crews outside."

Once more the millyard occupied the screen and Jud could see that some sort of an argument was going on between Eric Cates and Chuck Rogers.

"We're unable to pick up the conversation between Reverend

Rogers and Eric Cates, one of the younger leaders of the black community." Pendleton Crews' silken voice came from the set. "But Cates seems to be trying to argue Rogers out of going into the mill."

"The argument seems to be over," Crews continued, when Eric finally shrugged his shoulders and moved away, while Chuck approached the gate where an armed guard stood watching the scene. "We'll move in and try to pick up what Mr. Rogers is saying to the guard."

Before the reporter with the microphone could reach the gate, Jud saw the guard hand Chuck a portable electric loudspeaker like those used by police in riot control. When Chuck put the speaker to his mouth, his voice, many times amplified, burst from the TV microphone, which Pendleton Crews pushed toward him at just that moment.

"Al Porter!" The volume of Chuck's voice jarred the set until the station audio control cut it down. "Can you hear me?"

There was no answer for a moment, then a window on the top of the two floors of the mill was thrust open. Immediately, a moving police searchlight focused on the militant leader's face, glinting off the target pistol in his hand—aimed directly at Chuck.

"What's on your mind, Reverend?" Porter's voice was a bit slurred.

"He's high on some drug!" Kathryn Galloway exclaimed. "I've heard that tone in the voice of addicts brought into the Emergency Room."

"Which means he's liable to do anything that comes to mind," said Jud. "I've seen soldiers stoned on marijuana or opium go completely berserk."

"I want to talk to you, Al." Chuck's voice sounded distant now. Pendleton Crews had moved back at the sight of the pistol, and the microphone picked it up from the loudspeaker, plus an echo from a nearby building.

"Better not come any closer, Reverend." Al was obviously enjoying his role as principal in the tense drama. "I'm a dead shot with this little baby; bet I could center right between your eyes, if I tried real hard."

At the crack of the pistol, an overhead light near the mill entrance suddenly burst into fragments and the entire scene was momentarily frozen into the kind of tableau Jud remembered seeing in circus performances as a boy. Then there was a flurry of movement in all directions as people took cover, leaving only Chuck standing

228

by the gate and Eric, who had whirled in the instinctive reaction of the trained soldier to face the source of the firing, in the middle of the street.

Al Porter's high-pitched cackle of laughter floated over the scene from the window of the factory; in the glare of the portable floodlight, his face was contorted in an expression of fiendish delight.

"Break it up, Al!" Eric shouted angrily.

The target pistol cracked again, the bullet kicking up dust a yard from Eric's feet before ricocheting off to smash a window in an adjoining building.

"You ain't in charge no more, boy." Al Porter's voice was filled with contempt. "You started turnin' white the day Seth Wright gave you a white shirt and sent you off to college."

"Jud, look!" Kathryn exclaimed. "Chuck's going inside."

Jud's eyes swung from the two blacks to where Chuck had been standing by the gate, in time to see him disappear through the main doorway of the factory.

"Chuck must not realize Al is high," Kathryn cried. "Al will kill him."

"It's Eric Al really hates," said Jud. "I just hope he doesn't try to go inside too."

"A new development has been taking place during the confrontation between Al Porter, leader of the militant blacks, and Eric Cates, who heads the more moderate faction." Pendleton Crews' smooth tones poured over the scene. "Reverend Charles Rogers has taken advantage of the momentary diversion of Porter's attention to enter the factory, no doubt in an attempt to persuade Porter and his group to come out peacefully."

"Porter apparently realizes that Reverend Rogers is inside now," Crews added, when Al's head suddenly disappeared from the window.

Jud waited tensely for the sound of a shot from inside the mill, indicating that Chuck had reached the large carding room where Al Porter had been, but none came. Instead, another pistol shot was heard outside the building itself from the group around Jared Heath, and the sudden sputtering of an electric short circuit identified its target, the main transformer supplying power to the mill.

One instant the entire textile plant was aglow with light, the blue of its windows sharply contrasting with the glare of the police floodlights outside, themselves independent of any outside source since they had their own generators. The next instant, the entire building was bathed in darkness, until the searching beam of a floodlight was focused on the entrance to the mill.

Meanwhile, lights began to appear inside the mill, fluttering will-o'-the-wisps as the militants sought to find their way around by means of cigarette lighters, matches, and whatever was at hand.

"That cotton dust is explosive!" Jud was watching the scene, held by the drama of potential destruction, which had now been added to the situation, and unable to do anything about it.

"Pray God somebody inside remembers that before it's too late," said Kathryn, but a sudden gust of orange flame indicated that her prayers had gone unanswered.

The horrified watchers, hundreds on the scene itself and thousands by way of the television cameras trained upon it, saw the orange tide roll through the mill, as the flames rushed from one carding machine to another—each with its burden of highly inflammable cotton dust—turning the whole area into an inferno in a matter of seconds.

"Ladies and gentlemen, you are witnessing the death of an institution." The voice of Pendleton Crews had lost much of its composure in the face of the tragedy being enacted before the cameras. "Framingham Mills was spinning the cotton from which uniforms were woven for Confederate soldiers during the Civil War. Now, it is being consumed by flames that mark the end of a dynasty and perhaps the end of an era."

CHAPTER XXIV

Moments after flames gushed through the main carding room of the mills, Al Porter's followers began to pour from the building in panic, coughing and retching from the smoke. Fire engines were already converging upon the millyard and a rescue squad ambulance crew administered oxygen to the few who appeared to be in serious trouble from the smoke they had inhaled.

As for the fire itself, extinguishing it was obviously an impossibility.

The accumulation of cotton dust around the machines, as well as in every nook and cranny of the building itself, burned with almost the fierceness of gasoline, driving back any fireman who attempted to enter the building.

The offices where Horace Fellowes, the TV crew, and a few supervisors had been were located separately from the main structure of the mill and had been built later in the form of a one-story addition to the old building. Since it had a separate entrance, its occupants were able to escape as soon as the scream of sirens outside told what had happened. They gathered across the street to watch while flames continued to belch from window after window as the intense heat and pressure shattered the panes.

"I'm almost glad Al Porter was caught inside," said Kathryn bitterly as they watched the television screen. "But what an injustice for Chuck Rogers to die with him."

Jud could only watch in numb horror, bitterly conscious of his inability—or anyone's else—to help Chuck now. Then the voice of Pendleton Crews', almost stuttering with excitement broke in:

"Porter and Reverend Rogers are coming out!"

As the cameras swung to a close-up of the main entrance to the factory, Chuck and Al could be seen emerging from the entrance. Both were choking and coughing from the smoke but no one could doubt the reality of the threat posed by the pistol the militant was holding against Chuck's head.

"Hold your fire!" The voice of the police chief in charge of the considerable force of officers and security guards massed beside the mill entrance and across the street, some with high powered rifles, could be heard distinctly over the microphone.

Al and Chuck were moving across the street now toward Chuck's car, which was parked near the corner, but Eric Cates still stood where he had been when Al had fired the warning shot at his feet, separated a little from the rest of the crowd.

"If you hurt him, Al"—Eric's voice, too, sounded far away—"I'll hunt you down and kill you with my bare hands."

As the camera switched to a close-up of Porter and Chuck Rogers, now only a few yards from Chuck's car, Jud saw Al Porter suddenly twist his body so he could bring the pistol to bear upon Eric Cates. The sound of the shot seemed to echo instantly and Jud understood why, when he saw Al, too, start to fall and heard the excited words of Pendleton Crews:

"Eric Cates has been hit by Porter's bullet but Porter had to

231

turn in order to fire and a policeman with a rifle shot him. Cates is down and so is Porter. The police are converging upon him and Reverend Rogers, who appears to be unhurt."

"Thank God for that," said Jud as the telephoto lens centered on Chuck and Al Porter, now lying in the street.

Instead of making his escape, however, Chuck bent over the wounded man. True to his calling even in a time of grave personal danger, the minister sought to help the man who had held him hostage and, in his concern, ignored the pistol still clutched in Al Porter's right hand, which was pressed against his chest, where a spreading stain, sharply delineated by the magnification of the camera's telephoto lens, betrayed the gravity of his wound. Thus thousands of watchers saw Al's hate and pain-contorted face, when his hand moved the pistol slightly to center it upon Chuck's body and pulled the trigger.

The third shot, following so closely upon the other two—the first aimed at Eric Cates, the second the crack of a rifle as the police marksman brought Al Porter down—could almost have been an echo of the others. Then, as Chuck Rogers' body twisted halfway around by the impact of the bullet, the pistol dropped from Al Porter's fingers, bringing to an end the tragic drama that had moved so swiftly, once the flames started engulfing the mill.

"Porter appears to be unconscious," said Pendleton Crews. "Eric Cates seems to be seriously wounded and so does Reverend Charles Rogers, shot while he was trying to minister to the man who had held him hostage. Rescue squad ambulance crews are moving to pick up the wounded men now; the task of the firemen would appear to be only that of keeping the flames from spreading."

"Let's go!" Jud switched off the TV. "We're the nearest hospital to the mill and the ambulances will soon be here."

"Poor Chuck," said Kathryn as they hurried from Asa Ford's office. "I doubt if anyone else would have turned back to comfort someone who had threatened to kill him—"

"The same thing happened to me at An Tha," said Jud harshly. "The section of explosive bullet casing taken out of my brain at Letterman General was part of one I was removing from a Vietcong prisoner, when the North Vietnamese rocket hit the hospital."

"Why did Chuck stop to help Al Porter when he knew what Al was like?"

"I think he can give you the answer to that."

"If he lives—"

"Even if he dies, it would be the same; 'Love your enemies, do good to them which hate you.'"

II

The first ambulance arrived at St. Luke's in fewer than ten minutes after Jud reached the Emergency Room. Kathryn had gone on to set up the operating room, in case major surgery was necessary. The night laboratory technician was also getting a stock of type "O" blood from the refrigerator, ready for the expected emergency. Judging from the close range at which Al Porter had fired and the way Chuck Rogers had slumped over him, Jud doubted that there would be time for matching blood, so the universal donor type stocked for such emergencies would have to be used.

The first ambulance brought Eric Cates, already semiconscious and with his hair matted with blood from a scalp wound.

"This one's okay, Doc," said the ambulance driver. "The bullet must have just creased him. It's the reverend you've got to worry about tonight."

"Are they bringing him here?"

"Right behind us, but I'm afraid he's a Code Five. I saw the other crew putting the respirator on him as we were leaving the mill-yard."

The driver's diagnosis of Eric's injury proved correct, at least on superficial examination, the bullet appearing to have plowed its way along his scalp.

"Shave around the wound and put on a pressure dressing," Jud directed Dr. Montez, the least experienced of the four residents, all of whom were standing by. "We'll get an X ray before we sew him up later."

The whine of the second ambulance siren was heard outside while Eric Cates was being transferred from the mobile ambulance stretcher to one of the tables in a cubicle of the Emergency Room. Jud was at the door as the second stretcher was wheeled in, his fingers automatically reaching for Chuck Rogers' pulse.

"Code Five, Dr. Tyler," said the fireman ambulance attendant. "I lost his pulse a few minutes ago, but he's still trying to breathe."

Jud had already evaluated the gravity of Chuck's condition. The absence of any pulse at the wrist; the darkening pallor of his lips and ear lobes, denoting oxygen lack; the faint attempts at respiration—all betrayed a rapidly failing circulation.

233

"Any blood loss?" he asked the ambulance attendants as they lifted the limp body of the chaplain gently from the low ambulance stretcher to one of the wheeled tables, on which he could be moved to the operating room, if there were time for surgery—which at the moment hardly seemed likely.

"There ain't hardly a spot on his underwear where the bullet went into his belly. It must all be inside him, Doctor."

"Cut down set," Jud told the waiting nurse as the ambulance respirator was being exchanged for the hospital's Mark Four. "Cut off his clothes, Emilio," he added. "We've got to work fast and get some type 'O' blood into him."

While the Cuban slit Chuck's right trouser leg and exposed his ankle, the most available spot in the body for quickly reaching a vein by surgery, Jud put on gloves and dipped a sponge in scarlet-colored antiseptic. With his left hand, he swiped the ankle area just in front of the bone on the inner side, dropped a sterile towel across the foot, and, picking up a scalpel with his right hand, steadied it with his left while he made an incision about an inch long over the area.

"Blood ready?" he asked over his shoulder, as he probed briefly into the depth of the incision with a small curved forcep and flipped out the vein that could always be found there.

"Ready, sir," said another of the residents.

Nicking the vein wall with his scalpel, making just enough of an opening to slip a nylon catheter into it, Jud handed the other end of the catheter to the resident to make the connection with the transfusion set, while he reached for a suture to slip a loop of silk around vein and catheter. Making a tight connection and cutting the end of the ligature, he dropped the vein back into the wound, closing it with a dressing for there was no time to do any other suturing now.

Another nurse had started taking the blood pressure as soon as Chuck was placed on the wheeled table, following the standard operating procedure Jud had set up for grave emergencies, so everyone would know his or her duty and valuable time would not be lost while he explained things.

"His heart's beating but the pressure's hard to get," she reported. "I hear faint sounds at eighty."

"Diastolic?"

"I can't get that at all."

The information confirmed Jud's snap diagnosis of grave hemorrhagic shock. Loss of circulating blood from the arterial system because of damage by the bullet to a large internal vessel would immediately lower the basic pressure, called the diastolic, existing in the system between heartbeats. And since the blood now flowed only with the weak contractions of the heart muscle, a minimal amount of oxygen was being absorbed by it in the lung circulation, threatening vital areas such as the brain and the heart itself with death from sheer lack of oxygen.

Chuck was still making feeble attempts at breathing, as evidenced by the rhythmic tripping of the main valve of the respirator. But with the pressure dangerously low, the mere addition of blood was obviously not going to be enough to support the failing circulation during this crucial initial period of severe traumatic shock.

"Start some Aramine intravenously, Emilio," Jud directed the Cuban resident. "You can use the veins on the back of his hands. And inject 250 milligrams of methylprednisolone sodium succinate directly into the tube as soon as you have the solution going."

The injection of such a large dose of a synthetic corticosteroid, counterpart of a hormone produced by the adrenal glands, was a heroic measure. But then heroic measures were called for, if Chuck were to be kept alive until he could be gotten to the operating room and the damage done by Al Porter's dying shot repaired.

At the first signs of shock, whether from the impact of a bullet upon vital body organs, from hemorrhage as in this case, or from massive infection, the body fought back with its own protective measures, developed as a mechanism for either fight or flight through millions of years of evolution. Hormones produced by the powerful small glands above the kidney, themselves governors of vital life function, were poured out in a desperate attempt to preserve blood flow by constricting the smallest arteries and veins of the vast capillary blood vessel bed. First priority was to the brain and heart, and second to the muscles which—in the wounded animal—might allow it still to fend off an attacker and save its own life.

In severe cases of shock, however, the body's own measures—even the intervention of the powerful hormone secreted by the pituitary gland at the base of the brain—were not enough. Not only did the loss of blood need to be replaced as rapidly as possible therefore, either by blood itself or a substitute solution, but large doses of synthetic versions of the adrenal hormones must be added, hence the injection of methylprednisolone.

With every available measure which could be taken at the moment to combat shock now underway, Jud turned to an examination of the wound which, had the ambulance been delayed a few minutes in reaching St. Luke's, would have ended Chuck's life. Just above the navel, he was able to see the point of entry, an absurdly small spot that was hardly more than a puncture wound, because of the small caliber of the weapon from which the bullet had been fired.

Because Chuck was unconscious from the shock attendant upon the wound and the hemorrhage accompanying it, he could give no indication of tenderness or other signs that might have let Jud gain some insight into the degree of damage inside his body. But the presence of considerable muscle spasm over the upper abdomen, as the body instinctively tried to protect injured organs, could only mean that the damage was serious, possibly, judging by the degree of shock, an injury to one of the large blood vessels inside the abdomen. And when Jud moved Chuck's body to the side and pulled away the clothing from his back, he saw that there was no wound of exit, indicating that the bullet fired by Al Porter point blank at the man who had been trying to help him was still inside the body.

"Blood pressure's rising a little," the nurse with the stethoscope reported. "I think I can get the diastolic now at about forty."

"The Aramine is going, Dr. Tyler," Emilio reported. "And I've injected the prednisolone."

"Start moving him to the operating room then," said Jud. "We'll stop by X ray and snap a film of the abdomen to see where the bullet is."

III

By the time they reached the operating room, the heroic measures Jud had instituted to combat shock seemed to be having some effect. Chuck's systolic blood pressure had risen to eighty-five and the diastolic could be detected fairly accurately now at about fifty— still considerably less than the optimum for major surgery but better by far than the state of *extremis* in which the chaplain had been brought from the millyard.

"We'll have to do an exploratory laparotomy," Jud told Kathryn Galloway as they wheeled the table into the operating room. "Be ready for everything from multiple perforations to a damaged aorta."

"Are you going to operate?"

236

"Chuck's only chance of life depends on our being able to control the hemorrhage and repair whatever other damage has been done," he said. "I can't risk increasing the damage if my hand should slip."

"But you'll assist?"

"Of course."

"We will be ready by the time you've finished scrubbing. But I still wish the scalpel were in your hands."

"My brain—and everything I've ever learned about surgery—will be guiding it," he assured her. But he knew the answer didn't really satisfy either of them.

CHAPTER XXV

At the scrub basin where Jud, Emilio Fernandez, and Juan Valdese were standing, the Cuban looked up nervously from the stiff brush with which he was carefully scrubbing his fingernails. His dark eyes were filled with anxiety and Jud knew even before he spoke what was troubling him.

"I would feel a lot better if you were operating on Mr. Rogers, Dr. Tyler," he said.

"Things will go just fine, Emilio." Jud voiced an optimism he was far from feeling, but there was no time now to call in one of the general surgeons on the staff at St. Luke's. What had to be done must be done quickly—if at all—before the temporary effect of the measures he had instituted to allay shock wore off.

"What do you anticipate, Doctor?" Juan Valdese asked.

"I've seen bullet wounds cause every sort of injury you could imagine," said Jud. "This was a small caliber projectile without a very heavy powder load behind it, so it probably veered from the first body target it struck and could have gone anywhere."

The X-ray technician appeared in the doorway of the scrub room shortly before Jud finished scrubbing, carrying a film—still wet from the washer—in its frame. Jud took a look at it and felt whatever hope for Chuck's life he had allowed himself to entertain suddenly evaporate.

After penetrating the abdominal wall and the relatively soft structures beneath it, the bullet had struck a vertebra and literally burst into a half-dozen leaden fragments. What was worse, it had exploded the relatively soft body of the vertebra before coming to rest in a position—indicated by lateral views—close to, if not inside, the vertebral canal, through which ran the main nerve trunk to the body below that point, the spinal cord.

"*Madre de Dios!*" said Emilio Fernandez at the sight of the film. "I have never seen anything like this."

"Nor I—except in wartime," Jud agreed.

"What can be done, Dr. Tyler?"

"First we'll explore the abdomen and repair what damage has been done there. Then we'll see what we can do about that bullet."

"The spinal cord must surely be damaged?"

"Probably, but some nerve function may be left below the level of the wound. We'll have to preserve that if we can."

Dropping the scrub brush into the sink, Jud plunged his hands and arms into a basin of antiseptic, then lifted them so the solution would drip from his elbows instead of down across his hands, contaminating them once again, and moved into the operating room itself.

"His breathing is very shallow and the pressure is only eighty over forty," reported the nurse-anesthetist at the head of the operating table. "I'm carrying him mainly on oxygen with only a slight amount of anesthetic."

"Use as little as you can," said Jud. "How are we on blood?"

"There's plenty of stored type 'O,'" Kathryn Galloway reported.

"Substitute a unit of blood for the Aramine flask then," Jud directed. "We can't tell what we may get into here."

Fernandez had finished painting the abdomen with an antiseptic, and Kathryn now stepped up to the table with an aerosol spray can in her hand. Using swift even strokes, she sprayed the abdomen with a rapidly acting adhesive material, then stepped aside as Jud and Emilio Fernandez spread a sterile plastic sheet across the abdomen, where it adhered at once to the adhesive.

The draping was quickly finished and the table of instruments and dressings were moved into place across the patient's body. Jud took a sponge and tightened the skin of the abdomen, waiting for

238

Emilio Fernandez to make the first swift cut that would start the operation itself.

When it did not immediately come, he looked up to see the Cuban's stricken eyes centered upon the scalpel the nurse was still holding out to him.

"Make the incision!" Jud spoke sharply, recognizing that in the tension of having to operate upon the most important patient who had ever come into his hands, the Cuban doctor was frozen with apprehension and uncertainty.

"I—I can't," Emilio stammered.

Jud started to lash out at the other surgeon, hoping to break the bond of fear that held him immobile, but didn't. He'd felt the strength of that same fear of failure too often himself—and yielded to it—not to know that it would be unwise even to try to stir Fernandez into action. Almost by reflex, Jud's own right hand moved and took the scalpel from the instrument nurse.

"Tighten the skin," he directed, and the assistant immediately pressed upon the plastic-covered rectangle of scarlet-tinted abdominal wall with a sponge.

With the scalpel poised above the narrow space between the fingers of his own left hand and those of Emilio Fernandez, Jud concentrated all his will upon the fingers on the right hand holding the knife. When he sensed no answering response of contraction in those muscles which had for so long refused to obey the commands of his will, he felt sweat pop out upon his forehead beneath his cap and mask and knew a moment of sheer panic at the realization that his not being able to operate could only mean death for Chuck Rogers. And knowing this, he concentrated all the more upon freeing the nerve impulses generated in his brain by his will from the barrier which had held them back now for more than a year.

Then suddenly, he felt life spring into the muscles holding the scalpel and knew in an instant of soaring triumph that the miracle of the synapses had occurred, allowing tiny electrical currents to speed down his spinal cord, thence through the brachial plexus of nerves and along the main trunks to the muscles of his hand. As they reached the targets of the neuromuscular junctions, the scalpel suddenly came alive in his fingers, becoming once again the extension of his will it had been before his injury.

Even though intent upon his task, Jud heard Kathryn Galloway's sudden gasp as he brought the blade down in a swift stroke that laid the abdominal wall open from just below the lower end of the breastbone to well below the navel, slicing through skin and fatty tissues to expose the tough sheath of the rectus muscles beneath.

"Don't bother about skin bleeders," he told Emilio Fernandez. "We can get them later."

Dropping the first scalpel, potentially contaminated because it had passed through skin whose bacteria could not always be destroyed by any antiseptic, as well as by microbes inhabiting the sweat glands and hair follicles—many of them the ubiquitous staphylococci that were so often the villians of hospital infections—he took the second blade handed him by the instrument nurse. Slitting the sheath of the rectus muscle for the length of the incision, he reversed the scalpel and, using the blunt handle, separated the muscles to expose the lining membrane of the abdominal cavity beneath, the peritoneum.

"Suction ready," he called, for the dark color of blood inside the abdominal cavity was easily visible through the thin membrane.

Picking up a thumb forcep with his left hand, he tented up the peritoneal inner lining of the abdominal cavity while Emilio Fernandez seized it on the other side with a forcep, allowing him to nick it easily and insert the point of a pair of surgical scissors.

"Shall we save the blood for auto-transfusion, Doctor?" the instrument nurse asked, but Jud shook his head.

"There's too much danger of contamination from a possible perforation," he said. "We can replace better with type 'O' after we've stopped the hemorrhage."

With the scissors, he opened the peritoneum widely, ignoring the tide of dark blood that gushed out through the incision.

"Self-retaining retractor," he ordered and, when it came into his hands, inserted the blunt prongs into each side of the incision, spreading the ratchet control to hold the incision open widely and allow access to the abdominal cavity itself.

In the tension of locating and controlling the source of the internal bleeding, which he must do if he were to save Chuck Rogers' life, Jud had quite forgotten that the right hand, which now moved so swiftly and skillfully, obeying every impulse from his brain, had almost failed to respond in that first moment of truth. As Emilio Fernandez inserted the tip from the suction machine into the lower end of the incision, his right hand plunged deep into the upper half of the abdominal cavity, following by memory the track of the bullet, as he estimated it, from the point of entry to the vertebral body where it had come to a stop according to the X ray.

At first he wasn't able to detect any source of the hemorrhage other than a large and easily visible wound of the liver from which came a steady ooze of blood. Then, almost against the fragmented vertebral body which had been struck by the bullet, he felt a spurt of blood against his fingers that could only come from a badly damaged, if not severed, artery. Moving carefully in the depths of the incision, he pressed his index finger against the point of hemorrhage from whence the spouting seemed to come and felt the pulsating stream suddenly stop, telling him the main source was at least temporarily under control.

"Let Juan handle the suction, Emilio," he directed. "I need you to help me get exposure."

Once his initial freeze had ended, Emilio Fernandez was working smoothly. While Jud continued to keep the flow of blood under control with his finger, the Cuban doctor isolated the area with moist gauze pads until the point where Jud's finger touched a moderate-sized artery was adequately exposed.

"Caramba!" Emilio Fernandez exclaimed at the sight of the almost severed artery. "It's a wonder he lived this long."

"The blood pressure's falling again, Dr. Tyler," said the anesthetist "I can't get the diastolic any longer."

"Step up the flow rate on the transfusion, please," Jud told Kathryn Galloway. "And inject another ampoule of methylpredniso-lone."

With adequate exposure, Jud was able to put forceps on the torn vessel now and, using a slender needle with a strand of silk attached, ligated it on both sides of the tear.

Controlling the steady ooze from the jagged tear in the liver was another matter, however. In a patient who was in a better physical condition, he might have tried to repair the damaged portion of that vital organ. But in Chuck's case the degree of shock removed that alternative from consideration.

"We'll try to control the liver bleeding with an absorbable cellulose pack, Miss Galloway," he said.

Composed of a specially prepared cellulose compound which did not have to be removed, but was absorbed by the body gradually as healing progressed, these new surgical packs had largely replaced the older gauze ones with the always attendant possibility of a secondary hemorrhage when they finally had to be removed. Jud didn't delude himself into believing there was much hope, however. Exploring the damage done to the spinal cord was out of the question in Chuck's serious condition too. And even if he recovered from the grave abdominal wound, he would still probably be paralyzed from the explosive effect of the bullet upon the vital nerve trunks where it had come to rest.

Only a short time was required to pack the liver wound with cellulose. It appeared to control the oozing from the damaged area fairly satisfactorily and, when a full examination showed no other sign of hemorrhage inside the abdomen, Jud closed the wound and applied the external dressing.

"What are his chances?" Kathryn asked as he was pulling off his gown and gloves to apply the adhesive tape.

"Very poor, I'd say."

"I had the operator call Amanda at Provident and tell her Eric's all right."

"Any news from Mr. Wright?"

"I don't know."

"I wonder how things finally turned out at the mill."

"There's a small TV in the nurses' lounge," said Kathryn. "I haven't had time to look but I'll bring it into the supply room next door."

They were in time for the late night wrap-up, following the midnight movie. The wrap-up, largely a replay of tapes made during the dramatic series of events that had taken place at Framingham Mills, gave them no news, however, except that it had been impossible for the firemen to save the mill, with the conflagration raging through the highly inflammable cotton dust that had accumulated in every part of it through the years.

"What a waste it all was," said Jud dejectedly, as Kathryn switched off the set. "The mill destroyed. Chuck and Seth Wright dying—"

"I don't think Chuck would consider his death a waste," she said.

"Shot by a man he was trying to help?"

"Chuck gave you back your surgeon's skill, when you had to operate yourself or see him die. Don't you realize that?"

"I guess there hasn't been much time to think about it," he admitted. "But you know what that did for me, don't you?"

She nodded. "He made it possible for you to realize your dream of once again being a complete surgeon—now you must help him realize his."

"But he'll probably not be here to help."

"He will, if not as we knew him, then in some other way," she said confidently. "I'd better go. I'm going to special Chuck the rest of the night."

"I'll see that Eric gets sewed up properly, then I'll come and help you," he promised.

Eric was sleeping quietly from a hypodermic and barely roused while Jud injected the wound in his scalp with novocain, cleaned it, and sutured it. The skull X rays showed no sign of fracture, so he was reasonably sure there had been no serious damage from the glancing bullet.

While Jud was finishing the suturing, Amanda Cates came in through the small operating room where he was working.

"He's all right, Amanda," he said.

"I guess this is one time being hardheaded served him well."

"Is Mr. Wright gone?"

She nodded. "About an hour ago. Horace took Samantha home. Is there any chance for Mr. Rogers?"

"I'm afraid not. The bullet tore the left lobe of the liver into several fragments and then went on to smash a vertebra and the spinal cord. Kathryn is specialing him and I'm going to help her as soon as I finish here."

"I'll go home and rest until morning," said Amanda. "Then I can relieve her."

"Of course. Good night."

"Good night, Dr. Tyler."

CHAPTER XXVI

Chuck Rogers died shortly after seven the next morning. The transfusions Jud had initiated more than compensated for the external blood loss but they could not control the internal seepage of blood into the vast capillary bed of Chuck's own tissues, the network of microscopic vessels whose opening and closing controlled the flow of blood—and of vital oxygen—through every organ and tissue of the body. Trapped in the capillary bed by a circulation too sluggish to return it to the heart, blood had begun to lose fluid into the tissues, until vital organs had bogged down and were no longer able to carry on the vital life processes. The bullet that had literally exploded inside Chuck's body at such close range had set in motion the irreversible sequence of events that finally brought the end.

Dr. Wiley was eating breakfast when Jud came into the cafeteria about eight; Kathryn had gone home to change uniforms before beginning the day's duties.

"I suppose you heard about Chuck," Jud said as he put the tray down on the table across from the pathologist.

"Emilio and Juan were leaving when I came in. I hear you're cured."

Jud held up his right hand, flexing and extending the fingers. "The nerve impulses do seem to be flowing without obstruction," he said. "I guess you might say a minor miracle occurred last night."

"Not minor," Wiley corrected him. "Any way you look at it, the period since you came to St. Luke's has been a season for miracles. I'll admit that I never expected to see it, but I'm glad I lasted long enough."

Jud was still flexing and extending the fingers of his hand, as if unable to believe yet that they could move the way they were doing.

"I guess that's Chuck's last gift to you," said Wiley, echoing Kathryn's observation in the supply room just after the operation. "And he's happy about it, I'm sure."

"Is?"

"Do you doubt it?"

"I guess not—though there was a time when I would have."

"That time is behind you," said the pathologist. "The world's before you now, you know."

"Not *the* world, *a* world." Jud corrected him quietly.

"Then you're staying at St. Luke's?"

"Did you ever doubt that I would?"

"Only for a little while—at the start. I guess Chuck took care of that."

John Redmond came into the cafeteria and stopped beside the table where the two doctors were sitting.

"Sit down and have a cup of coffee, John," Jud greeted him. "You'll have to get your own cup, though—I'm too pooped."

"I'm too busy right now, thank you, Doctor," said the orderly. "I hate to interrupt you at your breakfast, but some of us think Mr. Rogers should be buried in the old cemetery at St. Simon of Cyrene. He loved the place very much."

"I know," said Jud. "But is there any room?"

"We found one spot, beside Henry—you know, the servant of Mr. Abijah. None of the white families who have people buried there wanted them close to Henry, so there's just room for one grave beside him."

"I don't know of any place where Mr. Rogers would rather rest, John," said Jud. "He told me the story of Henry once, so I know how much he admired him."

"Then it's all right for us to dig the grave there?"

"Unless someone in Mr. Rogers' family objects."

"I've already talked to Bishop Tanner about that. He approves and Mr. Rogers has no family that we know of."

"Please take care of the arrangements then. I'll guarantee the funeral expenses myself."

"The congregation wants to do that, Doctor; it's the least we can do for him now."

John Redmond moved away a short distance, then turned back. "A lot of people are wondering, Dr. Tyler," he said. "Will St. Luke's keep on, now that you're well again?"

"I'll keep it going as long as I can," Jud promised. "For whatever that's worth."

John Redmond's smile was like a blessing. "It's worth a lot to the people of Irontown, Dr. Tyler. And I'm sure God will help out too."

Jud smiled. "If he forgets, I suspect Mr. Rogers will be nudging him in the right direction every now and then."

II

It was late afternoon when three cars turned into the driveway leading to Seth Wright's mansion and came to a halt before the broad steps giving access to the heavy oaken doorway. Samantha and Horace were in the first car, driven by Albert Redmond. Joseph Morgan I and III were in the second car and Jud, Kathryn,

Amanda, and Eric Cates, his head encased in a turban of white bandages, were in the third.

The two funeral services which had been held that day were over: Seth Wright's in the morning from the cathedral with the bishop himself delivering the customary eulogy; and Chuck Rogers' that afternoon in the small cemetery of the Chapel of St. Simon of Cyrene. The bishop had presided there too, with the choir, led by Eric, chanting from a psalm set to the sort of barbaric rhythm Chuck himself had loved. Now they had returned to the Wright mansion at the request of Joseph Morgan I.

"I have asked you all to meet here this afternoon for the reading of Mr. Wright's will because you are all involved in one way or another," Morgan said, when they were gathered in the library.

"I should say at the beginning that Mr. Wright has always felt that his daughter, Samantha, was amply cared for under the provisions of her grandmother's will," said Joseph Morgan. "This accounts for the fact that there is no direct bequest to her under this will, except for this house. With that explanation, I'll proceed to read the will itself."

The terms were simple. Albert Redmond and his wife were amply cared for and there was a provision for funds to enable Eric and Amanda Cates to complete whatever educational programs they wished, though the money could be used for no other purpose. The remainder of the estate, which Joseph Morgan I assured the listeners ran into many millions of dollars, was to go to a charitable foundation in the name of Seth Wright, with Samantha, Horace Fellowes, and the Morgan firm of attorneys as trustees.

"You may be wondering where you are concerned, Dr. Tyler," Joseph Morgan said, when the reading was finished.

"I didn't expect to be included, Mr. Morgan."

"Although Mr. Wright has been ill for some time, he was a close observer of life in Framingham, Doctor. He had many friends and acquaintances too, who reported to him of happenings in the city. One of these was the remarkable accomplishment at St. Luke's and in Irontown of the Reverend Mr. Rogers and particularly yourself, since your return here. Though there is no mention of it in the will, I can assure you it was Mr. Wright's intention that much of the income from the trust indenture under the will should be devoted to Mr. Rogers' work and I am sure it will adapt itself to yours."

"I'm grateful, Mr. Morgan—for the hospital, for myself, and

particularly for Mr. Rogers' memory." Jud was still a little stunned by the revelation. "He did have certain plans—"

"Of which Mr. Wright was cognizant, I might say, and of which he approved," said the lawyer. "With the approval of Samantha and her husband, I plan to designate you agent for the foundation in putting these plans into effect."

"I approve—heartily," said Samantha promptly.

"So do I," Horace echoed.

"Do you accept, Doctor?" Joseph Morgan asked.

"I do—with one provision."

"What is that?"

"That no income shall come to me personally from the foundation."

"If that is your wish, of course we will agree, but—"

"Mr. Rogers and I had planned to convert St. Luke's into a clinic mainly for treating traumatic injuries and those not able to afford treatment elsewhere," said Jud. "If I am able to carry those plans out, I shall be fully compensated through professional fees. As for the dream of a community center for Irontown separate from my own plans for the clinic, I owe Chuck Rogers enough of a debt to see that these are carried out too, as he had planned. And here the income from the foundation will be of the greatest possible help."

"All of these things can be arranged, I am sure, Dr. Tyler." Joseph Morgan looked at his watch. "If there's nothing else, I have another appointment."

"What about the mills?" Jud asked, as he, Kathryn, Samantha, Horace, Eric, and Amanda were having sherry and cake in the library after Morgan's departure.

"I've been in conference with our directors since the fire," said Horace. "The money that we can get from the city for the land where the factory stood as the site of a new auditorium and coliseum, should enable us to rebuild Framingham Mills on the outskirts of the city as the most modern textile plant in the South."

"That sounds fine." Jud turned to Eric and Amanda. "I hope you two are going to stay in Framingham; we still need a good nurse at St. Luke's."

"I haven't changed," said Amanda.

"Chuck always wanted me to go back to college," said Eric. "I guess when you come down to it, a musician isn't really tough

247

enough to be a successful labor leader. I'm thinking of Juilliard—in connection with the sacred music department of Union Theological Seminary in New York."

"We don't have to ask what you and Kathryn will do," said Samantha. "It's written on your faces every time you look at each other."

III

The street lights had just begun to come on in the city below but dusk had already cast its daily spell of magic, hiding the ugliness of the ghetto, the dingy buildings that marked the downtown section of any large American city, the litter accumulated in the streets by day and never quite swept away completely during the night. In the distance, the glow of blast furnaces in the steel mills of Framingham was reflected from a low-hanging cloud to paint across a darkened sky a swath of brilliance that was also a promise of tomorrow's sunrise.

Jud and Kathryn had finished dinner at Spring Mountain Inn and now his right hand moved across the table to capture hers, with no vestige of the uncertainty that had plagued him as recently as forty-eight hours before.

"When are you going to marry me?" he asked.

"Would tomorrow be soon enough?"

"Tomorrow will be fine," he told her. "We can honeymoon over the weekend and be back to work on Monday."

She laughed. "No wonder you start so many controversies—always pushing people into doing things the way you want them."

"Do you mind—being pushed, I mean?"

"Not into marrying you—or even a weekend honeymoon. After all, we've still got a job to do—a bigger one, I suspect, than on the first day when you arrived at St. Luke's. So we can't waste time."

"But we have so much more to start with now," he said. "I owe Chuck a lot for bringing me back here—and most of all for making it possible for me to find you."

"Not most. Giving you back your surgical skill was that—and Chuck alone was responsible."

"I wish I could have rewarded him in some way."

"You did," she assured him. "Not every man can die, knowing

248

his dreams will be carried to fulfillment by someone as dedicated as he."

She looked up to the swath of brilliance still reflected against the cloud by the gush of flame from the stacks of the steel mills.

"I like to think that wherever he is right now, Chuck is speaking again the words he loved to quote from Ecclesiastes: 'The sun also ariseth and the sun goeth down and hasteth to his place where he arose!'"

"I guess Chuck's on his way there now," she added softly.